Wellington writer Philippa Swan trained as a landscape architect, with degrees from Otago and Melbourne. Her nonfiction book, *Life (and Death) in a Small City Garden*, was published in 2001 to critical acclaim. In 2006 her award-winning short story 'Life Coach' was selected for the NZ Book Month publication *The Six Pack*. A more recent story was selected for the LitCrawl short story competition. She has been a freelance writer for a number of lifestyle magazines for over 15 years, including as a columnist for *NZ Gardener* and *Cuisine* magazines.

'Philippa Swan's is an original voice that is articulate, humorous and disarmingly refreshing.' – *NZ Books*

PHILIPPA SWAN

THE NIGHT
OF ALL SOULS

VINTAGE

VINTAGE

UK | USA | Canada | Ireland | Australia
India | New Zealand | South Africa | China

Vintage is an imprint of the Penguin Random House group of companies,
whose addresses can be found at global.penguinrandomhouse.com.

Penguin
Random House
New Zealand

First published by Penguin Random House New Zealand, 2020

1 3 5 7 9 10 8 6 4 2

Cover and text design by Katrina Duncan © Penguin Random House New Zealand
Cover photograph by A. F. Bradley
Author photograph by Rebecca McMillan
Prepress by Image Centre Group
Printed and bound in Australia by Griffin Press, an Accredited
ISO AS/NZS 14001 Environmental Management Systems Printer

A catalogue record for this book is available from the National Library of New Zealand.

ISBN 978-0-14-377430-3
eISBN 978-0-14-377431-0

The assistance of Creative New Zealand towards the production
of this book is gratefully acknowledged by the publisher.

penguin.co.nz

MIX
Paper from
responsible sources
FSC® C009448

The letters survive, and everything survives.
The note was brought to her on a silver tray. She tore open the envelope with cold fury — no amount of words would absolve him now. She stopped in surprise at the brevity of his note.

The letters survive, and everything survives.
Two independent clauses bolted together with a conjunction. He graduated summa cum laude from Harvard. A hasty cursive script, but she wasn't fooled. His careless tone was well crafted. This was a note as calculated as it was casual.

The letters survive, and everything survives.
She'd begged him (countless times) to return her letters, but he always refused. What kind of man did that? Henry James called him incalculable. Yes. He was also a liar. Blackmail and desire. She would do anything for him, risk everything.

The letters survive, and everything survives.
Words that promised such love, underwritten with such vengeance. Words that held the power to destroy everything. Even now.

When I get a glimpse, in books and reviews, of the things
people are going to assert about me after I am dead, I feel
I must have the courage and perseverance, some day,
to forestall them.

Edith Wharton,
Personal diary, 1924–1934

CHAPTER I

Drawing herself up from a deep tide of consciousness, Edith opened her eyes. The vague darkness suggested a room, but nothing more. She sat quietly, watching the shadows assume the weight of walls, shapes beginning to form and take substance.

How extraordinary — to be here, to once again be *present*. She hadn't been present since . . . well, it must be 1937. The last thing she could remember was the comfort of Elisina's hand, her warm breath as she explained that Edith had suffered another apoplectic fit and the doctors wanted to perform a bleeding procedure.

Now that ended badly.

So this must be the afterlife — there was no other explanation. Certainly she had *written* about the afterlife often enough; but she couldn't recall anything quite like this. It appeared to be a room, small and featureless apart from a broken ceiling light. She could see several incandescent bulbs were missing, wires sprouting from empty sockets.

It was a little unnerving, to be honest, though that had never stopped her before. If she worried about nerves (or honesty) she would not have been a best-selling writer. Nor would she have seen Tunisia.

'Not sure about this, Edith dear.'

Walter! His chair was pulled up alongside as if they were in a waiting room. She cried with delight, reaching for him; but her body felt oddly cumbersome, weighted like a sandbag. And her outstretched hand (she saw) was oversized and ugly.

My God, she was *old*.

Retracting into her chair, tears stung. It was so unjust. She had hoped (and explicitly stated in her memoir) that the afterlife would be a place of re-lived youth; evidently, however, her wishes were to be ignored. Beneath the promontory of her jaw she could feel the swag of her chin. She wasn't ashamed of old age, but she would prefer young knees. Strangely, the past seemed to have lost its sequence, her later years already as distant as her youth. And her memory was as misty as a ghost story.

Thank goodness Walter was similarly old. She couldn't bear for him to be young again, with a roving eye. It was always hard work holding his attention; she would have no show now. He was still a handsome man, his white hair swept from a high forehead, a magnificent moustache hiding that small mouth. Forty years they had together. Edith stopped. It was too much; she felt — well, *underwhelmed*. Was it possible that human emotions in the afterlife were as limited as the furniture? Or was it that Walter's chair was slightly turned away? He was never one for a scene. More's the pity.

Until now, her thoughts had been vigorously steered away from the inescapable — those final hours when she had sat by his deathbed. She had been overwrought and weak with exhaustion. She had farewelled Walter with an honesty she hoped would endure for eternity. (Had she known their separation would be of a more *interim* nature, she might have tempered her tone.) Would he remember any of that? She hoped not.

In the shadowy light, Walter's moustache tilted as he pondered the pitiful light fitting. The dry familiarity of his transatlantic drawl was almost painful. 'Must be those ghost stories you took to writing, my dear. Never in the best of taste.'

It was quite true that she had 'taken' to writing ghost stories — but only in later years. Until the age of twenty-eight she couldn't sleep in a room that contained such things. But as to Walter's observation, she said mildly, 'You never did approve of my ghost stories, although I don't recall you complaining when Henry wrote *The Turn of the Screw*.'

Walter pressed his long fingers together and asked delicately, 'Have you been here — long?'

A man of such manners and form! Walter knew the etiquette of every situation (he would have done marvellously when the *Titanic* went down), but he was uneasy in these circumstances. As to his question — had she been waiting long? 'Not particularly,' she said, having no idea. Walter had always felt she did nothing *but* wait for him, all her life. She wouldn't let him assume she was waiting in the afterlife.

'Not one of your better ideas, my dear.'

'I'm not sure it *is* my idea.'

'Always interfering with the natural course of things, must be your doing.'

'You're probably right.' Edith was careful to keep a straight face. How could Walter possibly consider this her doing? Walter Van Rensselaer Berry, international lawyer and diplomat, sitting in a lady's wing chair! She burst with laughter, savouring the sheer physicality of being alive, but Walter coughed pointedly, so she stopped.

Only now did she notice her own chair was shabby and worn, though comfortable enough. It even rocked when . . . no, really? Reaching down, Edith pulled a handle and watched her legs float up. She paused at the sight of bloated feet pushed into carpet slippers. How awful: she had become *dingy*, like a character in a boardinghouse who collects her dinner from the servery. It was so unfair that women were always judged by their appearance — a fact she never forgot while writing her female characters, and certainly not while making arrangements with her dressmaker. Edith let her legs drop from sight.

It was, however, an excellent chair. She would have enjoyed something like this in her later years, around the time her preference shifted from a French *bergère* chair to a wicker bath chair with a rubber ring. Yes, this would have done nicely. Rocking gently, she pulled on the lever again, fascinated as her feet mysteriously reappeared.

'Must you?' snapped Walter. 'Always fiddling, and now see what your infernal arranging has done.'

'My *arranging*, as you like to call it,' she said with dignity, 'was largely restricted to picnics and the occasional sea voyage. I don't recall making arrangements for the afterlife.'

Walter flinched, twisting a degree further away to murmur, 'Went a bit Catholic towards the end, didn't you?'

No, Walter couldn't know that: he wasn't there at the end. Should she tell him that they were buried next to each other outside Paris, only ten minutes' walk from the Palace of Versailles? At least those had been her instructions, and she had every reason to believe Elisina had honoured them. Edith sagged at the memory. Walter's death had been too much to bear, his useless body . . . no, she wouldn't recall the end; it mustn't erase a lifetime — from their youthful escapades as part of the East Coast set to a later life in glorious Europe.

If only she could recapture a single instance together . . . yes, sitting on the terrace at Hyères in their twilight years. It was a summer evening with cabaret music drifting down on the night air from yet another wild party up at the modernist house on the hill. Walter was reading Dante — about a love that moved the sun and stars. Placing the book aside, he'd said with unfamiliar hesitancy, 'Would you say, Edith — I mean, with us — it's all been—' A searching pause and he tried again. 'It's all been *good*, hasn't it, my dear?' She was about to reply when a crack of laughter from the party above split the moment like an atom.

Now Edith faced Walter directly, taking comfort from his familiar profile: the small head and hauteur of his movements; the long-jointed frame like a giant insect. She reached out again, forcing her thick fingers to uncurl, but Walter ignored her. Leaning further, she waggled her fingers like a landed fish — still no response. She withdrew. No one could hurt her like Walter. She remembered now the bone-aching aloneness as she stood by his grave, followed by the business of soldiering on. Ten more years she endured, not giving up until her last dog died.

Edith shivered, sensing a cool breeze. She swivelled in her chair but — curiously — there were no doors or windows. The room remained empty except for the arrival of a badly worn rug. It was ludicrous to think she once wrote a best-seller on home decoration. With regard to drawing-rooms (if she remembered correctly) she mentioned the need for imposing proportions and a walnut console.

'Reckon old Henry will come?' Walter shifted at last to address her. His pale eyes were the only colour in the room. Now she saw three chairs were scattered about the place. Goodness, she hadn't envisaged such a possibility — *was* Henry coming? Directly opposite was an easy-chair (with dirty antimacassars) beside a Hepplewhite with a broken arm. Against the far wall was a spindle-backed oak chair that promised to be hideously uncomfortable. None had the gravitas to suggest an appearance by the great Henry James, which was just as well. Henry would be very surprised — with affectionate malice — to find the irreproachable Mrs Wharton hosting in such surroundings. This was not the sort of show she usually put on.

Clearly they were to be joined by others; but whom? Her life had been long and populous. *Long and populous*: the words sounded like a threat. Her mind crowded with faces. With panic she shook them away, clearing everyone until she was left with icy absence. Heart racing, Edith breathed deeply, determined to control herself. This was not the time to be overwrought; she must pull herself together and carry on, just as Walter had taught her. She must—

Of course, she remembered now.

At the age of twenty-one, Walter had taught her a brutal lesson about the importance of self-possession and carrying on. Brutal, yes, but it served her well. It was strange to recall that episode — not something she had dwelt on during her lifetime, a lesson that permeated her being like a parable. The original story, however, had become lost as the leading edge of her life sped towards the finish line. Yet now the memories in her overstuffed mind were spilling everywhere.

Yes, but what about those *other* memories?

Gripping the arms of her chair, Edith forced herself to confront those volatile memories she had so carefully locked away. They were memories she knew must be treated with care, approached with courage and a strength of mind. Were they safely contained — or did they wait in a dark recess of her mind, ready to ambush without warning? The idea was unsettling.

A chime of laughter rang through the room, and Edith watched the darkness pull back to reveal a delicate woman on a plump sofa. Good God, it was Lady Sybil Cutting. The impertinence of the woman was unbelievable. Some things never changed — even now.

Sybil was perched among silk cushions, gold hair shining under the electric light. It was infuriating to admit she was still attractive, but Edith found some solace in the papery skin and shrunken pink mouth. Sybil was a black widow, a woman who entrapped and devoured her mating partners; unfortunately most of them had been Edith's friends. In desperation, she'd once issued an edict begging that no one marry Sybil for at least a year. Edith tried now to recall the outcome, but her memory was unhelpful.

With a rustle of crushed tissue and a waft of violets, Sybil said, 'Walter, darling — isn't this a surprise!'

'A most delightful one,' he replied smoothly. 'You've never looked more lovely, my dear.'

Sybil trilled like a caged canary, showing small white teeth.

Edith stiffened. 'Good evening, Sybil.'

Sybil's violet eyes opened wide.

Edith gave a suppressed snort of laughter. Many of her unstable characters had been based on Sybil (a particular favourite was Lady Wrench with her outbreaks of hysteria and violent fits of fainting), but Edith didn't want Sybil here tonight. She had destroyed too many lives. Beauty and carelessness were such a devastating combination.

Tossing her head, Sybil said, 'I don't see why you had to arrange something so ghastly.'

'I believe you're in the wrong room,' replied Edith, with some authority. *I believe you're in the wrong room.* Her voice sounded ugly and imperious and echoed mockingly from the shadows. Adopting a more reasonable voice, she continued, 'I believe this is a literary evening —' was this true? — 'and you must leave.'

The lights flickered, and Edith gave a cry. Something was whirling through the air — a creature — landing softly in her lap. It took her a moment to recognise — Linky! her last and most beloved pet. With a sob of laughter she collected the dog in her arms, pressing her cheek against the silky fur until Linky gave a protesting snap. She hadn't changed a bit. The same inquisitive flat-pressed face, a row of sharp bottom teeth. Because Linky was small, people mistook her nature for that of a stuffed toy, but this was a devastating underestimation. Linky was proud and stubborn, dignified and independent; Edith couldn't think where this came from.

Overwhelmed, Edith was aware that her joy was matched by equal measures of grief. She had always hoped Linky would outlive her — but no. Saying goodbye to Linky had been a preparation for her own death; still painful to remember: the soft light of springtime as she stood by the small, freshly dug hole, feeling utterly alone.

Bracing herself, she looked directly into the alert eyes. Edith had always feared the knowingness of dogs, their reproach at being condemned to eternal inarticulateness and slavery. Linky stared back with a terrible, familiar expression that said: 'Why?'

Edith turned away, waiting for Linky's breath to slow and become heavy. There was nothing more comforting than the weight of a sleeping dog.

'Happy now?' asked Walter genially, as if he'd arranged Linky's arrival himself.

Edith felt a brimming love for this tall, distinguished man who found human communion so difficult. It wasn't his fault; he really did try — and that's when she loved him most. Walter hadn't always enjoyed her dogs, but he knew how much they meant to her.

The fire crackled, low flames warming the edges of the room. Beyond the mantelpiece Edith saw a high, crowded bookcase. 'Oh, Walter, look!' She reached out, aching for the weight of a book in her hands, the delicate creak of a spine, the vanilla-dust of an open page. Confound this useless body. Linky jumped to the floor, sniffing a basket by the hearth, and Edith pushed up from her chair. She balanced briefly before heading plod-legged for the bookcase. The floor swayed like a ship deck.

'Must you?' said Walter irritably. 'Wandering all over the show. Never could sit quietly.'

She could see her memoir on the top shelf: *A Backward Glance*. Reaching up, her attention was caught by something else — *À la recherche du temps perdu*. It was recognisably a first edition. Her heart rattled.

Removing the book, she opened the cover to read the inscription. Yes, it was Walter's copy. She scanned the shelves: there was only one volume. Why would a first-edition set of Proust be divided? It made no sense — and yet Edith had the feeling it was somehow connected to Walter's death. She drew a shuddering breath as the past moved closer, but her memory remained locked.

'What've you got there?' rapped Walter.

'Proust,' she said, casually replacing the book. 'Very poor condition.'

'It's not mine, is it?' His voice held the sadness of hope.

'No, dear.'

Next to her memoir was a copy of *Ghosts*, and she pulled it from the shelf. There was a picture of a bell on the cover — just as she had requested — but she hadn't lived to see this selection of stories published. The final story in the collection, 'All Souls', was the last she ever completed. Turning to the preface, she smiled at her words — that she could imagine a ghost more wistfully haunting a mean house in a dull street than the battlement castle. Above her, the ceiling light glimmered.

Swapping this book for her memoir, she stumbled back to her chair, collapsing into a paroxysm of wild rocking. She waited for calm, delaying the moment when she would be confronted by her own memories. The frontispiece was stamped by the Framingham Library, an issue slip below. She turned the pages to her earliest memory: a bright midwinter day, holding her father's hand as they walked along Fifth Avenue. Flicking past her European travels, she stopped at the sight of Walter's name — such a public declaration of love: *he fed my mind and soul.* She remembered now: writing after his death, she had been raw with loss; it was a stolen pleasure to declare her feelings. But something disturbed her.

This wasn't her style, this tone of defiance, shouting her love through a megaphone. Why had she written such things? Edith stared at the words, willing them to give up their secret.

She was about to speak when a loud chiming filled the room. An ugly Victorian clock hung on the wall, hands pointed to ten, its severe face reminding Edith of her mother. Bells sounded, sending her nerves ringing. She clutched her book, waiting for the noise to distil into a single note. Silence crept back into the room, but she sensed a stirring. Edith shrank as Teddy's eyes burned through the gloom with terrible lucidity. 'My dear—' she began, but her voice died away. Time slowed to a single heartbeat. She held her breath.

Surveying the room, Teddy rubbed his hands with anticipation. There was something awful about his robust vitality in this desiccated place. Edith stared at her husband's glowing white hair.

His voice boomed. 'Don't suppose Alfred's here? A fellow could do with a drink.'

Edith reappraised the room for new arrivals. There was no sign of a butler or a drinks cabinet, thank goodness. Her husband had the red flush of a man who had spent the day horse riding and drinking Château Margaux. So this was Teddy from their days in the Massachusetts countryside. It was chilling to be confronted with his good-natured stupidity and, as always, the possibility of violence.

Now he was whistling at Linky. The poor soul had always loved animals: his dogs and pigs, the poultry. Edith's heart softened, knowing the end of this story — his descent into madness and mayhem. The greatest tragedy was that Teddy lived a long life, his last ten years with a rug on his knees, face turned to the wall. Where was the justice in that?

Truthfully, she said, 'You look very well, my dear.'

Large hands slapped his knees. 'Never felt better, Puss, given the circumstances.' He chortled at this afterlife humour, bending to scoop up Linky. 'Bit of a show planned, eh?'

Oh, Teddy, he was hopeless; he'd be wanting dancing girls.

'A literary evening, apparently,' remarked Walter. 'I believe we're to enjoy a reading.' His voice was cleared of all emotion.

Edith rounded on Walter with suspicion, but his expression was blandly insouciant. She remembered now how in their later years Walter would become restless during her readings on the terrace at Hyères, preferring to prowl away like an old tom cat. He didn't want to be caught at the wrong party in town, would rather dance the Charleston at a waterfront hotel with women (let's be honest) like Sybil. The sort of women who made Edith seem wooden and coarse. Women whose prettiness counted for more than all Edith's achievements. It was never enough — the literary prizes and international sales, money and fame. She could never erase the changeling inside, the awkward child with big hands and red hair, a stubborn, forbidding jaw.

'Oh, God, a reading,' said Teddy, slumping in his chair.

'Oh, my,' murmured Sybil.

Really, the woman was insufferable, and she would only get worse. No one could talk like Sybil: her voice getting higher and higher until it was like the whizzing of a ceiling fan. Where was Henry when you needed him? But now, here was a thought — it could be worse. Two empty chairs were positioned by the fire, and there was a space on the sofa. The vacancies were ominously suggestive.

'Let's start,' she announced.

'Start what?' said Sybil.

Oh, for heaven's sake, the woman was doing her nails, a manicure set by her side. In desperation, Edith tapped her memoir. 'Perhaps I should read first.'

'Read what?' repeated Sybil.

Edith swung around, exasperated . . . Well, this was unexpected. Percy Lubbock was sitting on the sofa next to Sybil. His tweed trousers were neatly pressed, if a little short (she could see diamond-stitch on his socks). He wore his usual wire-framed glasses, and his moustache was neatly clipped. Percy was one of the Henry James set, and a picture formed in Edith's mind: a foggy Eton afternoon, lamps brought into the drawing-room. Henry was lumbering against the mantelpiece in full flight, surrounded by his coterie of admirers, all men except for Edith. Percy had sunk long-limbed in an armchair, while their host (the much-loved Howard Sturgis) curled in a chair beside the tea tray, knitting furiously. This was Henry's inner group, and Edith remembered those afternoons of quick laughter as some of the happiest hours of her life. And now Percy Lubbock was here; it was wonderful. But goodness, he'd be busy fending off Sybil — like most of Henry's friends, Percy wasn't the marrying sort.

'Percy, how nice to see you.'

Percy looked up, startled.

A nice enough fellow, and he wrote several quite good books. She must remind him — but no, Percy was already speaking with Sybil. Edith stopped: there was something strange about Percy's urgent whispering and Sybil's quick, bright movements. They were almost conspiratorial — surely not.

Edith held up her memoir. 'I wrote about you in my memoir, Percy. Did you read it?'

At Percy's expression of alarm, ideas began to rearrange in Edith's mind. There was something odd about Percy, if only . . . yes, she remembered now: they had travelled to Tunisia together. Was that odd? Percy had been down on his luck, writing to ask if he could stay with her. Mortified by his request, she appointed him her sailing equerry, and they had enjoyed a wonderful trip. She remembered the night they watched the moon rise over the Sahara.

So why this sense of unease? Something didn't fit. Her senses were sharper now, and the night's earlier joy was gone. Once again she was on defence; she could feel herself adopting the old habit of securing tarpaulins on-deck, pulling tight the covers and facing a stormy sea.

'Am I to understand,' said Percy formally, 'that you're going to read tonight?'

'Of course.' What else could they do?

Percy's lips twitched, and Edith sensed he was laughing at her. She flushed with annoyance — and something else: a recollection of having been angry with Percy before. But why? Edith shook her head, trying to dislodge the memories, but her mind remained locked. 'Tell me, Mr Lubbock, why did we lose touch in later years?'

Percy hitched himself up.

'Mr Lubbock? I demand an answer.'

'Oh, Aunt Puss,' came a voice directly opposite. 'You mustn't—'

'Trix — you're here!'

'So it would seem.'

Such a fine woman and a credit to the family, given — well — *everything*. Trix held herself so proudly, her features strong and hair defiantly upswept. She was deeply intelligent, and her tailoring was faultless; but she was so *severe*. By way of consolation, Edith said, 'I'm *so* pleased you're here.'

'I'm sure you would prefer Mother.'

Such a forthright manner! Like all the women in their family, Trix had never been one to equivocate — and, as usual, she was right. Edith *would* prefer her sister-in-law, the delightful if equally forthright Minnie Cadwalader Jones. And yet, if there were a family quota for tonight (what a terrible idea), then she could do worse than Trix.

'You always did have a thing for the supernatural,' continued her niece. Accusation hovered behind the words. This was too unorthodox for Trix, too unseemly — that her aunt should rattle up friends and family at this late stage. It was too much like high-jinks.

Edith was careful not to show offence, ignoring the vibrational tension that lay between them. Her niece had always questioned the taste of an aunt who insisted on publishing best-selling novels.

Bounding from his chair, Teddy took Trix's arm with boisterous affection. They were old friends who shared a love of trees, and Trix didn't seem to mind being treated like the village pump. Now Teddy ambled over to the bookcase with affected interest, hoping no doubt for a copy of *Practical Pigs*.

Trix angled towards Walter, cheerfully responding to a question. They had always got on well, both hiding their conservatism beneath an artistic exterior. It was coming back to her now — how badly Trix suffered as a child when her parents divorced. Edith's brother had flaunted his mistress in the window of Delmonico's Restaurant on Fifth Avenue — a scandal that thrilled New York society but drove a schism in the Jones family. Edith had sided with her sister-in-law Minnie and daughter Beatrix. Her brother (and by association her mother) never forgave her, but Edith had no regrets. Trix went on to become an acclaimed landscape architect, her work distinguished by a deep appreciation of classical Italian design.

It should have bonded Edith with her niece, their shared love of gardens; unfortunately, it was quite the opposite. While they liked to discuss plants, they were careful to ignore the obvious: that Edith always designed her own properties. First her American gardens at Newport and the Berkshires, later her French gardens. Edith never consulted her niece except on the most basic points of design; and, adding insult to injury, she had written a seminal text on Italian gardens! Yes, Edith understood Trix's irritation, but what could she do? She loved gardens as much as her niece.

While speaking with Walter, Trix was retying a silk scarf around her neck. The material was blurred with colours of algae and mud, and it went nicely with her brown eyes — unusually warm for such an aloof person. She was talking about Max-somebody, wishing he were here tonight.

Max? Oh, good lord — Edith had quite forgotten. At the improbable age of forty-two, Trix had married Max Farrand and — after the happy event — allowed her career to be subsumed by wifely duties. Extraordinary. Old Wet-Fish had been a professor of some sort, and they made a ghastly couple, self-referential and pompous. Trix even took up golf for the fellow — golf! And then what? Edith could only guess. No doubt they continued to sail smugly into the unreliable waters of old age in matching wet-weather capes.

Teddy was now perched on the sofa-arm beside Sybil, who was looking alarmed. Teddy took quite some getting used to, his Bostonian good breeding combined with something more agricultural. And he always liked a party. He appeared to have discovered a box of cigarettes under the sofa and was now blowing smoke rings, which rose majestically towards the ceiling. Percy and Walter were also smoking, ash dropping to the rug as they discussed old friends. Edith had declined a cigarette with the notion she might have given up.

Trix was standing in front of a large framed painting of mourners under a windswept sky. Twisting around, she said, 'Is tonight the night of All Souls?'

Edith was intrigued; this was not something she had considered — but, yes, it was quite possible.

'As I recall, you would always spend the evening sitting by the fire with friends.'

Not quite — Edith spent the night in the *memory* of friends — but how would Trix know? Her niece had been conspicuously absent in later years: too busy with other things, hoping Edith wouldn't notice or remember . . . and now look, they were back together!

Packing up her manicure set, Sybil waved towards the empty Hepplewhite chair. 'I want to know who else is coming.'

'There's no telling,' said Teddy cheerfully, 'but I'm here as Puss's husband. Walter's a lifelong friend, and Trix is family.'

Clasping his knees, Percy said, 'I believe I represent the writing fraternity, a contemporary if you will.'

No, Edith wouldn't go that far, and she felt another yearning for Henry.

'Indeed,' said Teddy. 'And Sybil, she's—'

'Comic entertainment,' said Edith.

Sybil shook herself like a small irate dog, and Edith was reminded of Linky, who was currently chewing on the rug.

'Doesn't explain our mystery guest,' said Teddy.

'One of Edith's enemies,' laughed Sybil, causing general hilarity — the consensus being that any number of people might arrive and were they short of chairs?

Edith ignored them. A mystery guest — it couldn't be . . . surely not with Teddy and Walter in attendance. That would be grievous. Trepidation forced her to announce: 'I would like to start reading.' It was hard to believe her voice had once been pitch-perfect in what now seemed the vast orchestral movement of her life. An authoritative voice had been necessary to succeed in a man's world, but that counted for nothing tonight; not in this democratic afterlife where people like Sybil felt at liberty to appear. Tonight Edith sounded like an off-key bassoon. Adjusting to a more conciliatory tone, she said, 'I'm not sure what else we can do. Walter, would you like to read Yeats? I saw him on the shelf.'

'I want to know about that business,' clipped Walter, nodding at a side table by Edith's chair.

This was unforeseen: a manuscript was stacked by a shining silver cigarette lighter. Edith leaned closer, her image blurring on the beaten silver surface. An envelope was there, too, and she opened it with fumbling fingers. Goodness, it was a letter from her editor — old Scrib! How wonderful. Fancy hearing from him again — he sounded just the same. Mr Scribner hoped that Edith didn't object to his making contact, or feel that he was interfering; but there was a consideration at hand, a matter about which he felt uneasy.

He would like to explain. Edith may not be aware of the current trend for reimagining well-known figures from the past. The English royal family had been plundered endlessly, and now literary figures were being subjected to similar appropriation. Mr Scribner was sorry to report that his own company was not immune to this publishing trend. Ordinarily it was not his problem, except when the company chose to publish novels regarding his own clients. On several occasions he had been forced to discreetly show his displeasure, and was pleased to report that the publishers had largely abided by his wishes. They had also taken to replacing their locks, along with other security measures.

Recently, however, a most regrettable incident had occurred when the company decided to publish a lurid novel involving Henry James. It was a highly fictional account of his love-life (as Edith would know, Henry didn't *have* a love-life) by a young writer making a shameless grab for fame. Several staff members were unhappy with the decision (particularly a young translator who had the misfortune to discover Mr Scribner reading the manuscript late one night). But management believed the novel would be a 'sure-fire hit'. The situation was deplorable, and while Mr Scribner didn't wish to disturb poor Henry, he felt he must express his displeasure — unequivocally. And he did rather well, although he hadn't appreciated the wastepaper basket was so close to the fireplace, and could only be thankful the damage hadn't been worse. Suffice to say, the company had replaced their smoke detectors and the novel was not published.

And now to the issue at hand: yet another novel of this kind had arrived, this one regarding Edith. The novella (yes, it was rather short) was not particularly alarming, but it *was* suggestive. Mr Scribner simply couldn't be *sure* whether to act on her behalf. Edith would be the first to admit to having been commercially ambitious. He hoped she wouldn't take offence at this, but she *had* dropped him in later years — all in the past now, but he felt quite unable to make a decision on her behalf.

The best solution, he felt, was for Edith to read the manuscript and decide whether she wanted it published. Mr Scribner wished to be clear: Edith should read the novella very closely and give serious consideration to the consequences of its publication. He must warn her that the world was now a vastly different place. It was difficult to explain, but Edith would read about something called the internet, along with other concepts such as unlimited broadband. As a fellow who couldn't work a gramophone, he felt inadequately equipped to advise her, but — if pushed — he would say the internet was a global consciousness, an existence where nothing could be hidden. That is to say, if something existed in the material world, it existed in cyberspace (yet another term — he apologised, but Edith should think of cyberspace as a kind of phantasmal interconnection); and once something hovered in cyberspace — well, this information was available to everybody. The democracy of this new medium was alarming and unprecedented.

Further to this point, he must warn Edith that in this age of the internet it was no longer possible to control her own image. To use modern parlance, Edith was unable to curate her own narrative. And while the internet was excellent for the purpose of research, as a social medium it was an uncivilised madness. In his opinion, the internet had all the screaming mayhem of an Elizabethan theatre pit.

And yet — he hastened to add — it was the most wonderful opportunity. Publication of the novella might mean the revival of all Edith's work, a new audience discovering her genius in the modern age. Edith would be pleased to know that, in many respects, her work was as relevant as ever.

Now down to business: if Edith were keen for publication, there was no need to act. The editors were unanimously agreed on publication. However, if Edith did *not* wish the novella to be published, Mr Scribner suggested that she burn the manuscript. One fireplace was much like another, and he was confident the publishers would not proceed, having only just installed a sprinkler system.

Mr Scribner hoped this letter found her well and he looked forward to catching up in the not-too-distant future, but these things were difficult to predict and in the meantime—

'Edith?' Walter was rapping his fingers with impatience.

'A letter from my old publisher, Charles Scribner.'

Walter's eyebrows lifted.

'They want to publish a modern novella about me.'

'What's Scrib got to do with things? I mean, he can't—' Walter shifted with unease, not wishing to be specific.

Indeed, old Scrib was dead like the rest of them. Edith tried to explain. 'He seems to — well, *know* about the novella, and feels I should know as well.'

'Why? Nothing you can do, stuck in this place.' Walter stretched his arm towards her. 'Here, pass it over.'

'No.' Carefully, she tucked the letter away.

'Then you must explain.'

Edith picked up the manuscript, enjoying the well-loved weight of an unpublished work. 'I would like to read the novella aloud, if no one objects.' She checked around the room.

Trix gave an equivocal shrug, while Teddy crossed his arms and gazed at the ceiling. On the sofa, Percy was watchful and Sybil plumped the cushions. Walter recrossed his legs and Linky snored in her basket; and directly across the hearth, the Hepplewhite chair remained empty.

Following in the Footsteps of Edith Wharton
— a novella

(1)

Coming home should be the easy part. But after thirty years following her husband around the world, Sara had been warned things could get complicated and she should prepare. According to *Back to First Base: Strategies for Repatriation*, Sara mustn't think she was 'coming home' — rather, she was returning to her passport country, and it was critical she be ready for re-entry. Sara thought this made her sound like an astronaut with immigration issues. And there was more. On arriving back, she should expect to feel anxious and alone. Lethargic. She should anticipate panic attacks in the supermarket and, since Sara and her husband had never before lived in Massachusetts, a definite sense of alienation.

Except it wasn't true. None of it. They had been in Lenox for three months and everything was fine. Austen was on a committee of some sort, and Sara relieved not to be playing tennis. She believed herself perfectly okay — until Austen suggested she might like to leave the house more often.

'I'm sorry?'

Austen had bought the book on repatriation, and now he explained it was important for Sara to integrate into the local community.

'But I've already done that,' she protested, '— at least eight times.'

'It's even more important now we're permanent.'

'Sounds a bit final.'

'We wanted final.'

No, thought Sara, opening the dishwasher to remove the dinner plates. Coming home had been Austen's idea. He wanted early retirement. As he explained, it was an adventure to disrupt the inevitability of their life, to take a side road and head off in another direction. Sara was flummoxed. It wasn't that Austen was leaving his retirement bonus so much as everything else: the international travel and exotic holidays, personal drivers and the clubbiness of accidental meetings in an airline business lounge — *and isn't the world a small place!*

But Austen thought it was the ultimate challenge for a couple who had been everywhere and done everything. He made returning home sound like a trip up the Himalayas. This was fine by Sara, who had discovered that life was pretty much the same anywhere, once you accounted for variations in weather and supermarkets. She just wanted to be finished with relocation companies.

Now Austen said casually, 'The club needs a new tennis co-ordinator.'

'You've got to be joking.'

Austen gave her a look that said: you used to like tennis. He was still perplexed that Sara hadn't joined the club, and Sara was surprised that he ever thought she *would* join. Wasn't that the whole point of being an ex-expatriate wife? That you didn't have to play tennis?

Austen was serious: she really did need an interest. 'A voluntary group — you know, you always said—'

'Yeah, I know.'

And so she opted to become a volunteer at The Mount, the historic home of Edith Wharton. She wasn't particularly interested in history, and had no expectations — yet her decision to volunteer at The Mount felt unsettling, as if it opened up a sense of *possibility*. Which was unusual because Sara only bothered with matters requiring immediate attention. Drop her anywhere in the world — Lagos, Mombassa, Brussels — and, if necessary, she'd soon find an emergency doctor. Of course there wasn't much call for that in Lenox, Massachusetts (pop. 5025), which was why, according to *Back to First Base*, Sara should feel irrelevant and undervalued, frustrated that her life skills were redundant, annoyed that she could no longer throw a dinner party by clicking her fingers at the kitchen staff.

Really? she thought. People actually did that?

*

Among other duties at The Mount, Sara was in charge of dusting the library. The books were too precious for commercial cleaners. But why would anyone trust a volunteer? Sara hadn't dusted in thirty years — she couldn't even get her own cleaner to dust at home. The library had over twenty thousand books (she could believe this), all from Edith Wharton's original collection. Apparently the restoration committee had performed a miracle in purchasing them from a private collector in England and having them shipped back.

Sara had refused to become a tour guide. Her life had been one long tour and she wanted something different, although the ghost tours sounded interesting. Apparently Edith Wharton had written three volumes of ghost stories — which, according to Mrs Newbold, head of volunteers, was no more desirable for being factually correct.

It was chilly in the library, but Sara didn't mind: it meant that visitors never stayed long. People found it weird that she liked the cold. They had such fixed ideas about expatriates — a life spent poolside, that's what they thought — and Sara never failed to disappoint. They assumed she would be more commanding after all those maids, and better presented after all those international shopping malls. And despite all the sun and chlorinated swimming pools, they never expected pale freckles and faded orange hair.

She was dusting the German section when Bernard arrived with a pile of books. Small and unshaven, he might in other circumstances — say, a fruit market in Istanbul — prompt Sara to check for her handbag. But here at the historic Wharton home, Bernard, dressed in black and potentially gay, was every bit the promotions manager. She had heard about him from Mrs Newbold, who said he was from Manhattan and 'really shaking things up'. His smile was friendly, and he was impressed to hear that Sara had no particular interest in Edith Wharton. He'd been fearing another graduate in post-structural feminist theory.

'You get many of those?'

A flash of bleached teeth. 'And volunteers hoping to see Laura Bush.'

'She comes?'

'Not much. So how're you liking Lenox?'

'It's very beautiful.'

'Don't worry, everyone struggles at the beginning. It's a small place. You got kids?'

'Not here.' This was her standard response and usually enough to shut down the predictable *Gosh, what an international family! All over the place — did you say Indonesia?* Mothers were the worst, implying that Sara's scattered family was a gross form of carelessness. As if to prove the point, each of her children had attached themselves to different parts of the world. Matthew was in Europe, Alice in Hong Kong, and Hugo was still looking. Sara could only hope he wouldn't destroy himself in the process.

But Bernard skipped all of this by saying, 'They'll be back. It's a great place to visit.'

'Sure,' said Sara, knowing it would never happen.

He looked at her curiously. 'How many countries have you lived in?'

'Nine.' These days she included Massachusetts, having decided it was as foreign as anywhere else. Possibly more so. At least when living abroad she attributed everything to foreignness. But now? She felt an even greater distance from her own life.

Sara waited for the inevitable reaction — nine countries! But Bernard didn't seem offended, and she continued to dust.

'You know what gets me, Sara?'

Turning, she was surprised to find Bernard right behind her. She liked the way he said her name. Maybe she could try that. *Well, Bernard*, she wanted to say, but she was afraid of calling him Brendan. She was no good with names — no point with people always on the move.

'If I say "Edith Wharton", what comes to mind?'

'No idea,' said Sara as an image of white roses bloomed. The Mount was such a beautiful place for a wedding.

'Most people think of Edith as imperious and Victorian, right?'

'To be honest,' said Sara carefully, 'most people don't think of her at all.'

'Ouch. Let's try again. If people *do* know about Edith Wharton, they misremember her as puritanical and repressed. You know, haughty and privileged.'

The camera in Sara's mind panned to a carriage in the driveway. A stout woman climbed out, dressed in Gothic black and bad-tempered as a crow.

'Wrong,' said Bernard, as if reading her mind. 'Wharton hung out with Henry James, sure, but she also lunched with a drunk Scotty Fitzgerald. And just because she was rich, people believe she dabbled in writing like it was flower arranging.'

Up close his face was blotched with brown spots.

'And Wharton had a secret that defied every misconception about her life.'

'Really?'

He shrugged. 'Not something we discuss around here, not with the weddings. Brand authenticity and all that stuff.'

'But—'

'Sixteen novels, short stories, poetry and non-fiction. Wharton achieved success *despite* her wealth, not because of it.'

Wow, Bernard was seriously into Mrs Wharton. He had to be gay. And she wanted to know more about—

'Read any of her books?'

'*Ethan Frome*,' she said, stopping to remember. She'd been a big reader when she was young.

'Required reading at high school. Bet you watched *The Age of Innocence*, thinking it was classic Wharton, all that Victorian melodrama and repressed passion.'

Sara had no idea.

Bernard shook his head. 'One of her few historical novels. Edith negotiated a massive advance and slick marketing campaign. Her books are just as relevant as Jane Austen, and don't get me started on Shakespeare — that guy gets everything. But Edith? Nothing but costume dramas.'

He pulled a book from the case. 'Wharton didn't just win the Pulitzer, she had the chutzpah to satirise it. And like Hitchcock she often gate-crashes her own stories.' He spun around. 'So how do we get people to read her again?'

Sara's mind went blank.

Removing another book, he opened the pages. 'I'm updating *The Glimpses of the Moon* to stage in the garden. Edith's first Jazz Age novel — Paramount offered fifteen grand for the movie options.'

Sara looked at the pile of books on the desk. Mrs Newbold had been thunderously clear: they mustn't be touched. The books were irreplaceable and must be protected from the public — that was Sara's job. She picked up one of the novels and turned the pages, dust layering her fingers. 'So what's the story about?'

'Nick and Susy, two international drifters in the 1920s. Charming but no money. They decide on a short-term marriage — living off the wedding presents, honeymooning in houses owned by rich friends. A pre-nup agreement. The marriage will be over when the freebies dry up.' He paused, raising his eyebrows. 'It all goes belly-up when they fall in love with each other.'

'Sounds great.' She liked the cynicism.

'Scotty Fitzgerald scripted the silent movie. In my version, I've got two international drifters who decide to get married. But then what?'

He didn't know? Sara explained: 'They sell the magazine rights to pay for the luxury wedding. A power couple is always worth more than the sum of their parts.' She knew this stuff, it was easy. Living in Singapore — second time around — she and Hugo had watched a lot of reality TV.

Bernard ventured, 'Susy could be runner-up on *MasterChef*. They take a film crew on their honeymoon — everything sponsored by Durex.'

Sara nodded. 'And secure a two-season series on cable. But ratings slump because—'

'Susy can't get pregnant!' Bernard banged his hands on the desk. 'Which is terrible because she's signed to a weight-loss company for the post-pregnancy diet. Dairy Queen sponsors the fertility treatment, but still no luck. The show's about to be dumped, but now they're really in love! But then—' He floundered.

Sara felt the intoxication of *knowing*, of someone being interested in her opinion. In fairness to Austen, he always tried when she said, *I thought we might have salmon for dinner*, which only made it worse. No wonder he wanted to return to America, hoping the shock might re-boot his wife. And now here she was — distinguishing herself with a knowledge of reality television! Hardly what Austen would have had in mind. He was never specific about his hopes for life back home, beyond autumn leaves and snowy Berkshires, but she could guess: Austen wanted to throw dinner parties for Thanksgiving, invite friends for a barbecue and watch the Super Bowl. A mythical version of home. Three months, and they still had no friends.

Bernard was now pacing the room: he wanted to know what happened to a cable series that was bombing.

Sara blinked, it was so obvious. 'Susy comes up with the idea of a celebrity divorce — you know, star attorneys and courtroom cameras. Ratings go ballistic, but Nick no longer wants her — she's too morally compromised. Plus they're divorced. But Nick is the love of her life.'

'Fantastic,' said Bernard. 'But the ending's got to be happy. It's part of our summer garden series.'

'Nick and Susy ditch the show before the divorce, and hold a press conference.'

Bernard whipped around: 'Announcing their desire for that

most elusive thing of all — can you guess?' He waited a moment before adding, 'Obscurity.'

Of course.

'The final scene is Nick and Susy happily managing a two-star motel in Anaheim.'

Sara laughed, surprising herself. She felt light-headed, weirdly unanchored — but not in the usual way.

'You like it?'

'It's great.'

Bernard's shoulders dropped. 'Try telling the others. They're more concerned about upholstery in the drawing room. I want this place to be interactive.' With no response, he continued. 'Wharton's work was often serialised in journals before she'd finished. Can you imagine the pressure? Like a screenwriter for Netflix.' He crossed to the windows overlooking the terrace. 'You know, she loved the garden.'

Outside, the mist was beginning to lift, the air sparkling and iridescent. Sara tried to imagine Mrs Wharton flinging open the doors, throwing instructions to a hovering servant. A staircase stepped grandly down a grass slope.

Bernard turned. 'Do you like gardening?'

God, no. The very idea filled her with boredom. Did Bernard really want a description of her garden? Three acres of lawn and shrubs. Last week she tried forcing bulbs into the ground under a tree but they didn't fit. Was that interesting? *Does your condo have a lap pool?*

And yet, when they first returned, Sara had briefly believed a garden might connect her physically with her new home, create a link with her own future. But gardens kept growing, wilful and subversive. Endless life cycles, senescence and death. It was creepy.

She said, 'You know the real problem with gardens? What no one tells you? They're never finished. They just keep going.'

'Isn't that the point?'

Bernard didn't understand. Caring for a garden wasn't like arriving at a freshly decorated apartment with a welcome pack in the fridge. Her life had been one of immaculate beginnings and clean-cut conclusions, and this was more difficult than it sounded — it was a real skill not to plan ahead. And yet it was critical. Even the most committed expatriate could be driven crazy by the dictates of head office — always being told what country to live in, and for how long. Not Sara; she adapted like a true Darwinian. She never played the long game or booked the theatre six months in advance. And she liked not having to worry about lasting consequences. There was no need since every new country provided a fresh start — always handy when the tennis committee turned feral.

Bernard was holding up another book to show her: *Italian Villas and Their Gardens*. 'Edith's first novel was set in Italy and hugely popular, so she wrote a non-fiction book on Italian gardens. She and her husband spent four months finding more than fifty properties, most overgrown and forgotten. I'm wondering, wouldn't it be great to re-create her trip and write a blog?'

Sara took the book from him, flicking past heavy blocks of text and strange magical drawings. 'Like that blog on Julia Child.'

'And made into a movie.' He pressed her, 'What do you think?'

'About what?'

'With your understanding of popular culture you'd be perfect. Revisit the gardens and write about them in a modern context.

Each blog posted on our website, plus a Twitter feed. Maybe a coffee-table book.'

'Why don't you go?'

'You think I can afford it?'

Sara turned another page. She never gave money much thought, just assumed it was unlimited like broadband.

'You'd be great,' he insisted.

Did he mean it?

Mrs Newbold's voice boomed in the foyer, welcoming the first visitors of the day. Sara picked up her feather duster, but the footsteps were already moving away towards the kitchen.

The garden was sparkling in the morning light. A series of terraces dropped to an avenue of trees, the skeletal branches misshapen by swelling buds, soil displaced by the thrust of spring bulbs. A flower parterre at the far end was newly planted, the annuals yet to form a coherent pattern. Sara watched sunlight burn through the last drifts of mist to reveal wooded hills glowing luminous under a delicate frosting of dew, a glittering lake in a damp hollow. It was very beautiful.

'So will you do it?'

Sara took a second to remember the question — a trip to Italy. 'We're not supposed to travel. It upsets the resettling process.'

'For how long?'

'At least a year.'

'Tough.'

Was this sarcasm? Sara couldn't tell.

'Can you write?'

'I started a sociology degree.'

'Perfect.'

Not really. She quit college when Austen got his first international posting. She didn't mind about her degree, was too excited about travelling. As she said to her friends, now she could put her studies into practice — you know, community initiatives and stuff. Except Austen's first posting was to Singapore, a gleaming city with no interest in Sara's views on social justice. And after two years, and a similar number of children, she found herself unable to decline the services of a sweet-faced Filipino nanny. By the time they got to Lagos, Sara was secretary of the tennis club and mother-of-three.

'You must be able to write.'

Sara wasn't so sure. The only writing she'd done since college was the annual Christmas letter: *This year we're spending Christmas in Dubai. Hugo is hoping to ride a camel!* It had seemed normal, but she was beginning to understand why relations with her sister were strained. And now Sara herself was living in America. Once again she had the chance to write a new version of herself. Except this was different. They were adopting a permanent life. Sara felt the visceral weight of the word — permanent — like something fused from permafrost and cement.

'Do I get an answer?' said Bernard. He was sitting on the corner of Edith's desk.

'Sorry?'

'I'm not blaming you, it's just—' He left the words hanging.

Only last week Austen mentioned a trip to Argentina. It was a suggestion light with cautiousness, given what it contravened, and what it implied — that life in Lenox was proving harder than he ever expected. Austen was learning that he could only play so much golf, attend so many committee meetings. That the skills of a prematurely retired environmental engineer were not required unless you counted a drainage problem behind the clubhouse. And without a frequent flyer card, he now found himself spending whole days at home with a spectral wife who floated about in a housecoat. Their future lay ahead like a long evening shadow.

'Sure, I'll go,' said Sara.

Bernard watched.

'To Italy. I want to write the blog.'

CHAPTER II

What an extraordinary evening. Setting the manuscript aside, Edith scanned the room with pleasure. The lights were blazing and the fire crackled. Linky was sniffing a sofa leg with interest, managing to ignore — with magnificent disregard — Sybil's attempt to kick her away. The little dog might appear demure, but she was stubborn as a mule.

Edith set her chair rocking again gently. To hear about her home had been an unexpected joy — as was knowing her books had been returned. When she left The Mount, she had closed the door on her memories, but she remembered now: it had been the house of her dreams, elegant and beautiful, with views that sent the spirit soaring. But it was also a place of horror and entrapment; and she'd had no choice but to leave.

The first chapter of the novella raised so many questions. Edith had faltered at the many unfamiliar words — blogs and websites; what was a Twitter feed? She could only suppose such things were related to what Charles Scribner called the internet; and it was the internet that would allow her work to be rediscovered. Edith glanced at the bookcase: there was an entire shelf of her books. For thirty years she had dominated the literary world and was even asked to finish Proust's last volume. She took great pride in her oeuvre; it deserved to be rediscovered. But seeing her books here, Edith felt her joy drain away: they were in a terrible state, tired and old-fashioned, neglected.

Feeling for Mr Scribner's letter tucked beside her, Edith's spirits revived. She had never given up, continuing to write and sell her work until the end. The world may have become indifferent, but that didn't stop her trying — not then and not now. Her last novel, following a group of modern American girls taking the British aristocracy by storm, was sure to have propelled her onto best-seller lists. It was a wonderful story, one of her best; and no doubt the final chapters were completed by a respected writer. Edith could feel the old stirrings of excitement. Writing was in her blood, and now she was back, with the most unexpected chance to restore her reputation.

'I do wish,' said Sybil, 'someone would explain what we're listening to. What on earth is a condo?'

'A large bird,' said Teddy.

'Twitter feed,' agreed Percy.

Imbeciles.

'I wanted to hear about my animals,' Teddy continued. 'And not a word about my stables.'

'A novella,' mused Walter. 'Not many published now, I suspect.'

'Scribner's are committed,' said Edith.

Trix clicked her tongue irritably. 'But you can't *want* the book published, Aunt Puss — surely not.'

What a peculiar thing to say — even by her niece! Of course she wanted it published. Now everyone was staring at her blankly. They couldn't be serious. Did they honestly think she would pass up the opportunity to have her name revived?

Apparently so. Look at them — all resigned to this banal non-existence, a universal acceptance of their hopeless fate. Well, she was cut from a different cloth. To have accepted her fate as Mrs Edward Wharton would have meant a lifetime arranging flowers.

Walter stretched his legs. 'Not sure about this, Edith.'

Frustration gripped her: why was he so obstructive? She felt close to tears, knowing she must fight. 'Surely you understand, Walter?'

'A long and successful career, my dear, leave it at that.'

The perceptible chill in his voice was like a reprimand. She deserved more support. Walter wouldn't remember his last days in the hospital when he wanted her close; holding her so fast that all the old flame and glory came back in the cold shadow of death and parting. He died one morning while she was hurrying to the hospital, without the chance to say goodbye. With a steadying breath, she said, 'You must agree it would be wonderful to have my name in print again, even if I'm not the author.'

Walter turned away, remarking to Sybil that dabbling in the modern world was beyond his comprehension; he could barely send a telegram — but, goodness, Sybil was looking well this evening. Shame about the dancing, but perhaps . . .

According to the novella, Edith was remembered, if at all, as a haughty and repressed Victorian. A bad-tempered old crow! Exactly what she had feared: a posthumous misremembering. It was utterly false. Her life had been as vibrant and overflowing as a Moroccan bazaar: house parties and travel; precious friendships; managing her career and finances — a vital life. It was everything that wasn't *this*. Why should she reject such an opportunity?

As if to disagree, Walter's mouth compressed. 'Not the natural order of things, Edith, interfering in the modern world.'

And to think he'd been her business advisor!

'You just want to be famous again,' said Sybil.

Trix straightened. 'You see? There's nothing to be gained by this.'

'You're wrong, Trix. I deserve better than to be forgotten.'

'I'm forgotten,' said Walter with dignity.

'Oh, Walter, I'm sure you're not forgotten.'

'Perhaps not entirely,' he conceded.

'But why?' asked Trix.

Edith regarded her niece levelly. 'I'm sure history has treated you well, Trix. Perhaps not as recognised as you deserve, but I suspect you're remembered correctly as a successful landscape architect.' While at the bookcase, Edith had seen a book on Beatrix Jones Farrand. From the spine it appeared a quality publication. She continued, 'Unfortunately, I appear to be misremembered.'

'I thought you were forgotten,' said Sybil, flipping open a compact mirror to apply a sweep of lipstick.

Good God, this was awful. Edith persisted. 'My question is: why?'

'Why what?' asked Teddy.

'Why am I misremembered? Why the image of a haughty imperious grande dame? A privileged lady who dabbled in writing. Where do such misconceptions come from?' Edith stopped. There was an intense silence, as if someone in the room had the answer. She hadn't expected this, hadn't believed there *was* an answer. 'Walter?' she said tartly.

'I've no idea.'

'Trix?'

'For goodness' sake, there's no point making everyone upset.'

'What do you know?'

'Nothing.' Her eyes slid to the sofa.

Edith swung around. Percy and Sybil were staring back like

a pair of Siamese cats. There was something about them — both English of course, but that wasn't unusual.

'Opening Pandora's box, my dear,' drawled Walter. 'I'd be very careful.'

'Walter's right,' said Teddy cheerfully. 'Best let sleeping dogs lie.'

Edith said, 'Any other meaningless aphorisms?'

'Have you ever considered', asked Sybil with unnerving lucidity, and Edith braced herself against the clear gaze, 'the consequences of being famous in the modern age?'

'I don't want to be famous, Sybil. I want to be remembered.' Why couldn't they understand? She simply wanted to participate in the world of literature. Nonetheless, Sybil's words echoed those of Mr Scribner: that Edith should think seriously about the consequences of the novella's publication. He had warned her: the world was a vastly different place.

'Dashed business,' said Teddy.

'But it's fascinating to hear about the modern world,' said Sybil. Bouncing up, she crossed to the mirror above the mantelpiece to inspect her makeup. She was so close that Edith could see the pink weft of her linen skirt, the sheen of silk stockings, her small neat ankles and low pumps. Her papery face was heavily powdered, eyelids smudged peacock blue. Smoothing her arched brows in the mirror, she said, 'I want to know how the war ended, what happened to my villa in Italy.'

No, surely not — *another* war? Edith sought to remember, searching her mind with a flashlight. Yes, she recalled storm clouds gathering once again over Europe, a screaming foreign maniac on the wireless. What happened to her homes in France? What happened to darling Elisina? It was terrible not to know.

Sybil pivoted from the mirror. 'Poor Edith — I believe you were gone by then. It was those Germans again.'

Edith replied stiffly, 'I'm thankful to have been spared. The Great War was almost the death of me.'

'Nonsense,' clipped Walter. 'You were a force to be reckoned with. Remarkable what your causes achieved, but you exhausted the rest of us.'

'Who won?' said Teddy with interest, as if he'd missed a horse-race and the possibility of a bet.

'We did,' replied Trix. 'Thankfully the second war was followed by a long period of peace.'

'I wouldn't call Elvis peaceful,' said Percy slyly.

'True,' murmured Trix, retying her scarf with care but unable to disguise her uncertainty.

Edith watched closely, aware Percy was playing a game of mortal last card. She was torn between wanting to stop the spectacle and hearing the final outcome.

'And The Beatles didn't help,' pressed Percy.

It was clear that Trix did not understand.

Percy smiled in victory before adding, 'I doubt they amounted to much, what with Love Me Do.'

'No idea what you're talking about,' said Walter testily, aware of having missed something — something involving Love Me Do.

Well, who would have guessed Percy would be the last man standing? He must have been a great age by the end. Disturbing that he'd had so much unsupervised time in which to make mischief. What did Percy get up to after they were gone?

Sybil laughed into the large gilt mirror. 'I want to hear more about the wife being re-booted.'

'The skills of a modern cobbler,' said Percy, keen to secure his advantage.

Trix knotted her brows. 'I wonder about a scholarship I set up, what happened to all my plans and papers.'

Sybil froze, her colour draining. 'I want to know about my grandchildren.' Turning, she surveyed the room with a brave smile. 'The oldest boy died before—' She broke off to gather herself. Everyone looked away as she returned unsteadily to the sofa.

Edith, however, was more interested in what her niece had said. Of course — papers: why had she not considered this before? What happened to the papers she had left behind in the care of Elisina?

On the sofa, Percy was attending to Sybil with an unpleasant solicitousness, his voice low and urgent. She was fussing with a handkerchief, dabbing the corner of one eye.

'You never would listen,' said Walter sharply.

Edith was confused; why should Walter be annoyed with Sybil? The woman had always been an emotional wreck; they were lucky she hadn't fainted on the rug.

Hooking one arm around his chair, Walter faced her directly, and Edith was stung to realise the words were meant for her.

'Gathering us tonight for your own advantage. You've no right.'

How could he say such things? Tonight she needed his support more than ever. Was that too much to expect? After a lifetime of loyalty their love was immortal, a love that defied the conventional and was always misunderstood by others. More passionate than marriage, it was a relationship of mind and soul, a bond that surprised and enriched until the very end, their sense of humour and irony pitched in exactly the same key. They never lived together, but Walter had been her travelling companion and social partner; he gave counsel on legal matters and read everything she ever wrote. She trusted his opinion above all else.

In truth, at the beginning she had hoped for something more … well, *more*, but in time she came to appreciate their unique understanding. If others had assumed their relationship was physical, she hadn't objected. On the contrary, it had served her well, proving every critic wrong when they called her cold and repressed, chaste and moralistic, emotionally empty . . . My God, her critics had been savage, but she had carried on. Battening down the hatches and gathering her friends closer, loving Walter more fiercely. All she asked for in return was loyalty and support.

'Oh, I wouldn't worry,' said Percy, crossing one leg over the other. 'The chances of Edith being rediscovered are absolutely zero.'

Edith glared with loathing. How dare he? 'You do realise that I was awarded an honorary doctorate in letters from Yale? Oh, of course — you were a writer as well, although I can only remember your little handbook on Henry. You took apart the great Master's writing like a mechanical clock.'

With a defiant bounce, Percy was up from the sofa and crossing to the bookcase. Edith had forgotten his height — his personality was of a smaller man, eyes like a fox terrier. However, Percy's clothes were neater than she remembered; he was no longer the rumpled young fellow she had known so well. His hair was smoothed and crisp, suggesting a recent trip to the barber. Edith caught her breath: it was the small domestic details that made their present circumstances so preposterous.

The others watched Percy peruse the bookcase. 'Peculiar collection — quite a few of your books, Edith.'

'I'm not sure that's peculiar.'

'*Ethan Frome* next to something called *Bonkers*. I suspect they're left over from a book fair.'

Odious man.

'Or a bookcase in a Helsinki youth hostel. Now this is interesting — something by James Joyce.'

'That's not remotely interesting.' She couldn't stand Joyce with his turgid schoolboy grubbiness.

'Published by Black Sun Press.'

Blood rushed to her cheeks.

'And something else — Walter, this may interest you.'

Edith stared in anguish as Percy pulled the copy of Proust from the shelf, carelessly opening the cover. 'A personal inscription, no less.' He crossed the room, pressing both books on Walter, who chuckled.

'My old friend, Marcel! Marvellous times we had together.'

Did Percy know what he was doing? Why select those two books? Would Walter understand the significance of Joyce — or rather, the publisher? Would he ask why the rest of the Proust set was missing?

Walter was reading Marcel's inscription, nodding with satisfaction. Edith knew the questions would come soon. She had no idea how she would respond. Briskly she said, 'Any other comments before I continue to read the novella?'

'I don't see the point,' said Walter.

'Surely you want to hear about Italy?'

'Not really.' He turned another page.

Oh, if only Henry were here; she desperately needed his support. Edith fixed her attention on the Hepplewhite, using all her strength to summon his arrival, but the chair remained mockingly empty. True, there was nothing about it that suggested Henry — the delicate arms (one slightly broken) and floral upholstered seat; it wasn't the style of furniture she could imagine him choosing to occupy. And would he really support her desire to be rediscovered? Henry had always admired her commercial success (no question about that) almost as much as he despised it. She could just picture Henry's response: grandiloquently crushing.

No, Walter had been her greatest supporter, encouraging her career from the start when she clumsily tried to write a book on home decoration. He had caught up the pages with good humour, and together they went on adjective hunts. But Walter wasn't helping tonight. Sinking with defeat, Edith saw he was deeply engrossed in Proust. She must stop him reading, stop the questions before they arrived. Quietly she said, 'Perhaps you could read poetry, dear?'

The bookcase was now shadowy and indistinct, the room dimmed in advance of a reading. Edith shivered with a premonition of someone in the room knowing too much, of a growing presence, a sense of foreboding. Her nerves rattled. 'Or we could discuss advances in archaeology? I see a book on the shelf.'

The lights flared, and a woman laughed. 'But Mrs Wharton, we're assembled to hear the novella. I insist you read.'

Edith started in fright. A woman was sitting directly across from her, smiling with unpleasant insistence. A woman so ordinary as to be unusual. She wore an ugly skirt of boiled wool; her amber necklace was like a string of barley sugars; and her cresting hairstyle could only be described as suburban. 'I'm sorry,' said Edith, flustered. 'I don't—'

'Consider me a fan,' the woman replied apologetically.

'I don't understand.'

'I always followed your career very closely.' Behind the heavy-framed glasses, her eyes burned with intensity. 'We have a great deal in common, Mrs Wharton. More than you could possibly imagine.'

Oh, for heaven's sake, she probably thought herself a writer. Edith knew the sort, with their unpublished scribbles and mildly hysteric fantasies. But that was no reason to gate-crash a literary evening and frighten everyone.

'I was also a writer,' she continued.

Of course she was.

A gesture of embarrassment: 'Nothing like you, but several novels and a collection of short stories.'

Walter shifted. 'Should we know you — er . . . ?'

'Gerould. My name is Mrs Gerould.'

Gerould. Edith tried to think. The name sounded familiar yet distant. Was she a minor notoriety or (worse) an obscure relative? No, it was more personal, like the faintest touch. Mrs Gerould was American — well spoken — and almost certainly from the Northeast. Edith searched the face for more clues: she had been pretty once, and married, obviously. Even the glasses gave away nothing: round tortoiseshell, the type once thought modern, but who was to know today? 'Did we ever meet, Mrs Gerould?'

'Once. A cab ride in Paris.'

She had the vaguest memory — rain-streaming windows and a gloomy interior. Sharply, she said, 'Who are you?'

Mrs Gerould responded with an apologetic shrug.

What a vacuous woman. She had no right to be here, delaying things with her amateur dramatics.

'I enjoyed the opening chapter,' approved Mrs Gerould.

Oh, good lord — now she was actually *knitting*. Next she'd be hanging out the laundry.

Mrs Gerould continued, 'Such a clever way to re-ignite interest in your writing.'

Walter laughed. 'Edith never did like to be forgotten.'

'Reviving the Wharton brand,' agreed Mrs Gerould.

She was surprisingly quick-witted.

'And the writer knows your work well — so sly and allusive, especially Sara dusting books in the library. It reminds me of your character Charity Royall in the library at North Dormer.'

So she had read the novella *Summer*. Not as conservative as she appeared.

'Perhaps,' continued Mrs Gerould, 'modern readers will be drawn to your more sensational material.'

Why did this sound like a threat?

'Sensational material!' tinkled Sybil. 'Let me guess: lace curtains in a drawing-room!'

'I was thinking of incest,' remarked Mrs Gerould calmly. 'That was a common Wharton theme. A brave woman to write of incest giving mutual pleasure.'

The room went silent; everyone was at a loss except for Teddy, who had found a copy of *Practical Pigs* under his chair.

Stirred by an idea, Edith said, 'Did you write the novella? Are you here under false pretences? You're not — well—' *You're not alive, are you?* What a dreadful question.

But Mrs Gerould said lightly, 'No, I belong here like everyone else. And I'm keen to hear the novella. I suspect we have some surprises in store.'

Mrs Gerould's enthusiasm was worse than Walter's protestations.

'But there's absolutely no point,' cried Sybil. 'Hasn't anyone considered the obvious? There's absolutely no point. Edith can't *do* anything about the book; none of us can. We can't change anything.'

Mrs Gerould regarded her thoughtfully before turning back to Edith. 'Could you explain again? I seem to have missed the beginning.'

Edith adopted a tone that warned against further questions. 'I've had a letter from my editor, Charles Scribner. The company wants to publish a modern novella about me. I assume they hold the rights to all my work and hope it will revive sales.'

'I heard you broke ranks with Scribner's.'

The woman knew far too much.

'You found them too stuffy, and poor old Charles Scribner behind the times. So you shopped around, selling *The Age of Innocence* to the highest bidder. Plus a further deal for four short stories about old New York.'

53

'I hardly see the relevance.'

'An astonishing achievement — you were the first modern literary agent. Unthinkable for a woman living far from New York to instigate bidding wars and aggressively promote her own work.' Mrs Gerould paused. 'So why did you become so forgotten?'

Exactly.

'You still don't understand,' insisted Sybil with mild hysteria. 'We're all stuck here because of Edith, and with no reason. Even if she wanted, she can't *change* anything.'

Mrs Gerould persisted. 'What did Mr Scribner say?'

'That publication is ultimately up to me.'

'I don't see how,' dismissed Percy. 'How can you let them know?'

'A séance!' cried Sybil, her hysteria forgotten.

'For God's sake,' snapped Walter.

'Oh, I don't know.' Sybil looked hurt. 'I found them rather fun.'

'We're not fairground ghouls.'

Mrs Gerould contemplated the low flames in the fireplace. 'You could burn it.'

Exactly the advice of Charles Scribner. However, this was Edith's decision; she didn't want others interfering.

'Burn the manuscript and it won't be published. Am I right?'

'Possibly.'

'But what if the fire goes out?' Trix regarded the flames with distrust. 'We should burn it now.'

For God's sake, her niece had never approved of an exhibitionist aunt who sold stories to the public. Clearly this extended into the afterlife.

'No panic,' said Percy, his moustache twitching with amusement. 'Edith's got a cigarette lighter.'

Of course, she had quite forgotten. Picking up the silver lighter, Edith was impressed by its weight: an object of substance and (more importantly) consequence. She was in control. She had a choice. The outcome of this evening was up to her; everything was in her hands: her future, the re-invention of Edith Wharton. With an intoxicating power, she ran her thumb down the spark wheel, watching a small flame burst to life. Her cheeks grew warm, and she let the cover click shut. Satisfied, she placed the lighter back on the table.

For just a moment, she had seen her reflection, slumped and beaten. It had been difficult to disassemble her features from the hammered surface of the lighter — except for her eyes: they had grown more and more distinct, giving out a light of their own.

'No sign of a fire extinguisher,' Teddy declared cheerfully.

'So everything is in your hands,' observed Mrs Gerould. 'Whether to publish or not. The re-invention of Edith Wharton. It's quite a decision.'

'Not really.' As far as she was concerned, there was no decision. She had taken risks throughout her career; she would not stop now.

Laying down her knitting, Mrs Gerould confronted Edith. 'Are you quite sure you want to be rediscovered? The past is so unpredictable.'

'This is about the future.'

Mrs Gerould shook her head. 'A dangerous business, rattling skeletons. You don't know what might come out.'

'This is my story. I know what's involved and have no reason to be concerned.'

'Such a common mistake to believe you can view your own life in its entirety. There are always unknown factors and other points of view. You know that.'

Apprehension breathed softly across Edith. 'I've no idea what you mean.'

'I'm wondering,' said Percy, hitching his trousers, 'what was meant in the novella about your having a secret.'

'I can't recall.'

'Wharton had a secret that defied every misconception about her life.'

She held her ground. 'It's called fiction, Percy. A small hook for readers, nothing more.'

'But—'

'But nothing. I tell you, it's fiction.' True enough, but her hands had shaken while she read this part. What had the writer meant? Edith had plenty of family skeletons — God knows, her family was worse than most — but nothing of interest to modern readers. So why hint at a mystery? It was almost a warning — about what?

Mrs Gerould said kindly, 'You haven't thought this through, have you?'

'I've no need to be worried, Mrs Gerould. I have nothing to hide.'

'Can you really tolerate your private life becoming public?'

'My life is already public. I made sure of that many years ago. If people want to know anything personal they can read my memoir.'

There. Finished.

A burst of laughter cracked the room. The lights flickered again. The laughter stopped, leaving soft folds in Mrs Gerould's skin.

Edith watched anxiously.

Mrs Gerould said, 'Your memoirs, Mrs Wharton, are so vague as to be misleading and so selective as to be deceitful.'

'That's not—'

'She's right,' said Percy.

Edith was astonished. 'I beg your pardon?'

'Bollocks, your memoir. The whole jolly lot.'

'The introduction to my memoir,' said Edith, opening to the first page, 'states that I will not record my every resentment of others.

I dislike the way autobiographies are judged by their vindictiveness and sensationalism.'

'Certainly,' agreed Percy, 'but a bit of truth might have been in order.'

'Nonsense.'

Mrs Gerould pressed on. 'Your introduction also states that having forgotten all your grievances, you would have to make the best of your unsensational material.'

Beneath the homely exterior of Mrs Gerould, Edith detected deep derision. Hesitating, she said, 'I believe that's true, yes.'

'And do you stand by those words?'

'I don't know — how can I?'

'If your memoirs are to believed, Mrs Wharton, nothing in your life might be considered . . .' Mrs Gerould paused before saying carefully, '*untoward*.'

'I don't know what you mean.'

'I believe you do.'

'You're referring to my parentage.'

A shake of her head. 'No, you were right to ignore such things.'

Mrs Gerould was aware of the accusation — that Edith was not her father's daughter. The allegation was outrageous. Her mother, Lucretia, was so cold and distant, always quick to condemn others, and repulsed by her child's habit of making up stories. Lucretia had quivered with discomfort when asked where babies came from, saying such things were 'not nice'. And later, when Edith had wanted to know what would happen on her wedding night, Lucretia's icy disapproval had deepened to disgust.

Could Lucretia really have slept with another man and borne his child? That was unimaginable — and yet it was possible. Nevertheless, it changed nothing: the precious bond between Edith and her father could not be understood or defiled by others. Her father was the only true person in her family. But he died prematurely, and the family would go on to destroy itself. Court orders and lawyers; estrangement and recrimination: the Jones family at war with itself.

But why hadn't she realised this before? Renewed interest in Edith Wharton would drag up so many matters best forgotten. Teddy didn't deserve renewed scrutiny; he was a decent man tormented by his own demons. Lucretia should be left in the past. As for her brothers, Freddy and Harry, they both had betrayed her. Her older brother, after flaunting his lover in the window of Delmonico's Restaurant, had taken the woman to Paris, where he was soon joined by Lucretia. Under his influence, Lucretia adjusted her will, and it took Edith years to redress the injustice. People assumed her lifestyle was funded by inheritance, but this wasn't true; she always relied on her writing. Any money she inherited was hard won in the courts.

And this was not the end of her misfortunes: her brother Harry was later ensnared by a woman calling herself the Countess Tekla. (Edith preferred to call her the smouldering rancune.) In Harry's last ten years, Edith saw him only once, an occasion when he screamed of her illegitimacy. Her real father (it was rumoured) was a red-headed young Englishman who had tutored her brothers then quickly headed out west, where he was killed by Indians. But it was also rumoured Edith was sired by an elderly Scottish peer with red hair and — like Edith — an interest in science.

Sex, inheritance and litigation: that was the Jones family. It was too devastating and private, and none of it was recorded in her memoir. Did she risk it all being dug up again? It was so frustrating; being dead made everything hard to control. Angrily, she said, 'I do wish, Mrs Gerould, you would tell us your Christian name. Who are you?'

'I thought you would have guessed by now.'

'This is not a parlour game. We once met and—'

'I always hoped for the honour of meeting you again — and here we are!'

Stupid woman, she appeared to be correcting a stitch of knitting.

Mrs Gerould placed down her work to focus directly on Edith. 'Have you thought about the rest of us? All dragged into your scheme.'

'Nonsense. This isn't about you.'

'It's about all of us, Mrs Wharton. Not that I mind my past being exposed to the public.'

Oh, this was ridiculous: what was the worst Mrs Gerould had ever done? Some domestic calamity involving soap powder? Edith said, 'We shared a cab ride, Mrs Gerould. If my life is to be reprised, I fail to see what role you would play.'

'I want to be played by Bette Davis,' said Sybil.

'I'm not sure that would be feasible,' said Mrs Gerould carefully.

'What on earth,' said Edith, 'is the woman talking about?'

'A film about your life,' responded Trix.

'Have to be a long one,' mused Percy.

Edith rounded on him, 'I keep telling you, this is about my writing, not my life.'

'No difference,' clipped Percy. 'Idolising celebrities. And judging from the novella, times are worse now.'

'He's right.' Walter rotated in his chair to confront Edith. 'Don't you agree? That we're all to be dragged into the business?'

'Oh, Walter, you'd love the publicity.' Her tone was breezy, but she was frozen by a terrible realisation. Walter had no idea what had happened after his death. He believed his life to be impeccable and beyond reproach (which was true), but it was also open to mis-interpretation, and there were events too painful for him to hear tonight. Edith felt confused and powerless. Picking up her memoir, she said, 'You're all mistaken and making everything so complicated. I simply want my work reprinted and marketed to a modern audience.'

'I would like to know,' demanded Walter, 'what you wrote about me in your memoir.'

Edith studied the patterned rug.

'Edith?'

'Too long ago, Walter. There's no point.'

'There's every point. A renewed interest in the life of Edith Wharton means we'll all be dragged into the business.' Unexpectedly, Walter thrust out an arm. 'Here, give it to me.'

'No, Walter—' She broke off at his insistence and reluctantly passed across the memoir.

On the sofa, Percy was saying to Sybil, 'As I recall, Edith wrote that Walter was the very meaning of her soul.'

Furious, Edith addressed the room: 'If anyone's interested, I wrote that Walter found me when my mind and soul were hungry and thirsty, and he fed them till our last hours together.' Yes, it had been a very public declaration of love. One had to grasp the few advantages of a long life because, God knows, there was little else to take comfort from.

'Not sure I understand,' said Teddy. 'I mean—'

'Dashed poor form,' broke in Walter, turning another page. 'Was this really necessary, Edith?'

'Believe me,' she said tiredly, 'it was extremely necessary.' She stopped — yes, but *why* was it necessary? She couldn't remember. Her very public declaration of love was genuine; she had been mad with grief, but it was also completely out of character. Why had she chosen to humiliate herself? Forcing herself to remember, a picture of Percy floated into her mind. God, she didn't need him there; he was already on her sofa. 'It was Percy,' she said slowly.

Percy swivelled around, eyes popping.

'I can't remember why — at least, not now. But it will come to me.'

'Poor Edith, your memory really has gone.'

'It's getting better. I remember you two are married.'

Percy blinked, and Sybil made a show of plumping the cushions.

She should have remembered sooner: Sybil and Percy were married. The idea was preposterous. Sybil had blazed through so many of Edith's friends — all vulnerable, sensitive men, all extinguished by a ruthless socialite. And finally Percy, hitherto protected by his own misplaced sense of superiority. Yes, Percy had become husband number three — or was it four? It had never occurred to her that Percy Lubbock was the marrying sort; he was just another of Henry's impotent satyrs. How wrong she was. Marriage was convenient for both of them.

Edith clasped her hands tightly with renewed distress. She had cut them both from her life — and now here they were, popping up like irrepressible corks, tittering on the sofa. Worse, they were laughing about her. This must explain her distrust of Percy — his marriage to Sybil — and yet she had the sense of something more dangerous . . . something about Percy's writing. Edith shook her head to clear the confusion.

Walter skimmed another page, saying icily, 'Why, Edith, would you publish such—'

'To protect your reputation,' she protested, and then, 'Oh, don't ask me more.' In truth, she couldn't remember; however, she was certain Percy was somehow involved.

Walter's thin mouth drew back in distaste.

Edith flushed deeply, recalling her description of his deathbed scene. 'I want to keep reading,' she said quickly, but Walter was fixed to the book. She had written of his last days, speechless and unable to move. A bitter consciousness of his failing powers.

The book dropped to the floor, and Walter leaned back so he was again hidden by the wings of his chair.

'I'm sorry,' she said more quietly, 'but I wanted everyone to remember you as the astonishing and gifted man I revered. The man I loved.'

A shadow fell across her manuscript and Edith jumped. It was Teddy. His hand landed on the back of her chair, and she began to recline. He loomed above, red-faced and horribly alive, like a mad surgeon. She tried to laugh, anxious that he was in an unmanageable mood. 'Teddy, please!'

He shook his head with baffled sheepishness. 'Wanted to see more about The Mount.'

With forced calm, she said, 'I suspect the next chapter is set in Italy.'

'Remember watching stars from the terrace? No place like it.'

Teddy was right, there was nothing like the fresh loveliness of The Mount, but his pleading ignorance broke her heart. Only nine years after completion, the place was sold. She was living in Paris by then, divorce imminent — as was the Great War. It would be many years before she returned to America, a short trip to collect her doctorate from Yale. That was all. She never saw The Mount again.

Large hands reached for the manuscript, and Edith found herself snapped upright. Shielding the pages, she said, 'Please, Teddy, sit down, you'll be more comfortable.' Teddy pulled away, ambling over to the fireplace to rest on his haunches, tickling Linky under the chin.

'Will you continue to read?' asked Mrs Gerould.

'I — well, of course.' Edith felt flustered. During her reading of the first chapter, Teddy had circled the room, chuckling and nodding to himself. But it was impossible to know what lay ahead.

Mrs Gerould's knitting needles flashed in the firelight. 'The writer hopes to catch the attention of the modern world. Can you imagine how?'

'The quality of my work, I hope.'

The flashing stopped as a thought passed across Mrs Gerould's face.

Edith tried to swallow, disturbed by the woman's expression; she looked like a stranded goldfish, all goggle-eyed and stunned. Edith willed herself to laugh, but her throat was dry.

'I'm very keen to hear the rest of the novella,' said Mrs Gerould.

The cool slide of pages in Edith's hand felt treacherous. Abruptly, she said, 'Let's read something else for a change.'

'But you must keep reading,' insisted Teddy. Swaying to his feet, he steadied himself. 'I want to hear about our trip to Italy.'

Oh, God, she recognised this Teddy from later years when violence lay just below the surface.

'Better read the damn thing,' muttered Walter.

'No, you don't understand.' She had no idea what revelations might come out. Her memory was becoming clearer, and she could sense something terrible. She must think. Mrs Gerould had asked how the novella would capture the attention of a modern world, which (she must concede) was a good question. The most obvious answer might be the family scandals — illegitimacy, litigation, and a lifetime of feuding. But that didn't fit with the novella's warning, one of the characters — Bernard — saying: *Wharton had a secret that defied every misconception about her life.* Nor did it fit the implication that the secret undermined the integrity of a white wedding. What was Bernard referring to? Certainly not a family feud. In Edith's experience, weddings seldom occurred *without* a family feud. This suggested something far more intimate. Something she could sense but not yet remember. Did the answer lie in the novella? Perhaps, although Mr Scribner said it was not particularly alarming; however, it *was* suggestive, and she should read it closely.

But how could she read aloud having no idea what was coming? She was afraid of Teddy's violence, and fearful what Walter might hear. Could she skim-read the manuscript while the others were otherwise engaged?

The room was warm and slumberous in the half-darkness, but Edith felt keenly awake. The novella had already fired a warning shot: the secrets of her life existed in the modern world. And Mr Scribner said (if she recalled correctly) that if something now existed in the material world, it existed as information available to everybody.

She mightn't understand the internet, but she understood that allowing publication of the novella would expose her life to inter-rogation — and in a place of uncivilised madness. How could she possibly agree to this when she didn't know what knowledge of her life existed? The question was this: if new readers were alerted to events concealed in Edith Wharton's life and went searching for the truth, what would they find?

The answer lay in this room tonight. She felt certain.

Obviously, the novella would provide answers, but perhaps not entirely. The bookcase was another possibility. Percy surmised the books were leftovers from a sale, but that didn't account for a first-edition Proust or a text on Beatrix Jones Farrand. Yes, she would take a closer look at the shelves — but there remained the uncomfortable and most obvious sensation: that someone in the room knew the secrets of her life. Why else had they gathered?

She always spent All Souls with memories of *friends*, which hardly described her company tonight — with the notable exceptions of Walter and Linky. They must be here for a reason.

Trix was the most obvious contender, having a family interest in the Wharton estate. However, Trix would also be the most difficult to question as she was constantly on guard. Walter and Teddy could be discounted, having both gone before her. What about those two traitors on the sofa? They weren't to be trusted, always circling like vultures. As for Mrs Gerould, the woman was a complete mystery. It was unnerving to recall her expression minutes earlier.

'Puss? I want you to keep reading.' Teddy was moving restlessly about the room, his face a hectic flush.

What else could she do? Opening to the next chapter, she began to read.

(2)

Tuscany

The crunch of gravel told Sara they were no longer alone on
the terrace. The other guests had already gone, rushing their
breakfast, and piling into the minivan heading for the Leonardo
museum — didn't Austen and Sara want to come? But Austen
shook his head, joking about a garden his wife had organised.
Okay, *ciao*, they laughed, collecting up their bags and cameras,
leaving in a cloud of dust through the vineyard.

At first Sara thought it was a boy weighed down beneath the
backpack that appeared around the side of the villa, but as the
pack swung around she saw it was a young woman. Short brown
hair and dark eyes. Watchful. As she walked towards their table,
she gave the twist of a smile. 'There's no one at the desk. I was
hoping for a room.'

'The manager's at the market,' said Austen, rising to pull out
a chair. 'Do you want to wait here?'

'Sure.' The backpack landed heavily on the ground, and the
girl sank into the chair. There was a slick of sweat across her
forehead. Dark eyes accused Sara of staring. Another twist of
her mouth.

Austen did his nice-guy thing, which usually got him
somewhere. He made the introductions and mentioned the
weather, but there was no response.

'Are you staying long?' said Sara, with no particular interest.
Is this your first posting? Got any kids at the international school?

The girl seemed to ponder the question longer than necessary,
making Sara uncomfortable. 'A few days,' she said at last.

Austen edged his chair closer. 'You're from . . . ?'

'New Zealand. Medora.'

Medora—?

'My name.' Awkward silence. Except she didn't seem to mind.

'We're doing a Medici villa today,' said Austen evenly, no indication he was offended. The girl had helped herself to a roll with small deft fingers. Sara felt sick watching her poke divots of soft bread into her mouth.

'Why?' asked the girl.

'Sara's writing a blog, retracing the gardens Edith Wharton wrote about last century.'

Sara glanced across the table at her husband. In the sunlight she could see the freckled skin where his hair was beginning to recede. Two lines were drawn down either side of his face like brackets, dividing lines between the two versions of Austen. One young, lean and eager, the other fleshy and complacent. With practice, she could switch between the two. But right now he had an assumed artlessness that meant he'd forgotten nothing. Only minutes ago she'd been saying they might as well give the garden a miss — no point, was there? She couldn't write the blog, it was hopeless and they might as well spend the day playing golf.

Austen said, 'Edith Wharton came to Italy in 1903.'

But the girl had lost interest, observing the view. Heat was already beginning to rise from the paving, the dart of geckos on a pale stone wall. Across the valley the hill flanks were spiked with cypress, a double-stitching of grapevines. Sara picked up her coffee mug, wondering why everything in Italy was painted with olives.

'I think I've read it.'

'I'm sorry?' asked Sara.

'Age — something.'

'*The Age of Innocence.*'

'Why gardens?'

Austen explained. 'We live near Wharton's property in Massachusetts — The Mount. Sara's blog is for the website.'

'What about you?' said Sara quickly, not wanting to field questions. 'Any plans for today?'

A shrug. 'Maybe the gardens at Villa Garzoni.'

'Really?'

'I'm a landscape architect.'

Sara felt the world become still. The crack of tree bark in the early-morning heat, the smell of eucalyptus. She heard herself say, 'The Mount often features in garden magazines — Lenox, Massachusetts — you must know it.' The girl shook her head, and Sara caught the clean scent of shampoo. She persisted, 'Edith Wharton even wrote a book about Italian gardens.'

'Sorry.' Now the girl was getting up — Melinda? — and hoisting on her backpack. 'I'll wait in reception. I don't want to miss the manager. You guys have a good day.'

'You too.' Sara was aware of having been insufficiently interesting. She felt irritated, as if the girl's opinion mattered — which it didn't. But what had she seen? A middle-aged American couple like any other, their good looks blurred by time. Sara could feel a space where the girl had been, like a lost possibility.

'C'mon,' said Austen, pushing back his chair. 'Let's go.'

*

The villa is reached by a dusty road through the Tuscan countryside. The property has had many owners, including the Medici family. The gardens have been changed often and it is difficult to know what parts are original. A nice large terrace garden slopes away from the villa with box hedges and lemon trees in pots. There are several fountains but they weren't going when we were there. There are plenty of trees around the outside of the garden which provide much-needed shade on a hot day, particularly for the bored husband. Edith Wharton says very little about the garden except for the fountain of a woman wringing out her hair. There is not much here for the general visitor but a very pretty drive. Why not stop at one of the many villages in the area, pick up some bread, tomatoes and fresh mozzarella. What better excuse for a picnic!

*

'Listen, Sara, this isn't quite what we wanted.'

Smothering her phone, she motioned for Austen to go downstairs and wait in the bar. Dinner was an hour away. She turned her attention back to Bernard. 'I didn't look at TripAdvisor.'

'Maybe you should.'

Sara focused on the collection of pottery plates on the wall — scenes of Tuscany and more olives.

'So, Sara, what are we going to do?'

'I don't know.'

'Did you start by describing the garden out loud?'

'Sure.'

'And you haven't tweeted.'

'It's hard to make gardens interesting.' Not even Edith Wharton could make them interesting. Sara was already stuck on the introductory chapter to *Italian Villas and Their Gardens*, blocks of text rising up like a Roman wall. What hope was there for her own writing? When she agreed to write a blog, Sara had pictured something chatty and informal, but who could be chatty about bench seats and petunias? And since when was she *chatty*?

Bernard was silent. A hopeless, weighted, what-the-fuck-are-we-going-to-do silent.

Sara dropped to the bed with familiar lethargy. This was the point where she always gave up, allowing everything to drift beyond reach. Golf was always an option — all that fresh air, and she didn't *hate* the game.

'I'm meeting with a guy from Simon & Schuster next week. What am I going to say?' More furious thinking. 'Look, forget the gardens, okay?'

'What?'

'We need another angle — a personal journey, discovering Edith's secret life. That might work, sex things up.'

'I don't understand.'

'I'll try Newbold, but for now I need everything rewritten, plus five hundred words on Gamberaia. Can you do that?'

'I'm not sure.'

*

'Everything okay?' Austen was regarding her closely.

Sara put out a hand to steady herself, unbalanced by Bernard's scathing despair. Now she saw that Austen was with the girl — Meredith, pixie hair and dark eyes, drinking beer straight from a bottle. Taking a seat, she pressed herself to speak. 'How was the garden?'

'Amazing.' The girl drained her beer. 'Baroque excess meets Tuscan topography. Very theatrical, but the flower terrace was like a municipal garden outside a town library — everything but a floral clock. And Pinocchio stalls everywhere.'

Sara pictured herself typing: *Baroque excess meets Tuscan topography. Everything but a floral clock.* Unfortunately, Edith Wharton didn't visit Villa Garzoni.

'So how was the Medici garden?'

Sara tried to recall what she had written. 'It's difficult to know what parts of the garden are original.'

'Material accretion.'

Under the girl's dark stare, Sara found herself being honest. 'The garden was quite boring.'

'But the villa is on a hillside with great views — right?'

'Sure, but I can't write about views all the time. Every garden in Italy has a view.'

'Hillside gardens around here showcase Alberti's treatise. He told rich city people how to design their rural retreats — loggias, shady groves, fountains, all that stuff.'

Sara felt herself flush. If the girl's point was to chastise, she was doing a very good job. And she hadn't finished.

'After years of people hiding in monasteries, the Middle Ages were over. Now the garden was for writers and philosophers to promenade while discussing stuff like Plato. A time of hopeful restraint, none of the wealthy theatrics that came later. That's why you found the garden boring.'

Wanting to change the subject, Sara said, 'Are you here to see the gardens you studied?'

'Not really.' She wiped her mouth. 'My thesis was on crops and drains — a classification system for traditional Māori horticultural ditches. So what are you doing tomorrow?'

'Villa Gamberaia,' said Sara, watching for signs of interest. The girl was supposed to be a landscape architect. 'You must know it.'

'Sure, but . . .' The sentence was left hanging.

'But what?' said Sara stiffly.

'The garden's only three hundred years old. It's got nothing to do with the development of the Florentine Renaissance.'

Sara sat back. She didn't know what to say.

'Look, I'm sure it's nice.'

The girl was trying to placate her! Sara smiled tightly. 'It's not a question of nice. Anyway, it doesn't matter. I'm not doing the blogs anymore.'

'Why not?'

'Because I can't write.' This was directed at her husband. 'Did you hear me?'

'Sure,' he said mildly. 'But it's early days.'

'Bernard wants it rewritten. He told me to consult TripAdvisor.'

'Bit rude.'

'Not really. That's where I got most of it.'

Austen was watching closely, an expression of pity and resignation.

'Right,' the girl said and made to move.

'Wait,' said Sara, putting out a hand. The brown eyes brightened, and she felt a buzz. Like electrical circuitry. A closed-circuit loop that excluded Austen. Of course, the girl was gay. This came to Sara with sudden and absolute certainty. She felt breathless. A loss of footing. Like Medora was the elder of them, knowing and unfathomable. Of course. Her name was Medora.

The dark brows quirked. 'Would you like me to come tomorrow?'

'Thank you,' said Sara. 'That would be wonderful.'

72

CHAPTER III

'I'm tired of reading,' said Edith. 'Shall we take turns to read something else?'

Firelight danced across vacant faces. Sleepiness had dulled their senses — but not Edith's; she was on high alert. Bernard's words had set off a warning bell: *We need another angle — a personal journey, discovering Edith's secret life. That might work, sex things up.* She had read hurriedly, not daring to look up. No more; she wouldn't read another word, it was too risky. She was beginning to suspect what might come. She would skim-read while the others dozed.

Sybil was the first to rouse herself, speaking quietly to Walter with a silvery laugh.

Edith ignored them, putting the novella aside to examine her hands. They were liver-spotted like an old map; the fingers thickened with age and knotted from years of writing. It was so frustrating to have to endure Sybil tonight. They should be enjoying the delights of quick conversation — Edith had always believed the air of ideas the only air worth breathing — but Sybil's ideas were as dull as cold mutton.

Walter stroked his moustache, saying, 'Sybil's been telling me about your stay at Salsomaggiore — do you remember?'

How could she forget? It had been a great misfortune to find Sybil staying at the same health spa.

73

'You were touring Italian gardens at the time.'

'I don't recall,' clipped Edith.

'Course you do,' laughed Teddy. 'You called the manager Twilight.'

Sybil showed her small white teeth. 'Because he wore a white evening tie with an afternoon coat!' The others joined her laughter.

Sybil had been with her first husband and about to settle at a Medici villa near Florence. Edith had adored Bayard, and their daughter would become a delightful woman and a good writer. It was bewildering that Edith liked all Sybil's husbands and lovers, yet Sybil was insufferable. Once, on hearing Sybil had thrown over her lover for his friend, and they were now engaged, Edith wrote: *I have been practicing liking it for 24 hours and am obliged to own that the results are not promising.* And on hearing Percy might become a husband, Edith had laughed — it was absurd! Apparently, so the story went, Percy had inadvertently dropped his cigarette down the back of Sybil's dress — and on fishing it out, Sybil had fainted romantically into his arms. However, Percy would have to wait eleven years for his turn, by which time Sybil had what Edith liked to call diminished trading capacity.

'I can't think . . . the deuce,' said Teddy, rising to his feet and looking surprised to find himself standing. Hands thrust deep in his pockets, he fixed his attention on the broken light. 'That Italian business, Puss, I mean, what the deuce was that about?'

'Please don't worry,' said Edith. 'I'm tired of reading. Let's read something else — we can take turns.'

'I'll read the novella,' offered Mrs Gerould.

Was she being deliberately difficult? Edith shook her head firmly, saying, 'Time for a change, don't you agree, Walter?'

But Walter was admiring the volume of James Joyce. 'Beautiful publication. My nephew had a fine artistic sensibility.' Stroking the binding, he added, 'Harry and his wife were publishers. Black Sun Press.'

Edith maintained her composure, but she was shivering inside. It was obscene to see that book in Walter's long, sensitive fingers.

'Edith?'

Everyone was wide awake now, watching with interest. Her voice tight, Edith said, 'I'm impressed to see the verbosity of Joyce so compressed, but I don't wish to hear him tonight.' Dangerous territory. She must move quickly, forestall the questions forming in Walter's mind. 'I'm sure you'd prefer to read poetry.'

Sybil squalled in protest, dramatically collapsing into the cushions.

'I have something to read,' said Mrs Gerould, holding up a file. 'My own work.'

Honestly, they were all the same, amateur writers — never left home without their unpublished manuscript. Edith said, 'Thank you, Mrs Gerould, but—'

'Oh, why not?' cried Sybil. 'It's better than poetry.'

'Come on, Puss,' said Teddy, resting large hands on his knees. 'I'd like to hear.'

Traitors and imbeciles, all of them. To Mrs Gerould, she said, 'Is it a short story?'

'Personal essay.' Already she was sliding papers from her file. 'I had several collections of my work published.'

'Marvellous,' said Percy.

The fellow was an idiot, but Edith was perturbed to see a gleam of amusement from Mrs Gerould — was she of a similar opinion? The idea was unnerving.

With an inscrutable smile, Mrs Gerould said, 'My later essays were criticised for being too socially conservative, and I'm trying to address this.'

'Of course,' murmured Edith.

'I hope you'll forgive the experimental nature.'

Oh, for heaven's sake, did she mistake this for a writing class? But Edith noticed the sheets of paper shaking — was there nervousness beneath Mrs Gerould's implacability? Fear crept into the room. Edith wanted to stop the woman, but it was too late.

Mrs Gerould cleared her throat to begin. 'The Mount, October twenty-first, 1907.'

Edith cried out — an ugly rasping noise like wallpaper ripped from walls.

Mrs Gerould was guarded, as if she had expected such a reaction.

Edith drew a stuttering breath. 'What do you mean by this?'

'A personal essay.'

'You weren't there.'

'True.'

'So you can't—' Edith floundered.

'Know?'

Chill spread through her bones. Instinctively Edith understood that Mrs Gerould had studied her writing closely, recognised the power of knowing — and, conversely, the vulnerability of not knowing. The irony was not lost on her. In the company of this mysterious woman, Edith was in the position of ignorance. Finding her voice, she said, 'But why is this necessary?'

'To hear the truth? It enhances our understanding of the novella — details of Edith Wharton's life will provide context.'

Edith's head spun. Who was this woman? Even her name — Mrs Gerould — seemed to conceal her true identity. And what had she meant: *We have a great deal in common, more than you could possibly imagine*? Was this a threat? It was intolerable not to understand. She demanded, 'Who are you?'

'A friend, Mrs Wharton, and I hope you'll come to appreciate my presence. And now, with your permission, I would like to read.'

What choice did she have? Pressing her hands together, Edith said, 'All right, let's hear it.'

With a small nod, Mrs Gerould began to read.

The Mount, Lenox, Massachusetts, October 21, 1907

The arrival of Morton Fullerton was a scene so finely executed as to be worthy of a novel. Edith watched from the shadows of the hall as he passed his hat and cane to the butler, stepping aside when his portmanteau was brought in. His presence in her home was so visceral it was shocking. The front door was closed against the drift of polar air while Mr Fullerton surveyed the luxury of her entrance hall, dark hair shining under the blazing electrolier lights. Suddenly his inspection stopped, and she flushed. He had known she was there all along.

'My dear Edith,' he said smoothly, 'what a delightful home, but I would expect no less.'

Edith stepped forward with apparent calm. Of course this would become a scene in a novel — how could it not? Later she would write: Every sensation of touch and sight was thrice-alive in her. For now she simply said, 'Welcome to The Mount. I'm so pleased you've come.' Edith listened to herself speak, aware of a glowing consciousness drawn around them. There was no indication that her nerves were stretched. She continued, saying that it was a shame he could stay only one night, but she was delighted he'd made the detour.

Now Grossie bustled in from the kitchen, red-faced and flustered: Mr Fullerton must be tired after his train journey — such a distance and, oh my goodness, all the way from Philadelphia! It was lovely to see him again, but he must freshen up for dinner. She would show him to his room — and my, weren't they in for a treat tonight. Mr Wharton had shot two ducks!

Escorted to the stairs, Morton turned with the promise of — of what? Edith's mind froze with incomprehension. The promise of something she did not understand, something she would not permit herself to imagine.

The Mount, October 21, 1907.

My readers, you're probably wondering why I've chosen to focus on this particular evening. Fair enough, Edith was always hosting dinner parties, so why recall this one, and rather an uneventful one at that?

Would you believe me if I said — for that very

reason! Writers look to the ordinary to illuminate
the extraordinary. They want to show the whole
world in a single grain of sand — or, in this case,
the story of Edith Wharton in a three-course
dinner.

Do you believe me? No, I'm sure you don't. You don't
want an ordinary evening. Why bother unless it's
important? In my defence, I may have underplayed
the drama of this evening — and, to be fair,
the following day's events become surprisingly
interesting.

But you're left wondering, why bother?

Does it help if I say a single evening can carry the
world? That a logical progression from cocktails to
postprandial cigars can be a vehicle for carrying —
well — pretty much everything? Believe me, this
dinner party has more baggage than a passenger
train. It's all there. Themes of feminism,
obligation, and class. The social context of upper-
class America in the early twentieth century.

But I sense you want a story that's specific,
weighed with personal significance. Filled with
telling details, for the truth is always in the
details. The exploration of an interior world and
the whispering of secrets. Am I right? Of course.

So what _is_ the answer? Why are we assembled to watch

this particular show? Because, well, all of the
above. Everything; it's all here, which is why you
should watch closely.

Edith Wharton is standing in the shadows when her
guest arrives, but what else? What is going on now
the unthinkable has happened and Morton Fullerton
is standing in her front hall? It's starting to
snow out and there's a drift of flakes across his
coat, and you just feel something's going to happen
when life takes on the surrealism of a film.

More context might help. Edith is forty-five years
old; remember, this is back when forty was old.
She's been married twenty-two years, and there are
no children: her friends call it a mariage blanc,
which should tell you something about her friends.
Divorce rates have trebled in the past three years,
but that's no comfort. Edith Newbold Wharton née
Jones is old-school, born into New York society
back when being a Newbold meant something. She's
a Rhinelander and related to Astors, a Jones from
'keeping-up-with-the-Joneses'. Yes, she's that
fancy.

Money? Not as much as you'd imagine. Not poor, but
you should see the outgoings (sixteen staff and
counting). But, as I say, things are changing,
and not least for Edith. Her latest novel,
The House of Mirth, has sold over 140,000 copies,
which by anyone's standards is huge. Plus it's

a wonderful book and should be on everyone's
reading list.

What else? She's a self-educated woman. Unlike
her brothers, there was no tutor for little Edith;
and her need to make up stories had an urgency that
alarmed her parents, watching through the keyhole.
She taught herself to read while lying on a rug in
her father's library, studying Goethe and Shelley.
It's said that she didn't like other women, but
that's not fair; it's just that most women couldn't
keep up. Edith is fluent in four languages. Her
husband, Teddy, a devoted anti-intellectual, went
to Harvard and was a member of the Knickerbocker
Club. Since their marriage, he's developed a
passion for poultry.

In the past six years, Edith has become a literary
powerhouse. She's written plays and short story
collections, novels and novellas. Two books of
non-fiction — and did I mention her poetry? All in
six years.

But what happened beforehand? Mostly just
marriage. She was a supportive wife who kept
herself occupied with housewifely things like
home decoration and gardens. And she was unwell:
neuralgia, insomnia, agoraphobia, and something
called women's problems. Make of that what you
will. As I said, no children, which is probably
not surprising and just as well because her

husband's got some hereditary trouble. But when
writing Mirth, Edith is surprisingly tender when
she describes holding a baby: the soft weight
sinking trustfully against her breast, the
rosy blur of the little face, the folding and
unfolding fingers. Obviously she's been thinking
about this.

And Morton? What does he see when Edith steps from
the shadows? A woman who's not beautiful, but
then she never was, that's easy enough to tell.
But she's got something. A sense of presence, and
a height Morton might wish for. Her auburn hair
is upswept — the maid was told to make a special
effort tonight — and her gown is low-cut Parisian,
accentuating her narrow waist and impressive
bust. Her nutcracker jaw, always so prominent
in photographs, is barely noticeable when she's
smiling. And tonight she's got a lot to smile about
because Mr Fullerton is in her foyer.

But he sees more. Attractive women are always
welcome, but Morton's preference is for people with
connections and influence. People of their time.
And this is Edith, especially since all New York
has been following the serialisation of Mirth,
crowding around the booksellers to find out the
latest. Some people claim to have unmasked the
characters; they recognise their great-aunts and
their lawyers. Acquaintances are outraged and
feel Mrs Edward Wharton has become rather too

commercial. Edith doesn't mind. With the proceeds
she's built herself a sunken garden.

More context: Morton has just spent two nights
with his little sister Katharine in Philadelphia.
She's clever but shy, pretty in a plain sort of way,
teaching English at Bryn Mawr. He's made a detour
to see Edith on his way to Connecticut to visit
their parents. Henry James warned Edith that Morton
wouldn't actually come, he's too unreliable.
But Henry was wrong because right now Morton is
standing in her front hall, and it's turning her
insides upside down.

Earlier in the day, Morton passed through New York.
It's possible he saw an enlarged photograph of
Edith looking, she believes, like a South Dakota
divorcée crossed with a magnetic healer. It's less
likely that he saw her name lit up on Broadway — the
stage play of Mirth did not go well. As Edith said,
Americans prefer their tragedy with a happy ending.
But, all the same, she is a woman with immense star
power, and for that Morton is prepared to overlook
a prominent jawline.

How well do Morton and Edith know each other? Not
that well. They met during Edith's recent stay in
France as afternoon guests at the same Parisian
salon. The glorious La Belle Epoque — you know,
Rodin and Rilke, Matisse — but remember, this is
Edith, she's not with this crowd. Her preference

is for the snobbish and élite salons of old French
aristocracy. It's almost unknown for an American
to be welcome here, except for Morton, of course.
Since then, Morton's come to her apartment for tea
on several occasions to discuss French translators
for Mirth. But, as always, what's left unsaid is
always more important.

And what is left unsaid? They both know Mirth is
going to be huge in France. Edith is about to be
a star on both sides of the Atlantic, and Morton
is excited by this. Because, for all his charm
and blue-eyed charisma, his stylish writing and
erudite conversation, he will never be famous. But
he's good at befriending those who are. Not that
it's any great hardship: being with Edith means
parties and good food, and he doesn't object to her
being three years older. She's still got plenty of
energy, and things are always happening. And never
underestimate her charm. When she wants, Edith
really is charming. Edith Wharton isn't all hauteur
and lorgnettes — she's got a great sense of humour,
and she loves a dirty joke. Yes, she's a snob, but
she loves to satirise pretentiousness. As long as
you're on her side, she's a lot of fun.

But you just want to know if Morton and Edith get
together. All that 'glowing consciousness' has
got to be going somewhere. Absolutely: we all want
this to work. When Morton Fullerton arrives in
her foyer, she's wound herself into a state — all

that 'visceral shock' and 'every sense alive'
stuff is true. But this is Edith. You really think
she's going to loosen her corset and hit the hay?
I'm sorry. Edith is the product of a society that
extinguishes women for such behaviour. The idea of
the irreproachable Mrs Wharton having an affair
is ridiculous: an affair will risk everything.
The House of Mirth is a sensation, but she's got
her eye on the future. Writing is her life. Already
it's bringing her fame, money, and, best of all,
literary credibility. Henry James is her latest
friend. She would be crazy to risk everything.

Are you still interested? You should be because
we're about to carry on with the evening; but
first it helps to know that Catherine Gross, the
housekeeper, is a substitute mother. Grossie's
been with Edith since she was twenty-two, an
occasion they celebrate each year with tea and
cake. In her memoir, Edith describes her real
mother, Lucretia, as disapproving and cold. And
her much-loved father would agree. In Mirth, Lily's
mother badgers her husband to death with requests
for money and clothes, and there's no prize for
guessing where this came from.

Edith has two much older brothers; don't worry,
I won't get biographical, but the age difference
is important. Anyone doing the math will discover
that Lucretia was thirty-eight when she gave birth
to Edith. Disgusting! That the remote Lucretia

should conceive a child at such an age! Lucretia
was a socialite and a snob, and she never forgave
the daughter who was a constant reminder of her
own shame. It didn't help that Edith's red hair
reminded everyone of the young tutor who taught
her brothers. Edith was a very public stain on her
mother's private conduct. But Edith had no time for
the rumours. She loved her dreaming father with a
certainty that left no room for doubt. But he broke
her heart when she was twenty by dying within sight
of the Mediterranean, and forever after Edith's
soul remained in Europe.

A quick word about the staff. It should be
mentioned that Grossie, along with the butler
(Alfred), chauffeur (Mr Charles Cook), and
secretary (Anna Bahlmann) will devote their lives
to Edith, and that should tell you something. What
about her friends? — yes, the same ones who snigger
about her marriage — well, that's awkward. The
old circle of friends and family loathe Edith's
commercialism and fame and are embarrassed by her
public indulgence in make-believe. And there's a
bigger problem: Edith's got a habit of pulling them
barely disguised into her writing. The old crowd is
giving her a wide berth these days. Society queen
Mrs Astor, Edith's cousin, was livid to read of her
husband's infidelities in a short story; suffice
to say they didn't attend the Wharton housewarming
party. But Edith doesn't care. She's bored by the
posh circle she was born into. She wants America to

be more like Paris, where intellectuals and artists party with the socialites. So Edith's turning her back on the Astors and Vanderbilts to form her own crowd.

A quick word about The Mount. Again, it helps to appreciate the context. Edith's first book was on home decoration, and it was hugely influential. She changed the way Americans designed and decorated their homes. Edith once wrote that The Mount was the only place where she was truly happy, and if you believe that you'll believe anything. But it should have been a place where she was truly happy. Let me describe it for you: a small, white mansion, grand in conceit if not actual size. The Mount sits on a low rise, and all the windows have shutters flung wide open, giving a startled expression — and yet the impression is secretive, enigmatic. The roofline is important: a cluttered eruption of cupolas and chimneys, dormer windows, even a small, balustraded balcony. It feels like the spirit of the house, captured within all its implacable solidity, can no longer be contained. Remind you of anyone?

The garden is a work in progress — remember, we're back in 1907 — just tree saplings and lots of empty space. The sunken Italian garden is the best part, designed after Edith got back from a garden trip to Europe. Inside, the house is everything she advocated in her book on homemaking: tall

windows and bowls of fresh flowers; an arcaded
gallery of bronze sculptures and potted orchids.
Edith elevated good living to an art form. But,
just remember: a perfectly presented life is no
guarantee of happiness.

So let's get on with the evening. It's fair to
say that when Morton enters the drawing room he's
surprised — very surprised — and not in a good way.
His life is pretty complicated right now, but he's
made the effort to visit. Why? Because, according
to friend Henry James, he can expect good company
and witty conversation. Edith hangs with the
literati these days, and Teddy's not afraid to raid
his wine cellar. But there's a problem. It's late
in the season, and everyone has gone. Edith smiles
with blithe apology — but on the inside? She's
dying.

So, who else is in the drawing room? First we've got
Teddy planted in front of the mantelpiece. Backlit
by flames, his hair is weirdly pink, his eyes
ranging wildly about the room. He's telling a story
about a stallion let loose in his stable. It's a
ribald tale told in old Bostonian style. 'By Jove,
I believed the old boy was dead!' He guffaws,
thrusting an empty champagne glass at Alfred, who
is passing with a bottle. 'Old boy was good for
nothing but sausages — and damned expensive ones
at that!' Teddy has told this story several times
this summer, and it's always been well received,

provoking raucous retorts. Not tonight. Not with
these people.

Teddy's sister, Nanny — picture an elderly maiden
aunt — is sitting on a low settee. She's flushed
and over-excited at her brother's performance.
Hands clasped in delight, her lace cap is askew.
She doesn't appear in the least bit alarmed by his
behaviour.

Teddy's mother is not so amused. Her lips are
snapped together, her mourning clothes like the
exoskeleton of a black beetle. Yes, this is Edith's
mother-in-law, which is not ideal, obviously,
but Edith always makes the most of the material
at hand. In The House of Mirth, old Mrs Wharton
is transformed into Mrs Peniston, a woman who
always sits on a chair and never in it. And more —
any attempt to bring Mrs Peniston into active
relation with life is like tugging at a piece of
furniture that has been screwed to the floor. Don't
worry, there's no chance of old Mrs Wharton taking
offence. None of Edith's family indulges in the
vulgarity of reading fiction.

Spare a thought for Morton — this is not what he
was expecting. Edith is a national celebrity. Her
latest work explodes with the energy of modern New
York: gambling, drugs, boom-and-bust Wall Street,
a kaleidoscope of trysts and divorce settlements.
All of America just loves this novel. And now

she's at her glamorous country estate with —
well, with this lot. Nanny sitting on the settee
with a piece of lace on her head. Old Mrs Wharton
glowering in black. Teddy talking gibberish. And
another fellow, Eliot Gregory, small and watchful,
strategically positioned in the corner. If Morton
hopes Mr Gregory will provide some intellectual
weight, he's about to be disappointed. Certainly
Mr Gregory has his own publication, The Idler,
but as the name suggests, it's not aiming high.
A gossipy little newsletter of innuendo, The Idler
delights in fallen socialites and extramarital
affairs. This is not exactly Morton's scene —
he graduated top of his class at Harvard, and now
he's the Paris correspondent for The Times of
London.

So why is Mr Gregory here? He doesn't seem
Edith's type, but — can you guess? This fellow
provided Edith with the scandals that made Mirth
so vivid. Edith couldn't possibly know such
things, and she's indebted to him. All the same,
she doesn't want him for dinner. Not tonight.
Edith's moving on to bigger things, and they both
know Eliot won't be around much longer. His snide
remarks are beginning to unnerve her, and he's
watching with particularly close interest.

Dinner is announced, and everyone heads for the
dining room. Edith is followed by her little dogs
skittering noisily across the parquet floor.

Catching her reflection in the mirror, she recalls
a line written this morning (a short story that's
coming along nicely): it was a face which had
grown middle-aged while it waited for the joys of
youth. True enough, yet tonight she seems almost
beautiful: the fashionable clothes, the softening
of her strong features, the proud bearing of
success. And the sense of Morton watching her.

Alfred throws more wood on the fire while the
diners discuss the weather. Outside the snow
continues to fall, and Nanny's already starting
to fret about their ride back to the village — she
doesn't trust motor-cars. Mrs Wharton eyes her
chicken soup with suspicion.

Morton takes up the conversation. He assumes
they're interested in the French serialisation
of Mirth — but no, Edith's accomplishments aren't
considered suitable for dinnertime. Or any time.
So Morton compliments Edith on her beautiful house.
He's charmed by the terrazzo galleries and potted
palms, the French doors and bronze statues. And
particularly the enfilade layout of the house —
très European, Mme Wharton!

Nanny gives a squeak of distress at this brazen use
of French. These old-money families like to boast
of their European origins, but as an actual place
Europe is horribly full of foreigners.

And so dinner progresses, halting and painful. Teddy
wants to talk about his livestock, but no one's much
interested. Edith says to Morton, 'Your parents must
be looking forward to seeing you again.'

Morton is startled, his wine glass paused in
mid-air.

Edith watches the customary control slip back into
place. But she's exposed a crack in the flawless
façade. Intriguing.

'Your parents,' she probes. 'I hope they're well.'

'Perfectly well.' His response is clipped and final.

Addressing the table, Edith says, 'Tomorrow
Mr Fullerton is travelling to his parents' home in
Brockton. His father is a most respected minister.'
This is directed at Mrs Wharton senior, still
stirring her soup. If the old bat is impressed by
Morton's links to the church, she's not showing.

Morton seems similarly taken by his soup, but
Edith presses on. 'And your sister, Mr Fullerton?
I believe you spent several days with her. How
is she?' While in Paris, Morton often spoke of
Katharine, and it seemed an enviable bond.

Morton's eyes are like blue snow-melt but warm
with recollection. 'Katharine is very well.

Quite the young woman now. It was a most enjoyable meeting.'

'I'm sure it was.' Edith could imagine the young Katharine infatuated with her handsome, accomplished brother.

Morton seems keen to remain on the subject of his sister. 'Katharine greatly enjoyed The House of Mirth and wishes to pass on her congratulations. She's excited to know I'm staying with you.'

Edith flushes.

'She would like to meet you one day.'

Eliot says pleasantly, 'I should think your social calendar quite free these days, Edith.'

He's referring to the swathe of upper-class New Yorkers who now keep a wary distance. Edith's got no problem with that — besides, right now she's more interested in the subject of Katharine. Looking around the table, she says, 'Mr Fullerton's sister teaches English composition at Bryn Mawr College. She already has a Master's degree from Radcliffe.'

Morton inclines his head with pride.

'Jolly good for her,' says Teddy.

'I'm not sure I approve of young ladies in education,' sniffs old Mrs Wharton. Teddy's mother and sister take their responsibilities as pillars of the local community seriously, treasuring their insularity and lack of education as they would a rare Anatolian ornament.

'Oh, I don't know,' says Morton smoothly. 'Women have a good deal to contribute to society.'

'We most certainly do,' says Nanny irritably. 'In the church and community. I don't see what good comes from education.'

'Far too serious, these college girls,' simpers Eliot. 'Don't you agree, Teddy? It's more fun watching them play archery.'

'Not sure I agree,' says Teddy. 'Look at old Puss here. You'd never believe she could write poetry with a figure like that.'

Edith demurs, as is expected, apologetic for her own intelligence. It's hard to believe she's got bigger things to worry about. Just yesterday there was a slide on Wall Street (a trading scandal), and the timing is terrible — her next novel is due to hit the bookstands any day. Her publishers are panicking, having agreed to her demand for a huge advance based on the success of Mirth. But her new novel? Charles Scribner is nervous. Apparently

what the American public want (according to old
Scrib) is another exposé of the élite of New York.
What they don't want is a novel set in a factory
town with themes of welfare reform. Which (as she
told Scrib) just went to show her fans weren't very
familiar with her back catalogue. But it's a worry,
no doubt about that.

And so the evening continues. Teddy is drinking
too much, waving Alfred over for another bottle of
wine. Alfred's eyes slide towards Edith, but she
can't help. Bending towards Teddy, he says, 'I'm
not sure we have another bottle of the '96, sir.'

'Course we have, man, don't be a fool. Saw it the
other day.' Teddy embraces the table with a crazy
grin.' Unless you've been helping yourself!'

Alfred flinches before resuming his composure.

Nanny laughs fatuously, her expression more silly
than usual. Morton straightens his cutlery, and
Eliot has the good grace to look away. Edith takes
courage to face old Mrs Wharton as if to say:
so this is the man you have raised. Are you proud
of him? Pointless, of course. His family maintain
the right to criticise, but the responsibility of
Teddy firmly rests with Edith. Not for the first
time she wonders: why should that be? Where does
the line of responsibility lie between a man's
family and his wife?

But old Mrs Wharton is having none of it. She's
already got her hands full with Teddy's father.
He's been dead for sixteen years, and someone's got
to do the mourning, but it's a delicate business.
While her devotion to grief is beyond reproach,
it also has the unfortunate effect of drawing
attention to her late husband's death — and no one
wants to be reminded of that.

Teddy's jaw is beginning to work like he's chewing
on gristle. Edith feels her own fear grow into
something she can feel and smell, something she
can hear. It's the memory of Teddy's father. She
recalls the winged-tipped collar of the attorney
making the terrible pronouncement of insanity. The
rattling of roasting pans in the asylum kitchen.
The endless doctors searching for an answer. The
experts always offering the latest treatment. And
the shocking end, a gunshot heard across a winter
field. Edith jumps, a silvery crash as her soup
spoon falls to the floor. Every nerve snapping, she
drags for air.

'Madam.' She opens her eyes to see Alfred. Such a
treasure, a dear and trusted friend. But right now
he's worried. 'Are you all right, Madam?'

She lays a hand on his arm. 'Thank you, Alfred. You
may clear the plates now.'

In the difficult silence that follows, Morton tries

again, addressing Edith directly. 'Henry sends his
best wishes.' To the others, he adds, 'Like Edith,
I am fortunate to count Henry James a friend.'

'I'm not really sure,' says Nanny worriedly but
unable to elaborate.

Eliot raises his fish knife and slowly rotates it.
Refracting blades of light circle the room. 'Not a
name we mention around here, old boy. Considered
something of a traitor.' Laying his knife back on
the table, he squares across at Morton.

Morton inclines his head in acknowledgment.
Henry's latest travel book, published as
The American Scene, hasn't won him any friends on
this side of the Atlantic.

'Traitor?' says Teddy. 'Marvellous fellow. Had
some wonderful times — isn't that right, Puss? Old
Henry developed a great liking for our motor-car.
We had some excellent runs in the countryside.'

'Yes, dear.'

'Gathering material for his book, no doubt,'
smirks Eliot.

'Material?' says Teddy, confused.

Eliot raises one eyebrow mockingly.

'I don't understand you, man. What's this material business?'

Eliot pauses while his next course is placed on the table. 'I merely suggested that Henry may have profited more from your hospitality than you realised.'

'What's he saying, Puss?'

'Please, dear, don't spoil your meal.' Alfred and the maid finish setting down plates and condiments, withdrawing to the edges of the room. Glancing around the table, Edith says, 'I hope you enjoy Teddy's duck.'

'An assault of vulgarity,' says Eliot, rearranging his cutlery with undue care.

Old Mrs Wharton quivers with distaste.

'Now what are you saying?' An ugly red stain flushes Teddy's neck.

'Henry's dislike of his own country. He called New York cheap, common, and commercial — and all too often ugly.'

Old Mrs Wharton permits herself the malicious smile of a Bostonian. She only moved to Lenox a few years ago.

'Not that Henry's opinion matters,' Eliot
continues blithely. 'No one reads the old boy these
days.'

'Your friends don't read Henry,' seethes Edith.
Poor Henry. He's writing himself into irrelevancy.

'My friends,' Eliot says delicately, 'were of great
interest to you not so long ago.'

'Fine fellow,' insists Teddy, filling his glass.
He holds it to the light, admiring the ruby hue.
'We'll see him soon, isn't that right?'

'Indeed,' murmurs Edith.

'What do you mean?' Nanny is aghast. 'You're not
going back to Europe already?'

'Well, we—' Teddy looks uncertain.

Edith picks up her cutlery, signalling the others
to follow suit.

'You can't go back again,' cries Nanny. 'You've
only just come home.'

'Calm yourself,' snaps old Mrs Wharton.

'But you know it does Teddy no good. All this
travelling. Why, last time—'

'No more,' shouts Teddy. The crystal glasses are ringing, an awful echo around the room.

'But your poor teeth,' trembles Nanny, wringing her napkin. Caught in her own hysteria, she seems unable to stop. 'And your ears. Doctor Kinnicutt said you must avoid excitement. You don't even like Paris. Last time you called it dreadful. And everything will happen all over again, just like before.' She swings around to Edith. 'It's all your fault. Everything. Teddy wouldn't be like this if—'

'Enough,' roars Teddy. 'Not another word. I'll do as I damn well please.' With a trembling hand, he throws back his wine in a single movement. There is a pause, a suspended moment, and a choking gargle. Wine explodes from Teddy's mouth, red-trailing spittle. A scarlet stain spreads across his shirtfront like a gunshot wound. Everyone gapes as he rises shakily to his feet, wretched and pitiable, wiping an arm clumsily across his mouth. Suddenly he erupts with fury, shouting at Alfred to do something, dammit man, get a napkin and clean up the mess. Nanny is weeping, his mother rigid with anger. A plate crashes to the floor, fleshy sauce splashes across the rug. Teddy continues to scream: it's the wine, he knew it — Alfred's trying to poison him. Edith jumps to her feet, rounding on her husband, easing him away from the table: everything is all right, he just needs to get changed, dinner can wait, if—

'Damn you, woman,' he spits, blazing with
inarticulate misery. With violence he shakes
himself free, and Edith stumbles against the table.
She rights herself carefully. No one moves. A dog
whimpers. Never before has Teddy mistreated her
in public, or in front of the servants. Even at
his most manic, Teddy understands that what takes
place in the bedroom stays there. She becomes aware
of Grossie steering Teddy away. Thank goodness
for Grossie. Beneath her flustered façade lies a
steely Teutonic loyalty to Edith that no one would
challenge. Edith turns to the table, careful to
avoid Morton, finding refuge in old Mrs Wharton.
She says, 'How unfortunate, poor Teddy. The wine
must have soured, but I don't think we should let
our dinner get cold.'

A glimmer of admiration from the old lady. Edith
feels a passing connection with Nancy Spring
Wharton, a bond of mutual recognition. They
understand each other. This weighs on Edith like a
death sentence. Picking up her napkin, she drops
into her chair and begins to eat.

*

So that's dinner. Nanny and old Mrs Wharton leave
in a hurry, fussing about the weather, while Morton
and Edith head for the library — ostensibly to
discuss Henry's book. Edith's having a difficult
time staying calm, but Eliot Gregory is hard on

their heels, a smirk on his face. They settle by the
fire, waiting for Alfred and Grossie to leave — and
then, unbelievably, Morton really does talk about
his essay on Henry's book The American Scene. Edith
doesn't like Henry's latest work: his writing style
conceals an illogical progression of ideas; he is
trying to justify a fixed conclusion. But Morton is
defensive: surely New York is sufficient argument
in itself? How can Edith defend the hideous
skyscrapers and Wall Street swaggarts, the money
and celebrity, the fashion for divorce?

No, she's not defending it, but she does require a
more rigorous approach to an argument.

But Morton thinks—

Eliot slinks away, bored beyond belief.

Now Edith is skittery with anticipation. They're
alone together in the library, and Morton's still
talking about Henry's work. He hasn't noticed
they're alone!

Edith mentions the weather and their car trip
tomorrow.

But Morton's laughing at Henry's admiration for the
Waldorf-Astoria, its aesthetic ideal a synonym for
civilisation.

Edith loathes hotels and is in no mood for irony.
Snow is falling heavily outside, and she's getting
desperate, aware of becoming strident and peevish.
Morton is so blinded by his devotion to Henry that
he won't hear a word against the Master.

Finally Alfred comes to extinguish the lights, and
they retire upstairs, parting in the gallery. Edith
goes to bed with all the agitation of a hot, gusty
wind. She continues to replay their conversation
in her head. There is something she doesn't
understand.

*

Next day is beautiful, a freezing blue sky and
glittering white world. Edith feels desolate.
This morning they're dropping Morton at Westfield
Station, and she'll return home alone (if you
discount Teddy and sixteen staff). Tomorrow
morning she'll wake to snow-melt and dead annuals.

But all this is forgotten on the ride to the
station — a dazzling motor-flight over blue
mountains and through avenues of amber-gold.
Swathed in hat and blankets, Edith feels the cold
biting through her veil. She laughs at Morton,
his dark hair whipped by the wind. In the front,
Eliot is shouting directions to the chauffeur,
but Charles Cook ignores his passenger, grandly
impassive as always. Edith and Morton edge closer

for warmth. They pass sawmills and farmhouses,
black Norway spruces and apple orchards. On the
flank of a steep hill, the wheels of the motorcar
begin to slide, and Cook pulls from the road and
cuts the engine. They're left in a blissful,
snowy hush. Edith looks at Morton as if this were
planned, arranged just for him. His eyes smile
back, glacial blue.

Climbing from the car, Cook ponders the problem —
he'll need to fit chains with Eliot's help. Edith
and Morton head for a fallen tree trunk, snow
breaking crisply beneath their feet. Edith is
conscious of her hem rimmed with damp. Morton flips
open a silver case, and she takes a cigarette,
leaning in for a light. She sits back, so intensely
aware of Morton's nearness that there's no surprise
in the touch he lays on her hand. They look at
each other in silence. Below lies a small village
hollowed in the New England countryside, the slim
white steeple of a church.

They smoke quietly for several minutes. It seems
Morton doesn't want to talk, and Edith's happy
enough with that. A shout tells them the chains
are fitted and they can leave. Morton follows her
back to the motorcar, stopping when she admires a
flowering witch hazel. She holds a branch in her
hand. Yellow pompom flowers bunch along bare wood.
The shredded flowers pop with carmine seeds. Edith
can smell the spicy fragrance on the ice-cold air.

She shows the plant to Morton, and he breaks off a
sprig for himself.

By the time they arrive at the station, Morton
is distracted, already focused on his trip to
Brockton. Edith should be offended — how can
his family be more exciting than the famous
Mrs Wharton? But she convinces herself that
Morton's distraction proves what a good family man
he is — when it comes to Morton, Edith is terrific
at convincing herself of all manner of things. The
train is late, and Morton tells her not to wait —
really, you can leave now. Edith heads back to the
motorcar with her head high, insides crumbling.
But don't worry, even before arriving home she's
convinced herself that Morton was worried for
her welfare. After all, it was icy standing on
the platform. And she's not going to give up this
easily.

CHAPTER IV

Edith was shaking with fury: damn this woman. How dare she recall those events with such clarity, and for what purpose? Revenge was the most likely explanation, but revenge for what? Or was she jealous? As a small-time writer, did Mrs Gerould resent Edith's international success? No, the essay felt too personal and deliberate. This was no minor writing exercise; Mrs Gerould's self-effacement was false and an exercise in reckless irresponsibility. While she was reading, Teddy had ranged about the room with loose-limbed madness, his mind too disturbed to understand his own distress. Occasionally, he gave a moan of despair or a gunshot expletive, balling his hands against the memories. It was terrible. To be reminded of his father's end was cruel.

And yet Mrs Gerould continued to read with a singular detachment, too caught up in her own story — as if it were *her* story. Who was she? It was impossible to guess her motive without knowing her true identity. One of the kitchen staff? Yes, that might explain things. Right now she was inspecting a stitch like a workhouse needlewoman.

Poor Teddy, it wasn't true that he spilt wine and disgraced himself — although, to be fair, it *was* an amalgamation of similar occasions. However (it must be admitted) everything else was correct. It was frightening how Mrs Gerould could recall those events with such bone-chilling clarity. 'You have no right,' seethed Edith, 'to use this evening for your own indulgence. Who are you? And what are you doing here?'

'She's right,' said Teddy, his large brow crumpled with distress.

Mrs Gerould remained motionless, having the sense not to further inflame Teddy. It was Trix who knelt by his chair, taking his hand.

'I'm not really sure,' said Teddy doubtfully, 'what that was about.'

'Teddy, darling,' soothed Trix, her features softening in sympathy. 'You mustn't worry.'

His voice rose, querulous. 'But I don't understand.'

'None of it's true.'

'But I remember. That's how—'

'No, the events were sensationalised until they became *untrue*.'

Teddy fell into worried muteness.

'Quite true, from what I hear,' said Percy to Sybil.

Edith pulled irritably on her sleeves. There was something about Percy — something, if only she could remember . . . but that must wait. She wouldn't be diverted from Mrs Gerould, who, to Edith's irritation, had resumed her knitting. With peremptory insistence, Edith said, 'I'm unsure of the relevance, Mrs Gerould, to recount events from so long ago. And don't give me any nonsense about grains of sand. This isn't a writing lesson.'

Mrs Gerould looked up from her work with such penetrating irony that Edith shrank back in discomfort. 'My dear Mrs Wharton, I should think you understand perfectly. There's so much to be gained by using the past, don't you agree?'

My God, how much did this woman know? She had such unnerving insight — as if she knew more about Wharton's life

107

than Edith did herself. What had Mrs Gerould meant when she'd said it was a mistake to believe past events could be seen in their entirety; there were always unknown factors and other points of view? As if Mrs Gerould were *warning* her. Nonsense, right now she appeared more interested in her knitting, a half-formed thing in a ghastly shade of flesh-pink. Edith examined Mrs Gerould closely: the remnants of a permanent wave; skin like soft-creased hide; the face of a gardener or a cigarette smoker; a woman who hung washing on a line behind the family house. It was ridiculous to be concerned.

'It's about themes and context,' observed Walter. 'The great Mrs Wharton chained to her fate by obligations and so forth. However, I don't see the significance, knowing you moved to France just a few years later.'

Teddy gazed at Walter, but his expression remained vacant.

Edith continued, 'You should be ashamed, appropriating my life for your own writing.'

Another penetrating stare before Mrs Gerould said, 'That's not true.'

'Of course it's true.' What had they been listening to, if not an appropriation of Edith's Wharton's life?

'My essay was based on your own writing, Mrs Wharton. I found *The Reef* particularly useful, but I used much of your writing. Your life provided so much material for your fiction. I believe your ghost stories were the most autobiographical, particularly when it came to marriage.'

'Quite the scholar, aren't you?' said Edith coolly. It was offensive that Mrs Gerould should hide behind Edith's own writing. But how clever (she hated to admit) to extract true events from fiction — Mrs Gerould knew her subject too well. The ghost stories had often equated marriage with entrapment, subservience and sexual violence. 'But why?' burst Edith, unable to disguise her fear. 'Why are you doing this?'

Mrs Gerould put down her knitting and regarded Edith with such kindly concern that she felt disconcerted. Events tonight would place Mrs Gerould as her adversary; yet Edith's instinct disagreed. How could she know such things? Had she really been a young member of staff? That didn't explain how she could write about events the following day — of course, the following day! Choosing her words carefully, Edith said, 'Trix, dear, you would've enjoyed hearing about the witch hazel. Always a great favourite.'

Trix responded with infuriating logic. 'You're confused with forsythia. I always used winter sweet.'

Typical Trix, unhelpful as ever. To Mrs Gerould, Edith said, 'Speaking of witch hazel, I wonder if there's an excess of *detail* in your story. After all, it's hardly important.'

Mrs Gerould's eyes held a challenge. 'A literary device, nothing more.'

No, the reference to witch hazel was a deliberate clue. What had she said earlier? *Truth is always in the details.*

Mrs Gerould shook her head with mock defeat. 'You're right, it's too obvious.'

Edith remembered now that on returning to the car, they had stopped to admire the witch hazel — but what else? Mrs Gerould wrote that Morton plucked a sprig for himself, but did she understand the folklore of the plant? Did she know that witch hazel only flowers on old wood, and always late in the season?

Several days after Morton's visit, Edith received a thank-you note. Morton had enjoyed his stay; her home was as beautiful as he expected and her company always a pleasure. She had read the note quickly, unconcerned by the polite detachment. It didn't worry her. In her hand was a sprig of witch hazel. It had fallen from the envelope and spoke more than words. They were both aware of the symbolism; she had explained about the late-blossoming of the old woman's flower. Opening a drawer, she removed a fresh journal and began to write. *The Life Apart: L'Âme Close.*

Her plans for Europe must be changed immediately. She and Teddy would be in Paris for Christmas! But she must hurry, there was so much to arrange — booking cabins, arranging transit for the dogs, securing an apartment in Paris. She must prepare The Mount for closure over winter, and deal with Teddy's mother and sister (which didn't bear contemplating). Excited, she wrote to Morton about her change of plans — they would see each other soon! But there was no response.

Now Edith held the steady gaze of Mrs Gerould. Clearly she understood the significance of the witch hazel and Morton keeping a piece for himself. There could be only one explanation. After picking the sprig, they had returned to the car, watched by two men. Charles Cook was Edith's friend and chauffeur; and he would remain in her service for another fourteen years, risking his life for her during the Great War. But Eliot Gregory? He was soon to disappear.

'I must assume,' said Edith, 'that you're acquainted with Eliot Gregory.'

'Not at all.'

'Damn it, who are you?'

A shiver ran through the room and Linky whined, scrambling into Edith's lap.

'Steady on,' murmured Walter. 'She's already told you.'

Mrs Gerould. They once shared a cab in Paris, yet the name Gerould meant nothing. However, the shadow of a memory was beginning to form. A pretty young woman in a Paris cab. The chance of discovery. A near miss. A disturbing secret. Yes, all those things — but who was she?

'Seems to me,' continued Walter, 'that tonight is turning into a dead loss. Not the first time you've over-schemed, my dear.'

Edith was stung. It was true her ideas didn't always run like clockwork. Not all her war efforts were successful, and her plans to help the impoverished Henry were clumsy if well intended. At least she tried. More than could be said for Walter with his immaculate and rarefied life. Annoyed, she said, 'I'm sorry you're not enjoying yourself, Walter, but I don't believe this evening is a failure.'

'You must admit it feels like a parlour game, Edith — one usually enjoyed by the middle-classes.'

He did have a point.

'I don't suppose you've got any playing cards? Or shall we play guessing games?'

Goodness, and people called her a snob.

His voice hardened. 'So what happened to the letters?'

She trembled as if a ghost were drifting across her grave. *The letters survive.* With an unsteady voice, she replied, 'Letters — what do you mean?'

'If we're to play guessing games, my dear,' — he smiled thinly — 'might as well achieve something tonight. I want to know what happened to our personal correspondence. You must remember, Edith — our letters.'

Oh, *their* letters. Yes, of course she remembered. Forty years' worth. His desk had been stuffed with their correspondence. After his death, she went to the apartment and poured them into a bag, sweeping out past the sobbing maid. She'd been protected from her grief by the immediacies of Walter's death, the many things that must be dealt with, knowing that devastation waited at the edges of her consciousness.

Tickling Linky behind one ear, she recalled that afternoon. She had destroyed the letters with such calm deliberation.

'Edith?'

'Gone. All the letters were burnt.'

'Well done.'

Blood beat angrily in her temples. 'With no help from you.'

'What do you mean?'

'What came afterwards.'

'I've no idea what you mean.'

No, he wouldn't care to know. Walter had stubbornly refused to consider what came afterwards (throw me on your roses!), but he cared enough to write a will he knew would cause her heartbreak. Was it a posthumous joke or an opportunity to reveal his true feelings? The flame of their relationship deserved a dignified ending, but this was denied by Walter's terrible coda.

Oblivious to her turmoil, Walter remained caught in his own memories. 'Remember Henry making bonfires in his garden? A lot of people slept easier knowing Henry burned everything.'

'Yourself included?'

'I was speaking generally.'

Edith allowed her memories to return — of being forced to protect Walter's reputation. Unfortunately, death was never the end of things.

'Let's hear more of the novella,' said Mrs Gerould, her voice light with challenge.

The file containing her essay was on the rug. Despite the unaccommodating nature of the Hepplewhite chair, Mrs Gerould had managed to settle herself comfortably. Edith appraised her thick stockings and leather brogues, her buttoned cardigan, woollen skirt stretched at wide hips. Now Edith understood: for some reason, Morton Fullerton had chosen to recount his visit directly to this homely looking woman. Mrs Gerould had no doubt been attractive when young, if a man liked the suburban type. Edith gave a snort of disbelief. Not the urbane Morton Fullerton. So why confide in a woman who admitted to being socially conventional? And why had Mrs Gerould been so keen to recall Morton's visit in such excruciating detail?

Edith checked the clock. Ten past eleven. Time was being wasted, and the situation was as incomprehensible as ever. After Morton's visit, Edith had started a diary and changed her travel plans, but what happened next? She couldn't remember.

Bluntly, Edith began, 'Let's be honest, shall we? If I'm to be published again, what will a new generation of readers discover about me? You say my memoirs are unreliable. Fair enough, but what other information is out there? Information of a more *personal* nature that survived my death?' She sat back to gauge the effect of her words. Someone here tonight must know — something at odds with a white wedding, something that might (God forbid!) *sex things up*. It was a marvellous phrase, and she could have made good use of it; certainly it would have been a welcome change from *dangerous allure*. However, this was no time to be distracted.

Her companions looked startled, but Trix was the most uncomfortable. Family always disliked the rattle of bones in the closet. 'Beatrix?' she ordered, 'what do you know?'

Trix scanned the room for an answer and stopped at Percy.

Of course, everything stopped with Mr Lubbock. After his marriage, Edith expelled him from her orbit (what had he expected?), but he was deeply resentful and survived her many years. The last man standing. So much unsupervised time to take his revenge. What did Percy do?

Light refracted from round glasses.

'Let me guess, Percy — your habit of writing parasitic books. I remember your act of literary treason when publishing Henry's letters.' Obsequious toad. Her memory was returning.

Percy bristled, ignoring Sybil, who placed a placating hand on his knee.

To the others, Edith said, 'Only four years after Henry's death, Percy published two volumes of Henry's letters. Despite all Henry's bonfires and ordering friends to destroy his correspondence, it wasn't enough. Percy grabbed what he could and published them.'

'A request by the family,' said Percy stiffly. 'They didn't want you involved.'

Family always won in the end, swarming the stage after the protagonist was gone. Henry despised his sister-in-law, but she controlled everything after his death; and the same could be said for Walter's dreadful sister. As for Edith's own departure — she outlived all her family except for the absent niece. It was her friend Elisina who stayed until the end.

When war was declared, they became instant friends. Cultivated and multi-lingual, Elisina Tyler was a beautiful, headstrong Florentine; a descendant of the Bonapartes and daughter of a *conte* and *contessa*. She was also shadowed by scandal. Madly in love with her second husband — and with a delightful son — Elisina had paid for her happiness by leaving four other children (and her first husband) in England. It was outrageous! Aristocratic Europeans thought her behaviour unforgivable, but not Edith — she didn't care. The Great War was raging, and Elisina was her Good Fairy, her aide-de-camp. Best of all, Elisina was a formidable committee woman.

Edith had never been one for good works, but she couldn't ignore the horror. Within weeks, Belgium was overrun and her beloved France under siege. She and Elisina opened a workroom for Parisian seamstresses (by then jobless after the fashionable ladies started sewing). Employing up to a hundred women at a time, Edith called on the support of everyone, including Walter, who found himself on the factory floor. Over in New York, Minnie Cadwalader Jones was scrambling to find a market for all their lingerie. Needs must, and so forth. Meanwhile, on the front line, two thousand young Frenchmen were dying every day.

Civilian refugees poured into Paris, dazed and deafened, sleeping on street benches and in railway stations. This was a scale of devastation beyond anything she and Elisina could manage. They turned to organising a network of committees; fundraising for charities to establish refugee hostels, orphanages, and (finally) convalescent homes. When peace was declared, Edith watched the troops march along the Champs-Élysées. Utterly shattered, she sought her own peace away from Paris. War may have been her finest hour, but it broke her heart.

But war *did* bring Elisina, her dear friend who stayed until the end. It was Elisina who wheeled her outside to watch birds on the lawn and leaves falling into the pond. Elisina vetted the endless well-wishers waving her to the great discovery of what lay beyond, the limitless spaces. And Elisina was beside her at the end, when Edith, circled by doctors with their hopeless 'bleeding' experiment, finally surrendered. Elisina's was the last face she saw.

Yes, but what happened next?

After the funeral, Elisina would have gone through everything. Such a tiresome job. Edith's life had been committed to words, and she left behind so much: notebooks, diaries, letters, so much of everything. No doubt Elisina kept the parcel marked

'For My Biographer', but what about the rest? She had already burned all correspondence with Teddy (under Edith's instructions), but did she read Edith's erotic stories of incest? What about the private letters and diaries? Everything was left for Elisina to decide.

Elisina Palamidessi de Castelvecchio. She was a woman who knew the pain of social ostracism, and she wouldn't have wished Edith's posthumous reputation to suffer a similar humiliation. It was likely that, to protect Edith's good name, she burned everything

Or was this Elisina Tyler, wife and mother? A woman who devastated her first family to become the ferociously loving wife of Royall and mother to William. A woman who understood the importance of a tight-knit family. For this reason, she might have consulted Edith's only living relative, Beatrix Jones Farrand. They would already have been in contact over Edith's will — it was quite possible that Elisina told Trix about the explosive papers. If this were the case, they would have been destroyed. Trix was a conservative woman, scarred by the scandal of her parents' divorce. She would consider the papers intolerable.

Or was this Elisina, her chief war officer? Vice-president of the American Hostels for Belgian Refugees. Vice-president of the Children of Flanders Rescue Committee. Chairwoman of the Franco–American Committee of the Viennese Children's Fund. Did Elisina honour the spirit of their friendship by becoming (once again) the efficient aide-de-camp? Edith could imagine her sorting and itemising everything: contacting biographers and curators of university collections; negotiating rights to the material and arranging for it to be catalogued and valued for auction.

Or was Elisina simply overwhelmed by grief and paperwork? Did she hand everything to Edith's literary executor, Gaillard

Lapsley — a man who, in all probability, put everything into cardboard boxes and promptly forgot them.

What had happened to her papers, her journals, private letters and erotic writing? Were they burned, or did they survive? Most importantly, what happened to her secret diary — *The Life Apart: L'Âme Close?*

Enough, she was drifting. It was imperative that she deal with Percy. Edith regarded him coolly, saying, 'I've nothing to be ashamed of, Mr Lubbock. I tried to protect Henry's legacy and can only be thankful your books were forgettable. That was their only memorable aspect.'

Sybil's eyes glittered. 'You wouldn't make jokes if you knew.'

The others held their breath, except for Percy, who polished his glasses with fastidious care.

'Percy?' said Edith. 'What is your wife referring to?'

'A book of memoirs,' said Trix.

'But why should anyone read about Percy?'

'No, he wrote about *you*.'

Edith swung back to Percy. 'Nonsense. We hadn't spoken for years. You knew nothing of my early life in America and nothing of my later years.'

'I spoke to people,' said Percy haughtily, clutching his wife's hand as if to shelter her from the unpleasantness.

'God forbid,' said Edith with feeling, and then, 'You must have breached my legal rights.'

'Not at all. Gaillard Lapsley requested that I write a memoir.'

Edith was stunned. How could Gaillard do such a thing? He was her literary executor. This was too painful.

She heard Walter say, 'Don't upset yourself, Edith. It's all in the past.'

'Gaillard should have protected my legacy from a parasite like Percy.'

'Now don't you see?' insisted Trix. 'Why can't you leave things alone?'

'I want to know what Percy wrote about me.'

'Percy is the least of your worries.'

They glared at each other. A silence lay between them like a sullen weight. What else did Trix know? Linky bristled, giving a low growl as the lights dimmed into darkness. A flicker, and the lights were on again. Nothing had changed except Mrs Gerould was now standing at the bookcase. Pulling a volume from the shelves, she murmured, 'Yes, I thought so. Percy's little book, *Portrait of Edith Wharton*. Most interesting, I remember now.' She held it up. Gold letters sparkled in the light.

'This is very tedious,' said Sybil with a petulant toss of her head. 'You know, I actually wish Edith would keep reading.'

'No,' said Edith. 'I want to hear what Percy wrote.'

Mrs Gerould took her seat and opened the book. 'Such a mean-spirited book, I don't know where to start. Let me see, Percy describes your house parties at The Mount as full of gaiety and fun of a very simple sort.'

'Simple?' Edith's mouth dropped open.

'That you were more amusing than well-bred.'

Edith allowed this to sink in before facing Percy. He was gazing intently at the ceiling. She demanded, 'How could you write about my house parties at The Mount? We didn't meet until later.'

'No,' said Sybil clearly, 'but I was there.'

Edith shook her head, uncomprehending.

A coy sweep of long lashes. 'With my first husband.'

Oh, God, she remembered now: Sybil arriving at The Mount as the young English ingénue, Mrs Bayard Cutting.

Mrs Gerould continued. 'Sybil's opinions are littered throughout the book, although she's never identified as Percy's wife, just some shy little Englishwoman. She describes you as cold and snobbish at home, while in Italy you're overbearing and money-grabbing. And Percy called your novels "pretty little tales" written in the margins of a busy life.'

In disbelief, Edith said to Percy, 'You *do* know I won the Pulitzer?' It was hopeless. The insufferable prig had got the last word after all. People said life wasn't a race, but they were wrong. Outlive your adversaries, that was the key. The last person standing got to write the final draft of the script. In her case, it was the hideous Percy. Edith understood now: this was the final version of herself presented to the world — the haughty Mrs Wharton, a grande dame, overbearing and pretentious.

Damn the infernal Percy Lubbock.

Mrs Gerould continued. 'Nothing about your Pulitzer prize or honorary doctorate. Nothing about your war effort or the Chevalier Award.'

'Unbelievable.' Edith shook her head — to think the innocuous Percy Lubbock was such a traitor. It was true that she ignored him for the last years of her life, so deep was her disgust for Sybil, but nothing could justify this memoir.

Mrs Gerould carried on with unpleasant insistence. 'Percy paints you as an intellectual and social snob, always grabbing for new experiences with no depth of understanding. A woman charming to her friends but aloof to others. He presents you as Mrs Wharton the endless hostess, demanding faultless perfection. And Mrs Wharton the bully, even in the garden. That it was a stupid little plant that ever dreamed of dodging your eye.'

'What a peculiar thing to say.'

'And dogs.'

Edith held still. 'What about my dogs?'

'That you surrounded yourself with small dogs of the yapping and whining variety.'

Edith collapsed back in her chair, resting one hand on Linky. The small dog gave a snuffle, burrowing more deeply into her lap. It was unconscionable that Percy had repaid her hospitality with such spite.

'Am I mentioned?' enquired Walter with polite interest.

A pause as Mrs Gerould fixed on the book, seeming unsure how to respond.

With horrible premonition, Edith quickly said, 'No more.'

'I would like to know', said Walter, 'what Percy wrote about me.'

'Oh, Walter, why bother?' Her voice had a forced carelessness. 'Nothing but the ravings of a non-entity.'

'If we're all to be rediscovered in this little scheme of yours, Edith, I want to know how I'm portrayed. It's clear Percy entombed you as the imperious Mrs Wharton. I would like to know how posterity views me.'

With obvious reluctance, Mrs Gerould leafed through the pages. She read for a minute before saying, 'Percy says you were dry and supercilious.'

A fluster from the sofa, as if a feather bolster had exploded.

'But that you were an insatiable reader and a hard worker, a good linguist and traveller. That your practical experience often helped Edith.'

'Indeed,' said Walter. He stroked his moustache lingeringly.

Mrs Gerould looked at Edith. 'But none of your friends thought you better for the surrender of your spirit to the control of such a man.'

Edith felt her eyebrows rise. She had suspected as much. Some of her friends viewed Walter as her gatekeeper, but it wasn't true. He was her soulmate.

'Percy says — no, I'm sorry.' Mrs Gerould shook her head. 'Some things are best left unsaid.'

Reaching out, Walter ordered, 'Here, give me the book. Throw it to me.'

A moment of indecision.

'Please.'

The book landed at Walter's feet. He swept it from the floor and began to read. All eyes were on him, trepidatious. His long fingers swiped over a page, lips pressed thinly as he tore it from the book.

Sybil gave a cry of fright.

Crushing the sheet in one hand, Walter took aim. The ball of paper landed in the fire: a brief conical flare, and it was gone.

There was a profound silence.

Walter cleared his throat. 'Percy writes that I have the harshness of a dogmatist, the bleakness of an egotist, and the pretentiousness of a snob.' A faint smile of disbelief. 'And a deep vault of egotism sealed against the currents of sympathy and humanity—'

'My God,' breathed Edith. She couldn't believe it — even of Percy Lubbock. However, Walter wasn't finished.

'—creating a chill that lowered the temperature of life all round it, deadening its charm and cheapening its value.'

The room was the temperature of a morgue. No one moved.

'How dare you?' Walter snarled. 'You sycophantic parasite.' He was white with anger, body quaking with suppressed violence. Taking aim, he spun the book through the air. It flew in slow motion, whirling across the room. Percy threw up his arms to protect himself, glancing the book towards Sybil. She screamed, a shattering pitch that cut the lights. Sybil whimpered like a sick animal.

Linky jumped to the floor, disappearing behind Edith's chair. The sobbing continued, Percy making low noises of sympathy. The darkness endured. Gradually there came a sound of Linky scratching on the rug. The room slowly lightened, and Sybil began to quieten. Percy was solicitously attending to his wife, dabbing a trickle of blood on her temple with a handkerchief. Opening a compact mirror, Sybil began to repair her makeup. Tears stained her powdered cheeks like a braided river. The memoir lay split open on the rug.

Walter was hidden by the wings of his chair. He was drumming on the armrest with a long, bloodless hand, a red seal ring on his small finger. Walter's behaviour was quite inexplicable — even in the face of such provocation. He was usually the embodiment of Old New York, a tribe of people who dreaded scandal more than disease, and placed decency above courage; who considered nothing more ill-bred than 'scenes' — except the behaviour of those who gave rise to them. However, Walter had caused a scene tonight.

As for the man who had given rise to the scene, Edith was no longer surprised Percy Lubbock had written about her. Of course he would have profited from their friendship. Marrying Sybil would have come with its own set of problems: a difficult woman and expensive to keep happy. Money, spite, publishing: a terrible combination. But the depth of his treachery was breathtaking.

Portrait of Edith Wharton: no doubt Percy mentioned her want of good looks — he would have enjoyed that. She could just imagine his patronising tone of malicious endearment. Nor would Percy have been constrained by his lack of originality and creative thought. He would have simply retold the same old stories: that she was too fashionable for Boston and too intelligent for New York. That she wrote in bed, leaving the pages on the floor for the maid to collect. That she despaired of American hotels — such crass food, crass manners, crass landscape! *What a horror it is for a whole nation to be developing without the sense of beauty, & eating bananas for breakfast.*

No doubt Percy mentioned the bons mots that had been so spontaneous and witty at the time; but they would be worn and unpleasant when recounted with such a deadened hand. She knew the stories: her enjoyment at the expense of her wealthy, uncultured neighbours in Lenox. *The XYZs, they tell me, have decided to have books in their library*. Or being shown around an opulent home, the owner saying, *And I call this my Louis Quinze room*, to which Edith replied, *Why, my dear?* The Frenchman who approved of The Mount but disliked the bas-relief in the entrance hall, to whom Edith said, *I assure you that you will never see it here again*. Percy would have enjoyed her entombment, nailing the door on her mausoleum.

Edith felt her resolve strengthen. Percy Lubbock would not have the last word. She would be rediscovered as the Edith Wharton who wrote about Wall Street tycoons and material girls at the Met Gala, of celebrity gurus and spiritual vacuum cleaning, a sleepless goldfish kept awake all night by electric lightbulbs. She would be correctly remembered as a woman of her time. And yet . . . publication of the novella would mean open season on the life of Edith Wharton. She couldn't be sure, exactly, what might be revealed, but her memory was beginning to return.

She and Teddy travelled to Paris before Christmas along with their staff and two small dogs. There was still no word from Morton, and Edith felt a deep shame. How could she have imagined Morton Fullerton would be interested in a woman like herself, a woman without delicacy or charm? It was humiliating to have misread the situation so badly. Her secret diary lay untouched.

They settled into an apartment on the rue de Varenne, and she wrote again, politely informing Mr Fullerton of her arrival. Again there was no response. And then — suddenly — he was everywhere. Overwhelmingly present. He regularly sent notes, and they had tea together to discuss the translation of *Mirth*. When Morton suggested an evening at the theatre, she agreed. The play was Italian, and since Teddy objected to the language there was no chance of his joining them.

They had a private box swagged with red and gold velvet. Edith was intensely aware of everything about Morton. His reaction to the play, his light movements, the soundless interplay of their bodies. In her diary she wrote, *Looking now & then at the way the hair grows on your forehead, at the line of your profile turned to the stage.* Partway through the play, the leading actress became so overcome with passion that she found herself unable to send away her lover. Edith was careful to fix her attention on the unfolding drama, her profile composed and distant. She could feel Morton lean close, warm breath against her cheek, his words: *That's something you don't know anything about.* She shook at the unknowingness of intimacy.

It was a perfect romance. As delicate as the spring blossom along the quays of the Seine. A playful delight: *Meet you at the Louvre at one o'c, in the shadow of Jean Gougon's Diana.* A drama of tea gowns and rushed whispering at the theatre. Morton was the perfect leading man — a dashing journalist, scholar, and poet. They spoke the same language: *I have found in Emerson just the phrase for you & me. 'The moment my eyes fell on him I was content.'* Together they barrelled through the countryside in their motor-car (laughingly named Hortense), with Henry James holding forth in the passenger seat, all twinkly-eyed indulgence at the flights and fancies of his two protégés. It was perfect — utterly perfect — and how often can that be said of life? Always the writer, she relived the events in her diary, adding: *This must be what happy women feel.*

And then came the evening that changed everything. They were in her drawing-room, Morton bent over some papers, his black hair shining under an electric light. Edith watched him with musing contentment.

Morton raised his head. He seemed to have read her thoughts. There was a second's pause, which Edith mistook to be shared joy, before a cruel mask slipped over his face. His smirk was mocking, voice ugly: was this really what Edith was content to settle for? A quiet night by the fire? A relationship as sexless as her own marriage?

Edith was sick with shock. Unable to answer, she allowed him to continue.

He was tired of the playacting; the low-cut gowns and flirting; the mock-modesty. He wouldn't wait much longer; this wouldn't sustain him. How could she expect it to be so? He would seek satisfaction elsewhere.

She told him to leave.

Rising to his feet, he nodded curtly and was gone.

Edith watched the flames burn low. Grossie arrived, fussing about the room, and Edith sent her away. Midnight passed. Eventually she picked up a pen to write, *Dear Morton* . . .

(3)

Tuscany

Heat shimmered through the windows, dust rising behind
the car. Blasted by the air conditioner, Sara pulled on another
sweater. From the back seat Medora had been answering their
questions with surprising enthusiasm. They heard all about
her life in New Zealand — her mother owned a sheep stud,
and her father was a loser. Austen wanted to hear about the
sheep stud, so Medora explained: Coopworth mostly and some
Texels, but they never bothered with ram hoggets because of the
reliability issues, '— you know, like, *gross*'.

'What—?' said Austen.

'Ram hoggets don't have as much semen as two-tooths.'

'That's a problem?'

'Sure. The libido of a ram hogget often outstrips their semen
supply.'

Ouch.

Medora wanted to hear what places they'd lived, so Sara
reeled off the countries like the ingredients for a stir-fry.
Her list was broken by Austen reminding her of Nigeria —
remember? — which Medora found hilarious. Sara listened to
her laugh for a second before joining in. Austen glanced across
in surprise.

Sara watched the rushing blur of olive trees out the window.
She liked having Medora around. The girl had no opinion on
their expatriate life. For thirty years Sara had lived in a self-
justifying sphere — *Don't our kids pick up languages easily!* — and
she'd been unprepared for the hostile reaction her life provoked
back home. But Medora? She absolutely didn't care.

They parked on a gravel verge shaded by a tree. Sara pulled her bag from the trunk and looked up. The plain square Villa Gamberaia had ochre walls that tumbled with creepers. No wonder Edith loved it — and now it was Sara's job to capture this beauty in a blog. Could she do it? She slammed the trunk shut with unnecessary force. There was no room for failure. This was her last chance.

Large gates opened on to a gravel courtyard. Along one edge tall stone dogs sat on a low wall, facing out across the valley towards the distant spires of Florence. Medora was wearing the same stressed jeans as the day before, but her tee-shirt was clean and hair damp. In the car, Sara had been aware of a fresh soapiness, and now she could see the imprint of pegs on her tee-shirt. She pictured Medora washing her clothes in a hotel basin, drying them on a line over the bath. Medora turned and smiled, as if reading her thoughts. This was the first time Sara had seen her teeth. Regular and white, they were blunt like they'd been levelled with a metal file. It made Sara's spine tingle.

'See you later.'

Taken aback, Sara watched Medora walk away. She'd assumed they would see the garden together, but the girl was already gone. Dropping to sit on the wall, she flipped open Edith's book on Italian gardens and began to read . . . *the most perfect example of the art of producing a great effect on a small scale.* She blinked, urging the words into action, but they remained sullenly shut. Gazing back across the valley, she squinted against the diffuse blue sky.

Why was she doing this? There was no reason to make herself feel useless. Right now she could be in a café with Austen, dragging a conversation from the floor of her brain: *Why don't we buy some pottery?* But was that what she wanted, really?

Because sitting in a courtyard café with Austen would mean no Medora. At least now she had Medora's absence and the sense of possibility. Turning a page, Sara willed the words to crack open and reveal their meaning.

*

Austen lowered himself to the pool edge and looked into the shallow water. A scatter of tarnished coins lay on the bottom. Low-denomination euros, plus some other currencies he didn't recognise. What were people supposed to do in a garden? How long could you stare at a plant? And in a place this small, you couldn't get a decent walk. If their son Matthew had joined them, they could've been playing golf. Frankfurt wasn't so far — but Matt had just switched banks, and it was a busy time of year. He was sorry, but just couldn't swing things.

Sara didn't seem to mind. When Austen relayed this conversation to her, she'd nodded in agreement as if it were prearranged, of no particular consequence — like a picnic cancelled for bad weather. Austen was careful to hide his irritation, unsure if he felt more betrayed by his son or his wife. Not that Sara's complacency was new. Only Hugo could penetrate her indifference — even a phone call from a beach bar in Asia was enough to unhinge her. But an agitated call from Alice about a test having placed her on the autism spectrum had left Sara unmoved. She'd said only, *That's odd, it's usually a male thing*. And that was the end of it. Austen had felt impotent fury on behalf of his prickly daughter. Sara called the kids global nomads with no sense of belonging. She said this lightly, without regret.

Plunging his arm into the pond, Austen tried to prise a coin from the bottom.

'Got cash-flow problems?'

It was the girl. Dropping her daypack to the ground, she joined him on the pool edge. Too close. Austen moved further along. In the sunlight her hair was plum-coloured, sticking up in quiffs. Her face was shiny from the heat.

She took in the shell-nubble walls. 'I like it.'

Austen wasn't so sure. It seemed a little tacky.

'A nymphaeum. Like a natural grotto, only more architectural.' Her eyes scanned the walls, then shot straight at him. She was too close, he couldn't focus. Humour shadowed her mouth. 'It's a Roman thing. Nymphaeums were often part of the dining room. Splashing fountains and dripping moss helped diners feel better when they were drunk and bursting. Those classy Romans.'

Austen laughed.

'Why does your wife care about blogging?'

He felt his smiled wiped, like pushing 'delete' on a smart board. 'It's a good opportunity, and it fills her time.'

'Odd way to describe a life. Fills her time until when?'

Austen looked away, irritated.

'That's an aim in life?'

'One day you'll understand, Medora. Life is a continual process of lowering your horizons.'

'Lucky you're not a motivational speaker.'

He grinned, despite himself. 'It's not the big stuff. Life is about getting through. Years with nothing to show.'

'I can't believe I'm getting Pink Floyd.'

'I can't believe you know Pink Floyd.' They watched the splash of water. He said, 'You always want to be a landscape architect?'

'I started with geography. Then I got interested in other stuff.'

'Like drainage systems.'

'My anthropology lecturer used to talk about the supermarket of life. He said it was our civic duty to experience as much as possible.'

Austen fixed his attention on a parapet.

'Particularly in the aisle of physical intimacy.'

Keeping his eyes fixed, he said, 'That's an unusual thing to say.'

'Professor Restieaux was a very unusual man. Odd that someone so well acquainted with pre-European Polynesian family life could be so forgetful with his own.'

She was having him on, Austen knew that. A consummate liar. Nevertheless, he was impressed. She was trying him out, testing the water. He knew this from the young recruits at work. They were all the same, beautiful young women with immaculate academic records. They scared him with their bulletproof confidence. They came from a world he didn't understand — speed dating and internet sex. He had no wish to understand. Of course some of them would try it on — he was a guy on the top floor. He knew it wasn't personal, just an automatic reflex. Like a depth sounder sending signals into the unknown, trying to gauge the topography.

Austen never responded. Not because he wasn't tempted. Occasionally he was. But he knew what the fallout was like; he'd seen the mess. Like coming across a car smash with people wandering around dazed and scattered. You couldn't put things back together, not after something like that. Not properly. Sure, he was tempted when Sara kept getting more removed. It was like living with someone underwater. Sometimes he just wanted to remember what it was like to connect with another human being. And then, without warning, Sara would look at him, really *look* at him, and say something simple and true, like,

Home can never exist for us now, and he got that feeling of the abyss. There were days when he would stand in his office gazing down on yet another city, convinced the plate-glass windows were ranch sliders, that he could lift a latch and step outside. The co-existence of normality and terror, the way a head might split open like a watermelon.

Medora was trailing her fingers through the cool water. 'Professor Restieaux taught me everything I know about polygamy in postcolonial Micronesia.'

'Was that useful?' His voice was flat, disinterested. He was getting tired of her.

'Y'know, I always feel like I'm missing something. I can appreciate these old gardens in an intellectual way, but that's all. I'm not overwhelmed by enchanting loveliness or elusive charm. Just doesn't do it for me.'

'What does do it for you?' He heard the reluctance in his voice, didn't want to ask. Nor did he want to be stranded in the uncertain waters of silence.

'I hoped it would be these gardens — a stairway touched by Ligorio, a fountain admired by Cosimo de' Medici. But it's not like that. Not with the restaurants and car parks. What does it for you?'

He felt his guard slip. 'I'm not sure I know what "it" is anymore.'

'When a trapdoor opens inside, and you feel yourself falling. That stumble on the stairs just as you go to sleep.'

Standing by a plate-glass window and stepping outside. Half-turning, he said, 'I was on a Delta flight to St Louis when we hit turbulence. The oxygen masks dropped.'

She shook her head. 'How about lying in the grass with closed eyes on a sunny day when a cloud passes over?'

'Closing the drawer on a well-organised filing cabinet.'

'Pulling a bottle of vodka from the freezer on a hot day, icy glass pressed against your mouth, and the kiss of condensate.' She continued, 'A finger drawn lightly down your spine. Lips pressed against closed eyelids.'

'We should get going.'

She leaned towards him. He felt her intention a second before her breath touched his temple. 'A body pressed hard against hotel sheets.'

He scrambled away, aware his discomfort was comical. Like an outraged bride. He was embarrassed by her expression, ironic and amused.

'Oh, there you are!' It was Sara, standing at the entrance all flushed and distracted. She surveyed the garden, bemused, like she'd been expecting a homewares department.

Austen was irritated by his wife's lack of intuition. Sara had never been suspicious of him. Ever. Never had a reason, of course — but an affair was always an available option. No thanks to her that he ignored the opportunities. It would have never occurred to her, engrossed as she was in her muffled world. At times he wondered if *she* were having an affair. What else could account for such absorption? But a few desultory checks had shown nothing, and he could only conclude that Sara was absorbed in herself. Unbelievable. Even now. She walked straight into a dramatic set piece — Medora coolly composed by the pool while he was flung against the wall — and still she suspected nothing. Moments like this he could do with a little support. A little female intuition could go a long way around here.

Medora was laughing at something — loud, almost honking. Of course, he thought. Why should Sara suspect anything? What was there to suspect? Now Medora was up on her feet, hoisting her daypack over her shoulder. 'I've been reading about the garden when Edith came to visit. It was owned by a beautiful Romanian called Princess Ghyka. She was restoring the villa.'

Sara was stroking the rough surface of a pumice wall, her expression uncertain.

Medora continued. 'She hated men but loved the garden. It's said she swam in the pools at night.'

'What a great story.' Sara stopped. 'I don't suppose — well, this afternoon I'm writing about the garden, if—'

'Fine with me,' said Medora.

*

Blog: Villa Gamberaia

Few could be immune to the magic of Villa Gamberaia. Little wonder it influenced Mrs Wharton's own garden at The Mount. There's no lovelier place on a hot afternoon as fountains splash in shady corners, distant Florence turning hazy-blue. And there's no better guidebook to Villa Gamberaia than Mrs Wharton's own writing. Her text is incisive, and her analysis always sharp.

The design of the garden, in her own words, combines logic and beauty. On the subject of beauty there can be no question, but logic? The garden plan is best understood when viewed from the upstairs loggia, a view that Mrs Wharton undoubtedly enjoyed. While this is not achievable for most visitors, don't despair. Just as much enjoyment can be had from exploration; every corner of this garden is surprising and rewarding.

Let's picture the garden when Mrs Wharton came to visit. What she made of the owner, Princess Ghyka of Romania, we can't imagine. The beautiful princess was living in the villa with her lover, an American woman with the fabulous name of Miss Blood. Mrs Wharton was impressed by the well-preserved nature of the garden, but she didn't approve of recent changes to the fishpond made by the princess. What had been simple plots of roses and vegetables were now the elaborate water parterres we celebrate today.

Which raises the question of historical authenticity. While we regard Villa Gamberaia as the perfect Tuscan Renaissance garden, it is relatively recent and greatly modified (not least after Nazi occupation, requiring yet more restoration). Nonetheless, beauty and history effortlessly combine to create something unique and magical. Sun-filled terraces with dancing fountains, cypress-scented boscos with depths of green. A citrus garden of potted lemons and crisply clipped box. And always, the ghosts of the past.

*

The next day when Sara arrived on the terrace for breakfast, she found Medora already at their table, the orange juice finished. Taking a seat, she said, 'Bernard loves the blog.' It was true. Sara had spoken to him last night after dinner — he couldn't believe the improvement. He loved the way she brought the garden alive, a seamless fusion of history and design. Sara had mentioned Medora, but Bernard wasn't interested. Tomorrow he was pitching to the publishers — they were going to love the project as much as he did. This thing would really fly.

Listening to Bernard, Sara had watched her reflection nodding in the bedroom mirror. He was talking about his elevator pitch and how he needed a marketing plan. It made

Edith sound like a product. Not that Sara minded. Bernard was lucky he didn't have to read *Italian Villas and Their Gardens*. Bernard's voice lowered — remember that stuff he said about Edith's love-life? Forget it. Mrs Newbold went nuclear. Laura Bush agreed to be patron of the Summer Series, and Newbold wanted to keep things tasteful.

'I'm not surprised he liked the blog,' said Medora, helping herself to a bread roll. Pushing her plate aside, she began buttering it on the glass table. This morning she was wearing jeans and another fresh tee-shirt. Sara could just make out the soapiness of a shower.

'Only, he wondered—'

'What?'

'Not so much garden stuff.'

Medora started to laugh.

'More lifestyle content.' Sara was defensive without knowing why.

'Lifestyle.' A smile tucked into the corner of Medora's mouth.

'Like picnics, and not so much Wikipedia.'

Medora's brow quirked. 'Bernard has very high standards.'

'But why — I mean, with your qualifications—'

'—would I use the internet? I don't have a library here.'

'No,' agreed Sara, but something didn't feel right.

'YouTube mostly,' said Medora, her mouth full.

Medora's table manners were terrible. She had no use for utensils and took up the table like it was a land occupation. Last night she'd joined them for dinner at Sara's insistence: it was the least they could do. Austen had been annoyed, couldn't see the need. He'd been uncharacteristically curt. They ate in an overpriced trattoria, and it turned out Medora was vegetarian. She spent the whole night looking at Sara's chicken parmigiana like it was a thing to be pitied. And Medora felt no obligation to be engaging, her answers monosyllabic. It was left to Sara to save the evening.

Back in their hotel room, Austen had said Medora was creepy and weird-smelling. Sara explained that Medora was a lesbian, which probably explained why she didn't use perfume — besides, what was wrong with soap? She refrained from saying she liked the smell, that it reminded her of small children, of bath-time and clean pajamas.

But Austen refused to believe Medora was gay.

Sara wasn't surprised. Guys could never tell these things, but women knew — and Medora definitely was. But she hadn't meant to say lesbian out loud. It was too defining. Medora was different in a way she couldn't understand. Repellent and beguiling at the same time.

Austen still wasn't convinced. Nor was he happy. That's when Sara started to get worried and hoped he wasn't coming down with something. Was he feeling okay? The last thing they needed was a medical issue. Which was when Austen got angry, locking the bathroom door to have a shower — at which point Bernard rang. And this morning Austen went running before Sara was up. She had come to breakfast alone.

'I'm leaving today.'

'What?' Sara stared. In the sunlight, Medora's skin was unexpectedly soft.

'After breakfast.'

'But you can't.' Sara's mind scrambled with panic. Medora couldn't leave now. It wasn't thinkable. Her hand shot across the table. Another low-voltage connection, like a small electrical pulse. She forced herself to maintain contact. Such brown eyes. Incalculable. 'Please, Medora, just one more night. We'll pay for your room, no problem. I need help rewriting my first blog, the Boboli Gardens.'

Medora tipped her head to one side, an unspoken question.

'What I mean is, could you write it for me?'

'And the Medici garden?'

'That too.'

'But I'm going to Florence today, an exhibition. I'm not slave labour.'

'No, but—'

'You're expecting a working holiday without pay.'

Money. The girl wanted money. Fear forced Sara to look directly at her. Enigmatic. Unfathomable. 'How much?'

'An hourly rate of forty euros?'

Sara's breath caught. It was exorbitant. But what choice did she have? It was obvious Medora had already decided a price. She was following a preconceived course of action, had already plotted the co-ordinates of a plan in which Sara was now trapped. The thought was both terrifying and intriguing. How long had she been plotting? And how far back did this go?

'Of course,' said Sara. She was aware of Austen approaching the table. 'But please, don't—'

'—tell Austen?' The girl shrugged.

'Morning.' He was at the table, bending down to kiss Sara. Pulling out a chair, he sat down, flushed from his run, hair wet from a shower. He looked healthy and tanned. Untainted. Smiling across at Medora, he said, 'So, you're leaving today?'

CHAPTER V

It was difficult to read the novella with everyone otherwise occupied. Trix had listened closely to the descriptions of Villa Gamberaia
before taking a book across to show Walter. Thankfully he was
now calm, and Trix was back in her chair. Mrs Gerould had set
aside her knitting to tickle Linky, while Sybil continued to huddle
in the sofa, a handkerchief pressed to her temple. Percy was now
some distance away, seated at the other end of the sofa, with the
reduced appearance of someone chastised. The two were avoiding each other. The book lay on the floor between them in mute
recrimination. Oddly enough, it was Teddy who was most attentive,
crossing his arms and nodding at the carpet.

Edith had been wary while reading, but no one noticed the
mention of her love-life or Mrs Newbold's wanting to keep things
tasteful. Edith had hurried this passage, keeping her eye on Teddy.
She had been delighted by the monumental Mrs Newbold —
a woman cast in the image of Edith Newbold Jones Wharton; it was
a nice piece of writing.

'Edith?' said Walter impatiently.

'I'm sorry?'

'Trix and I have been speaking,' he said distinctly, 'about the
fine art of biography. Not Percy's pathetic little scribbles, but

the sacrifice and dedication required of a gifted biographer. As I was saying, it's an act of heroism.'

'Indeed,' replied Edith absently. Her attention was taken by the book on Trix's knee. It appeared (from looking upside down) to be about the life and gardens of Beatrix Jones Farrand. The same book she had seen earlier in the bookcase. Yes, it was a quality publication. Lucky Trix. She had no fear of her dark secrets being exposed or any untoward revelations about her and Wet-Fish. Even her career involved nothing more salacious than angiosperms.

Perhaps that explained why Trix was here tonight, representing the values of Edith's childhood. Old New York: a place where the unusual was regarded as either immoral or ill-bred; where people with emotions were not visited; where authorship was still regarded as something between a black art and a form of manual labour. Yes, Trix was a fitting representative; she was so resolute in her determination to carry to its utmost limit that ritual of ignoring the 'unpleasant' in which they had been brought up.

Little wonder Edith moved to France.

Walter continued with deliberate carelessness. 'I imagine my own career was covered after a time. Not my wish, of course, but still — a judge on the international tribunal in Cairo must have been of some interest.' He waited, but with no reply forthcoming he prompted, 'Edith?'

'Oh, my dear, I tried.'

'What do you mean, you *tried*?'

'I asked Mr Fullerton to write a biography.'

'Excellent.'

'Yes, but he never got *around* to it.'

There was an astonished silence before Walter said stiffly, 'Well, he missed an excellent opportunity. A most prestigious commission.'

'Yes, dear, that's what I said.'

A burst of laughter came from the ill-mannered Mrs Gerould. Edith glared, and after an awkward period of indecision the woman picked up her knitting.

Trix turned another page, wistful and composed. Edith could see a pergola weighed with wisteria, and architectural plans for a reflection pool. There was a photograph of Wet-Fish standing in a doorway, Trix sitting beside — Of course! Why hadn't she realised sooner? A biography must have been written on the life of Edith Wharton. Why was she so slow-witted this evening? A biography would tell her everything she needed to know — more specifically, whether her secret diary had been kept and discovered.

Edith craned towards the shelf containing her novels, straining to see. So much of her work was here, but what about a biography? With fixed determination, Edith levered herself up and lurched for the bookcase. It must be here, somewhere.

'Aunt Pussy,' said Trix with asperity. 'What on earth are you doing?'

'Nothing, my dear.' She continued scanning the books. If a biography had been written on the life of Edith Wharton, it wasn't here. Her disappointment was acute. Then she caught a flash of red binding. A collection of her works. Pulling the volume from the shelf, she was impressed by the cover — her literary executors had been of some use after all. The contents page had a list of the novellas, short stories and — Edith stopped. At the bottom, like a provocative afterthought, was *Appendix: Life and I*. Her private memoir had been published.

Astonishment sent her spinning. Clumsy with distress, she dropped the book on the floor, and Linky growled. She heard Trix cry out, and her arm was taken. Leaning heavily, she marvelled at her niece's strength, and together they moved slowly across the room. Edith collapsed in her chair.

'Aunt Pussy, you mustn't frighten us.'

Edith reached to clasp her hand. 'Such a comfort, my dear, having you here tonight.'

A small nod, but Trix was bent awkwardly. She straightened, removing her hand to put distance between them. The moment had passed, the warmth gone. Returning to the bookcase, Trix picked up the book. 'A collection of your work,' she said, carrying it back to her chair.

No — don't read it.

But Trix was already rifling through the pages. 'Another memoir. *Life and I*.'

Mrs Gerould nodded with irritating authority. 'Your published memoir was such a polished presentation of your life. But you once likened life to a tapestry, the real business hiding behind the display side. I'm guessing this unpublished memoir has you standing around the back, viewing the knots that hold everything together.'

Was there anything this woman *didn't* know?

Edith said briskly, 'Only three chapters. It was never finished.'

Mrs Gerould went to stand behind Trix's chair, looking over her shoulder as she skimmed the pages.

What were they reading? How, only days before her wedding, seized with such dread of the whole dark mystery, she summoned up courage to appeal to her mother and begged her, with a heart beating to suffocation, to tell her *What being married was like*. At her mother's look of icy disapproval, Edith persisted, *I'm afraid, Mama — I want to know what will happen to me!* The coldness of her mother's expression deepened to disgust — surely Edith had seen enough pictures and statues to know men were made differently? To Edith's confusion, she ordered: *Then for heaven's sake don't ask me any more silly questions. You can't be as stupid as you pretend.*

Lucretia's scolding was so extreme that Edith had sworn off the whole business until she had been married several weeks.

The shame made her burn even now: the virgin marriage bed; a husband driven to showgirls; a misery that triggered ten years of illness.

Trix maintained a studied expression of concentration on the volume. It was Mrs Gerould who said, 'I assume you didn't want this published.'

'Not particularly.'

Trix slammed the red volume shut. 'If you'd let me deal with things, I would have erased everything.'

Exactly. Edith closed her eyes, listening to the rapid-fire beat of her heart. So her memoir wasn't destroyed by Elisina. It survived and was eventually discovered and published. If publishers bothered with three chapters of a private memoir, they would publish anything: poetry and experimental fiction, letters and personal papers . . . a secret love diary.

The Life Apart: L'Âme Close.

A sensational love diary that would forever cancel the misconception of Edith Wharton as a prudish Victorian. It was a literary bombshell and marketing gold — a fact not lost on the novella's author (Edith felt sure). Charles Scribner must have known this, weighing it against Edith's commercial ambitions, and been unable to decide. But how much detail from her love diary was in the novella? Scrib said nothing too alarming. Probably some insinuations that raised red flags; enough to encourage readers to find out more. And (if she understood correctly) what existed in the material world existed on the internet, an excellent place for research.

She finally understood Scrib's concern: her love diary was on the internet and available to the modern world should anyone be inspired to search for it. The contents may also be in the pages of the novella. She would stop reading aloud; her companions must not hear such things. Besides, there was no reason to keep reading; she knew everything needed to make a decision. Publishing the novella and reviving the works of Edith Wharton would draw attention to her secret diary. This was Charles Scribner's concern, a decision he couldn't make. And now it was her decision.

Walter spoke with impatience. 'Edith? I don't understand. What's everyone going on about?'

'An unpublished memoir.'

'My God! Is there no end to this?'

'It was private.'

'Should've been burnt. Don't tell me there's more undying love.'

'No, Walter, you're quite spared. I promise. There's nothing about love; it's mostly about my mother.'

A ripple of laughter from the sofa.

'If this memoir survived,' said Mrs Gerould, 'there must be other material. Can you remember what?'

'Some short stories that might surprise. Secret journals and experimental fiction. I forget what else.' Edith felt her heart thump at the thought of her secret love diary.

'Experimental? In what way?'

'As you say, incest was not unknown in my writing.' Ignoring Walter's stir of anger, Edith continued. 'A graphic story about a father and daughter enjoying the mutual pleasure of lovemaking and the terrible consequences.' She shrugged. 'I was exploring my limits, nothing more.'

'A disgrace,' flared Walter, 'having people read your sordid tales.'

'Thanks to Percy, I'm considered puritanical and overly interested in flower arranging. I doubt my erotic writing would provide much interest.'

'But what if you become popular again? Is that what you want — a collection of Edith Wharton pornography?'

'I doubt the publishers would allow such a thing.'

'Nonsense. Who cares to protect your legacy now?'

'You might be right; after all, that was always your job.' She tried to recall what Percy had written about Walter — that none of her friends thought her better for the surrender of her spirit to the control of such a man. Damn Percy Lubbock, there was some truth to it.

Every blade-stroke through the water brought them closer to the question. Walter was about to propose! They had spent the summer holidays exploring Bar Harbor and the island, avoiding the adults. Heedlessly boastful, they discussed art and archaeology, and (of course!) literature. Anything that set them apart from the others. Walter said, *It is easy to see the superficial resemblances between things. It takes a first-rate mind to perceive the differences underneath.* She caught her breath. Walter was holding up a mirror to her own future. Being with him meant she could be a writer. At night she lay beneath the mosquito net, sheets tossed to the floor, excited with wonder: *Can this be me? Can this really be happening to me?*

The swell from a small fishing boat washed against the canvas of their canoe. Waiting for it to pass, Edith re-arranged the layers of her muslin skirt. Behind her, Walter continued to slice the surface with his paddle. She felt a wave of panic. He still hadn't proposed! Tomorrow he was leaving for Washington to continue his law studies.

She refused to believe he could be so indifferent to her feelings. It must be part of a plan. Of course! That would explain things:

Walter was purposely delaying the moment. How very like him! To increase the dramatic tension, force a deliberate heightening of their own story: the desperate rush of a proposal set against the ticking hours. She felt her agony turn to exquisite pain, a tormenting pleasure. He would propose any minute now, she was quite sure. As if in response, Walter laid down his paddle, allowing the canoe to drift. Edith held her breath.

'About time we headed back, old girl, don't you think?' he said.

That night they dined at Roddicks Hotel under the blazing scrutiny of the summer crowd. It was now or never. Even Lucretia was positioned with the other mothers, an expression of suppressed superiority. To think, the serious Edith Jones was about to capture Walter Berry! This was even more amazing as she was damaged goods, given a previous engagement had been cancelled by the groom's family, who found Edith unnaturally intelligent.

Walter was magnificent. He ignored the summer crowd with a lofty disregard, smiling as their expectations turned to confusion. They had clearly underestimated him, mistaking him for one of their own with his good looks and breeding, his athleticism. But no, Walter was set apart by his intellect and fine sensibilities. Why should he conform to their conventional ways? They were nothing but sport-mad philistines. Walter (and by association Edith) sought to occupy the republic of the spirit; they wanted no part in this parochial and insular world of braying idiots. Walter set his own course even when it came to that most hidebound ritual of all: engagement.

Edith held herself proud. She could barely eat, fixing her mouth into a smile that stayed in place all evening. Gazing into Walter's loftily mocking face, she had never felt so close to him. They were in this joke together. Her skin was sore from mild sunburn, and her jaw ached. Edith laid her large hands on the starched white tablecloth and was reminded of the high altar at her father's funeral. She bled with loss but would not be defeated. By the time dessert arrived, the crowd was restless, confusion turning to derision. Nothing betrayed her shame. She assumed a disregarding pride that would last a lifetime.

Next morning she came downstairs to bear the final humiliation: Walter had left the hotel without saying goodbye. He had elegantly removed himself from her life with no promise of communication. Horror crashed over her like a North Atlantic wave, Lucretia standing scornful on the shore. Walter had carelessly broken her heart, amusing himself by making a spectator sport of rejection.

Two years later, on a cold day in April, she married Teddy Wharton, arriving at the church without bridesmaids or a bouquet. Her older brothers thought him a fine fellow, and her mother approved of his Boston breeding. Edith approached the church clutching her prayer book as if to defend herself against the demands of marriage, but it wasn't enough. She was about to marry a large blustery man, twelve years her senior and with a working knowledge of animal husbandry: it brought little comfort to a frightened bride. But Teddy was also a kind and patient man. It would take a month until, suspecting fear was turning to neurotic hysteria, he finally penetrated his wife. She would later write of the large double bed as a fiery pit scorching the brow of innocence. She would describe the new bride's dull misery as she endured her husband's rough advances. It was a cruel experience.

She and Walter made contact many years later, and he became her mentor and advisor. She bore him no ill-will for his behaviour at Bar Harbor. She now loathed the young Edith Jones and took malicious delight in befriending that poor creature's tormentor. After her divorce, people wrongly assumed they were lovers; that Mrs Wharton was *still* waiting for a proposal! Gradually, as the threat of any prospective Mrs Walter Berry faded, their relationship settled into something more honest and enduring. Edith could offer Walter nothing more than she already did: her writing, thoughts and soul. And Walter accepted as much as he was capable of.

Several years before his death, he wrote to Edith recalling that day at Bar Harbor: canoeing in the bay and dining at Roddicks. Walter wondered why he *hadn't* proposed, for it would have all been good — and then the slices of years slid by. He wrote that he never 'wondered' about anyone else, *and there wouldn't be much of me if you were cut out of it. Forty years of it is yours, dear.*

Reading his letter, Edith had shaken her head; it was so typical of Walter, revisionary and romantic. He always did prefer the literary version of life. But the truth of their relationship was much more valuable. As a divorced woman living alone in Europe, it was vital to have Walter, a man held in such high esteem, as her companion and travelling partner. He secured her social reputation and protected her from innuendo. No doubt their friends wondered about the specifics of the relationship, but in time they were simply Walter and Edith, for which she was eternally grateful. And (if anything) Walter benefited even more from their arrangement than she did.

'I rather think,' observed Percy, 'that Mrs Gerould has more to read.'

Edith saw the papers were back on Mrs Gerould's lap. No, absolutely not. The woman was wildly unpredictable. 'Thank you,' said Edith firmly. 'We appreciate your wish to contribute, but since you're not a writer—'

'But I *am*,' insisted Mrs Gerould. 'I told you earlier — oh, not in your class, obviously, but I wrote several novels and collections of short stories. We were once published in the same edition of *Scribner's Magazine*, do you remember? Along with my brother Will.'

Edith gasped with disbelief, her mind in turmoil. Light glanced off the woman's glasses. It all made sense. She even recognised her inscrutability. Why hadn't she guessed? 'Of course,' stammered Edith. 'Please go ahead, Mrs Gerould, I'm interested to hear.'

Paris, 1909

The windows of the cab were smeared with rain.
In one corner sat Mr Fullerton, his back to the
driver, watchful with suppressed energy. Next
to him sat Carl Snyder, young and oversized,
an oceanographer with freshly washed sandy hair.
Until now his pleasant face had held an expression
of surprise — finding himself in the company of the
famous Mrs Wharton! But he was becoming wary now
Mrs Wharton had declared an Interest in Science.
Of particular interest were freshwater snails
and the theory of evolution, and she was hoping
Mr Snyder could further her understanding. But
Carl Snyder was painfully aware that his expertise
lay in the field of ocean currents and that he was
unable to help.

Across from Carl sat a young woman with pale
skin and dark hair, wide-eyed and shy. She was
in Paris for the day, having arrived from a

convent in the country. And Mrs Wharton herself,
stylish and busy, instructing the driver and
wiping condensation from the windows, concerned
with lunch arrangements and the difficulties of
weather.

The cab came to a stop, and Morton Fullerton opened
the door to a blast of showery air. Stepping on to
the running board, he prepared to jump a puddle
to the footpath. A note dislodged from his pocket,
catching in the showery blast. It fluttered
within the cab. Slowly, it came to rest on the damp
floor and lay between the three passengers. Blue
notepaper, crisply folded but already beginning
to soften. Heavy black ink through lightweight
paper. Large scrolled writing. Morton, struggling
with his umbrella, was now speaking to the doorman
at the gallery and alerting him to his companions.
Inside the cab it was hushed.

After a moment's indecision, Carl Snyder leaned
forward to collect the note. His hand was large,
lightly covered with blond hairs. He held up the
note, and the two women considered it in silence.
Only now did Mr Snyder become aware of a charge in
the air, watery static like a lightning-strike
in rain. He stared at the note as if it were an
unfamiliar sea creature. He tried to produce
his easy smile, but it snagged. He gulped as if
underwater. A brief hesitation, then he passed
the note to Edith.

```
Swept from his hand, the note disappeared. Gone.
But the silence remained, made louder by the
noise outside the cab. Rain continued to hit
the footpath. Newsboys shouted, Dreyfus trial
adjourned! Morton called for the ladies to hop out,
gesturing with his open umbrella. It pulsed like a
jellyfish in an ocean current.

The women prepared to leave, gathering themselves
and rising awkwardly within the confines of the
cab. Accidentally, a look passed between them.
Fleeting and weighted. Meaningful. Although
meaning what, exactly, neither woman could be sure.
```

Mrs Gerould slipped her papers back into the file. Folding her
hands together, she waited, her expression as unreadable as ever.
Edith eased back in her chair, heart clattering in her ribcage.
To hear about that cab ride again! The streets of rain, the dropped
note, she and Katharine looking at the folded blue paper in the
large grip of the young oceanographer.

Of course she could see the resemblance now. Why had it not
occurred to her? Mrs Gerould was Morton's adored and much
younger sister. After her studies in America, she'd spent a year in
France. They met only once, on that rainy day in Paris. Katharine
had been a budding writer and shyly showed Edith a poem. Soon
after her return to America, Katharine had married. Edith felt
herself relax. Katharine Fullerton Gerould. That explained why she
knew about events at The Mount. Morton had arrived from Bryn
Mawr where he'd stayed with Katharine, and (if Edith remembered

correctly) the two were to meet again at their parents' home in Brockton. A perfectly reasonable explanation. Katharine may have even seen Morton slip the sprig of witch hazel into the envelope, though she wouldn't have understood the significance.

But why write about a note dropped in the cab? Clearly it had made an impression. Edith smiled. 'How nice to see you again, Katharine.' And she meant it. Many years later, Katharine had written a complimentary review of *The Glimpses of the Moon*. Edith continued, 'I understand what you meant by saying we shared a common interest. My friendship with your brother lasted many years.' She stopped. Katharine's expression was difficult to read — sceptical, even amused. Not what Edith had expected. Quickly she looked away, saying to the others, 'This is Katharine, Morton Fullerton's sister.'

Sybil asked bluntly, 'So what was it?'

Edith was confused. 'I'm sorry?'

'The note. What did it say?'

'I've no idea. How could I possibly remember?'

'But you wrote it.' To Katharine, Sybil probed, 'What do *you* think it said?'

'I really don't know.'

'But you believe Edith wrote a note she didn't want you to read.'

Katharine replied calmly, 'Perhaps.'

'Oh, stop it,' said Edith, exasperated. 'Why would I write notes to Mr Fullerton? I was a highly successful author with some standing in Parisian society. Why would I jeopardise everything by writing silly *notes*.'

'Because—' began Sybil, but Edith would have none of it. She wouldn't allow this woman to make insinuations in the presence of Teddy and Walter.

'What *exactly* are you saying, Sybil?' Edith was aware that

151

Walter had become very still, and Teddy was restless like an autumn wind. She must stop this stupidity. Even if readers of the novella discovered the secret life of Edith Wharton, it must not ruin this evening. They were two separate worlds, and she would keep it that way.

Sybil seemed about to launch another attack, but she was too slow.

'What you're accusing me of is unthinkable, Sybil. I was a married woman in her forties and raised in conservative New York society. It is deeply offensive. No one would believe such a thing.' Edith sat back, exhausted. Unsure where to look, she studied the light fitting, bulbs glimmering with indifference.

'I only accused you of writing a note,' said Sybil sulkily.

Edith eyed her with suspicion. 'Like an infatuated schoolgirl?' Sybil sniffed.

'Perhaps you're right,' mused Edith. 'It is inconceivable that the dashing Mr Fullerton should indulge himself with a plain woman such as myself. I apologise, Sybil. Clearly I misunderstood you.'

Sybil busied herself by sweeping imaginary hairs from her skirt, as if to incriminate Linky.

'My heart was always with Walter. You know that.' She glanced quickly at Teddy, but his features were clouded with confusion.

Walter pulled himself up, saying testily, 'Thought we were done with that business.'

'I'm sorry, Walter, but if Sybil insists on making insinuations, I can only insist on speaking the truth.'

'But is it the truth?' asked Katharine.

'Of course,' said Edith. 'Walter and I spent forty years as companions. That must tell you something.' She didn't add that they were buried next to each other in the tilting flatlands of Versailles. Bone-dry soil (no place for a gardener) on the margins of a major road. A terrible place. However, that's where she chose to rest. Next to Walter. The ending she chose for her own story.

'You two never married,' observed Katharine.

'Marriage is not always an indicator of love.'

'But you hoped for marriage before . . . well—'

'Indeed,' clipped Edith, another quick glance at Teddy. He was following their conversation with no apparent understanding.

Percy was telling Sybil that Edith never mentioned divorce in her memoir. 'Poor fellow's barely included. After twenty-eight years of marriage, he simply fades out.' Sybil was nodding, gold hair bobbing in the light. 'At least I dealt with the business in a fair and tasteful manner. And never —' he turned to Edith '— did I apportion blame.'

Edith absorbed herself with a loose thread on her armrest. Across the room she could feel a distressed shifting.

'Puss?'

'Take no notice, Teddy.' She went cold with fear.

More shifting as Teddy sorted the confusion in his head. Slowly he said, 'I remember you went to Europe and left me behind.' He paused, and the room waited. A sudden gulping sound as if Teddy were being submerged under breaking memories. His voice was incredulous: 'Sold the house — I remember now, you sold The Mount. The stables and my animals.'

'You were unwell, Teddy. It was too much for you.' She cast about in desperation. There must be some way of diverting his attention, to stop this progression of thought.

His voice swelled with indignation as he levered himself up from his chair. 'And our motor-car. How dare you sell—'

'We needed the money, Teddy. You . . . well—'

'Went a bit crackers, old boy,' said Walter clearly. 'Took off with Edith's money. Off to Boston, bought yourself a bachelor pad.'

'A bachelor pad.' Teddy's face clouded with concentration. A smile broke in dawning memory. Dropping back into his chair, he gave a low chuckle. 'I did, didn't I?'

Dancing girls. Teddy embezzled her money, installing two dancing girls in a house he bought in Boston. There was no malice intended; he was swinging wildly from depression to irrepressible madness. It was hard to know which was worse. He gallivanted about the place with his women, signing them into hotels as his wife. Edith once came across her name in the register of an unfamiliar hotel and noting the previous entry of a 'Mr and Mrs Edward R. Wharton', said wryly to a friend: 'Evidently, I *have* been here before.'

After that she did what she could from the safety of Europe. His ridiculous sister was no help, refusing to believe Teddy was unwell. Edith arranged all the doctors and sanatoriums, the health spas, but there was only so much she could do. She was starting a new life in France, and she divorced Teddy for adultery.

Now Teddy began rocking, happy in the memory of dancing girls in a Boston clapboard. Edith watched, aware his mind would soon start searching the darkness that lay ahead. She must move quickly. Casting around the room, she fell on Katharine. The knitting was on the floor like a discarded prop, as if her role this evening were finished. It was unlikely that Katharine Fullerton Gerould knew much more. She had been in a French convent at the time, and afterwards sought the haven of American suburbia. No, despite her mysterious allusions, Katharine had nothing more to contribute. Edith's attention switched back to Teddy. He had pulled himself up, but his eyes were milky. 'Can't seem to remember what happened—'

'Wonderful holidays, Teddy. Switzerland and fishing trips. Motoring through Europe.' An endless string of health retreats. He was a travelling circus interrupted by a series of breakdowns.

'Yes, but where did we live? I don't remember—'

'Too long ago,' said Walter. 'Can't remember myself.'

'Yes, but—'

'Citizens of the world.'

'Oh, right.' Teddy looked doubtful, as he indeed might. Teddy's days of roaming would soon be restricted to the grounds of an asylum.

But Edith could see that questions were continuing to form in his mind. Aware of the need for diversion, she seized the novella, but haste made her clumsy, and it spilled across the rug.

Walter swept up the pages, pausing with interest.

'Thank you, Walter,' she said quickly, stretching out as far as possible, muscles tearing. 'If you could—'

Fortunately, he lost interest, passing the pages back and collecting the books that lay by his chair. Holding up the volume of James Joyce, he said, 'Published by my nephew — Black Sun Press. Magnificent boy and a fine intellect. No doubt he became an accomplished writer.'

What nonsense: Harry Crosby had arrived in Paris after the war, and Walter mistook his eccentricities for talent, introducing him to the best writers and publishers. But the boy had no aptitude or discipline, producing nothing more than bad poetry, self-published, of course.

'But why', asked Teddy with a whining insistence that sent Edith's blood cold, 'did Nanny look after me? Where were you, Puss?'

'Enough about that, old boy,' said Walter. 'We're talking about my nephew. Do you remember, Edith, taking tea with Harry and his wife at my apartment?'

'The first time I had the pleasure of their company,' she said drily.

'And the dog, magnificent specimen. Only I can't remember—'

'Narcisse Noir,' said Edith. 'A whippet as I recall.'

'With a diamond-studded collar.'

'That's right.' It sat on the silk settee next to Walter. The similarity between the two was ridiculous. Walter and the dog both sitting upright, all hauteur and disdain, their small heads turning deftly. Edith would have laughed if she weren't so angry. Walter spent the afternoon flirting urbanely with Harry's wife Caresse, and she repaid the compliment with seductive teasing. As always, Edith played along like a fool, as if she couldn't see what was happening, though she knew more than anyone else in the room.

'And another dog,' mused Walter.

'I don't recall your giving any of my dogs such consideration,' said Edith stiffly, adding, 'Another whippet called Clitoris.'

Silence.

When it came to his nephew, Walter lost all discrimination and taste; but it was a challenge, even now.

'What became of his beautiful wife?'

'Caresse.' She knew he'd get to Caresse sooner or later. Like all men, Walter worshipped her. Not that Caresse was her real name. She was born Polleen Peabody.

'Marvellous entertainers. Famous for their parties in Saint-Germain.'

At the mention of parties, Sybil became interested. 'Who are you talking about?'

'My nephew Harry Crosby and his wife.'

Sybil's eyes grew large.

Did Sybil know? Quite possibly. Quickly Edith said, 'I would like to keep reading.'

But Sybil wouldn't be deterred. 'Did you really attend their parties?'

'Sometimes,' said Walter with feigned carelessness.

'I heard Harry Crosby had a library filled with model ships and sea chests.'

'Quite true.'

'And entertained while lying in bed.'

Walter hesitated. 'I'm not—'

'It's true,' insisted Sybil. 'Guests dined at tables in the bedroom, everyone eating oysters and caviar, drinking champagne. Zebra and bear skins on the floor, Harry wearing a gold kimono.'

Edith had heard the same stories. But Sybil wouldn't have seen the skeleton at the bottom of the stairs confronting departing guests, its jaw open with a pink rubber condom for a tongue.

Percy snickered. 'I can see why you chose not to attend, Edith.'

'Really, Percy? I understood you thought me ill-bred.'

Percy's face closed shut.

Infernal man, and now they were wasting breath on the madman. 'We should—'

'What became of Harry?' asked Walter.

'Oh, Walter, it's too long ago.'

'Did he stick to poetry? He was starting a novel.'

'I'm not sure.'

'And children? The boy needed stability. I thought a family would help.'

'Please don't concern yourself,' she said. 'It's in the past.'

'But dash it, Edith, I would like to know.'

'There's no point.'

'Would someone please tell me,' asked Walter, his voice simmering, 'what happened to my nephew?'

Everyone looked startled. One of them here tonight was sure to remember. The sensational end to Harry Crosby had been splashed across every newspaper on both sides of the Atlantic. Harry would have liked that; he'd always been enthralled by death.

'Please. Someone tell me.' Walter's voice was tremulous with pain.

'I'm sorry, Walter. This is all my fault.'

'That we should hear the truth?'

'The truth is seldom glorious, and the price is often too high.'

'I remember,' said Sybil suddenly.

'No!' cried Trix.

'Only I can't—' Sybil's brow wrinkled with unaccustomed concentration.

Trix turned furiously on Edith, willing her to intervene. But what could she do? Throw another book at the woman?

'If only—' worried Sybil, tapping her temple, aware her moment of glory was fading.

'Stop her, Aunt Edith,' pleaded Trix.

Edith stared back at her niece. She was so contradictory, this fireside lady with her large gardening hands and an unexpected anguish on Walter's behalf. If Trix really wanted to, she could silence Sybil by wresting her to the floor. Edith could not; she was an old woman with creaky knees and a perverse ambivalence over the whole thing.

'Tell me,' repeated Walter more urgently.

'Something in the newspaper,' continued Sybil, drumming her temples. 'It was everywhere. Percy, you remember?'

'Not sure that I do.'

'Oh, if only I could remember.'

Walter was ashen with anticipation, mouth working and cheeks hollow.

'My aunt would like to keep reading,' said Trix, her jaw set.

Edith shrugged. It was out of her hands; there was nothing she could do if Sybil remembered. She felt like she were drifting down a river, hearing the storm of an approaching waterfall: the exquisite terror of the inevitable. Walter was about to learn what sort of man his nephew really was. The man he chose to be executor of his estate. The man he decided was better suited to dealing with his legacy than his lifetime companion. Just a little joke, a bit of gallows humour.

Sybil flushed pink. 'Of course,' she said triumphantly. 'I remember what happened to Harry Crosby.'

'If my aunt won't read,' snapped Trix, rising from her chair, 'then I will.' Before Edith could guess her intention, Trix had swept up the novella and was carrying it back to her chair.

'No, you can't—' But it was no use.

Trix was already flicking the pages and clearing her throat. The lights slowly fused into shadow, and Trix began to read.

(4)

'More wine?' said Austen, holding up the bottle.

Sara shook her head, watching as Austen refilled his glass.
He was drinking more than usual but seemed happier now
Medora was no longer eating with them. On their second
night, Medora had spied wild rabbit on the menu — turned out
she wasn't a vegetarian at all, was fine about anything caught in
the wild. She explained this while sucking on the little bones of
an animal that, as she said, had been happily hopping about that
afternoon. For someone who never used makeup, she had chosen
that evening to wear pink lip gloss, which smeared with rabbit
fat around the rim of her mouth. Sara had been revolted but
found herself drawn to the smeared lip gloss.

Medora had explained — while tipping the little carcass
upside down and delving into places Sara wished she wouldn't
— that it was also fine to eat road kill. Not something she
made a habit of, though she did once eat a seagull, but she drew
the line at hedgehogs on account of ringworm. She grinned,
exposing blunt teeth. Sara wondered where Medora was eating
tonight and said suddenly, 'I've given Medora money for
dinner.'

At first she thought Austen hadn't heard, as he continued to
chew. Then his eyes shot up. 'How much?'

She hadn't expected him to be so specific, so confrontational.
Like a cool draught through an open window. She said evenly,
'Not much. She always eats at cheap places.'

'You pay all her meals?'

'Just dinner.' This wasn't going well, and she still hadn't
explained the payments for each blog.

Austen took up his meal again, giving his veal more attention than it required. Sara gazed around the restaurant: posters of the Amalfi coast, Chianti bottles crusted with candle wax. Where was the line between cliché and authenticity? She had no idea. But thank goodness there wasn't a piano accordion like the Italian place in Singapore. 'Of course I pay her,' she said. 'Why else would she be here? Especially the way you're behaving.' This wasn't particularly fair. Around Medora he was scrupulously polite, but his features suggested otherwise. Like he was handling contaminated goods.

Austen chewed another mouthful of veal. 'Medora should be happy with free transport and five-star accommodation. Not a bad way to see Italy.'

'She still has to put up with us.'

'Oh, I don't know, you two seem happy enough.'

'What's wrong with that?' Slicing her steak with unnecessary care, she added, 'You can't expect Medora to hang around for nothing.'

'What do you mean?'

Everyone regarded Austen as the nice guy. It was the crinkled eyes that gave the impression of good humour. People didn't see him like this, righteous and irritating.

'Sara? It's her choice. She can leave whenever she wants.'

Sara flushed. 'Do you know what this means to me?'

His tone irritated her. This was a conversation they shouldn't be having. It was unfair to expose her paltry little ambitions, like lifting a rock and watching a small helpless animal in the light.

Putting down his fork, Austen said carefully, 'Have you thought — well, if you can't write the blog, maybe—'

'Maybe what?'

'Give up. No shame in that.'

'And play golf.'

His eyes crinkled. It was the expression that always allowed her to give up — but not now. With cool indifference, Sara began moving slices of fat to the edge of her plate. He wasn't being fair. Compared to most expatriate wives, she'd never been a problem. Presentable enough without being expensive, a supportive wife who maintained her independence. She'd never fallen drunk into a swimming pool at a party (surprising how often that happened) or slept with the gardener (not unheard of). She hadn't bemoaned her lost career or raided the pantry for brandy before lunch. But none of that mattered anymore. Once you walked away from the expatriate life, none of it counted. The least Austen could do was support her now. Sara put down her knife.

*

They were two hours from the lakeside town of Stressa when the rain stopped, steam rising from the motorway. Austen flipped his sun visor down against the streaky light. The silence in the car was like static electricity, twitchy and irritating. Medora had been needling Austen again. Sara liked the claustrophobic feeling; she could smell Medora's clean skin. It was bizarre that she knew less about Medora than ever. Was that even her name? Why did she never use her mobile phone — no texting or checking emails. She seemed insular in a way that wasn't right. And so unpredictable. Just when things were going smoothly, she disappeared without explanation. And always driving Austen crazy. Just now she'd been bombarding him with questions: how did an environmental engineer come to work for an oil company? Why did he retire at such a young age? Did he really believe the petrochemical industry was socially responsible in Nigeria? What did he *do* all day? Sara took a sideways glance at her husband. His jaw was in lock-down.

Sara was opening a bag of peppermints when her mobile rang — Bernard, as excitable as ever — was this a good time to call? Her blogs were getting a fantastic response, everyone loved them. Plus he'd had confirmation from the publishers. A glossy book on Italian gardens — full-colour photographs, not too much text. Now he was thinking about a cookbook — you know, rustic and regional. Bernard rang off, promising a radio interview.

The ferry from Stressa dropped them at a conical island in the middle of the lake. Developed over three hundred years ago, Isola Bella was inspired by the Hanging Gardens of Babylon; but, as Medora said, it looked more like a giant cruise liner. She and Sara were standing on the top terrace, hanging over a stone balustrade. The terraces below were stacked like a series of plant-tumbled ship decks. Sara watched Medora write: *It's like the Lusitania just crashed into a conservatory at Kew Gardens.* Pointing to a flowering shrub, Medora asked, 'What's that stuff called?'

'No idea.' It was ridiculous. Neither of them had any idea about plants.

'Tell me about The Mount.'

Sara took a moment to adjust — what about The Mount? She'd only volunteered there for a couple of months. 'What do you want to know?'

'Edith had the place built for herself, right?'

'Yeah, she wrote a book on home decoration, and The Mount showcased her style.'

This was according to Mrs Newbold, who had taken Sara on a tour that first day. She'd followed Mrs Newbold's regal bulk upstairs to a charming high-vaulted gallery of gauzy light and floor-length windows. Fresh pastels and French cream furniture. Mrs Newbold caught her breath and continued. In 1897 Edith Wharton published *The Decoration of Houses*, a book that changed how Americans designed and decorated their homes. Edith argued for classical proportions and clean lines, harmony and simplicity. She hated clutter and being swamped by her own furniture. The book was a rallying cry against the Gilded Age of grandiosity and confusion, when Queen Anne chairs were crammed into Louis XIV ballrooms. It was also a direct hit on her mother. Edith was mocking her childhood home when she repudiated drawing-rooms that were festooned with lace and ruffles, plush little tables covered with knick-knacks. Floral wallpaper and curtains that looked like lingerie. Her book sold very well.

Back downstairs, Mrs Newbold opened the dining-room doors with a flourish. A glass table was set with china plates and crystal glasses, a tall vase of almond blossom. She explained: Edith was a perfectionist who strove for nothing but the best in gardening, cooking, furnishing, and housekeeping. A Wharton house-party was always an occasion of fine food and conversation, even afternoon excursions — motor-flights through the countryside, walks in the garden, a legendary Wharton picnic.

Sara had found herself fixed with an unassailable smile: Edith Wharton was the original Martha Stewart.

Medora squinted against the sun-sparkling lake. 'So why did she leave?'

'Leave what?'

'Edith only lived at The Mount for — what — six years?'

Sara shrugged, gazing across the lake. It was an intense, uniform blue, like a deeply run bath. It looked almost fake.

Walking back to the ferry, Medora mentioned casually that her money was running out. She needed an increase, but no more than fifty euros an hour. That should be enough.

Sara could feel Medora's words wrapping around her heart and squeezing tight. It was hard to breathe.

'You heard,' said Medora, breaking off a lavender head.

'Listen, Medora, I can't—'

'Austen.'

'Sorry?'

'You're about to say Austen will have a fit if he finds out.'

Exactly.

'Why should he know?'

'It's not that easy.'

'Sure it is. We go to a market and buy a cheap jacket, tell him it cost five hundred euro. There's no receipt, and he won't know.'

Sara shook her head. 'I know you think we're wealthy, but I would never spend that much on a jacket.'

'So?'

'Austen might get suspicious.'

'You mean he isn't already?'

Sara felt light-headed. Being with Medora was like drinking wine in the sun. Everything became fluid and untraceable. There was no solid benchmark for what was right — or true. Sara knew it was disingenuous to use arguments from her normal life.

'Just remember', Medora continued reasonably, 'that I never planned to stay in Italy. Everything's so expensive.' Her open honesty caught Sara's breath. 'Does that help?'

Of course not. None of it made sense. 'What sort of market?'

'Dunno. Let's wait until Padua, it's a student town. There's bound to be cheap, styley stuff there. I can help.'

'Thanks,' said Sara, and she started to laugh.

*

Bernard rang at midnight, his words faster than usual. Things were going crazy — like, *really* crazy. The lawyers were scrambling for the rights to all Edith's work. The publishers wanted her novels made into audiobooks, starting with *Twilight Sleep*. But there was a problem with the blogs. They needed a whole lot more.

'It's not that easy,' said Sara, peering at her bedside clock. 'The gardens are all over Italy.'

'Edith managed, and she didn't have the autostrada.'

'She took four months.'

'Ten more gardens.'

'Wait until Rome.'

'We need gardens from everywhere — like Genoa.'

'We're not planning Genoa.' Sara lowered her voice as Austen hauled on the bedcovers.

Bernard hadn't finished. He'd been looking at a Genoa garden, Villa Pallavicini, which was amazing, a series of scenes that worked like a play — a prologue and three acts. Plus a Chinese pagoda.

Sara wasn't sure she'd heard correctly. Did he say a Chinese pagoda?

'And we need more variety. Everything looks the same.'

'They're all Italian gardens.'

'No more hedges, okay? More anecdotal stuff, Italian family picnics. Which reminds me, I'm working on other ways to leverage the situation — you know, monetise our position.'

Sara waited.

'We'll start with small stuff — gardening gloves and notepaper.'

'You mean merchandise.'

'Exactly. And with Edith it could be anything — picnic rugs, tea towels, umbrellas.'

'Wow.'

'I need you to mention this stuff in the blogs.'

'Like umbrellas.'

'Exactly. Write that Edith never went picnicking without her umbrella — or a rug.'

'And tea towels.'

Bernard stopped. The line crackled with suspicion.

'It's a great idea,' said Sara, and she meant it. Bernard wanted to sell Edith like a fake Rolex.

'Don't forget the radio interview tomorrow. Talk about Edith as a style icon. But don't mention the Wharton merch — at least, not yet. There might be some pushback.'

*

It was late afternoon, and Sara was waiting in their hotel room for the phone call. They had arrived late in Padua after Austen took a wrong exit off the motorway. Now he was trying to find a park. Sara sat on the bed, smoothing her notes. Most of it was written by Medora — anecdotes about Edith's trip, ideas about her writing. Medora was an expert now she'd downloaded Edith's complete works on her e-reader, and she was relentlessly curious.

But it was Sara who fronted the blogs and interviews. She was running on adrenaline and making up for lost time — a lost *lifetime*. Her kids were now following her online — even Hugo. Alice rang suggesting Sara have her thyroid tested.

The door clicked open, and she saw Austen had the suitcases.

Landing them on the luggage rack, he was about to say something when Sara's phone rang. It was the station manager — was she ready? Sure. They discussed time zones for a while, and Sara was about to mention the weather when she found herself suddenly on-air. The interviewer, *Call me Leonard*, had a radio-rich voice so naturally interested that Sara relaxed. Yes, she loved the gardens, and it was wonderful to be reading Edith Wharton, amazing what the woman achieved. It was so much easier to travel now with internet banking and TripAdvisor. Edith had to deal with slow trains and broken-down horse conveyances.

Leonard was impressed: Sara had obviously formed a connection with her predecessor. 'What about Edith's writing? Did you enjoy reading her books? There were quite a few, weren't there?'

'Sixteen novels and loads of other stuff.'

'Incredible. Have you read everything?'

'Well, no,' said Sara carefully, 'but I'm excited to be on a journey of discovery.'

'Any recommendations for your readers?'

'Absolutely,' said Sara (scanning Medora's notes). 'Start with *Summer*, a novella that's short and devastating, with Wharton raging against female oppression and the double standards of the patriarchy. Or how about *Twilight Sleep*? New York in the 1920s with mystical gurus, Hollywood producers, and gay designers. And here's a favourite — 'Xingu', a short story that brilliantly satirises a book club. And every Kardashian sceptic should read *The Custom of the Country*.'

'No way.'

'Absolutely. The themes are the same — personal betterment and consumerism, the value of social currency. Wharton is as relevant as ever, and the whole thing going crazy. A re-issue of her ghost stories, a compendium of her New York stories, and everyone after the movie rights for *Custom*.'

'And the blog, Sara — how's that going?'

'A huge following. The publishers are working on a book of Italian gardens, plus merchandise — gardening gloves and notebooks. Even a cookbook!'

*

Austen stopped unpacking. A cookbook? First he'd heard. And Sara had never mentioned merchandise. Now she was explaining that her next blog would be posted from Padua — she couldn't wait! Her followers would absolutely love the gardens. Maybe a video blog.

Austen removed a pair of runners from the bag and chucked them under the luggage rack. Amazing how quickly Sara had slipped into the role of minor celebrity, a brittle excitement and insincerity like stale perfume. Authority over a subject of which she had little knowledge. Austen threw his now empty suitcase into the wardrobe with satisfying force. He motioned to Sara that he was going out. But Sara ignored him, too busy talking.

Walking out the hotel entrance, he searched around for a café. This was the medieval part of town, close to the university. He took a seat outside Café Sport. Across the square, students were sprawled on the soft-stone steps of a church, a banner unfurled and forgotten. He watched a large tourist coach try to enter the square. Two old men began shouting and waving, and the bus retreated. He ordered an espresso and pulled on a sweater. His cellphone rang. It was his son. 'Hey, Matt, changed your mind?'

Matt had promised to ask his girlfriend again. Despite living together in Frankfurt, Sophie spent most of her time in London. 'Sorry, Dad, we're pretty busy.'

Austen kept quiet. Passive. Directed.

'Any other time, you know—'

'Your mother would love to see you.'

'Sure, but—'

Austen listened to his son's words slipping through the opaque waters of deception. He watched the students across the square preparing to leave, collecting their bags and rolling up the banner. He wished it were Alice on the phone, her clipped conversation and absolute view of the world. A patents lawyer in Hong Kong, she only rang on Thursdays, and if this was unsuitable she waited until the following Thursday. As for Hugo, shaggy and oversized, he was too shambolic for a mobile phone. Given the chance (and the airfare) he would probably join them in Italy. A terrible idea. Austen had seen it all before. His arrival promising so much, then Hugo leaving days later, with Sara in tears and the place a mess. Along the way he would have cleared the bathroom of meds and helped himself to any loose change (and some not so loose). At Sara's insistence, Austen always tried to remonstrate with Hugo, making clear his transgressions. But it was like trying to scold a bewildered puppy. Austen always ended up shouting at the boy like he was a lunatic.

'Hey there.'

It was the girl, ditching her bag under the table and dropping into a chair. She was wearing a scrappy little dress like a squeezed-out dish rag. He hadn't seen her coming, her olive skin and dark eyes. The dress made her look smaller. She must be close in age to Alice, though his daughter would never dress like that. With a flash of insight, he said, 'Your family, they're originally from Italy?'

She grinned. 'Lombardy and Ngāti Tūwharetoa.'

He didn't understand.

'My grandfather was Italian. After working on the tunnels in northern Italy, the company sent him to New Zealand, an underground hydro-power scheme. My grandmother was from a local tribe, and they married.' She signalled a waiter. 'So where's Sara?'

'Doing a radio interview.' He stopped before adding, 'She wants a Kardashian on the cover of a Wharton re-issue.'

Medora surveyed the square like she was searching for another topic. 'Sara's got a unique take on the world. Fragmented. Kaleidoscopic. Like an ageing internet native.' Ordering a Limonata from the waiter, she continued, 'I love her cynicism. Must be from living in so many countries — the random links, a brain like a scattergram.'

Austen wasn't sure this was a compliment, but it made Sara sound intriguing.

Medora's drink arrived, and she began sucking through a straw. She grinned. 'Like my dress?'

'Well, I—' He struggled and gave up.

'That's okay. I found it in a market. It'll be better after a wash.'

She seemed to be getting younger as he watched. And smaller. He wanted to ask, *So who are you, really?*

She sucked the remains of her drink and wiped her mouth. 'Right now I smell like someone else. It's an odd feeling. Kind of liberating. I like to imagine who owned my clothes. I suspect this belonged to a gypsy girl who sneaked into Italy strapped under a Contiki bus.'

'It does have that look about it.'

'Or the illegitimate daughter of an Italian count who died in mysterious circumstances.'

'The count or his daughter?'

She laughed. 'Haven't decided yet.'

So tell me, Medora, who are you? Really? He smiled. 'How about a beer this time?'

CHAPTER VI

Trix had barely finished reading when Katharine Gerould queried, 'I don't see how anyone can talk on the telephone while they're sitting in a town square.'

No, Edith couldn't understand either.

On the sofa, Sybil was telling Percy that she had never found Edith a gracious hostess — quite the opposite. Percy nodded, saying it was ironic to hear The Mount was now a wedding venue, having begun as a place of divorce. Sybil kicked him swiftly, a nervous glance at Teddy.

Edith had enjoyed hearing about the cookbook, and wished Grossie were here to share the joke — the idea of Mrs Wharton in the kitchen like a scullery-maid! About to share the joke with Walter, she stopped.

Walter was white-faced and sepulchral, his eyes fixed on Sybil. Leaning forward, he said, 'You must remember. Tell me, what happened to my nephew.'

'Your—? Oh, yes, I remember.' Sybil gazed around; the room was bristling with expectation. 'He had a mistress called Caresse, but that wasn't her real name.'

'You're wrong,' barked Walter. 'Caresse was his wife.'

Sybil seemed confused. 'Well, I know he had a mistress in New York. He shot her before—'

'No,' cried Trix, but it was too late.

'—killing himself. They had matching holes in their temples.'

Edith listened to Walter's inward reflection. It seemed to pulse with sorrow.

Quietly, he said, 'How old was he?'

'Thirty,' murmured Edith.

It had occurred only two years after Walter's death. The bodies were found in a New York studio. Crosby had his arm around the woman; the soles of his feet were tattooed with Egyptian symbols of the sun. It was believed that he spent hours alone with the body before killing himself, but there were so many theories. The headlines were blazing and sensational: COUPLE SHOT DEAD IN ARTISTS' HOTEL. It was called a murder–suicide pact, but who was to know? Harry's life was picked over in the press — the drug-fuelled parties, his money and women. He was supposed to be lunching with his wife, mother, and uncle J.P. Morgan when he shot himself. Too much money. Too many drugs. So much of everything, he hadn't known the value of his own life, treating it like a work of art. Unfortunately, he wished the same for his death.

'The boy had a bad war,' said Walter shakily.

It was true. At sixteen he had volunteered as an ambulance driver, bringing the dead and wounded back from the front line. He saw things no one should. But that's what he wanted. Death excited him. 'I can't believe,' Edith broke, 'that you made Harry Crosby executor of your estate. Were you mad?' She stopped. She hadn't meant to speak out loud.

'You have no right to ask that question, and I've no intention of answering it.'

Walter was right. She didn't deserve an answer; but his decision had been unforgivable. She had been sick with grief, exhausted from spending weeks by his bed. To be told Harry Crosby was executor of his estate — the boy was at the horse races when Walter died! And he was already showing signs of insanity. Edith did her best, arranging a state funeral in Paris that was attended by the American ambassador and the oldest families. But she was a wreck. Shrouded in black, she'd barely got through the ordeal. However, what came later that day was so much worse.

Furious hammering reverberated through the heavy oak door. Shouting and more hammering. Cries from the French police-men — *Ouvrez la porte!* Grossie had been propelled from the kitchen by the shouting and was now sailing brokenly about the entrance, an ocean liner burst from its moorings. She gave another cry at a fresh thundering at the door, wringing her hands: *What's happening, Ma'am? What should we do?* Grim-faced, Edith turned to the drawing-room. It was her favourite room, with its golden light and fresh-cut flowers, the tall doors to the garden, all green serenity and French-clipped precision. It made the current spectacle there all the more grotesque. Harry Crosby was a comedy of insanity: Dante's inferno, her worst nightmare. The grinning fool was circling the rug, panting and perspiring. No longer the matinée idol, he was the fairground idiot.

'They followed you.' She was incredulous.

'Car-chase from the crematorium.' He grinned, pupils spinning. 'Sirens and flashing lights all the way from Paris.'

She should feel compassion, but his arrogance made that impossible. They had seen the same war, both been at the front line to witness the enemy. Such an experience should demand a greater appreciation for life — not least out of respect for those who died. Not Harry Crosby: he treated everything as a joke, including the ashes of his uncle. He was jittering about the room like a marionette, still clutching the urn. God forbid, was he about to drop it? He must be on drugs, or chasers thrown back after the funeral. Edith stepped forward. She must take the blessed thing, or poor Walter would be spilt across the rug.

'Give it to me,' she ordered.

Crosby's smile wavered. He looked like a confused puppy who had been expecting praise, but he handed her the ornate silver urn.

It felt cool. What had she expected? Blood warm or fiery from the furnace? She weighed it in her hands. This was Walter, heavier than she expected. She buoyed it gently, as if to find familiar comfort in its weight, but it meant nothing. She recalled Walter's long-limbed body, the tilt of his small head, his eagle-sweep — these couldn't be equated with this weight. She thought of his strong teeth, blue gelatinous eyes, bones and mucus, soft veins, all incinerated into dry rubble. This had no meaning either. Yet she could feel his still presence. She could feel his undivided loyalty and quick defence of her work; his painful absences and mocking laugh; his casual vindictiveness. He wrote: *forty years of it is yours, dear*. Edith weighed the urn in her hands: yes, this is what she could feel. Forty years.

'Oh, ma'am,' cried Grossie from the door.

Edith turned in shock. For a moment she had forgotten.

'Ma'am, what should we do?'

'Let them in,' clipped Edith.

'You — what?'

'I said, let them in.'

The door was opened, and policemen piled into her home. It was like the worst kind of French farce, a bungling joke of bureaucracy. The ashes must be interred in consecrated grounds. By-laws were to be observed.

Compost, Walter had laughed — sprinkle me on your roses!

But it seemed she could not. The police would not allow it.

So she arranged for Walter to be placed in the flatlands of Versailles, near a yew tree. And ten years later she would rest alongside.

'Poor Caresse,' murmured Walter.

She could only just make out Walter's figure, sunk low in his chair. He was the victim of her desire to be published again, and his sadness was her own. She hadn't meant this to happen — for Walter to hear the truth — and yet the truth wasn't her fault. Walter was suffering to learn the consequences of his own decisions. He was being forced to endure his own aftermath. And the past wasn't finished with; she knew there was more to come.

Edith endeavoured to compose herself before saying, 'Caresse continued as a publisher in Paris and produced some fine work.' Nothing Edith would read (Hemingway and his ilk), but it was true that Caresse retained a level of dignity after the headlines faded, becoming well respected in the publishing world.

Walter nodded sadly. 'She would have inherited my book collection. That is some consolation.'

'A wonderful collection,' said Trix, encouraged by this glimpse of light.

'Over eight thousand books, many extremely rare. That's what first brought us together, Edith, remember? Our shared love of books. I hope you found some to your liking.'

Some to her liking! Walter's book collection was extraordinary. His will allowed her to have first choice of the books, the remainder going to Harry Crosby.

'The Conrads,' he persisted. 'Did you keep them?'

'Thank you, indeed.' It was true, she did keep the Conrads, along with his Lucretius and Rimbaud and the poems of Victor Hugo.

'And Whitman?'

'*Drum-Taps.*'

He nodded with approval. He was holding Proust, turning the book over in his hands. 'And my collection of Proust, obviously you took those.'

'I had my own copies.'

'Of course, but I can't help wondering—'

Edith held her breath.

'—what happened to my set. Why would a complete set of first editions, all personally inscribed, be broken up?'

'I'm not sure this particular bookcase makes any sense.'

'But why would a book of such tremendous value be placed beside a book on motorcycle maintenance?' He smiled sadly. '*Remembrance of Things Past*. Marcel and I had some wonderful times together.'

'I did hear rumours,' said Percy.

For heaven's sake, now what was Percy saying?

'What rumours?' Walter was motionless.

'That Harry Crosby sold your books.'

'Edith?'

She was confused. She had been expecting something else; that Percy was about to make unpleasant insinuations about Walter and Marcel. But he was talking about the books. Without thinking, she said, 'Yes, the boy got rid of everything.'

'But you chose the books you wanted?'

'Fewer than a hundred. That was all Crosby allowed.' The reprobate had pursued her relentlessly, wouldn't leave her alone.

He wanted all the books, believed they were his legacy — what right did she have to them? She hadn't the energy to defy him.

'I'm sorry.' Walter's voice was filled with grief. 'My dear, you can't know how sorry.'

To her surprise, she burst out laughing. A crazy, braying sound crashed about the room. A rush of air bubbles filtered her bloodstream. Linky barked, and she broke off. She tried to order her words carefully, as if drunk. 'But it doesn't matter, does it? Has anyone thought about that? Nothing matters. It's over. Finished.'

'No,' said Katharine. 'Because that would mean nothing ever mattered. And that's simply not true.'

'But it's pointless if we can't change the past.'

'It still matters.'

'What if I told Walter the truth?' Edith felt giddy with carelessness yet was unable to look at him. 'Percy said Harry Crosby sold all your books. You probably think he entrusted them to a private collector, hopefully one of repute. But, being Harry, this may not be the case — he could have entrusted them to a smart young dealer. Or worse, your collection might have been sold at a book auction, picked over and broken up, dispersed to all parts of the globe like the Irish diaspora. But tell me: does it really matter?'

Walter hesitated before answering. 'I'm not sure.'

She continued. 'Just think. Does that explain why your first edition of Proust has been separated from other volumes in the series? Does that explain why it's sitting on a bookcase with a book on motorcycle maintenance? A bookcase that, for all we know, comes from a youth hostel in Helsinki. Again, does it matter?'

'A ridiculous question.'

'Why?'

'Because no one would break up a first-edition set of Proust's work.'

'Crosby did.'

'I don't believe it. The boy loved books, even if he sold them.'

'But he didn't sell them. Percy is misinformed. Harry Crosby *gave away your books*.'

Walter digested this, then ventured, 'To family, I hope. The J.P. Morgan foundation?'

'Not exactly. You see, Harry was searching for spiritual enlightenment. He was dissatisfied with life. Apparently a clever wife and trust-fund income weren't enough. Not even the books. So Harry went to Egypt to consult a wise man.' Laughter bubbled through Edith's blood. 'And the wise man said: "My wealth I measure by the things I do without." And Harry, bless him, decided to rid himself of anything that felt burdensome — not the money or beautiful wife, of course — but it did mean—'

'—the books.'

'Yes. Baudelaire and Flaubert, the lot. Every day after coffee he would leave a priceless book on the table for the waiter. Just a bit of fun. But even that became a burden — eight thousand books is quite a lot to dispose of. According to Caresse, he began walking Paris with heavy bags, handing books to barmen, cab drivers and people on the street. Sometimes he would sneak them into antiquarian bookshops along the Seine, pencilling in ridiculously low prices. Just a bit of fun.' She stopped, drifting in the shallows of silence, until she became aware of a slow sea-whisper. It was the sound of Walter breathing. 'You see? Why should we care what has happened? It's finished.'

'Easy for you,' remarked Katharine. 'Knowing your books were returned to The Mount.'

'Perhaps.'

Trix was restless with agitation. 'So why torment poor Walter?'

Indeed.

'The past can always throw a shadow forward,' observed Katharine, 'but only if we allow it. How unfair to make Walter suffer for his mistakes.'

'You may be right, and I apologise.' Edith felt bitter regret. Her initial joy at seeing Walter was gone. Everything was too painful. She cast about for something to relieve the pain, a glimmer of hope. But there was no hope in the room tonight. All they had was the past. Observing the bookcase, she said, 'Walter, dear, would you like to read Yeats?'

Walter's expression was one of utter disbelief, and it cut her to pieces, his look of repulsed incredulity. A look that seemed to ask was she mad, completely mad? A look that said the events of tonight had undone him — and now she wanted him to read *poetry*. God, if there were flowers here she'd be up and arranging, fussing over the décor. Her vanity and craving for attention had unleashed the hounds of Hell — all the things that should be buried and finished — but she was like a gravedigger exhuming their history, pulling bones from the mud. Walter twitched with fury, rising and falling in his chair.

Edith cried out as he lurched forward, his long arm sweeping the novella from the table. He tore at the falling pages with gibberish ferocity, intent on destroying every word.

The first page ripped apart.

Edith cried out again, urging him to stop. The lights flickered, and tangled wires exploded into blue sparks.

Percy rose, stumbling in a flashing staccato. Gathering the pages from Walter's flailing arms, he dumped the shambling pile into her lap. Edith held the papers close, looking up to thank him.

Percy held still, considering. The lights slowed to a low burn.

She smiled wistfully: 'Do you remember our trip to Africa?'

His mouth tugged: of course — the trip of a lifetime. 'You were very generous, and I always regretted that we—'

'I know,' she said quickly.

He stood awkwardly for a moment before moving way.

She understood: married to Sybil, Percy never had a choice; how could she blame him? Her other friends who married Sybil all escaped by premature death.

Walter was sunk back in his chair, chest heaving from the exertion. His face was tight with malice when he spoke. 'As I recall, Edith, you funded Percy's trip to Africa, paying his bills until he found the next person to bleed like a literary bloodsucker.'

'Better than a cocksucker,' murmured Percy from the sofa.

Walter turned slowly, wary as an animal sensing danger. Blood rose to his cheeks, and a shudder went around the room. His lips moved before his words became audible. 'You dirty little sneak. Nothing but a barrow-boy selling gossip about your friends to the highest bidder. People of esteem and accomplishment.'

'That's quite true,' agreed Percy. 'Henry James was an excellent source of income. So many letters. Particularly when you were coming to stay at Lamb House.'

Edith cried out for Percy to stop. She hated the desperation in her voice, but this mustn't continue. She had allowed Walter to hear the consequences of his will, but never this — he didn't deserve this.

Percy's moustache quivered with mischief. 'Henry wrote several letters ahead of one particular stay.'

Walter viewed Percy with cold disgust.

'Take no notice,' ordered Edith.

'They were published by your nephew,' Percy went on softly. 'A beautiful little book, *Letters from Henry James to Walter Berry*.'

Walter's fingers renewed their nervous drumming.

'Percy is insinuating an unsavoury relationship,' said Edith abruptly. She would not allow Percy the pleasure of toying with Walter.

At length Walter said, 'I don't understand.'

'Your letters,' she persisted. 'You left everything to the madman.'

'Harry?'

'Of course Harry. You didn't think he would profit from your papers?'

'You can't blame Harry Crosby,' said Percy. 'Walter bequeathed the letters to him. What was he supposed to do? He was a publisher.'

'He was insane,' snapped Edith. 'And you encouraged him to publish the letters.'

Walter seemed unable to follow. 'I thought you burned my letters.'

'I had no right to burn everything. Only our personal letters.' She was distressed at his state of disbelief. Was he recalling Henry's words? The ardent yearning and physicality: *You are victor, winner, master, O, Irresistible One — you've done it, you've brought it off and got me down forever.* 'Why on earth did you leave Crosby your letters?'

'I was trying to help him.'

'He was beyond help.'

'Oh, stop it,' exclaimed Trix. 'You know what Henry was like, always writing suggestive letters. It didn't mean anything. It was horrifying what he wrote to poor Mother.'

Edith's mouth quirked. It would take more than a letter from Henry to shock Minnie Cadwalader Jones.

Even Walter managed a shaky smile. 'The old boy did get a bit florid in later years. And his handwriting was devilish to read.'

'Let me see,' said Percy, feigning the strain of recall. 'Ahead of Walter's arrival, Henry once wrote, *I shall have nothing for you but a great gaping mouth.*'

There was a collective gasp.

Clasping his knees piously, Percy stared at the ceiling. 'And what was the other line? Oh yes: *I must feel your weight and bear your might.*'

'Good lord,' whispered Sybil, glancing uncertainly at Walter.

'*. . . think of me therefore as just a waiting, panting abyss . . . .*'

Walter's slow blood rose to his cheeks again. 'Damn you, Percy Lubbock, no better than a parasite, living off the crumbs of others. Worming your way into our company — and how do you repay us? With betrayal after we're gone. It's abominable.' With spitting vehemence, Walter launched himself upright. Edith was amazed at his height, blocking the light. Sybil shrieked. Percy froze; his neck jack-knifed to take in Walter.

Walter's hands were balled. With malevolent fury he made for Percy, but he stumbled, his foot catching on the rug. A scream and a sickening crack; he collapsed to his knees. Panting, he sprawled across the floor, one arm outstretched.

Edith cried out, throwing Linky aside, but she was too late. Trix was already there, choking with tears — was he hurt, could he move? With a horrible dignity, Walter twisted his upper torso around like a reptile, staring up at Edith, haunted and cadaverous. Written with hate, he hissed, 'Damn you, woman.'

Collapsing back, she listened to Walter crawl to his chair like an injured animal. The only noise was the ticking of the clock, the sea-swell of her heart. How much more could they endure? Walter had been her life. After his death, she had been empty on the inside — and now, finally, they had the chance to be together again. But their reunion was too great to bear; it was deeply regrettable. The secrets he'd been forced to confront tonight were cruel and unnecessary. Despite a lifetime together, so many things had remained unsaid; and tonight they had been mercilessly exposed.

When she first met Walter, she believed herself competing with the pretty young ladies on the verandah at Roddicks — and this was true, in a way. She could remember his sliver of irritation as she fought for his attention, plunging with increasing desperation into Baudelaire's theories of social justice. Many years later, inviting Walter to The Mount, she declared: *If I could find a fairy who would suit you I should secure her at once.* Such self-effacing humiliation to admit she wasn't pretty enough. And although the threat of another Mrs Walter Berry dissipated, the pretence did not. More than thirty years later (Walter almost seventy!), ahead of his visit to Sainte-Claire, her home in Hyères, she wrote: *I shall try to import fairies from Cannes.* This was the jocular disguising of an unspoken truth that demeaned them both. Layering over a secret understanding.

Her presence in Walter's life always inured him against innuendo and rumour, allowing him to enjoy the company of Marcel Proust and friends without risking shame and disgrace. She protected his impeccable career as an international diplomat. Walter was far removed from those ruined by social and legal forces, men like Oscar Wilde dying destitute in Paris. She had done it because she loved him — as her oldest and dearest friend.

But only a year after Walter's death, Harry Crosby published the letters that confirmed him as a closet homosexual. Walter's reputation as a ladies' man became a joke, and by the time her memoir was published five years later, the pretence was pointless. Nonetheless, she did her best, making a public declaration of love. Once again, she reprised her role as the woman Walter refused to marry, the companion who waited while he flirted with pretty young women. She extended a lifetime of public humiliation well beyond his death.

But it wasn't enough — not enough to counter the physicality of the letters, Henry writing, *I shall have nothing for you but a great gaping mouth . . . think of me therefore as just a waiting, panting abyss.* At the time of Crosby's publication, she was distraught with grief for Walter, a grief pure and singular. But Crosby annihilated that. Her grief became fractured and confused. She had tried to decipher what Walter's response to Henry might have been. Encouraging? Vainly ambiguous? In off-guard moments her mind tried to picture what took place behind the shuttered façade of Lamb House. Most likely it was just another of Henry's hopeless infatuations encouraged by Walter's ego.

She was not naïve. Even when Edith was a child, social dandies were as much a part of New York society as old spinsters. Her happiest days were spent with Henry and his male admirers, all archly affectatious. Life was a form of fiction, and they were all characters. Edith had joined the mock displays of outrage, innuendo, and suggestive intrigue; truth suppressed beneath witty wordplay. It was unthinkable that Percy would later marry — was it for his own protection? Had Sybil understood she was part of an illusion?

But the letters were so shockingly real, so *corporeal.* Edith's only relief had been knowing she would never face Walter with such knowledge. But she was wrong, they were together again. She had once written (shortly before her death) of the difficulties for a ghost: their need for silence and continuity, their preference for the small hours; the impossibility of finding standing room in a roaring and discontinuous universe. Yet — unbelievably — she and Walter had found each other in this primeval gloom; and she desperately wished that it weren't so.

Walter's books were spilled across the floor in a horrible reminder of what had occurred. Edith wanted to sweep them from sight but felt unable to move. The others were watchful, unsure how to respond. Walter was angled away, and Edith dropped her head in despair. He had paid a terrible price for her indulgence. The truth had been brutal, and she regretted his pain.

The ticking clock, a metronomic march to oblivion, filled the silence, along with something else: the delicate sound of loose pages being turned — the novella — as Katharine began to read.

'No, please,' said Edith. She was afraid of what was to come. Walter mustn't hear the truth. He would be devastated to learn that Edith wasn't an entombed, sexless creature but a woman who loved with all her being, and who was loved in return.

She remembered now: it was the most perfect affair. What could be more beautiful than a springtime romance in Paris? *Meet you at the Louvre at one o'c, in the shadow of Jean Gougon's Diana.* She couldn't help smiling as her chair rocked gently. Was she about to hear of those weeks again?

That would be intolerable with Walter seated alongside. She must stop Katharine from reading. But goodness, the room was warm. The lights dimmed, and Linky was snoring in the firelight. 'Please, you mustn't read,' she said weakly.

But Katharine appeared not to hear.

'Please don't—' Looking up sleepily, Edith saw it was twenty past eleven. Even the clock seemed to be slowing down. There was something important she must . . . What? No, it was gone. No reason to worry. It was so much easier to rest quietly, allowing the words to wash like waves against a canvas canoe.

(5)

Throwing back some painkillers, Sara lay on the bed for a while. The radio interview had been exhausting. Trying to be smart and funny. Trying to be somebody else. It left her empty of everything except a headache. And she hadn't meant to mention the merchandise — she'd been carried away by the momentum of the interview. Bernard rang afterwards, furious that she'd gone on about gardening gloves and the cookbook. Just stick to the blogs, okay? And the book on Italian gardens.

Thank goodness Medora wasn't around. She would have made weird faces, been scathing about Bernard's schemes to commercialise Edith. Sara was trying to hide Bernard's more ambitious ideas (the cookbook) while tacitly encouraging him. Of course she was. With no blogging project, there was no Medora.

Feeling on edge, Sara opened her laptop. In Austen's absence, she could check the internet. Typing *Medora* into the search field, she waited. Medora: a town in Billings County, North Dakota, population 112.

She thought for a moment, then tried *Medora, New Zealand*. A documentary on the Medora basketball team had screened at an international film festival. And a schooner called *Medora* sailed into the Auckland port in September 1879. Sara was aware of prevarication, a deliberate postponing of her real intention. Now she tried *Medora Edith Wharton.*

Medora Manson — Character in The Age of Innocence. *The eccentric old aunt of Ellen Olenska. Medora raised Ellen after the deaths of her parents. A penniless itinerant, Medora is repeatedly widowed and tolerated by society only because of her family connections.*

So her hunch was right. Only now did Sara allow herself to picture their breakfast on the terrace that first morning. In the rush of the others leaving, Medora had paused around the side of the villa and overheard them speaking. Sara had been telling Austen that she couldn't write a garden blog about Edith Wharton. After joining them, Medora claimed to be a landscape architect but left before she could be questioned. Then she spent the day researching on the internet. By that evening, she had come up with: *Baroque mastery hits Tuscan topography. Everything but a floral clock.* Perfectly formed, expertly delivered, and Sara had fallen for it. Medora admitted having read *The Age of Innocence* and must have remembered Medora's name.

But why? Why give herself a name from an Edith Wharton novel? Maybe it appealed to her sense of humour to highlight the stupidity of her companions. Or maybe Medora really didn't care if they discovered she was a fraud. Whichever way, it didn't make Sara feel great. But nor did it change anything. She couldn't write the blog alone.

*

Padua Botanic Gardens. They were sitting on a stone bench in the *hortus conclusus*, enclosed by a high stone wall. The neatly laid-out garden plots were marked with iron fences, and the fountains were resting. Over the circular wall came the sound of a school party, but inside it was quiet and earthy-warm under a lowering sky. Putting down her notebook, Medora said, 'Tell me about Teddy.'

Teddy?

'They were married for twenty-eight years,' said Medora, dark-eyed with irony.

'Oh, sure.' It was unsettling now Medora was a Wharton fan. It should be useful — at least Sara didn't have to read *Italian Villas* anymore — but why ask about Teddy Wharton? She said, 'No one really mentions him. I think he spent a lot of time outside.'

A quick smile. 'Tell me about the garden.'

'It's beautiful, especially the trees.'

'Teddy helped plant them.'

Sara was unsure of her point. 'The garden falls away from the house, with terraces and an avenue. The Italian garden is the best part.'

Medora nodded, appearing to give Sara's words more thought than they deserved.

'It's difficult to describe.' Sara could feel the watchful eyes and braced herself against: *You're supposed to be a garden blogger*. But the words never came. Just a thick earthy silence. Sara was so relieved to be spared the marital point-scoring that she wanted to lay her head on Medora's shoulder. She tried again. 'In spring the garden's really fresh, like so — *green*.' She gave up, saying, 'Why do you want to know about The Mount?'

'Just wondering.'

'It's got nothing to do with our trip.'

Surprise lightened Medora's face. 'Gardens were always a part of Edith, she carried them with her. Don't you wonder how she felt being here? Seeing these beautiful old gardens with Teddy?'

'Not really.'

Opening her notebook, Medora began to write in a slow crab-scrawl. Sara tried to recall what she'd heard about left-handed people. They were wired differently. Something about their brains, but she couldn't remember what. Medora had small hands and blunt fingers.

Sara said, 'Bernard wants more gardens. He said there's one in Genoa with a pagoda.'

'Did you check *Italian Villas*?' Medora picked up the book, skimming the pages. 'There's one here.'

'With a Chinese pagoda?'

Sara edged closer to see the page. Light drizzle had left a fresh dampness to Medora's skin. Sara was aware of the soapy scent of her shirt and something musky beneath.

'Edith calls it ridiculous.' Medora turned a page and began to read: '...*guide-books still send throngs of unsuspecting tourists who come back imagining that this tawdry jumble of weeping willows and Chinese Pagodas, mock Gothic ruins and exotic vegetation represents the typical "Italian garden", of which so much is said and so little known.*'

It seemed so senseless to Sara. 'Why would Bernard want us to travel across Italy to see a Chinese pagoda?'

The book slammed shut. 'We could always make it up.'

Sara was careful not to betray the buzz she felt whenever Medora said 'we', the assumption of a partnership. 'You mean, we don't go to Genoa?' Her voice was light, no indication of the delicate shift in balance — that Medora could now dictate their travel plans. 'How do we make up gardens? ...Oh, I get it.' They would write about the gardens without visiting them.

Medora was silent

Sara felt pleased to have understood so quickly. 'No need to visit every garden. We research them on the internet, but how—'

'Most hedges look the same. We use generic photos of you beside a hedge, or sitting by a pond.'

'Bernard wants a Chinese pagoda and a weeping willow.'

Medora dropped the book into her bag. 'I'm sure we can find

a willow somewhere, but it's crazy to include a pagoda that Edith hated. It's a great idea, don't you think?'

Sara was drawn to Medora's mouth. She wanted to rub her thumb across the sawn-edge teeth. It wasn't her idea to falsify the blogs, but embraced by Medora's inclusive smile she was happy to share the credit. She felt pleasure in her own unease, dragged further into a shadowy entanglement, aware that any retrospective explanations to Austen would be damning. The ethical parameters of her life were moving. They were in this together.

*

The jacket was an ugly olive colour and made from rough material that made Sara scratch. The pockets were stitched on the outside, and the seams frayed. It wasn't really her thing, but Medora said it looked great, adding, 'You still need a tee-shirt,' and rummaged through a pile. They were in a bargain shop with a strange smell. 'And a slouchy leather bag.'

They hadn't found a market, but Medora had decided this place would do fine. They had stopped at a money machine, Medora leaning against the wall to watch Sara punch in her identification number and pass over the money. Now Medora dumped a silk shirt and a silver necklace on the counter — they needed expensive-looking stuff. Sara wasn't so sure. She had no idea how she would explain a shopping spree with no receipts or shopping bags. But she wondered if, like Medora, she had reached the point where explanations were no longer necessary. Specifics and accountability seemed futile.

'What do you reckon?' Medora was holding an orange tee-shirt against Sara.

She checked herself in the mirror. 'Not my colour. Not with *this*.' She waved despairingly at her hair.

'That's why it's so great. A discord that kind of works.'

Sara continued to study their reflection, Medora's dark hair against her own. It reminded her of another time, shopping with her daughter for a school prom. They were living in Surrey, the children at an international school. Alice was laughing in the changing room as Sara ferried dresses back and forth. Except it had never happened. Alice went shopping with her friends and bought some Amish-looking thing. And Alice never went to the prom anyway — some drama that was never explained. She spent the evening in her room angrily practising the cello. But the vision — shopping for a dress together — remained in Sara's mind more clearly than if it had really happened. Which was probably best. Such intimacy would have been awkward for them both.

*

After a quick lunch at the tabac, they were back in Sara's hotel room to write. It was freshly decorated, the windows opening on to a square. Tomorrow was a long drive down to Viterbo.

'Where?' said Medora.

'Central Italy, close to Villa Lante.'

But Medora had no idea about that either. Villa Lante was one of the most famous gardens in Italy. Even Sara knew that. Medora no longer seemed interested in pretending to be a landscape architect, just as Sara had given up all pretext of writing. Medora was sitting at the writing desk with her laptop. She was a fast typist and strung her sentences together quickly. Occasionally, she would stop to look up, as if an elusive adjective might be perched on the curtain rail. According to Bernard, the publishers thought Sara had a very natural style of writing.

Sara threw her phone on the bed. She had managed to book an extra room in Viterbo — a premium double. This was all becoming very expensive. She put out a hand to steady herself. Sometimes Sara felt afraid when she was alone. It was like standing beside an open window in a storm, feeling an eerie suck of air, straining against a force that might sweep her from sight. She had that feeling now.

It had begun to drizzle again, and the room was dim. Yesterday she had been pleased by the yellow walls and dark covers, but now she was oppressed by them. She could hear someone next door, movements that heightened her sense of distance. She wondered what time Austen would return. He was wandering through the old university.

Medora stopped typing. 'What do you think?'

Sara pulled up a chair.

The Padua Botanic Garden. They both agreed it was interesting — the world's oldest surviving botanic garden — but not worth a detour. However, Villa Barbarigo was stunning. Deep square pools and long canals; a boxwood maze. Medora called it a Walter Garden, explaining that Walter was Edith's travelling companion, a real uptight dude. Sara was confused: she didn't know much about Edith, but she was pretty sure Teddy was the husband. But Medora said she was referring to later years, when Edith always travelled with Walter Berry. Sara remembered dangling her legs over the pool edge and watching an orange carp slip up to the surface; a green silence of avenues and distant fountains. Classic and tasteful.

Medora laughed. According to Wikipedia, the Barbarigo garden was an allegory of man's progress towards his own perfection — just like Walter.

Sara blinked, watching the hotel room fill with watery light, a sun-shower passing across the town square. Medora closed her laptop and began massaging her shoulders. Sara wanted to offer a back rub, but Medora had gone over to the bed, opening *Italian Villas*, which was jammed with Post-it notes.

'Do you think a garden can reveal anything about its owner?'

'Not really.'

Medora settled back. 'You know Edith had an affair, right?'

How could Medora know that? Sara had thought it was an in-house secret. She recalled Bernard lowering his voice to talk about Edith's secret love-life. Medora must have read about it on the internet.

'Morton Fullerton. A real charmer and totally hot.'

Was this the same Edith Wharton who complained about conifers?

'No one ever guessed except Henry James. He was crazy about them both, but sometimes he got in the way. Edith wrote about the affair in a secret love diary. We should include that stuff in the blog.'

'Bernard said not to.'

'I thought he'd like that kind of thing. Great marketing potential.'

'An affair confuses the brand, apparently. All those white weddings.' Sara always adopted an ironic tone when talking about Bernard.

But Medora was serious. 'Sure, weddings bring huge money, I bet they need every cent to run The Mount. What they do is incredible.'

Sara felt irritated. This always happened — wanting to say the right thing but losing herself in the process.

Medora continued. 'Do the couples mind? Like, do they even *know* Edith was divorced?'

'But she wasn't divorced, not at The Mount, so I guess that doesn't count.' Now Sara could feel the slow burn of Medora's derision. She felt like telling her about the cookbook — Bernard had even come up with a title: *La Casa Aperta — The Open House*!

Looking up with a lazy smile, Medora said, 'I wonder what Edith would make of the internet.'

'Despise it, I imagine.'

'She was always an early adopter, first with electric lights and a motorcar, even a luggage lift. But the internet? Maybe you're right. Edith curated her life with such suppression — and now look, her private life is available to everyone. I bet she'd hate to see her work infantilised into study notes. And, boy, would she loathe a brain-dump like Wikipedia — so much information with no understanding. But her love-life? Sometimes I have the feeling Edith *wanted* the world to know.'

Medora stretched, her tee-shirt pulling up to reveal her flat midriff, paler than Sara expected. She tried to swallow, unable to drag her eyes away. The beginnings of a tattoo snaked beneath the waistband of Medora's vintage jeans. The tail of a dragon. Maybe a lizard. Next to Medora's head was the form of Austen's pajamas beneath the cover. Striped boxers and an old Chevron tee-shirt. The juxtaposition seemed deliberately provocative.

'It's a tuatara,' said Medora.

'Sorry?' said Sara, flushing, aware she was staring.

Medora pulled down her waistband to expose more of the tattoo, the body of what appeared to be a lizard. 'A tuatara,' she explained. 'Native reptile of New Zealand. They've been around since dinosaurs and are considered *taonga*, or a special treasure.'

Sara nodded, forcing herself not to look away. Her mouth felt dry. Medora pulled up her waistband, and Sara turned to the window, watching raindrops coalesce and smear with grey dust. She felt agitated, unsure of herself. She wondered what the head of a tuatara was like.

'I've been reading about her gardens in France,' said Medora. 'Do you know about them?'

'Not really.' She was still fixated on the tuatara.

'Edith spent the rest of her life in France. Two homes, completely different, like flip-sides of a coin. Pavillon Colombe was near Paris and described as elegant and beautiful. A garden of lilies and dark pools, close-clipped hedges. And every winter she went south to Hyères, to a restored monastery called Sainte-Claire. The garden sounds amazing, almost subtropical, with succulents and stuff. Her friends thought it bad taste, but Edith loved it. Burnt-orange soil and the heat-hazed Mediterranean, a jasmine dawn.'

Medora had rolled onto her side, head propped on one hand. Her hip bone was pale against the bedcover. The rain was heavier now, sealing them from the outside world.

Sara felt a ringing in her head. The glowing intimacy of a hotel room, the vibration of a minibar. She gripped the radiator, her mind blank, trying to think of something to say. 'So what did you mean about Walter?'

But Medora's smile was kindly, like she could read Sara's mind and knew she was afraid. Hitching higher on her elbow, she said, 'You don't seem like a mother. I forget that about you. What's it like?'

Sara was taken aback. 'I'm not sure.'

'Really?'

She didn't want to be reminded that Medora was probably the same age as her daughter. It made everything wrong. But Medora was expecting an answer, so she said, 'I was never subsumed by it. There was always a part of me watching. It should have meant more, all those ear infections and hockey games. It never added up to something I could count. I'm not even sure it changed me.' Unlike her sister Linda with her low-slung breasts and grandchildren hanging off her arms, rummaging in her bag for vitamin E cream. Linda still lived in their old Chicago neighbourhood. Every week she posted another family celebration on social media — a shambolic mess of step-relations and godparents, neighbours and anyone occupying the spare room. Her sister's life was weird and unsettling, but thankfully not genetic.

'Tell me about Austen.'

Sara wasn't sure that she'd heard correctly. The rain was heavier outside, and in any case Austen wasn't someone she wanted to talk about. Not with Medora.

'How long have you been married?'

'Thirty years.'

'I can't imagine what that feels like.'

'Like having two arms. Just a fact of life.'

'But relationships change over time.'

'So do arms.'

Ignoring this, Medora said, 'Do you think Austen's happy? I mean, you've just spent thirty years with someone moody.'

'Of course not.' Sara felt her allegiance shift, her voice defensive. Everyone liked Austen, this wasn't fair. 'Usually he—'

'So it's me?'

'It's everything.'

'He doesn't want you to be a success.'

'He doesn't like deception.'

'A strong moral code. I like that.'

'Are you really a landscape architect?'

'Of course.'

'You overheard us talking on the first day at breakfast. About the blog and Edith Wharton.'

Medora was still, watchful.

'How did you know that stuff?'

'Wikipedia.'

'But so quickly.'

'High-speed internet.'

Was she joking? 'And your name—'

'What about my name?'

'Nothing.' It was tricky to see in this light. Suddenly Sara felt deathly tired. She wanted to move across the room and lower herself to the bed. Lie quietly. Nothing more. Tell Medora how much she mattered. That she was sorry for her failings — her emotional dishonesty and keeping her feelings hidden. She wanted to trace a line across each dark brow, run a finger lightly down her face. She wanted to press her lips to the corner of her mouth and breathe her skin. Sara allowed herself to become submerged in these possibilities, a drifting desire, knowing she was protected by her own instinct for safety. Her body would never move. She knew that. Impulse had long dissipated in the years of marriage.

Medora's shape rose from the bed. Sara shrank away with a conflicting desire that Medora should come to her. But she was at the door, and Sara felt a shameful inadequacy flushing her body with heat. She wanted to call out, but the door opened, the girl was outlined in the light. It closed again. Sara swallowed, remaining motionless. The slap of rain against the window became the passing of time. She waited for several minutes. Transfixed. Waiting for Medora's return.

It was the cold that disturbed her, a chill on her skin that seeped into her consciousness. She moved towards the bed. Careful not to disturb the indented form, she lowered herself into the musky warmth.

CHAPTER VII

Katharine quietly placed the novella on the rug. The fire was lower and the room dim.

'Can't be right,' said Teddy, a nervous flush across his cheek-bones. 'I mean, it's not right, is it — Puss?'

'Please, Teddy, don't worry.'

'But it's not right, that's what I'm saying.'

'No, it's fiction.'

'Not that.' He shook off her words like a dog. 'I remember the fellow. Always falling over him in Paris.'

Edith didn't dare move.

He continued slowly, as if working out a difficult puzzle. 'And rumours, people saying things. But I knew you wouldn't do that sort of business — not with me, not with any man.' His face cleared. 'That's right, isn't it, Puss?'

She willed the questions to vanish. 'Of course, dear. You always thought my stories were make-believe nonsense. You could never see the point.'

'But it was true, all along. What people said. So my question is—' Teddy cast about the room as if searching for a question that might be hiding behind the furniture.

Everyone in the room waited.

'So my question is this . . .' His eyes locked onto Edith with sudden shocking connection, so powerful it made her blood run cold, so visceral she could feel the steel clamp of his hands. Slowly rising from his chair, he demanded, 'My question is this: how could you divorce *me* for adultery?'

Crushing her cigarette in the ashtray, Edith stood up. Dirty lunch plates lay on the table, crumbs scattered across the red-check cloth. Two smeared wine glasses. The scene would be slovenly were it not for the sunshine, the sound of dogs and children, a singing canary. Edith tried to smile, a nervous smoothing of her skirt, but Morton was all suave deference, holding her chair, taking her arm. Together they crossed the small courtyard, a glimmer of sunlight through the chestnut tree. The other diners took no notice as they stepped into the dark recess of the country hotel. It took several seconds for Edith's eyes to adjust before seeing the steep and narrow stairs. She did not ask how Morton knew the hotel and the arrangements necessary to book an afternoon room. She was light-headed from wine and a sense of unreality, like a dust mote hovering between the branched layers of the chestnut.

They reached the small upstairs hallway; Morton removed a key from his pocket to unlock the door with a mechanical click. It swung open. Standing back, he allowed her to enter. She fixed her attention on the room: it was clean and bare, the floor freshly swept. A patterned cover lay on the double bed with its simple iron bed-head. Sunlight filtered through the window. She could see the branches of the chestnut tree laced with filigree flowers. She thought: this room has been waiting all along just for the two of us. All the weeks of prevarication and nervous confusion, the silly misunderstandings. Even her final lingering over a cigarette in the courtyard — all postponing this moment. But why? She was here now, quite ready. Closing the curtains, she turned. Morton was leaning against the closed door, watchful, his expression thoughtful. The date was May 9, 1908. The first time they made love.

'Absurd, isn't it?' said Teddy, tall yet stooping. He looked about the room. 'To think of Mr Fullerton fucking my wife. Not the sort of thing a fellow should hear about, not about his *wife*. But — pardon me, I remember —' a high-pitched laugh, 'we're no longer married. You divorced me for adultery. Isn't that right, Puss?'

Edith swallowed thickly, unable to speak.

'I begged you not to. Remember? I was unwell — my teeth, and a buzzing head.' He spoke so quietly, she almost couldn't hear him, but she knew exactly what he was saying. He repeated himself, voice hoarse with wonder and pain, 'You divorced *me* — for adultery. How could you do that?'

Now he swung around to Katharine, and she drew back in fear. 'You knew about them, didn't you? Hinting in your little story. Making fun of me, saying I was always drunk.' Seizing the file, he shook it. 'Stories that weren't true. Spilling wine — that never happened, did it?'

'No.' A frightened whisper.

The file hit the wall, and Linky whimpered.

Teddy was on the move now, staggering around the room. He stopped at Sybil, who gave a smothered cry. 'And your spiteful tales, calling us common. There was nothing common about The Mount, damn you. A beautiful home. Shame on you. And shame on your spineless husband.' He rounded on Percy. 'How dare you write about my divorce — you've no right. Boasting that you didn't lay blame when you were too spineless to take sides.'

Percy stuttered in agreement.

'But you're wrong, because my wife was to blame, tupping her fancy stallion.'

Percy just shook his head, transfixed by the terrible sight of Teddy.

'And you,' Teddy spat at Walter, 'my so-called friend. Gone like the others, rats deserting a ship. Left me alone, nothing but hospitals and doctors. Locked in a room, abandoned by everyone including my *wife*.' Now he stopped to confront Edith. 'Did you hear me?'

Edith nodded dumbly.

'Spreading my name around town like muck. Publicly shamed. While Lady Wharton waltzes off to Europe to fuck Mr Fullerton.'

'It's finished,' said Edith. 'It means nothing.'

'Nothing?' He looked astonished. 'Damn it, woman, what do you mean "nothing"?'

Edith held the bloodshot eyes. He couldn't hurt her now.

But a horrible grin took possession of his features, voice mocking: 'Holier than thou, Mrs Wharton, like Mother-fucking-Superior.' Choked and glottal, he wiped his mouth to continue. 'To think what I put up with. Thought yourself so clever. Never mind old Teddy. Just the fool you married when old lover-boy here disappeared.' A jerk in the direction of Walter.

'Please, Uncle Teddy,' pleaded Trix. 'You mustn't—'

Teddy continued to fling obscenities at Edith. Not his fault he went searching for what a man should get at home. Made to feel like filth, a dirty sickness to bother his oh-so-pure wife. Whiter than snow. Except she wasn't, was she? Too busy fucking like a bitch on heat. While he—

'No more,' barked Walter. 'Do you hear me?'

Teddy planted his large hand on the back of Edith's chair, forcing her to look up.

'How could you do that to me?' he whispered.

She shook her head.

'Our beautiful home. The only place I was happy. But you dressed me up and took me to Paris like one of your lap dogs. A fish out of water with all your clever friends. Dumped me in sanatoriums when I became a bother. I just wanted to be home. My home and animals. That's all I wanted. A place to get well.'

Shaking with fear, Edith watched the tears fall down his creviced face.

'You left me in a mad-house. How could I get well in a place like that?'

Edith turned away.

'I just wanted my home.'

She could barely hear him, a whisper of breath on her cheek. He watched her a moment longer before shambling away back to his corner, now in darkness. She heard the creak of his chair, a low sobbing. The sound brought back terrible memories, all the times she had held his shaking body, filled with dread at their unknown, unknowable future. Now she knew what was to happen, and so did Teddy. He would continue to slip inexorably into madness, creating mayhem along the way. He would not take the pre-emptive measures of his father, cutting short the misery of his life. He had always been a stubborn man; and not even insanity could curb his determination to live out every miserable year, seventy-seven of them in all. He would be cared for by the overwrought Nanny, but Nanny went first, and Teddy would spend the last five years of his life alone with nothing but the grim triumph of his existence.

There came a raw cry of grief. The fire flickered as if to go out. Soulful cries filled the room. It was terrible; Edith covered her ears, but she could hear Walter entreating Teddy to stop. The noise continued, painful and heart-rent.

How could she have divorced him?

Towards the end of their marriage, Teddy had had a string of women and trouble with money. He had embezzled large amounts of her savings for gambling and drinking. He had admitted this in a fashion similar to this evening — with howling sobs interspersed by violent shrieking and recriminations. Even Henry, always a defender of Teddy, was horrified by one such scene, writing later, *you must insist on saving your life by a separate existence*, which is what she eventually did. Teddy continued his escapades around the world, unrestrained and on the loose; and in a fit of spiteful mania he sold The Mount.

An uneasy calm settled on the room, despite Teddy. With his face turned to the wall, he had lapsed into incoherent muttering, a low, rhythmic beat broken by an occasional raised word as he fought the voices in his head.

'Well, who would've thought, my dear?' said Walter with lazy spite.

Edith did not move.

'You still have the ability to surprise me.'

'You wouldn't have wanted the truth.'

'The truth is abhorrent.'

She understood his hurt. Walter might have suspected Edith was attracted to Morton — but a sexual liaison? Never: it was inconceivable that Morton should desire a woman whom Walter did not want! But she sensed that Walter had always felt *something*, and he found it disturbing. His suspicions would always fuel another frenzied round of flirting with other women.

Yet Walter never minded about Teddy — quite the opposite. They got on well together. There was simply no reason to be jealous:

everyone knew the Wharton marriage was in name only. Certainly he wasn't threatened by Teddy's intelligence; there was no competition for Edith's mind. Teddy was a livestock man who admired his wife like a well-bred filly. Walter was probably relieved (Edith had felt) that she was a married woman, allowing him unfettered access to the famous Mrs Wharton without any obligations. And afterwards? If Walter had any sense of duty to formalise his relationship with Edith, he gave no sign.

So why did Walter never suspect that Edith and Morton were lovers? Why was it so impossible to believe?

Because Walter was attracted to Morton himself.

Despite his feigned indifference, it was suddenly so obvious: his heightened, watchful interest in everything about Morton, always wanting to discuss him, savouring his success like a fine wine. Whenever he learned they would be joined by Morton, Walter's eyes would glitter, a high flush across his narrow features. Only in his letters would he permit himself overt displays of affection about that 'fine fellow'.

And now, finally, the truth. Poor Walter, it was a double betrayal.

Linky began to stir, and Edith stroked the silky ears until the little dog became drowsy. Her thoughts were drifting. It had become a closed chapter in her life. She had been the star in her own drama, playing the lead role of adulteress. The streets and *salons* of Paris became a theatrical setting, the secrecy of longing staged in a Parisian season. *I don't suppose you know . . . the quiet ecstasy I feel in sitting next to you in a public place . . . while every drop of my blood in my body whispered 'Mine-mine-mine!'* She had been radiant with love, glowing with sensuality. For the first time she felt truly beautiful. Morton ripped through her ordered life, turning it upside down. She experienced everything, mad with desire. Morton said: *We are behind the scenes together.*

'Well, that settles it,' said Trix, her features harsh and angular.

'Settles what?' said Edith.

'Burn the novella. There's no point reading more, although the damage is done.' A momentary pause before she burst: 'How *could* you?'

'Allow Katharine to read?'

'No. I mean, *everything*.'

Teddy was gently banging his head against the wall, and Walter's outrage had chilled the room.

Trix reached to the floor for the novella.

'*No!*' shot Edith.

Katharine saw her chance and quickly swept the pages into her lap, folding her hands like a sentinel.

Trix jerked to her feet. Holding her chair for support, she turned ferociously on Edith. 'You knew the affair would be used to sensationalise the novella. You guessed at the very beginning.'

'No, my dear, I've been unaccountably dull-witted.'

'Literary prostitution. Selling scandal for fame.'

'That's not how I would describe it.' Yes, she might become known as an adulteress, but Edith hoped that readers of the novella would be more understanding and see her as a woman with the courage to love. Calmly, she continued, 'I always envied your marriage, Trix. Why should I be judged so harshly for wanting happiness?'

'It's called adultery.'

'The world appears to have changed. Remember the opening chapter of the novella — how *The Glimpses of the Moon* was to be updated? I admit the revision made little sense, but it's evident my romance would barely be a scandal now.'

'So why does the novella draw attention to your affair? You know as well as I do — for *marketing* purposes.' Trix managed to make 'marketing' sound like something a plumber might remove from a blocked drain.

Trix was right; Bernard's marketing world sounded voracious. Some things didn't change. Even when *Mirth* was published, Scribner's put a wrapper on every copy saying *For the first time the veil has been lifted from New York society!* Edith had been appalled (she was related to half New York's society), and insisted the wrappers be removed. Poor Scrib, he even apologised for his somewhat exotic spirit of enterprise. But many years later she was happy for *The Age of Innocence* to be sold as an exposé of New York society with advertisements screaming: *Was She Justified In Seeking A Divorce?* By then she had accepted the need for aggressive sales tactics.

It seemed the author of the novella was of a similar opinion.

Trix was twisting her fingers as she paced the rug. 'But why keep your secret love diary? That's what I don't understand. You should have realised it would be discovered.'

Edith was silent.

'Why not destroy it, build bonfires like Henry?'

'I couldn't destroy my own work.'

'But you must have known—' Trix stopped.

Edith kept very still.

Collapsing into her chair, Trix said, 'I don't believe it.'

Walter seemed tense with anticipation. 'What are you saying, Beatrix?'

Trix glared at Edith.

'Beatrix? I demand an answer.'

'You *wanted* the diary discovered.'

Edith stared at the flames, trying to remember. She left the diary behind — yes, but for what reason? She couldn't believe it was a deliberate act, more a decision made through inaction. She asked that Teddy's letters be destroyed but nothing else. Even on her deathbed, she never asked Elisina to burn *The Life Apart: L'Âme Close*.

Why did she leave her secret diary behind?

The answer came to her in a flash: because the world had already consigned her to history. She was criticised for being out of touch, her writing old-fashioned. And it would only get worse after she was gone. What could she do? How could she change such misconceptions after her death?

There was no precise plan, nothing predetermined. She could not control her posthumous image, but she *could* allow for possibilities — and so she left the door open, that was all. She left the door open to unknowable eventualities. And now a modern novella would 'sex-up' the iron-clad image of Edith Wharton; and she had learnt for certain (from the most recent chapter) that details of her affair were available on the internet.

Lifting her gaze to the watchful Trix, she said, 'It was nothing premeditated, my dear. I simply left things to providence. Is that so unreasonable?'

'You were organised enough to leave papers for a biographer.'

Surprise caught her. 'You spoke to Elisina?'

Trix looked away with a flush of ... embarrassment or anger? 'Your estate. Of course we had dealings.'

Dealings? What did that mean? About to ask, Edith found herself under renewed attack from Trix: 'Do you really want the novella published, even now?'

'I haven't decided.'

'Dash it, woman,' breathed Walter.

She held her ground. 'I've nothing to be ashamed of.'

'What about your reputation?' Trix shook her head with dis-belief. *'Our family reputation?'*

Edith burst with laughter, setting the lights blazing.

She could feel Walter's irritation like friction in the air. She hadn't imagined it would be this challenging. And what about Katharine — how did she feel about the novella being published? Edith could read nothing in the woman's poise, but she felt sure the work was safe in her hands.

Sybil turned to her husband and sniffed. 'You never mention Fullerton in your memoirs.'

'Didn't know about him. Nobody did — not that sort of business.'

'Nonsense. What about the housekeeper?'

Edith was watchful. It was true that Grossie knew what was happening, adopting a magnificent discretion without request.

'People were very gracious with their time,' said Percy stiffly, 'including Lady Tallandier. I was hardly going to include licentious stories from a dead housemaid.'

Obsequious creep, how dare he disparage poor Grossie?

Beside her, she could feel Walter shifting, as if rearranging his memories. But it couldn't be done; to reconsider a forty-year rela-tionship through a different lens was impossible. She could feel the slow beat of her companion's pain. She regretted this. If only she could comfort him by saying her affair with Morton changed nothing. But she would be lying. It changed everything. Morton Fullerton undermined the very basis of her relationship with Walter: that Edith had been eternally loyal, always waiting for his attention.

If only she could tell Walter that her writing stopped when he died, but that wasn't true either. She always credited him for her achievements as an author — a truth they maintained throughout her career. However, when he died, she simply carried on. She published three more novels and continued to write until she was physically incapable. On the bookshelf she could feel the presence of *The Buccaneers* like a recrimination.

Poor Walter.

'You knew,' said Sybil, her blue gaze fixed on Katharine. 'All that business in the cab about the note.'

Katharine looked amused. 'Of course.'

Edith spoke sharply: 'You didn't understand at the time.'

'Of course I did.'

No, Edith was certain. 'Morton explained the situation after your marriage. That day, in the cab, you were so—'

'Innocent?'

Edith disliked her mocking expression. 'Your brother was worried that you were too devout. He said—'

Katharine burst out laughing. 'I was engaged at the time.'

'No, you were in a convent!'

'My life was complicated, and my fiancé was not an easy man. I needed solitude to think.'

'Your fiancé was not Mr Gerould?'

Katharine's smile was reflective. 'No. Gordon proposed after my first disastrous engagement.'

'Disastrous?'

'My parents thought so.'

'They disliked your fiancé?'

'My parents adored my fiancé, Mrs Wharton, but they didn't approve of our engagement.'

'I met them once — your parents — and greatly enjoyed their company.' A sudden thought caused Edith to inhale sharply. The memory of her own audacity! Taking tea in the front parlour of the modest clapboard in Brockton. Katharine's father was a minister with a crisp manner and kindly demeanour. His wife was handsome and clever, completely besotted with her son. Edith had arrived in the guise of a famous author. His parents would never have suspected she was their son's lover. *Would you care for more tea? said Mrs Fullerton, picking up the silver tea strainer.*

'They knew you were lovers,' said Katharine.

'I beg your pardon?'

'Don't you see?' said Katharine with a quiet intensity that was frightening. 'Why are you so blind to the dangers?'

Edith was shocked. 'What dangers? I thought you wanted the novella published.'

'I want you to understand the full cost, Mrs Wharton. Your accounting is a little . . . limited. You know my brother was no Prince Charming, so why this charade of romantic love?'

'You're quite mistaken,' said Edith gripping her knotted hands together. 'It was perfect.'

Katharine's look was derisive. 'A perfect month of love before returning to America.'

'Yes, that's right.' She held Katharine's gaze with every ounce of resolve. She felt like a passenger on an ocean steamer who is told there is no immediate danger but that she had better put on her life-belt.

'But that wasn't the end, was it?'

A trapdoor opened inside. Edith heard herself say, 'Endings are seldom clear-cut, but for the purposes of story a springtime in Paris is ideal. A story that is self-contained, complete and — I hope — available to a new generation of readers. All recounted in my diary.'

Katharine shook her head. 'But a wider truth would be known by others.'

'No one else knew about the affair except Henry and dear Grossie.'

'And my family. My parents were very grateful for your help. Will was always in financial strife, and they weren't wealthy.' To the others, she said, 'Will was being blackmailed, and Edith helped pay the blackmailer.'

Edith held her breath.

Walter demanded, 'Is that true, Edith?'

Katharine knew too much.

'You astound me. To degrade yourself in such—'

'That's enough,' clipped Edith.

'But why?' asked Trix, aghast.

'It's difficult to explain,' said Edith, knowing full well why she had paid Morton's blackmailer.

'A form of insurance,' said Katharine.

'I suppose so,' replied Edith.

'Against what?' Trix asked.

Truthfully, she said, 'I was afraid for our future together. I hoped paying his debts would secure him. That he would feel morally obliged to stay.'

'Fullerton sounds like a hustler.' Walter's words dripped with venom.

Katharine laughed. 'He had no sense of moral obligation. Not to anyone — not even you, Mrs Wharton. Am I right?'

'If only I'd known Morton as well as you.'

'Perhaps.' Her face was enigmatic. 'Do you know why he was being blackmailed?'

'Not entirely.' She had chosen not to know.

'Did you know he had an affair with Lady Brooke?'

'No.' Edith was intrigued. Lady Brooke was a forceful woman and at least fifteen years older than Morton. As the wife of the

White Rajah of Sarawak, her social standing was prestigious. The Rajah was a powerful man and very handy with a firearm. 'There was evidence of an affair?'

'Oh, yes,' said Katharine. 'All sorts of papers.'

'His landlady.'

'She kept everything, scheming old harridan. Mother was furious, and my poor father tired of paying his debts.' At Edith's look of surprise, she continued. 'He was always extricating my brother from what they called Will's love episodes. Father even knew about Lady Brooke. That was around the time Will and Camille parted. Mother was very upset; she was so fond of her.'

Who was Camille?

'And Mireille.'

Never heard of her either; they were obviously not women of society.

Katharine regarded her with sympathy. 'Curious you know so little when you were so generous to my brother. So risky when you don't know the full story.'

'Of course I do. It's my story.'

'It's more than your story. Your picture of events is so incomplete.'

Walter was stiff with indignation. 'Can't believe it of either of you! How much did you lend the fellow?'

'Nothing directly,' said Edith, relieved to be distracted from Katharine's penetrating eyes. 'Mr Fullerton received an advance from Macmillan's for a book on Paris. That was Henry's idea. The advance came from my bank account. Of course, he never did write the book, nor did he return the advance.' Now she looked straight at Katharine. 'Henry called it Morton's exquisite art of never quite pulling the thing off.'

Katharine's suppressed smile was unexpected. Edith said, 'Did you know Henry reworked Morton into *The Wings of the Dove?*'

'Of course. Merton Densher. A charming journalist who persuades a dying heiress of his love. I believe my brother was flattered.'

Even now it was difficult to dismiss Morton's breath-taking expediency. 'Tell me, who was Camille?'

Katharine's face tightened. 'Camille Chabert, an opera singer — of sorts. More of an entertainer. And a daughter, Mireille. A sweet child. Even after the divorce they stayed in touch.'

Edith leaned forward, unsure she had heard correctly. 'I'm sorry, Katharine, I don't understand. After who divorced?'

Katharine seemed genuinely surprised. 'You didn't know Morton was married?'

Edith tried to laugh, but her throat jammed, and she could only stammer, 'Absurd. He never married — I know that for a fact, he would have told me. Morton could never, I mean—' Her voice became clogged. The lights began to spin, and in the distance she could hear Katharine's voice, insistent and clear: it was perfectly true, they married in Portugal and remained in contact all their lives—

'An affair with a married man,' said Walter, every word a bullet.

'But why?' asked Trix. 'Why—'

'Demean myself?' Edith was trying hard to hide her shock. That Morton had been married all that time. She couldn't believe it.

'With a married man—'

'I didn't know he was married.'

'And their child,' said Katharine.

'Morton's child?' The floor opened. Edith felt an emptiness seep to the edges of the universe. Morton was a father? She tried to find her voice, but it was no more than a whisper. 'He never said . . .' She trailed off.

'He never accepted the child as his.'

Edith was unable to speak.

'A little girl. Mireille. She became quite a character. But her mother and I lost contact over the years.'

A baby girl. How could Morton have ignored a child? The depth of his deceit still had the power to stun. She struggled to breathe; the lights were out of control, leaving circular trails of colour. The wires began to spark, a series of small electrical explosions, and the room was filled with fireworks. Edith felt herself slide into darkness.

(6)

He could feel Medora watching from the shade as he
photographed a hillside spring. It was a difficult shot, the
trees creating angular chunks of light. Austen fiddled with his
camera, aware that he'd been joined.

Medora reached out to catch the water, causing it to splash
and sparkle. She smiled. 'The source of the whole garden.'

Austen clicked on his lens cap.

Turning her hand against the flow, Medora said, 'From here
the water travels down to the theatrical drama of the grand
terrace. The trees keep getting pushed out like stage wings, the
garden architecture becoming more dominant.' She was silenced
by the arrival of a couple in matching rain jackets. Austen
indicated the stairs, and she followed him down, coming out by a
pretty fountain tiered like a wedding cake. The light was smoky-
blue under liver-spotted plane trees. Medora watched him
take another photograph before saying, 'Have you noticed the
walkways are never positioned on the central axis? Only water
gets that honour. The axis of the garden is mostly implied. That's
why you get that irritating feeling of something unresolved.
Have you got that?'

'No.'

'Like an itch you can't scratch. A low-level frustration. By the
time we reach the Fountain of the Moors it's a dénouement.
Everything gets resolved in this huge rush — an overwhelming
sense of relief as everything releases in this dramatic climax.' She
grinned. 'If you get what I mean.'

He looked away.

Dropping to the edge of the fountain, she said, 'You remind
me of my father.'

Austen was caught by her expression, open and curious. Joining her on the edge, he said, 'I thought he was a loser.'

'Did I say that?' She seemed puzzled, shaking her head. 'He's a fund manager.'

Austen started to laugh, but he wasn't sure why.

'His daughter Stephanie is a week younger than me.'

Austen felt his laughter dry up. He didn't understand.

'He's a regular family guy. Right down to the Labrador.' A short pause, then she said, 'Do you have a dog?'

'No.'

'Sometimes my mother calls me Persephone — goddess of the underworld, queen of the shadows.'

The stone edge felt cold beneath his palms.

'He paid her to keep quiet.'

'And did she?'

'Sure, until I was ten. That's when we turned up at Stephanie's birthday party. I was in my party dress. I didn't understand that we hadn't been invited.'

Austen held still.

'They had pink and white balloons. Even a magician. I'd never been in a house that big. Even the front door was huge. And trees. It was almost a park.'

He shifted uneasily. It was like listening to a private conversation. He didn't want her to continue, but he didn't want her to stop.

'Stephanie had just started a new school. Her mother was pleased to be meeting her new friends. She gave us a lovely welcome and pretended not to notice my present was wrapped in old paper. We went through to the back garden where there was a swimming pool and a table of party food. And so many kids. I got confused when I saw my father — I wasn't expecting him.

He was carrying a massive cake, and I thought it was for me. I got so excited: I hadn't seen him for months, and he had a birthday cake. Funny thing is, I can't remember what the cake was like.' She shrugged. 'I can picture everything else. Calling out to him, the pool water as I ran past, his expression — I try not to remember that — but the cake? Sometimes I think it was a princess cake, but that's just a guess. Whenever I look at it directly, the cake sort of explodes.' She paused before saying, 'It was my grandmother who bred sheep. I used to stay with her whenever my mother got sectioned.'

Austen waited.

'The psych ward.' She kept her focus on the fountain spray. 'So, tell me about being an environmental engineer.'

He relaxed, pleased to take the conversation where she wanted to go. 'Water quality, looking after discharge. I started as a process engineer, but my job title got changed. I was never going to save rainforests, Medora.'

'Did you make the world a better place?'

From side-on she was perfect. A small upturned nose and gently curved neck. He looked away. 'I stopped it getting a fraction worse.'

She nodded.

A picture came suddenly to mind, something he hadn't thought about in years. 'There was a guy who came to my son's childcare centre. Environmental educator. Pulled up in a massive sport utility painted with birds and trees. Told the kids to care for the planet — it would be theirs one day unless they kept using fossil fuels. Then he roared off to another school.' Austen shrugged. 'I always biked to work.'

'Is there a moral to the story?'

'Not really.' Medora's face was angled upwards to the sun. Her lashes were dark against pale-olive skin pulled tight across her cheekbones. He said, 'You still think I'm guilty of selling out.'

'I don't think guilt is absolute.'

'What do you mean?'

'More like a sliding scale of culpability.' Medora dipped her fingers into the water, then drew a cross on the chalky stone edge. She looked up. 'There are so many types of guilt — by neglect or association, a slow accretion of sins that finally tips the balance.'

Austen was intrigued that she had given it so much thought.

'Guilt is just a judgement call — and who's to judge? An old man in a wig who drinks too much and bangs the stenographer after work on Fridays? Or the moral majority, using outrage to cover their own dirty secrets?' Drawing another chalky cross, she added, 'The only thing that counts is your conscience. Only you know the extent of your guilt.'

Austen wondered what had prompted Medora to so carefully consider this. He was about to ask when she said, 'I once lobbied against a cellphone tower near our school.'

'Did you win?'

'No, but I got a year of free texts.'

'So much for youthful conscience.' This came out wrong, too accusatory. He was sorry.

'We all have our price.' Now she was defensive. 'Do you know I'm on the payroll?'

Austen didn't understand.

'You don't know, do you?' She shook her head. 'Strange. I always thought marriage would be creepy, the closeness and scrutiny. But it's not true. I suspect I'd enjoy the deceptions of married life.' A short laugh before she added, 'Fifty euros an hour, plus expenses.'

Austen stood up, shoving his hands in his pockets. He rocked back on his heels.

'Professional rates. I want my academic qualifications and writing skills recognised.'

'Sure. I understand.' Confused and annoyed, he headed for the balustrade. The village of Bagnaia lay below, a jumble of orange roofs, wires strung between antennae.

After a couple of minutes, she joined him, leaning her bare arms on the stone. 'Edith really loved this garden. She's so perceptive. She said it's a garden as rich in shade as water. That's pretty smart.' A quick grin. 'Plus she figured everything out by herself, no Wikipedia.'

'An Edith Wharton cookbook,' said Austen. 'That's what they're planning.'

Medora stared at him.

'Gardening gloves and notebooks. I forget what else.'

She turned back to the view. 'Edith wasn't interested in food.'

'But she was interested in marketing.' He knew this because Sara had told him. He'd been questioning the gardening gloves, wanting to know what came next — Wharton soy candles?

'Sara knows nothing about Edith.' Fixed on the view, she added, 'One day I'd like to finish my degree.'

'But you—'

'Mostly geography. Sort of related to landscape architecture. I did some botany papers and urban design. But I never finished my degree. Things got complicated.' She turned to face him. 'I heard Sara on that first morning saying she couldn't write the blog, so I stayed around to help.'

'Thanks, kid.'

'I like to think you mean that.' Her voice was teasing.

He was prepared this time, the whisper of a kiss touching

his temple. He turned quickly to see her surprise as he opened his mouth against hers. His eyes shuttered against everything except the rattle of overhead leaves, the mosaic of sun and shade. He raised his hand to push her away but pulled her closer.

It was the crush of leaves that alerted him. The bustle of bags, the breathlessness and Sara's *Isn't this amazing!* He steeled himself, but she was admiring the view, dropping her bags to the ground and hauling out her books. Had she seen them? She must have. But Sara was carrying on as usual, distracted and absorbed. Austen scanned the low, burnt-orange hills.

That night, as he tried to sleep, the picture kept scrolling through in his mind. Pulling Medora close. The feel of her body. Her musky scent and bubbles of laughter in her throat. And the possibility of something in her eyes before he caught her mouth. Triumph — was that it? And her body against his. Pliable, a tensile strength that amazed him. Hip bones pressed firm against him, urgent, no disguising how she felt. Or what she wanted.

Ripping back the sheet, Austen sat up. The nights were getting hotter as they travelled south. He'd cracked open the window but it made no difference. He ran a hand over his face. Medora was imprinted on his mind as he bent to kiss her. The only time he'd ever caught her off-guard. He tried to swallow, but his throat was dry. Sweat ran down his back. Swinging his feet to the tiled floor, he reached for his water glass and drank hard, splashing the remainder on his cheeks. Then he sank back on the bed and stared at the ceiling. Sara's breath was light and even, the carefully measured breath of someone awake.

*

Their hotel room wasn't ready when they arrived in Viterbo, the manager promising it would be available by four. 'That late?' said Austen, but the manager just shrugged. *Presto. Presto.* So now they were wandering around a part of town that wasn't anywhere. An auto-repair shop and a Chinese take-out, prefabricated buildings and empty lots. This was not the Italy of tourist brochures.

'This part was probably bombed in the war,' said Sara.

'That was a while ago.' Austen glanced up at the sky. Drizzle clouds had condensed into something heavier.

'We could call Medora,' Sara continued. 'There's no point getting wet.' Medora's room had been ready on arrival. She'd given them a quick wave as the lift door shut. 'Austen?'

But he was already crossing the road for a cash machine. Sara looked into a dusty shop window at electric razors and Casio alarm clocks. Of course she'd seen them kiss yesterday, but what of it? Impossible to understand, no point even trying. It was beyond her reach. Except for her response — that was something she could control. She had taught herself this in Lagos when Alice had asthma attacks that blasted her body like a sandstorm. Sara had often cried at the thought of leaving her baby behind, buried in the dry red soil. Stupid. She learnt to curb these fantasies and stick to useful things like Ventolin. The immediacies of here and now. Medora would be gone soon. She and Austen would resume their life, continue as before. There was nothing to be gained by a scene.

Medora would be gone soon. She waited for her response. But nothing. The words made no sense.

Now Austen was shoving his wallet back in his pocket, staring at her strangely. He said, 'I'll need to make a transfer. We're churning through the money.'

Sara kept walking. They must be close to the town square.

'Sara?'

'I bought a jacket in Padua, it was quite expensive. I'll show you when we get back.'

'You paid cash?'

'It was a market.' She forced herself to hold Austen's gaze. She had never deliberately lied before, but it was surprisingly easy. 'And other stuff.' Sara unzipped her sweater to show her tee-shirt.

Austen blinked.

'Not my colour, I know.'

'I like it.'

'Really?'

'Sure, it goes with your hair.'

*

They didn't get into their room until late afternoon, Bernard ringing just as the door closed. Twenty thousand Twitter followers! Incredible. Sara was scheduled to speak at the opening night of the summer series, 'The Art of Civilised Living', alongside Laura Bush. And the garden book was already in pre-production. What did Sara think?

Sara thought everything was getting a little too *House Beautiful*.

There was a small pause. Sara felt a rush of air, as if a lift door had shut in her face.

'I'm sorry?'

Sara persisted: the gardens were all the same, it was hard to make them interesting. Most of the anecdotes were fabricated anyway — the family picnics and rainstorms. She needed more to work with, why not Edith's love-life?

Bernard's voice changed gear, laboured as he explained: that idea was never going to fly. Who would be interested in the affair of — well, let's admit it, Edith was no oil painting. Sure, things might be different if she were beautiful but . . . Bernard's voice trailed off at the insurmountable problem of Edith's face.

Sara waited.

But merchandise — now that was a winner. No need to worry about Edith's looks when they could use the name. Wharton was synonymous with elegance. Everyone knew Whartonian meant stylish, and anything Whartonesque was expensive. She could be a luxury brand.

Sara wanted to think Bernard was a jerk, but she couldn't. She had to believe in a Wharton franchise, something to provide a future with Medora. Was that possible? Whenever Sara thought about what came next, after this trip, she felt hollow with fear. Whenever she tried to look directly at the future, it was empty.

Putting down her phone, she saw Austen was in a bad mood, annoyed their room overlooked a car-repair shop. Absently, she said, 'The garden book is already in pre-production.'

'What about Medora?'

She was tired of this argument. 'There's nothing wrong with having a ghost writer.'

'Be careful, Sara,'

Did he know she was paying Medora? Or had he guessed they were writing about unvisited gardens? Yesterday Medora had spent hours on TripAdvisor inventing visits to Vicobello and Villa Visconti. But she was getting irritable, fed up with writing the blogs.

Now Austen was going on about authenticity. Did Sara really want to be part of something so infantile, this mindless pursuit of fame?

'It's called public validation.' These were Bernard's words, his response to her own concerns. They sounded crass when thrown at Austen in this elegant hotel room, but caught in the momentum of her argument she had no intention of losing ground now. 'Do you have an issue with that?'

'Not if you're sixteen and want to be on *X-Factor*.'

'You think I'm too old?' Finally a reason to be angry.

'I think you're worth more than this.'

She loathed him. 'And you're in a position to lecture about morality?' Danger lay just beneath the surface. Her head felt light, fingers tingling.

His eyes flickered across her face.

'Oh, for God's sake.' Sara picked up her bag. 'I'm going to see Medora, tell her the news. At least she'll be happy for me.'

The door closed heavily behind her. She was alone in the hall, a deep-pile hush except for a housekeeping knock in the distance. Where was Medora's room? She had no idea. Heading for reception, Sara fortified her fury at Austen — he had no right to belittle her. He couldn't deal with her success, the idea that her life was finally changing.

Nearer reception, Sara felt her resolve waver under the recall of his withering look. She had nothing to be ashamed of. Austen's problem was not her pursuit of fame but that she was an ambitious older woman. Not completely true either, she had to concede, arriving at the entrance. Austen had always supported her in the past. But she was determined to stay angry lest other shadows take shape. Medora. The fact they would soon be alone together.

The same manager was on duty. Sara was aware that twenty years ago he wouldn't have been so indifferent. 'Medora Manson,' she said politely. 'Could you tell me her room number?'

He gave no sign that he understood.

'We all arrived this afternoon. You remember. Her room was ready.'

'*Partire*.' A flourish of satisfaction.

'I'm sorry. I don't understand.'

'This afternoon she gone.'

'No, she arrived this afternoon. We all did.'

His head tilted to the entrance. 'Gone. *Partire*. Out the door.'

Medora must have gone for a walk. Sara felt let down. She didn't want to return to Austen, but what could she do? She could see it was now raining heavily outside.

'With her — what you call bag-pack? And no coat.' He shook his head.

'Backpack? I don't understand.'

'Change plans.' Now he was cheerful in the face of Sara's shock. 'Check out. But you pay two nights. I have card number.'

'You're mistaken.' Sara tried not to panic. Stupid man, he was confused. He couldn't know Medora's intentions. But her backpack? Oh, God, why?

Now he waved towards a key on the board. The room had been checked but nothing missing. Maybe coat hangers. That was all.

Turning, she made unsteadily for a sofa. What had happened? Medora was fine this afternoon. Quiet, perhaps, but that was all. Had she been preoccupied, making plans? Sara recalled the cheeky wave as the lift doors shut. Had something bad happened? Should she call the police? Of course not. She should ring Medora's phone.

Fumbling with the autodial, Sara waited. A mechanical voice answered, impartial, unhelpful. The cellphone was switched off or out of range. Sara had known that would be the case. She also understood that Medora had left freely. What sort of person did something like that? Sara felt a sweep of shame. Clasping her knees, she was aware of cold air drifting through the entrance doors with the arrival of more guests. They were talking and laughing loudly. She must seem a strange spectral presence in the foyer, unmoving, gripped with anxiety. What could she do? Questions crowded her head like angry protesters demanding answers. Where was Medora now? What about Bernard, her blogs, the whole project? What would happen? She had no idea. Control — she must control herself, stick to the immediacies. Medora was gone. That was all. Except it wasn't all. Sara desperately wanted to see her. She wanted Medora to walk into the foyer, laughing and wet. She wanted her more than anything.

CHAPTER VIII

At the edge of her consciousness, Edith could hear a low murmur of voices. Sybil's laughter fissured the darkness. She was telling a story about her niece: 'The most wonderful piano player, even as a child. She'd just finished playing for the Whartons when Edith said loudly, *Well, Teddy, it may be just as well that we never had any children. Just think, one of them might have been musical!*'

The others joined her laughter, enjoying themselves at Edith's expense, and she felt the seep of sadness. Always the outsider. All her life *the soul sits alone and waits for a footstep that never comes.* A lonely marriage followed by the public humiliation of Walter's lifetime refusal to marry. But just for a moment — that first month with Morton — she had believed she might be joined by another, that life might become otherwise. Together they would occupy the republic of the spirit. But she had been deceived — all along he had been a husband and father.

A baby girl. How could he ignore the existence of his own daughter? Quite easily, it would seem. Just another complication to be avoided, a situation that offered no opportunities. That was Morton. Why acknowledge the existence of a child? It might cost him; certainly it would be inconvenient. Even so. It was unfathomable to disown a child.

Rousing herself, Edith rapped against the armrest.

'Oh, Aunt Puss,' broke in Trix. 'You frightened us.'

'Then I apologise.' Briskly smoothing her skirt, she allowed Linky to jump into her lap. At the periphery of her vision, she could sense Walter — the long supine body, head cast in the shadows. Cautiously she ventured, 'Walter?'

'Yes, dear, I'm here.' His voice was tired, a sadness that hadn't existed before. Edith swallowed against her bitter regret, knowing something had been destroyed tonight. Forty years of complicity. While their romantic attachment had been a fabrication, wasn't everything? And forty years of complicity weighed considerably more than a moment of truth. She was sorry for what had been wrecked.

The evening was drawing to a close, and she felt a cloud pass across her heart. Soon they would be apart again. But in the meantime? There was work to be done.

Across from her, Katharine was inspecting her hands, twisting the wedding ring on her finger. She looked up when Edith began to speak. 'Katharine, you spoke earlier of Morton and his wife — Camille, was it?'

Resting her hands, Katharine responded. 'Yes, a wild thing. Morton once threw her out a window. She was upset about his affairs, but they remained lifelong friends. After marrying in Portugal, he returned alone to Paris, moving back with his landlady. That's when he met you.'

Edith nodded, she remembered the small crackling fire in Rosa de Fitz-James's *salon*, the cream silk blinds and walls hung with red damask. She had been in conversation with a playwright when her attention was drawn to a watchful Morton, jolted by his intensity. For her it was a wondrous flowering, the possibility of love. For Morton, she now understood, it was simply the next episode.

Katharine spoke. 'Did you ever meet the landlady?'

'The scheming harridan? No, I never had the pleasure.'

'To begin with he called her a fair-haired siren.'

'I suppose he wrote that to your parents.'

Sybil was astonished. 'Why did he live with a woman who blackmailed him?'

Katharine smiled. 'My brother was not a wealthy man, Mrs Lubbock.'

'But—'

'Expediency,' rapped Edith. 'While it's true Madame Mirecourt blackmailed Morton, I don't believe she charged rent. At least not in a monetary sense.'

Sybil's eyes were wide. 'Madame—?'

'Her stage name. She was a minor actress in vaudeville and musical comedy, and at least seventeen years older than Morton.'

Walter stretched lazily, his voice cutting like a knife. 'Charming who you chose to . . . associate . . . with.' Having conveniently forgotten his own affection for Morton, Walter was now rewriting history to fit this new viewpoint.

The irony was not lost on Edith. She had also been forced to re-evaluate her history with Morton. At the time of their affair, Madame Mirecourt was nothing but a shadow; only later did she picture Morton crossing the gardens of Les Invalides after their own lovemaking, returning to his landlady. And now, in these unexpected circumstances, she must re-imagine Morton as a husband and father.

Trix was shrill with indignation. 'I could never believe you had an affair with a man like that.' She seemed not to care that Katharine was his sister. 'How could you?'

Edith was confused. Trix seemed to be suggesting that she'd always known about the affair, which was impossible. Trix hadn't known about the diary and couldn't know about the affair. Edith shivered as if someone had drifted across her grave. She must think. What were the 'dealings' between Trix and Elisina? Why would—

But Trix was on attack again. 'It was never enough, was it? Nothing was enough for the insatiable Mrs Wharton. All your homes and travel, clothes and famous friends. You always wanted more. Even a—'

'No—'

'—best-selling writer. So why—'

'Exactly. Don't you see?' Edith waited for her niece to collect herself. 'Trix, have you ever contemplated how similar writing is to gardening?'

Trix sat back, glowering.

Edith continued. 'Both take years of learning and great patience, a ruthless eye for the extraneous. Weeds are not so different from adverbs.'

'He was a liar.'

'I didn't know that at first.'

'I still don't understand.'

'Gardening books won't make anyone a gardener. A true gardener can only learn by getting their hands dirty.' It was a terrible metaphor, but it would have to do.

Trix was silent, watchful.

Edith said gently, 'You do understand what I'm saying?'

'You were already a successful writer.'

'No, that's not entirely true.' Until Morton, her best-realised character was Lily Bart, a woman unable to confront her own sexuality, much less act upon it. Always at the point of crossing the threshold, she would withdraw. Edith continued, 'My career as a writer couldn't be sustained within such personal limitations, let alone flourish. A writer cannot observe life from the sidelines.'

Without warning, a moment — pure and vivid — flashed into her mind. They were at the theatre together, watching the beautiful young woman on stage unable to send away her lover. Morton's breath was warm against her ear: *That's something you wouldn't know anything about.*

He was right.

That was all she ever wanted. To know what other women knew. It amazed her even now that, with the exception of Henry, no one ever guessed the truth. She was baffled by their imperceptibility. Surely they must wonder from where her insights into such primitive human passions came? But no. When she wrote *Ethan Frome*, her critics marvelled at her understanding of the poverty-stricken lives of the New England villagers — how could she possibly know such misery? Nobody stopped to question how she could write of the aching need of Ethan every time he passed Mattie Silver's bedroom door. Not even Walter questioned the source of her writing — and, perhaps, given later revelations, this wasn't surprising.

Katharine said, 'It's one thing to break from personal limitations, quite another to choose a man like my brother.'

'It wasn't a choice so much as compulsion.'

'But you came to understand his true nature.'

'My dear, he was your brother. I don't wish to—'

Katharine folded her hands. 'I understand my brother better than anyone.'

No. Katharine was a devoted sister, but Edith had known the intimacy of a lover.

'You still don't understand, do you?' said Katharine steadily.

'I knew your brother better than anyone. Morton and I were lifelong friends. We even caught up shortly before — well, the end.'

She was almost seventy when Morton came to visit her at Pavillon Colombe. Stepping from the carriage, he paused on the platform for a moment. They studied one another, taking in their altered appearances, before he slid smoothly forward to kiss her on both cheeks. She was aware that her figure had thickened, and he would probably think her stout. She was also conscious of her face having slumped, her skin weathered, but she'd never been beautiful. At least she now enjoyed the democracy of old age and the advantage of strong posture and expensive clothes.

And Morton? What of him? Her first impression was of a small man — not stooped; he had remained dapper and upright. But without the vigour of youth he was physically diminished. Edith found this surprising; she had not remembered him as so slight. His hair and moustache were as dark as ever, suspiciously so, as if smoothed with black dubbin. It gave him the cheapened look of an ageing lothario. He let go her hand but continued to absorb her appearance with vivid blue eyes.

She indicated their direction. They would walk; it was no more than a mile through the village of St-Brice. On the way he must tell her all about Paris. What was happening? She had no reason to visit — couldn't stand the place, such a racket — but she loved to hear the news.

He thought this funny: Edith practically lived in Paris! He told her that the city was quickly heading this way, devouring the countryside — so unlike what he'd seen on his previous journey to this area, when he'd travelled past orchards in blossom and budding vegetable gardens. But now? The view was terrible, nothing but dreary backyards and soot-crusted buildings.

They continued out of the station and turned left along a road of small shops, passing a *salon de coiffure* and *boulangerie*. Edith wondered if Morton had deliberately recalled that particular train journey when they had been together in springtime twenty-five years ago. After waving Henry off at the Gare du Nord, they had caught a local train to Montmorency, only a few miles across the forest from here. The fields were fresh with early crops and the newness of spring, reflecting her own sense of beginnings. She had felt young. On finishing luncheon together in a shady courtyard of a small hotel, she had lingered over a cigarette before following Morton up the narrow stairs to a simple room. She remembered a flowering chestnut outside the window, the soft filigree flowers. It was such a long time ago.

Now she turned to Morton, saying blithely — indeed, the sprawl of Paris was abysmal, but she was a countrywoman and would stay that way. Paris could spread all it liked. No business of hers.

Morton gave a quick laugh.

Edith was careful to keep a neutral expression, hiding her distaste. His skin was smooth and leathery, incised with a series of sharp vertical lines. This was not the skin of an ageing gentleman or a weathered labourer; this was a man who had lived the high life in sunny climes. But more shocking were his teeth. Yellow, cracked, several partially broken. She remembered what was said of Morton now: that he lived in reduced circumstances with his common-law wife, a woman who was little more than a charlady. Edith had forgotten this at first, dazzled by his highly polished shoes and cane. Only now did she notice that his clothes, while immaculately pressed, were worn. His glory days were behind him.

Yes, glory days. Morton had done well for himself. His book on international politics, *Problems of Power*, was published sixteen months before the Great War broke out; his timing was perfect.

Morton became a respected political commentator; King George even sought his advice before declaring war.

Then war took up everything. Morton contacted her several times, but she was too busy to see him; her commitments were all-encompassing. They drifted apart though she continued to believe he would turn up when she could be of use. But no, a natural silence fell between them that was to last many years. He never became wealthy, but he was at the disposal of those who were. He consorted with statesmen, generals, and industrialists. He moved among American millionaires and the French aristocracy. In America, he stayed at the Waldorf Astoria, and while at the French Riviera he stayed on board private yachts. When Queen Mary came to Paris, she always invited him to tea.

Edith occasionally heard about his conquests and his victories. They sometimes caught up, but nothing more. Morton had no eternal hold on her. She had gained far more from Morton than she ever lost. And she was never bitter about him; not in the least, always remaining in desultory contact. Without regret or yearning, they became distant friends.

They were met at the front door of her home by Grossie. She was tying the strings of her apron around her girth, wispy grey hair about a reddened face. Morton was delighted to see her, taking her hands: to think the inimitable Miss Gross was still with her mistress! And to finally see Pavillon Colombe!

They went outside to the flagstone terrace, crossing the lawn to a gate overhung with roses. Edith pointed out her potager and cutting garden, the fruit-laden orchard. Morton declared himself delighted by everything. Turning for the house, they stopped by a circular fishpond in a dappled glade, sunlight catching a single jet of water. Morton looked keenly into the pond for goldfish, telling Edith that he didn't require reading glasses.

Such a vain man; he always was.

Showing him into the library, she knew he would appreciate the soft-pastel walls and bowls of freesias. She left the doors open to the terrace, letting in a drifting scent of orange trees. Grossie brought them tea, and they talked of Walter. It was four years since he had died, and Edith was only just emerging from the darkness.

Morton was fulsome in his praise for Edith — she was *still* writing international best-sellers!

Edith was irritated by the implication, acutely aware of her public image as a popular writer disdained by the critics. She didn't care, not after Henry's distress at becoming irrelevant in old age. And only eighteen months after Wall Street crashed, she was relieved to have the money.

Besides, Morton had no right to occupy the artistic high ground. He had long since sold out to the commercial benefits of journalism — which brought her to the point: would he be interested in writing Walter's biography? She could think of no one better. It would be a prestigious undertaking, the biography of such a distinguished American and pre-eminent Parisian. Would he consider it?

'Most certainly.'

But Morton never did write the biography. Several months later he returned with an idea to publish the poems of his friend Bliss Carman. Edith was impressed by his manuscript, but suggested Morton tone down his admiration for the fellow, particularly his photograph. Morton had always been susceptible to beauty — in himself as much as in others. As for Walter's biography, she would have to find somebody else.

Edith remained quiet, lost in memories. She rocked her chair, reaching down to pull the lever, watching her legs slowly rise. It was the most wonderful chair for tired old legs; she could almost drift—

'What on earth is that?' Katharine was staring in astonishment.

'I'm not entirely sure myself,' said Edith truthfully. 'But it's wonderfully comfortable.'

'I believe,' said Percy, 'it's called an American comfort recliner.'

'You *are* a fountain of information,' remarked Edith. 'Who knew we'd be so indebted to your longevity?'

Percy's moustache bristled. 'You always had a thing for modern novelties.'

'Is it comfortable?' persisted Katharine.

'My dear, would you like to try?' Edith was surprised that Katharine hadn't had a chair like this at home, and yet . . . it was difficult to reconcile suburban Katharine with the passionate young woman who wrote poetry in a French convent.

'I would rather hear about your love diary, if you don't mind.'

'Not at all,' said Edith with a breezy insouciance she didn't feel.

'I imagine it's become a literary triumph. The perfect romance recorded by a writer at the peak of her powers.'

Edith felt she was being pulled somewhere she didn't wish to go, but she couldn't ignore Katharine's observation. She nodded, 'That's quite true; even while hopelessly in love I never lost my powers of observation. It was like a part of me was always watching — do you understand?'

'Of course.'

'I confess to idealising our love — I was a writer — almost as if things were taking place outside of myself.' Edith turned to the fire. 'That's why I called my diary *The Life Apart: L'Âme Close.*'

'A romance that was beautifully recorded in a diary and kept forever. A diary you hoped would be discovered, allowing for, as you say, future possibilities.'

Edith nodded.

'And yet,' continued Katharine with relentless penetration, 'your diary *was* discovered, and you're still regarded . . . well—'

'I know,' said Edith quickly, wanting to forestall any elaboration. The novella called her an imperious Victorian.

'Haughty and privileged,' said Percy.

'Puritanical and repressed,' sparkled Sybil. 'And what else? . . .'

Please, no.

'A bad-tempered old crow.'

Ignoring them both, Katharine persisted, 'Why didn't it work? Why didn't the discovery of your diary recording an illicit *grande passion* correct your image?'

Edith had no idea except that it was terribly unjust.

Katharine smiled sympathetically. 'I imagine some historians were excited at the discovery of a secret love diary. It must have caused quite a stir in academic circles.'

'But not enough to shift public perception.'

'No, a secret affair should have caused great excitement in popular culture.'

Edith raised a hand to her hair. It was drawn back severely and secured by a clasp. Her earrings were large but (she knew from experience) unable to disguise her elongated lobes. She sighed. 'Perhaps my image is just too intractable and beyond re-invention.'

'Or perhaps the love diary never reached beyond the shrouds of academia.' Katharine sat back in her chair. 'But now you have another chance. If the novella is successful, it will prompt popular interest in Wharton's private life.'

Katharine's words recharged the excitement Edith had felt

earlier, before everything started going awry. She could feel her energy returning.

Katharine looked curious. 'So how does your diary finish?'

'Like most diaries, it's simply abandoned.'

'That's very convenient.'

Convenient? What an odd word.

'And convenient that you and Morton remained friends.'

'You have no idea about my relationship with your brother.' Was this true? She was no longer sure of anything, and no closer to the truth.

'I know more than you'd find comfortable. Let me ask you a question.' The quietness of Katharine's voice belied the challenge in her eyes. 'In the early summer of 1908, you sailed from Le Havre for New York, leaving behind your new lover after a blissful month together. A month detailed in your diary. But what happened next, after arriving at The Mount? Can you tell me?'

'How could I possibly remember?'

'I'm sure you do.'

'What do *you* think happened?'

'Nothing,' replied Katharine promptly.

What an exasperating woman. Edith said tersely, 'Then why ask?'

Katharine's face was stripped of pretence. 'I'm right, aren't I? Absolutely nothing happened.'

Edith avoided replying. Even now the memory was draining.

The night before her departure, Edith laid her clothes on the bed as if preparing for her own funeral. For the past month, she had been truly alive, love revealing a world she had never known existed.

But now the old obligations were regaining their control, and she was leaving for America.

Seated at the writing desk in her cabin, Edith wrote through the loneliness, beginning her new novel, *The Custom of the Country*, taking grim delight as Undine Spragg stormed onto the page tossing her red-gold hair. Ruthlessly ambitious, Undine considered divorce nothing more than an unpleasant necessity as she climbed her way to the top. And yet, for Edith, divorce went against everything she had been bred to believe; and her brother's divorce had precipitated a tumult of sin, scandal, and financial ruin. But while at her writing desk in the company of Undine, with the sway and shift of the ocean liner beneath her feet, Edith set out to destroy the marriage plot. Undine Spragg was proof that divorce no longer had consequences. It might reduce one's immediate value in the marriage market, yes; but the effect was only temporary. Undine (named after a commercial hair curler) allowed Edith to explore her own conflicting feelings about divorce.

As the ship made its way into port, Edith stood on deck, surveying the New York skyline. The city of her childhood was continually being torn down and rebuilt. She was a stranger to this place, and yet she was an outsider in Paris, like a pendulum that swung between old Europe and the New World. This couldn't continue — that much she knew — but for now duty called. Teddy met her at the port, and together they travelled to The Mount; arriving home, she heard a key turn in her prison-lock. She was trapped in her elegant hilltop home.

Edith's need for Morton became desperate and all-consuming. Her first letters to him were written when the buds on the lime trees were still swelling. Her words were aching and full of love. *Hold me long & close in your thoughts. I shall take up so little room, & it's only there that I'm happy*. Playfully she recalled their first luncheon together, observing other guests, *the moist hippopotamus American with his cucumber-faced female — do you remember?* Often her letters were distraught: *You chained at one end of the world, & I at the other.* But Morton's letters in return were short and unsatisfactory.

She felt the first whisper of fear.

By mid-summer the lime trees were almost touching. Next year they would enmesh into an avenue. Next year. The weight of her life shifted and settled more heavily. It was now three months since she had waved farewell to Morton at Le Havre. How trusting she had been, how confident in her own powers to hold this distinguished lover from a distance. How blissfully unaware of the real torment that was to visit, shrouding her like a slow death: his silence. She continued to write, insistent and despairing. For days she sat at her desk or stood numbly at the window overlooking her garden, trying to find words that might touch him.

Dear, won't you tell me the meaning of this silence?. . . What has brought about such a change? Oh, no matter what it is — only tell me!

. . . didn't you see how my heart broke with the thought that, if I had been younger & prettier, everything might have been different—

But this incomprehensible silence, the sense of your utter indifference to everything that concerns me, has stunned me. It has come so suddenly. . . This is the last time I shall write to you, dear, unless the strange spell is broken. And my last word is one of tenderness for the friend I love — for the lover I worshipped.

She stood up to open a window. The heat was getting worse as the summer dragged on. The lawn was cracked and the plants parched. She couldn't breathe for hay fever. Everything looked dull; even the clematis had died. The door of Teddy's bedroom clicked open and closed, footsteps receding along the gallery.

Her days became solely focused on the mail delivery. Sometimes she almost wished its delay. As long as the mail was yet to arrive, there was hope. She became acutely attuned to the clopping hooves of the postal buggy arriving in the forecourt, knowing the mail was being passed to Alfred, who would place the envelopes on a table in the entrance. Often she would remain in her bedroom, forcing upon herself a dignity of indifference until her secretary brought up the letters. On more restless days, she would emerge from her bedroom, slowing her descent down the staircase. It always ended the same way. A sickening scan through the envelopes, hope persisting until the very last.

Back at the desk, she picked up her pen. Her novel lay untouched and mocking. She could barely make entries in her line-a-day diary, and her secret love diary was a painful joke. She could write nothing but explicit poetry: *Nay, lift me to thy lips, Life, and once more / Pour the wild music through me*. Gone was the usual routine of writing from bed, a frenzy of words and torn-off pages falling to the floor. Even her afternoons, once busy with gardening and hosting guests, were now spent drifting and lethargic in her bedroom. Goodness knows how Anna filled her days; there was nothing for a secretary to type. Certainly she wouldn't let the poor woman see her poetry: . . . *and into my frail flanks, / Into my bursting veins, the whole sea poured / Its spaces and its thunder; and I feared* . . .

Impatient, Edith returned to the window. It was still oppressively hot and airless. The mail should arrive soon. Her only accomplishment now was to caution against hope. There were moments when she almost argued herself into thinking Morton's silence more natural than his continuing to write. She couldn't allow herself to believe he'd forgotten her, that the whole episode had faded from his mind like breath from a mirror.

Edith opened the drawer of her desk and removed a vellum envelope bearing her name in bold, elegant hand. *Mrs Edward Wharton*. She unfolded the letter within. Dear Henry had warned her against Morton, and now his distress at her agony was humbling. Yet he believed, still, that some light would absolutely come to her: *Only sit tight yourself & go through the movements of life. That keeps up our connection with life — I mean of the immediate & apparent life, behind which, all the while, the deeper & darker & the unapparent, in which things really happen to us, learns, under that hygiene, to stay in its place . . . . Live it all through, every inch of it — out of it something valuable will come — but live it ever so quietly; & — je maintiens mon dire — waitingly!*

She placed the letter away and turned for the door. Walter was due tomorrow. She must go through menus with Grossie, pick flowers for the library. Would Walter suspect anything? He always accused her of being overbearing when she was upset: she must watch that. No doubt he would think Teddy the cause of her agitation. Evenings would be awkward, with Walter wanting to hear about Undine. But she had nothing to read except poetry, and she wouldn't be reading erotica in the living-room after dinner — doors open to the terrace, night sounds floating in on a scent of hemlock. She smiled. Only at night did she manage anything close to peace. The sylvan sweetness of the night air, moonlight shining on the big terrace overlooking the lake. And only at night did she make peace with her home and relinquish the feeling of being chained to her destiny.

Smoothing down her dress, she closed the door behind her, stopping to breathe the blessed cool of the gallery. Through an open window, she could hear Teddy down in the forecourt, loud and blustery, followed by the gruff reassurances of Cook. They must be inspecting the motor-car. Her footsteps echoed as she made her way to the staircase. She could hear the sounds of a pony leaving the forecourt. The mail must have arrived. Her heart sped with anticipation as she slowly descended the stairs.

But no. It would be another five months until she heard from Mr Fullerton. She was spending Christmas in a country house in England and had formally written to request the return of her letters. *You have — if they still survive — a few notes & letters of no value to your archives, but which happen to fill a deplorable lacuna in those of their writer.* It was over, that much she knew, but she also knew the importance of protecting her reputation, especially now she understood Morton's true nature.

She was in the drawing-room when a butler brought the letter on a silver tray. She recognised the handwriting (of course she did), tore open the envelope with cold fury — no number of words would absolve him now — and beheld the brevity of his note. *The letters survive, and everything survives.*

Two independent clauses bolted together with a conjunction. He'd graduated summa cum laude from Harvard. It was a hasty cursive script, but she wasn't fooled. His careless tone was well crafted. This was a note as calculated as it was casual. *The letters survive, and everything survives.* Words that promised such love, underwritten with such vengeance. A breezy insouciance. The close-breath of threat. *The letters survive, and everything survives.*

She'd begged him (countless times) to return her letters, but he always refused. What kind of man did that? Henry called him incalculable. Yes. He was also a liar. Blackmail and desire. She would do anything for him, risk everything.

Edith stirred. Opening her eyes, she began to stroke Linky. She had always known that dogs had souls, and it was no surprise to her that Linky was here tonight. They had been such close friends. She looked around the room. The fire was a low crackle. Teddy was in darkness, giving an occasional whimper, while the others were reading. Walter had opened the small volume of James Joyce, and Trix was studying the biography on her life, her shoulders quaking as if holding back laughter, but Edith couldn't be certain.

'Trix, dear?' she said anxiously.

Her niece raised a face ravaged with pain. 'Why? Why are you making us relive our past?'

Edith shook her head wordlessly. Something in the biography — but what?

'Our garden at Bar Harbor, you remember.'

Of course she did. As a young woman Edith had canoed in the bay with Walter, and many years later Trix and Wet-Fish had settled on the island.

Katharine was watching with concern. She appeared torn between wanting to comfort Trix and respecting her privacy. Edith knew Trix would prefer to compose herself, and she sought to divert Katharine with an explanation: 'Reef Point Gardens, Mrs Gerould, was a school for horticulture and gardening. Display gardens and plant collections, a library and herbarium.' Typical Wet-Fish. Anything to commemorate his legacy.

Trix shook quietly.

'Trix?'

'There was a fire. Only two years after I lost Max, a fire razed the property.'

'Oh, my dear.'

'I rebuilt everything at huge expense, for the memory of Max.'

'Of course.'

'But tourism suffered, and I had problems with money. I even had to sell my jewellery.'

Surely not the Cartier diamond chain? Edith had bequeathed her diamonds to Trix.

'I sold the place for a housing development.'

A housing development?

'And destroyed the garden.'

Now Edith understood the lines of sadness in her niece's face, the quiet defeat. When Edith's own garden at Hyères had been destroyed by a frost, she felt she might die from the pain. She could remember the terrible slashing of foliage, the sound of axe-blows, plants torn from soil. It took every last reserve to start again. *How dangerous to care too much even for a garden!*

'Perhaps,' Edith began uncertainly, 'we are too concerned with events after we've gone.'

Trix glared, her face tear-stained. 'That's why we're here — because of your obsession with your reputation.'

'I mean our material possessions; do they matter now?'

'Easy for you, knowing The Mount was restored and your books returned.' Trix shakily turned a page of the biography. 'It says here that I achieved, in my own way, as much as my distinguished aunt.'

Edith was careful to keep composed. Their careers were incomparable.

'How would you feel,' asked Trix, 'if your properties in France were demolished?'

248

'Very upset, I'm sure, although it shouldn't matter.' Which was true, but Edith felt certain her properties were safe. Both had great historical significance long before she bought them.

Closing the book, Trix said bleakly, 'I already knew about your affair well before tonight.'

Edith felt the draught of a terrible truth. It couldn't be — she wouldn't allow it — but the draught was gaining strength. It was like trying to slam a cellar door against a gale-force wind. How could Trix have known about the affair? Only Henry and Grossie knew (and now, she discovered, Katharine's family). The only possibility was Henry, but he admired and respected Trix too much to have told her.

Against her will, Edith raised her head to Trix. 'I don't understand.'

'I heard about it after you — well . . . had *gone*.'

'You saw my love diary?' Edith felt a flicker of hope. Had Elisina shown her the diary? It was conceivable.

Trix shook her head with impatience.

No, that didn't explain Trix calling Morton *a man like that*. In her diary, Edith had shown Morton to be the perfect gentleman and lover. With hard-fought calm, she said, 'Perhaps you should explain.'

'It was something distasteful. A poem.'

Edith's head spun. No — how was that possible? She tried to concentrate, but her mind was in chaos. Trix couldn't have seen the poem, that much she knew, because—

'I can't remember what it was called.' Trix shook her head as if to dislodge something unpleasant. 'Something about a train station.'

'"Terminus",' said Edith quietly. A poem written on her soul.

Trix's face distorted with disgust. 'That's right, it was called "Terminus".'

In the shadowy corner, Teddy's agitated soul stirred. He appeared to be nothing more than a discarded pile of clothes. Edith watched with fear, saying to Katharine, 'Would you mind reading more? I'm keen to hear how the novella concludes.'

Trix looked startled. 'I thought you wanted to hear about the poem?'

'I do, yes, but I'm aware of time passing.' The room already felt sleepy ahead of another chapter. Teddy was rocking, blurred and indistinct, as if withdrawing from the scene. Edith wanted to hear about the poem — of course — but not at the risk of disturbing him again. More time, another chapter, and Teddy might be gone.

(7)

'You need to ring Bernard.' Austen's face was set.

Bernard had been trying to contact Sara for days, but she refused to take his calls. Austen had been making excuses for her — a stomach bug, problems with her phone. But Bernard was getting frantic, and Austen was sick of the whole fucking thing. 'I'll tell him next time, Sara. I'll tell him everything.'

Sara continued to eat, giving more attention to her lunch than it deserved. A shrink-wrapped egg sandwich. They were at a service stop by the autostrada, traffic screaming from behind a line of trees. A bird hopped onto their picnic table and began picking at crumbs. Of course she knew Bernard had to be told. It was three days since Medora's disappearance. She and Austen had stayed in Viterbo until this morning, hoping to hear from her, but nothing. 'I wonder where Medora is now,' said Sara. It was a pleasure to say her name out loud. Almost provocative. She took another bite. Medora was gone; that much she understood.

Austen blinked at the sound of Medora's name. He said evenly, 'Enjoying the money, I imagine.'

Austen knew about the money?

'She duped you, Sara, pure and simple.'

A flash of irritation. 'She worked hard.'

'You're defending her?'

'How did you find out about the money?'

'Medora told me.'

A scream of traffic. A sense of disbelief. Medora told him about the payments? Why would she do that? Placing her sandwich carefully on the wrapper, Sara looked at him. Betrayal made her angry. 'Did you know she pretended to be a landscape architect?'

'Sure.'

Another wave of pain. 'And did you sleep with her?'

'Jesus, Sara.'

Incredible. To have this conversation, saying these words to her husband. This was a new existence, weird and unpredictable — yet the words came so easily. She didn't really believe they slept together, Medora's silky legs parted around Austen. It was repulsive — and Medora would think so, too.

*

Austen crushed his lunch wrapper and headed unsteadily for the bin. So Sara had seen them kiss. Nothing he could do about that. He looked back and saw Sara dab her mouth delicately with the paper towel like it was fine linen. She was taking forever to eat, chewing like a masticating cow. He was taken aback by his revulsion. Especially at her jacket. An ugly green thing that hunched on her shoulders like a sullen animal.

Dusting her fingers, Sara said, 'You know her name's not Medora, don't you?'

His surprise was too quick to conceal, but he countered, 'Let me guess — Persephone?'

A blank stare, and Austen felt a ridiculous sense of loyalty to the girl. So Medora hadn't explained her upbringing — the crazy mother and absent father. But maybe — here was a thought — that wasn't true either. He said, 'Just a guess. What's her name?'

'I've no idea. Medora Manson is a character in *The Age of Innocence*. I looked on the internet.'

No clue to her real identity. No way of tracking her. The concern that had dogged him for days, unspoken and elusive, now took weight. Medora was untrustworthy, but she was also fragile. Why did she leave? So many potential reasons — not all of them flattering to himself — but no definitive answer. He could only hope she was safe.

*

Their hotel room in Rome looked down on a street of expensive shops. Austen leaned on the window railing and watched a woman saunter past, her small dog lifting a leg on a potted tree. A liveried doorman stood in front of a plate-glass window. A black limousine waited in the street. Austen was determined to enjoy his stay. Even their room had touches of Rome — the gilt-post bed and marble bathroom. From the fridge he pulled out a half-magnum. He poured two glasses and carried one into the bathroom, placing it on the vanity. Sara was in the shower, the room filled with steam. Taking up his own glass, he headed for the computer. Time to clear his emails and check their bank accounts. A barrage of Vespas prompted him to check the street. Refilling his glass, he returned to the computer and pulled up Google. Sara was right — Medora Manson was an eccentric old aunt, a penniless itinerant.

Any clues? Not that he could see. He recalled Medora arriving on the terrace that first morning, struggling under her pack. No, she'd had no time to research. Medora was the first name that came to mind. She had admitted having read *The Age of Innocence*. Pulling his chair closer to the desk, he checked Sara's emails. Bernard was still frantic. He didn't care that Sara was unwell, he was building momentum — maybe another Broadway production of *Mirth*. But he needed more material, and fast.

Austen stopped. A series of new blogs, the last posted only an hour ago.

'What is it?' Sara was at the bathroom door wrapped in a white robe.

'Seven more blogs.'

'What?' She was beside him in an instant. 'But how?'

'Must be Medora,' he said, more calmly than he felt. 'The last blog was posted an hour ago.' Clicking on the most recent entry, he watched as words filled the screen. Sara leaned forward and together they began to read.

*

Parc National Office, Hyeres

Yeah, I know, you're expecting a blog from Rome. You want to read about Villa d'Este, the garden of 500 fountains — am I right? One of the most amazing gardens. EVER. But I'm at a government office in the south of France — like, wtf?

Hands up, all the Wharton fans out there. Any guesses why I might be in Hyeres? Ring a bell, anyone? You at the back, speak up!

Didn't Edith Wharton once own a house in Hyeres?

Damn right she did.

So now I'm at Sainte-Claire, her home above the old coastal town of Hyeres. I'm sitting in the sun, and I'm reading a plaque on the wall. It's a quote about how much she loved this place, especially the garden, that it's a paradise like no other, the *Cielo della Quieta* to which the soul aspires when the end of the journey draws near.

She loved this place — like, *really loved* it. Her last 18 years were spent

254

between here and Pavillon Colombe, her home outside Paris. But me? I think she loved this place the best. Once, when the garden got hit by a late frost — a real stinger — and the plants were pretty much wiped out, she went to bed with pneumonia and a broken heart. And, like her garden, she almost didn't survive.

So now. I'm seriously off-piste, and there's gotta be a reason. Why Sainte-Claire? Is there a point to all this? Absolutely. Let's start with the fundamentals. The idea of following in Edith Wharton's footsteps.

Retracing the gardens Edith & Teddy discovered in 1903 is a great idea — only it's too easy. SatNav and the autostrada. Lunch bars at the gas station. And when you get to the gardens? Tearooms and gender-neutral toilet facilities. But Edith took over four months to discover these places. Some of them were literally covered in climbing plants.

And then, guess what? Turns out you guys didn't want gardens anyway — too boring! Why bother when you've got Wikipedia? What you want, apparently, are travel stories with picnics. Cellar-door sales. Hand-painted pottery. Artisan cheese with artisan bread. Locally sourced tomatoes and — well, fuck me — did we get confused with a lifestyle blogger?

Sorry. Let's get back on track. Let's get back to *Edith*. I know, she's not exciting like artisan bread, but bear with me — I think you'll be surprised.

Moving to France just before WWI, her voluntary work was amazing, but she was shattered by the end. And she was finished with Paris (overrun with American soldiers and construction equipment), and bought two properties in rapid succession.

Pavillon Colombe is in the village of St-Brice, some 20 kilometres from central Paris. It was trashed during the war, but she transformed the place into a Whartonian home of elegant restraint. Leafy and gracious. Clipped ilex and deep pools. You get the picture.

But Edith hated spending winter here so . . . *when winter comes, and rain and mud possess the Seine Valley for six months, I fly south to another garden, as stony and soilless as my northern territory is moist and deep with loam.*

Yes people, we're in the south of France. But not showy Cannes or Antibes where most American expats hung out. Edith chose the forgotten corner of Hyeres — and yessir, another make-over. This time an old nunnery built into the ruined walls of a castle above the town.

Let's have a look around, shall we? We'll start with the view.

The terrace looks straight down on medieval Hyeres. Angular orange roofs cling to the hillside. At the base the town becomes spacious and orderly; large 18th-century TB sanitoriums, hotels with formal gardens, palm-lined avenues. Beyond this lie the coastal plains. In Edith's day they were vineyards and orchards, but now it's car parks and light industry warehouses, a massive Casino Marche. Sure, the wide bay looks the same, but it's hard to ignore the coastal strip of housing developments, seaside hotels, and fast-food outlets.

But it's still beautiful, a sweeping bay fringed with silver-blue grass and salt marshes. Wide white beaches and rolling surf, the confetti-fleck of kite surfers. And, in the distance, pale in the salt-glazed air, lie the archipelagos and islands low beneath a wide-curved Mediterranean sky.

*

It was wonderful to hear Medora again. Sara focused on the voice, an intensity suppressed by flat vowels and irony. She wanted to press her palm against the computer screen to bring her closer. She tried to picture Medora. Only an hour ago she had been — where? A dirty café, surrounded by sun-stupid backpackers posting drunken photos. Not Medora, *the archipelagos and islands low beneath a wide-curved Mediterranean sky*. It would be warm in the café. Sara could taste her skin-scent, the golden sheen of sweat, boyish jeans on angular hips. Gripping the chair, she felt a rushing need. She wanted Medora more than anything — to swap this luxury suite for a dirty backstreet hotel with a sagging bed. It was her fault Medora left; what reason did she have to stay? If she could be with Medora right now, it would be different.

'Are you okay?'

Sara squinted into the gold, streaming light. Yes, she loved Medora, but would she see her again? Would she be given another chance?

'Interesting,' said Austen, turning his attention back to the screen. Scrolling down, they continued to read.

*

And the house? Elegant and charming, almost modest. Twin crenulated towers at each end of a low stone building. French doors opening onto a terrace. Picture Edith settled in a wicker chair shaded by two pollarded plane trees (now palm trees), gazing out to the coast. Below the low, curved stone wall the old town tumbles down the hill.

But wait. I'm peering through the dusty windows and thinking — whoa, this doesn't look like Edith, not the woman who said every drawing room should have a candelabra. If I were to put a style on this place, I'd call it Municipal Head Office. Sure, I get that parks staff have modified her home for practical reasons — but *ceiling tiles*? And there's no telling what remains of the original interior under all the cartons and dusty computers. Not to mention fire alarms and partition walls. Let's stay outside.

Ready for the garden? I hope so. But first let's get an overview: the property rises up behind the house in a series of organically shaped terraces carved into the hill face, and continues to climb up to a single ruinous castle tower. Here, finally, the garden gives way to the wild maquis.

Right. Let's go.

Leaving the terrace, you're absolutely *swallowed* by a tropical jungle. Tangled and green. Jewel-sparkling flowers. I'm Indiana Jones pushing along narrow paths to discover pergolas and pavilions, tiny brilliant lawns. I'll tell you this for free: Sainte-Claire is a garden of *topography*. The whole place is ruled by contours and the sheer *heft* of the hillside. Sinuous high stone walls bear the weight of higher gardens while making space for clearings below.

So, people, do we need plant names — yes? Sure. For you I can hop into the garden beds for labels — now, what've we got, salvias and lantana, lilies and iris and, let me see — oh, sure, we've got ourselves some roses! Sniffy-sniff. The air is scented with floral notes — what do we reckon, everyone? Chanel No. 5?

Bold colours hit the canvas like Gaugin gone mad in Tahiti. Flamboyant. Provocative. I'm expecting a tiger soon. Striped orange canna lilies. Castor oil plants. Hibiscus and datura. Palms and plumbago.

We're still going up, team. The terraces are getting narrow. Flowers are exploding like it's fireworks. More plants? Sure. Pixellated flecks of grevillea. Electric-blue echium. Scarlet aloe. Orange montbretia. Righty, I'm over plants, let's talk about something else. You know what? This isn't Mrs Wharton serving up another posh garden. This place is *wild*.

Higher still, and I'm starting to *sweat*. Leaves are looking dusty tucked in the warm-grey rocks. Now the plants are stocky and robust, punctuated by skyrocketing cypress. Question: have you ever foraged on a Provencal hillside for wild herbs? Ever picked gnarly bits of rosemary for the roast lamb? How about silver thyme for the cassoulet? No? Me neither. But that's what it feels like. Spiky grasses and echium. Wild herbs. Plants adapted to climatic extremes. Hot summers, cold winters. A strong coastal wind.

Did you know Edith was a Darwinian? Sure thing. Lily Bart failed to — wait — you what? You haven't read *The House of Mirth*? Come on, people, *keep up*. Lily Bart failed to adapt to her environment and, boy, did she pay the price (plot spoiler) BIG TIME. Here a plant will do the same. Anyone want a free lesson in biogeography? It's right here, folks, just keep your eyes open. Rockeries spring from the stone-exposed hillside. Higher again, and the plants are turning fleshy and succulent, aloes and ice-plants moulding themselves to ground contours.

And finally the tower. We've got ourselves a breeze-blown view of the Med. The upper limit of the garden. It used to segue into the maquis, but now there's an ugly mesh fence. Wind-blown pine needles and plastic bags. Through the fence I can see bits of the old garden: prickly pears and giant American agaves in a scatter of broken glass and crushed stone. Wind-tossed olives, their leaves more silver than green. Crippled judas and soft-needled casuarina.

'Did you ever think to check her passport?' Austen's eyes were still on the screen.

He was worried, she could tell, preoccupied with Medora's disappearance. But was it a paternalistic sense of responsibility or something more?

'Of course not,' she said. 'Who knew she'd vanish?'

'She mentioned someone once. Her anthropology lecturer — funny name. French.'

Was there a point to this?

'Montreux.'

'That's a jazz festival.'

'Something like that.' He scrolled down to another block of text.

*

So. We've done the garden. Now what? Let's start with Edith's legacy — as a gardener and designer. How influential is this place?

Bad news, folks. Around here it's pretty much forgotten. A small mention in a tourist brochure. Nothing at the tourist office. Any garden-lover in Hyeres gets directed right past Sainte-Claire to Saint-Bernard — a Cubist garden 200 metres further up the hill. Can you believe it? People walk right *past* Sainte-Claire and don't even notice — too busy worrying about theories of lineal perspective and who brought the sunscreen.

This would break Edith's heart. Believe me. She never had any time for Saint-Bernard — not the house or the garden, although she liked the owners when they weren't throwing parties, the gramophone making a terrible racket. Younger guests at Sainte-Claire said they were playing Cole Porter, but she didn't care. Jazz, that much she knew.

Worse, her friend Walter was always restless on such nights. Not even W.B. Yeats could hold his attention. Kind of embarrassing, really, Walter going on about whether he should join them up the hill. Pablo Picasso. Jean Cocteau. It was just an act. Everyone knew Walter would get sniggered at if he took his grandiloquent ways up there. Sure, in Antibes his silver tongue and snobbery brought a tinselled class to the showgirl scene — but Saint-Bernard? They'd laugh themselves stupid. Edith thought them a bunch of exhibitionists — not least Dali with that moustache making a hirsute mockery of all others. Drugs. They were all at it.

But you — what? Oh. You really want to see the Cubist garden. Fair enough, be my guest.

Edith would say it's all very loud and modern. Most people think it's just *small*. And simple. A triangular geometry of low plants and concrete. You can definitely try this out at home, folks — a bag of cement and some coloured stones, a few ground covers. Incredible to think the Cubist gardens caused such a fuss at the 1925 Paris Exposition. Garden magazines screamed that the apocalypse had arrived. But in the end I'm guessing Edith would say it's just a conceit. No allowance for the natural rhythms of a garden. No soul or sense of time passing. *No ecology.*

*

Sara shook her head. 'I don't think—' She was interrupted by a buzzing from her handbag — her mobile phone. It was Bernard.
   'You're in France?' His voice was disbelieving.

'Well . . . yes.'

'And?'

She was unsure how to respond.

'Old Newbold is pretty pissed about the blog, Sara.'

'She is?'

'Calling our garden at The Mount sexually repressed. What's that about?'

What the hell had Medora written? Leaning over Austen, she scrolled down.

'Sara?'

'I'm trying to attract a — well, wider audience.'

'Leave that to me. Now what?'

'Sorry?'

'Will you go to Rome?'

'Of course.'

'One last garden, that's all.'

'What about the other blogs? Were they . . . okay?' Sara held her breath. She had no idea what Medora had written.

'Short on detail, but mostly fine.'

She exhaled, light-headed with relief.

Bernard's voice was shadowed with suspicion. 'You were supposed to be unwell — and now you've visited seven gardens and turned up in France. What's going on?'

'Nothing. I don't see the problem.'

'Are you really writing the blogs, Sara?'

'What do you mean?'

'They don't sound like, well—'

'Like a middle-aged woman?'

'You mentioned someone joining you. A couple of weeks back.'

'I don't remember.'

'Okay, so tell me about your final blog. Why are you writing about The Mount?'

More furious scrolling.

'Look, Sara, don't blow it now. Stick to Italy. We're nearly there. Some major sponsors have signed. Even the media is following the story. Just stick to the brief. One more garden, okay?' He rang off with a reminder: make the last blog sharper. Not so much of that garden shit.

*

Oops, sorry. I got off-topic. Where was I?

Oh yes. The legacy (or not) of the gardens at Sainte-Claire. Sometimes it gets name-checked as a notable garden of France, but only because of the Wharton association. Nothing more. Yet French garden historian Michel Racine argues that Edith Wharton is one of the great designers, her work just as good (if not better) than the professionals on the Cote d'Azur. I'm with that guy.

Sure, in plan form Sainte-Claire doesn't announce anything new, and maybe that explains the obscurity. It's no Cubist garden. Nor does it have the mathematically derived perspectives of a classically designed garden. No avenues. No quincunx of pear or bilateral symmetry. Let's face it, this garden is actually a little hard to represent on a plan.

And that, my friends, *is precisely the point.*

This is a garden that responds to the *ecology* of the site, founded on environmental principles that (in 1918) were only just being understood. Edith was familiar with the wilderness movement (she's known to have read

Andrew Jackson Downing and Thoreau, was an admirer of Ruskin). Her niece, landscape architect Beatrix Farrand, was a great friend and admirer of William Robinson, author of *The Wild Garden*. Together they would've discussed the work of landscape architect Frederick Law Olmsted. They had both seen Gertrude Jekyll's naturalistic plantings at Munstead Wood in Surrey.

But wait — there's more. A whole lot more. Because Sainte-Claire is more than a study in ecology. Edith has unleashed all the promise and capacity of the site. Given the freedom of climate, she's gone crazy, creating a garden of unexpected vibrancy and explosiveness.

Really? Is this the same Edith who dressed her characters in whalebone corsets?

Sure. So how can we possibly explain the PASSION of this garden? In this garden she's broken the bounds of her own elegance and good taste. This is pandemonium — almost chaotic. Yessir. This is the garden of a passionate gardener, but, more stunningly, a garden of passion. A garden perfectly adapted to the rocky hillside. Native flora entangles with fecund and sensual exotics. Spiky cacti and flamboyant succulents. The *joie de vivre*! Edith exalts in exuberance and profuse abundance. Sensuous and heavily perfumed. A wild pleasure ground of rocky terraces and theatrical vigour.

Sorry, got a bit carried away. But obviously we've got a question. And the question is this: how can we possibly correlate this place with her sexually repressed Italianate–Victorian garden at The Mount?

I'm gonna leave you with that one.

Sorry about my diversion to France — *excusez-moi!* — but you'll understand in the end when I bring everything together. Because, guess what?
We're going to finish where it all began — at The Mount.

Because, you know what? In a rush to give you all that anecdotal
shit about *lifestyle,* I forgot that Edith's book on Italian gardens is a
great how-to manual. She's got some really good advice on garden
design. So, how's this for an idea: let's run the ruler over her own garden.
Let's see how The Mount measures up. That'll be fun, don'tcha think?

And in the meantime, guys, give my question (see above) all the consideration it deserves . . .

*

'Restieaux,' said Austen, pushing back his chair and going to
stand at the open doors. It was quieter outside now, the shops
closed and Vespas gone; a dry wind was blowing across the
doorway, small dust-eddies in the air. 'Her anthropology lecturer
was Professor Restieaux.'

Sara wanted to remain alone with Medora on the hillside, the
smell of rosemary on salt wind. She heard herself say, 'I don't
understand why it's important.'

'Might tell us what university she went to.'

Sara's attention was jolted by the concrete reality of a
university. Medora seemed so ephemeral, as if she only existed
within the sphere of Sara's consciousness. Even her stories of
sheep breeding seemed unreal. Most likely were.

Austen went back to the computer. His voice was flat when,
after several minutes, he said, 'You should probably see this.'

Sara felt the familiar flare of irritation. Why couldn't he

understand? She didn't need to know more about Medora. She knew everything she needed to know. Medora had constructed the person she wanted to be, and that was enough. God knows, that was something Sara could understand, had done all her life.

With reluctance, she went over to the computer. Her heart thumped, blood rushed to her face. A photograph of Medora — younger, but no less defiant. Her name was Lizzy Field. Below was a photograph of a middle-aged man with a neatly trimmed beard. Professor Restieaux. His specialty was pre-European Polynesian culture. *Murder Accused Goes to Trial.*

Austen clicked on a link.

At first it was believed that his wife, Henrietta Restieaux, died of natural causes — but of what, exactly? An autopsy revealed the presence of an acrylamide monomer. She had been poisoned. Professor Restieaux was arrested.

It was established that Professor Restieaux had been having an affair with a graduate student. Her name was Lizzy Field. According to friends, the affair had been going on for more than a year. Professor Restieaux denied it.

He was charged with murder.

Now it was suggested that Lizzy may have been responsible. Sources said that she was obsessed, had wanted to marry the professor, pestering him to leave his wife. Most likely Lizzy poisoned Henrietta Restieaux. The girl was delusional. Had no sense of reality.

The police believed that Lizzy was involved, that she had encouraged Professor Restieaux to kill his wife. She was charged as an accomplice. Lizzy Field denied everything. There was another photograph of her. She seemed to be getting younger.

There were stories. It was said that Lizzy was a Goth, interested in satanism, that she cut herself. After her first court appearance, the charges were withdrawn. Insufficient evidence. The police were frustrated. They weren't looking for anyone else in connection to the crime.

The court trial of Professor Restieaux went ahead the following year. He was found guilty of murder and sentenced to seventeen years without parole. The stories of Lizzy Field continued: that she was promiscuous and known to take drugs. But there were no more photographs. She seemed to be disappearing.

It was reported that Professor Restieaux had the right to appeal and, according to his lawyer, would be availing himself of this judicial right. But the night before Professor Restieaux was to be transferred to a high-security prison, he was found hanging in his cell. Of Lizzy Field, nothing more was said.

*

That night he dreamed of her. She was sparkling with malice. He reached to pull her close, but her silk dress slipped through his fingers. She was dancing in the light, and he saw that she held a glass bottle, shards of colour revolving through the sky. They were drenched in a stain of emerald and indigo. Again he tried to catch hold, but she slipped away, tossing in waves of strobing light. With a final lurch he caught her, and they tumbled to the floor. She lay under him, a gleam of triumph in her eyes, arms above her head. She began to move against him. Brilliant light swept their bodies, pulsing and rhythmic. His body moved harder, a convulsion that overtook him, tumbling him into shallow waves that crashed against the shore. He heard someone cry out. Clutching at the silk dress, he found it empty. She was gone. Only her laughter remained. Straining to breathe, he felt himself being strangled. Slowly and deliberately. His lungs compressed as the dress wrung itself more tightly, snaking around his body.

He jolted upright, hauling in cool air, running a hand through his hair. His heart was hammering, an echo inside his chest. He was confused. He couldn't remember where he was. It took several moments until parts of the room assembled themselves into coherency. Their hotel room in Rome. He remembered: Medora was gone. Then the revelations of yesterday. The poisoned wife and sensational court case, the suicide of the professor and, always, the vanishing and predatory Lizzy Field. About to get out of bed, Austen found himself caught in ropes of sheet. He was wet, and not only with sweat. He felt a wave of shame. He waited for his heart to settle. Beside him, Sara faced away, no pretext of sleep. Quietly he eased himself back, staring at the ceiling, grit forming behind his eyelids.

It was the sound of a cellphone that eventually woke him. He felt hungover, disoriented — at first he thought he was at work. He heard Sara answer, a moment's silence, her murmured response. He wasn't sure what alerted him, perhaps her stillness. He sat up before another wave of shame as he remembered the dream.

Sara was looking at her phone on the table. 'That was Medora,' she said absently. 'She arrived in Rome last night and wanted to know our hotel. She'll call by later.'

CHAPTER IX

Sainte-Claire: what a blessing to relive the beauty of her country home. The place was so clear to her: the classic simplicity of a book-filled room, long curtains falling from iron rods, the Persian rugs and vases of flowers, a staircase with wrought handrails. Sainte-Claire had been a home of great happiness when her life was drawing to a close.

Yet something disturbed her while Katharine was reading, something about her home — a question. Katharine read on, and Edith drifted into memory, breathing in the thyme-salt wind. Her question — yes, she remembered now.

What were ceiling tiles?

About to speak, she heard Walter say, 'Damned nonsense, don't know why we bother.'

Poor Walter, mocked for his grandiloquent ways: he would hate that. But Edith had enjoyed hearing of his silver tongue bringing a tinselled class to the showgirl scene. That was Walter exactly!

'I agree,' said Trix. 'We should have burnt the novella at the start, but it's too late now, the damage is done.'

Edith felt her nerves rattle. Before the latest reading, they had been discussing 'Terminus', and it was imperative that she understand. Trix knew about the poem — but how? There had only been one copy — unpublished (of course!) — and she had burnt it, along with all Morton's letters. So how could . . . oh, God, Edith sank back in despair. Only one copy, and she had loaned it to Morton. Such blind trusting faith! Morton had the manners and grooming of a gentleman; but (she now understood) he had taken her poem home and, while sitting by lamplight with a fresh sheet of paper, had copied out her work, word for word. For his own purposes. 'Terminus' had continued to exist after she destroyed the original. But how could Trix know about the poem? She had no link with Morton — the thought was laughable if it weren't so horrifying.

Tentatively, Edith began. 'Trix, about my poem. I—'

'Oh, don't worry,' she drawled. 'I doubt it survived.'

Edith straightened with indignation. She would not have her work dismissed in such a tone. Coolly, she said, 'I'm not worried, Trix, I remember every word.' Not her finest work perhaps, but certainly her most raw, penned with blood and irony.

Now she noticed that Katharine was restless, the file back on her lap. Edith felt panicked — did she have the poem? It was incomprehensible. Morton would never give something so disturbing to his little sister. With urgency, she demanded of Katharine: 'Do you have the poem?'

'No, I never saw it.'

Edith's relief was short-lived. There was something in Katharine's demeanour that compelled her to probe: 'But you heard of it?' She watched closely as if everything tonight hinged on the coming words.

'Oh yes. I knew all about "Terminus".'

The gentle rock of Edith's chair brought no comfort. Two other women in the room tonight knew about 'Terminus'. Edith could feel herself moving closer to the flame of truth, the heat of the furnace on her cheeks. She must step closer, knowing it might cut her last ties with Walter. Quietly, she said, 'Go on.'

Katharine hesitated, but at Edith's encouraging nod she said, 'It was written in the aftermath of making love. It takes place in a railway hotel — I believe it was the Charing Cross Hotel in London.'

Such a detail: as if the scene of the offence added to the guilt of the couple.

'So it's true,' murmured Trix.

Edith flashed: 'Must it be true? Do you really think I spent a night in a railway hotel with Morton, and afterwards, while lying in soiled sheets, wrote a poem? Does that sound like me?' This was her old defence. She had always been protected by her age and her past — and the image her mirror gave back to her.

There was bitterness in Trix's reply. 'You were happy enough to have your affair used for promotional purposes. Who knows what else you're capable of?'

'You do understand that I wrote fiction? Imagine if all my poetry were mistaken for being autobiographical. You know, I once wrote of a hermit and a wild woman.' Edith tried to laugh, but the sound died, and her face became a rictus. She wished to discover the truth — yes, but not at the expense of a confession; she would continue to defend herself.

'Fiction!' laughed Sybil viciously. 'The only way you could experience life.'

'No,' responded Katharine. 'Edith Wharton — the writer — was a woman who risked everything.' Directly to Edith, she said, 'Am I right?'

Edith held herself against the charge, knowing she was losing ground. She was being propelled back into her past, to a place to which she wished never to return.

'She was a writer who experienced the beauty of love, but also the degradation. A woman who was made to pay with servility and humiliation. A woman who survived.'

Laying a hand on Linky, Edith remembered what she had written in her diary: *I have drunk of the wine of life at last, I have known the thing best worth knowing, I have been warmed through and through, never to grow quite cold again until the end.*

'Am I right, Edith?'

Slowly nodding, her tears began to fall.

After a torturous summer at The Mount, she was finally leaving for Paris. The prospect of seeing Morton again was terrible. She arranged to visit England first, spending a month with old friends.

Her trip was a triumph, every day crowded with friends and accomplices. Everyone wanted a piece of Mrs Wharton, the celebrated and successful American writer. England was a whirlwind of parties and engagements. Henry took her to meet George Meredith, her literary hero. She partied at Clivedon with the young Waldorf Astors. J.M. Barrie accompanied her to his latest production at the West End. It was exhilarating to feel so *esteemed*. She managed to push Morton to the back of her mind until, while staying in a large country home, she received his message.

Arriving once again in Paris, all her trepidation and confusion returned. In her mind she played and replayed the coming confrontation: Morton must acknowledge her pain at being so abruptly and inexplicably cut. He must be made to understand her aching uncertainty. She was even prepared to apologise — perhaps he'd found her awkward and inarticulate? It was true; she'd been so afraid, had felt everything too deeply. But most of all she wanted Morton's love — and, if that weren't possible, she would settle for his friendship; anything but his silence.

Ahead of their meeting, she sought to disguise her fear. She schooled herself to be dignified, adopting a deportment of calm indignation: Morton had behaved abominably, but she was prepared to give him a second chance (of course!) — but he must work to regain her forgiveness and trust.

How misguided she was.

Nothing could have prepared her for the humiliation. Morton was glacial, contemptuous; he saw no reason to be contrite.

Reeling with shock, she became imperious and shrill. He couldn't treat her like this — a woman such as herself!

Morton made no effort to hide his distaste; she did herself no favours by behaving in such a manner.

Edith was appalled by his indifference. Could this be the same lover to whom she'd gifted her innermost self? Anguished, she tried to reason with him. Surely he must understand how she felt?

No, Morton wasn't interested in the past — what was the point? Edith had made her choice. She was here now, wasn't she?

In the blaze of his contempt, she shrank into submission.

Yes, this was a new phase in their relationship: one of desperate humiliation. Despite the lies, this was a sexual union stripped of all pretence: she no longer expected to be treated with dignity or respect but was grateful for anything he chose to give. She came to understand these new terms and to abide by them. She had no hold over Morton, no right to expect anything more than he chose to give. When he suggested a night together in a railway hotel, she was sick with gratitude.

How could she willingly subject herself to such degradation? Because she had no choice. She simply wanted to participate in this common human experience. How could she not have him? The alternative was so much worse: for the rest of her life she would write of characters who did not take their chance at love; were not bold enough for the journey, retreating into a rage of conformity, unable to spend a night in a railway hotel with their lover.

The memory of it was more vivid than anything in the room tonight. Every detail was branded on her mind with startling reality. The faded bedcover, grey sheets starched and wrung; watching Morton from the bed with pleasure. He turned from the mirror to smile, everything about him radiating satisfaction. His moustache glistened black as boot polish; his blue eyes were all indulgence and triumph. Now he applied himself to the mirror again, fussing with his cravat and smoothing imaginary creases from his crisp white *plastron*.

Oh, God, she thought, falling back against the bolstered pillows. *And the low wide bed, as rutted and worn as a high-road, / The bed with its soot-sodden chintz, the grime of its brasses.* Languid with pleasure, she gazed about the room, taking in the grimy carpet and wallpaper in the morning light. The black marble mantelpiece, the clock with a gilt allegory under a dusty bell, the high-bolstered brown-counterpane bed, the framed card of printed rules under the electric light switch. She wasn't the least disheartened by her surroundings. Far from it: to her writer's eye it was perfect.

Suite 92, Charing Cross Hotel.

She could feel the rumble of a train deep within the bowels of the building, the shriek of a departure from below her window. *The shaking and shrieking of trains, the night-long shudder of traffic . . . .* Only now did she become aware that it was still raining. It had rained all night. *The black rain of midnight pelted the roof of the station.* Rising from the bed, she pulled tight the belt of her night robe and crossed to where rain streamed against the high-perched windows, reducing their vast prospect of roofs and chimneys to a black oily huddle and filling the room with the drab twilight of an underground aquarium. She could see a clock in a tall building beyond the railway.

Seating herself at the writing desk, she began to make order of the strewn sheets of paper. She heard Morton go through to his own room, collecting his suitcase and belongings. She switched on the red lamp, flushing the commonplace room with magical shadows. Now Morton was back in front of the mirror and pulling on his jacket. He flicked an imaginary speck and tugged at his sleeves. *Here, in this self-same glass, while you helped me to loosen my dress, / And the shadow-mouths melted to one . . . .* His case was placed on the armchair by the fireplace. Edith studied the blotched marble top of the chest of drawers, the electrolier overhead. She committed to memory everything about this dull and featureless room, allowing it to take possession in her mind, every detail pressing itself on her notice with the familiarity of an accidental confidant. Whichever way she turned, she felt the nudge of a transient intimacy. *Yes, all this through the room, the passive and featureless room, / Must have flowed with the rise and fall of the human unceasing current, / And lying there hushed in your arms, as the waves of rapture receded, / And far down the margin of being we heard the low beat of the soul . . . .*

Now Morton's mouth was pressed against her neck. 'The insatiable Mrs Wharton,' he murmured, and she smiled in triumph. He must leave now, he said regretfully. Henry would be waiting downstairs, ready to accompany him to Waterloo. But he would write as soon as he reached America — he promised.

She did not respond.

'Edith? Do you believe me?'

'Of course.' Scepticism flooded her body like molten lead. She felt the draught of his departure but did not wait to hear the door close. Taking up her pen, she began to write.

Terminus

Wonderful was the long secret night you gave me, my Lover,
Palm to palm, breast to breast in the gloom. The faint red lamp
Flushing with magical shadows the common-place room of the inn,
With its dull impersonal furniture, kindled a mystic flame
In the heart of the swinging mirror, the glass that has seen
Faces innumerous and vague of the endless travelling automata
Whirled down the ways of the world like dust-eddies swept through a street,
Faces indifferent or weary, frowns of impatience or pain,
Smiles (if such there were ever) like your smile and mine when they met
Here, in this self-same glass, while you helped me to loosen my dress,
And the shadow-mouths melted to one, like sea-birds that meet in a wave—
Such smiles, yes, such smiles the mirror perhaps has reflected;
And the low wide bed, as rutted and worn as a high-road,
The bed with its soot-sodden chintz, the grime of its brasses,
That has borne the weight of fagged bodies, dust-stained, averted in sleep,
The hurried, the restless, the aimless — perchance it has also thrilled
With the pressure of bodies ecstatic, bodies like ours,
Seeking each other's souls in the depths of unfathomed caresses,
And through the long windings of passion emerging again to the stars . . .
Yes, all this through the room, the passive and featureless room,
Must have flowed with the rise and fall of the human unceasing current;
And lying there hushed in your arms, as the waves of rapture receded,
And far down the margin of being we heard the low beat of the soul,
I was glad as I thought of those others, the nameless, the many,
Who perhaps thus had lain and loved for an hour on the brink of the world,
Secret and fast in the heart of the whirlwind of travel,
The shaking and shrieking of trains, the night-long shudder of traffic;
Thus, like us they have lain and felt, breast to breast in the dark,
The fiery rain of possession descend on their limbs while outside
The black rain of midnight pelted the roof of the station;

And thus some woman like me, waking alone before dawn,
While her lover slept, as I woke and heard the calm stir of your breathing,
Some woman has heard as I heard the farewell shriek of the trains
Crying good-bye to the city and staggering out into darkness,
And shaken at heart has thought: 'So must we forth in the darkness,
Sped down the fixed rail of habit by the hand of implacable fate—
So shall we issue to life, and the rain, and the dull dark dawning;
You to the wide flare of cities, with windy garlands and shouting,
Carrying to populous places the freight of holiday throngs;
I, by waste land and stretches of low-skied marsh,
To a harbourless wind-bitten shore, where a dull town moulders and shrinks,
And its roofs fall in, and the sluggish feet of the hours
Are printed in grass in its streets; and between the featureless houses
Languid the town-folk glide to stare at the entering train,
The train from which no one descends; till one pale evening of winter,
When it halts on the edge of the town, see, the houses have turned into grave-stones,
The streets are the grassy paths between the low roofs of the dead;
And as the train glides in ghosts stand by the doors of the carriages;
And scarcely the difference is felt — yes, such is the life I return to . . . !'
Thus may another have thought; thus, as I turned, may have turned
To the sleeping lips at her side, to drink, as I drank there, oblivion.

The room was deathly quiet. Edith watched the bulbs above gently pulse. She heard the rustle of silk on the sofa, and beside her Walter stretched creakily. It was Katharine who spoke first, saying, 'I knew the poem existed, but never imagined I would hear it recited by the author. It was a great privilege.'

'Are we still supposed to believe it's fiction?' quivered Sybil.

Edith consulted the clock: a quarter to midnight.

'Of course it's not fiction,' said Katharine.

'So why pretend otherwise?' Sybil pressed her lips together with distain.

Edith allowed Katharine to answer. 'Because it contradicts the narrative. A spring romance in Paris doesn't usually involve a railway hotel in London. Am I right, Edith?'

'I'm no longer sure,' she said, slow with lethargy. 'I seem to have lost control over my own story.'

'An idealised story.'

'I prefer to call it abridged, or possibly truncated — that would be accurate.'

'But I don't see', said Trix, 'how you could be so blind. You still haven't considered how I came to hear about the poem.'

No, Edith hadn't considered this, nor did she want to. The pieces lay scattered in her mind. With enough application she could put them together — but, dear God, she would rather not.

'Oh, for heaven's sake,' snapped Sybil, 'I'm tired of that poem. We're supposed to be reading the novella. I want to know what happens next.'

'She's right,' said Percy.

Edith appealed to Katharine. 'Would you mind?' They must be nearing the end. She was worried about returning to The Mount, but it was easier than trying to order the confusion in her head.

(8)

It was late morning when Medora finally knocked on the hotel-room door. Sara was in a state of bored agitation. She had spent the morning alone, Austen having left hours ago. He couldn't see the point of waiting. When the knock finally came, she opened the door and was struck by how much smaller Medora seemed. She wore a red-checked lumber shirt and the same worn jeans, oblivious, it seemed, to the heat. Sara stood back so the girl could pass, closing her eyes at the familiar scent.

If she expected Medora to be contrite, she expected too much. Not even a careless nonchalance. Nothing. The girl was oblivious to the distress caused. 'Nice room,' she said, heading for the balcony. She inspected the view, then she was back inside, hunting through the fridge. 'Did you read the blogs?' she asked as she cracked open a bottle of orange juice.

Sara nodded. Medora had posted seven more gardens, each blog peppered with anecdotes — a fashion shoot by a fountain, a sudden thunderstorm. Her imagination was boundless. Her name wasn't even Medora. 'I'll get your money today,' Sara heard herself promise. 'You've worked so hard.'

'Don't bother,' said Medora, her hand trailing along a gilded chair.

'Please—'

'I said no.'

Sara felt the sting of her words. 'At least let me pay for the last garden. Villa d'Este. I hoped we could visit this afternoon.'

'You're kidding, right?' Medora dropped into the chair.

'I've booked a driver.'

Medora tipped back her head and finished the orange juice.

'We were worried,' said Sara. 'We felt responsible.'

Medora made no response.

Sara recalled the sensational headlines, the lurid details. Medora seemed so small. 'Did you really go to France?'

Medora looked surprised. 'Of course.'

'You promised a revelation in the final blog.'

'Just a theory.'

Sara began collecting her books and camera, a jacket and handbag. There was only just time for lunch before their car was due.

*

High above Rome, the fresh air made Sara spin, and it seemed Medora felt the same way, laughing as the driver raced up hairpin bends. Now they were standing in front of the villa, the garden falling steeply away, under a sky whitewashed with heat. After the turmoil of the past few days, Sara felt almost delirious — the sheer improbability of their being together, her own power of survival. And pure, simple joy. She watched Medora shuck off her lumber shirt to reveal a white top and a band of olive skin above her jeans. Catching Sara's gaze, Medora raised her eyebrows mockingly.

Sara felt alive to everything. Being with Medora gave the world a cinematic brilliance, magical and surreal. Even Medora's powers of description seemed to have infused her. Down a flight of stairs, they dropped into bruise-blue shadow and silence, glinting shafts of light. Sara pushed her notebook into her bag, not wanting to break the enchantment. She could feel the age and mystery of the garden, the ghosts of the past. Cardinal d'Este barking orders to his architect. Henry James struggling for breath. Piano notes from an open window as Franz Liszt tortured over *Fountains of Villa D'Este*.

Water imprinted every scene. Even out of view, the sound of water was like piped music. Fishponds lay in glassy sheets, the Ovato Fountain played a crashing crescendo, the shaded walk of one hundred fountains slow-dripped onto a fringe of ferns. The soft-stone garden crumbled into tangled undergrowth. And Rome was a constant presence, a distant, outspread glory beneath the red haze. Sara couldn't remember having ever felt so alive. She watched herself: movements overly deliberate, her world saturated with the sense of icy water and moss, the crumbling, fallen statues. Medora seemed just as sensitive to the garden, her hushed voice and blatant stare, blunt fingers lingering on stone. In the black shade of a cypress she laid a hand on Sara's bare arm, and it burned her skin.

Leaving the garden, they instructed the driver to drop them near the Spanish Steps. Sara wanted to see the Trevi Fountain, and Medora's hotel was close by. They stopped by the fountain, and Sara searched in her purse for a coin, tossing it into the water, eyes closed. When she opened them, Medora was standing so close she could see the radiating flecks in her irises.

'What did you wish for?'

'I didn't,' said Sara. 'I never wish for anything.'

The quirk of a smile.

The crowd swarmed around them like a maelstrom, a chaos of Vespas and shouting hawkers. It had the effect of isolation. They were disembodied from the crowd, stranded in a slipstream. Together alone.

'Would you like coffee?' said Sara, tongue-tied and clumsy.

Medora paused with silent intensity.

Sara was aware of this moment taking weight, that a conclusion was imminent — one way or another. That everything depended on her. Again the sense of heightened reality. Awareness of a moment that would be revisited time and again. That its meaning would become apparent later when pieced together in a larger picture.

Medora's eyes darkened. 'My room's nearby.'

This was the moment Sara had played so often in her mind. But now she was a confusion of thoughts. A failure of words.

Medora waited.

Sara's anger flared and died. Why did Medora make everything so difficult? 'I'd like that,' she heard herself say. 'To see your room.' Stupid. Like a mother wanting to see her daughter's college dorm.

'That's not what I'm saying.'

The honesty of Medora's reply stripped Sara of all self-delusion. She was painfully aware of how she must look, her hair frizz-dried with the heat and dust of Rome. She knew she was unpleasantly flushed, her body soft and freckled. Never had she felt so unattractive, standing next to beautiful Medora. Or so old. Never had life seemed so beyond her reach.

Drawing a deep breath, Sara watched herself. With cool detachment, she observed that her desire for Medora made her girlish and naïve. She knew Medora would discard her afterwards without a second thought. Medora would destroy her and walk away. And this was a pain Sara could endure, to lose everything — if only Medora would suffer as well. But no, the girl was untouchable.

Despair gave Sara courage. She leaned forward, so close she could feel the forcefield holding them apart. Medora blocked the light and silenced the crowd. Sara continued to press against the repelling forces. Their lips touched and parted. She mouth-breathed the scent of Medora, running her tongue lightly inside the rim of her lips. A touch of her hair. Then slowly she withdrew, the memory imprinted. She watched Medora's eyes open, somnolent and sleep-drugged. Sara smiled and thought, *This is like being happy.* She allowed her fingers to lightly feather the beautiful cheek.

The storm had passed, the open window had closed. She was safe from herself. She would not be whirled down the ways of the world like dust-eddies swept through a street. Stepping back, she let the surging crowd drag them apart, Medora's face fading like breath on a mirror.

*

Austen knew she would text. He'd already had a few beers in a small dark bar where the waiter insisted on speaking English. He wandered outside, the late sun bleached and golden. Medora was standing by the Trevi Fountain in jeans and a white tee-shirt. She seemed preoccupied, removed. Austen had no problem with that. He took her back to his bar, and the waiter treated them like old friends. After that they ate pizza and walked the crowded footpaths. From an upstairs window came the sound of a television newsreader and the crash of kitchen pots. He wiped warm cheese from his mouth and pointed to a night market. He bought her a red dress and a sketch of the Trevi Fountain. She got changed in the bathroom of another bar while he ordered dirty martinis. She returned, beautiful and exotic, flashing a smile at the barman. She threw back her drink, set the glass on the marble counter, and ordered another.

After that they found themselves in a crowded burlesque show. They stood at the back, Austen clutching a beer. The fat lady was singing, but the show wasn't over. He tried to explain, but Medora couldn't hear. He indicated the door, and she nodded. They headed along a lane, creeping into the back row of a picture theatre. *La Dolce Vita*. Austen went to sleep with his head on her bare shoulder. She woke him before the end, and they crept out again, along a lane to a nightclub. Austen thought he might have dreamt this scene before, but not so loud. Medora shouted in his ear, offering him some pills, but he shook his head. He watched her dance. She had her eyes shut, wafting like an underwater plant. Then her eyes flicked open, and she was gone.

He followed her along another lane, wondering how she knew her way around. She stopped, pulled open a glass door, and they were in a small hotel foyer. A young man at the counter was asleep, head on his arms. A staircase spiralled tightly up into the dark. He followed her, pressing himself to one side as a couple came down. She went along a short corridor and unlocked a door, leading him inside. The door closed, and Austen leaned back for support. He tried to focus on the mosaic floor, could hear Medora in the bathroom. He took several steps towards the bed, lumpy and worn, fell forward, relieved at the embrace of soft black oblivion. The dream came to him again, Medora dancing in the light. This time her dress was red. Her skin was bare, and his hands caught the curve of her back. Her laugh was soft and low. He woke up, hard and urgent. Pinning back her hands, he caught her laughter in his mouth.

He woke in the morning with a headache that locked his eyes shut. He reached for her, but the bed was empty. Shock hit like cold water. He sat up, forcing his eyes open against the pain. She was gone. The room was empty. Except for the red dress. It hung on a coat hanger at the window, casting a diaphanous ruby glow over the shabby room. Not until he was dressed and letting himself out did he see the message pencilled on the chipped door. *Call me, LF xxx*

*

Sara was awake all night. She showered at four in the morning and went back to bed. Hugging herself, she watched the sky turn from violet to gold. She knew without doubt that Medora was beyond reach. Sara had been given a choice — between safety and chaos. How could she change the habit of a lifetime?

Only now did she understand that what began as self-preservation amid the currents of so many cultures had contorted. Her life was an act of self-justification, a self-supporting scaffold. *Aren't our children lucky — the whole world is their playground!* She survived, but it was at a terrible cost. Even when the children lived at home, they were lost to her, keeping their bedroom doors closed. And when they left home, Sara hadn't minded — it was the natural course of things; she was inoculated against loss. *If there's one thing I've learnt, it's resilience!*

She hadn't started this way, it had been a gradual process, but one scene stayed with her: Alice having a late-night asthma attack in Lagos. It was terrifying. Austen was away (of course, he was always away), and they rushed to an after-hours medical centre. Sara argued with the doctor, who wanted to inject Alice with a used needle. She had screamed at him, lunging while her daughter convulsed on the bed. But, shockingly, Sara stopped, hit by ice-clear clarity like the blast from a freezer. And the sense of stepping back, the way death is sometimes described. A long hallway. The act of walking away from everyone she loved.

Calmly she bundled Alice in her arms with no idea where they would go next. And above them the fan revolved slowly. Green walls ran with condensate. A scatter of needles lay in a metal tray.

Now Sara could feel her self-contempt growing. Her smug sense of accomplishment at every suppressed feeling, pleasure when things didn't hurt. Sara felt a loathing for her life conducted at such distance. She knew in the coming days she would lay out her failings for closer inspection. Hold every lost moment to the light, turning it over with wonder. Grief lay ahead.

She swung from the bed and crossed to the full-length windows, long sheers billowing softly in the golden light of Rome. Was this the moment when everything changed? Probably not. But she could make herself a promise: to never again live by proxy, protected by her own detachment. To never congratulate herself on self-preservation. She would reach out to her children, make small offerings of connection, knowing rejection was possible. If Alice agreed, they could visit Hong Kong, and maybe she could try ringing Matthew once a week. And Hugo? What could she do with him? He was so vulnerable, his life reckless and chaotic. He could so easily destroy himself, taking her with him. She had always understood this. Hugo was the reason she continued to steel herself against life. She couldn't save Hugo, but did she have the strength to try? She didn't know. She didn't have all the answers, but this much she did know: she would engage with her life and determine her future.

Sara made another cup of tea and began to pack. She took her clothes from their hangers, watching herself fold them to perfection. Everything outside this room had no bearing. No meaning and no relevance. She wouldn't think about Austen. She wouldn't speculate on where he was, how he spent the night.

She had made her choice and would live with it. But it changed everything. She would never forget this feeling of loss.

She had just finished another cup of tea when a card slotted into the door, and Austen entered the room. The door closed behind him. He was unshaven, eyes bloodshot. Any closer and she would know the smell of alcohol and deceit. Of musky olive skin. Pulling tight her satin wrap, she said, 'The final blog, it's been posted.'

*

Righty. We're at the business end of things now. I've got myself packed and heading home. Thanks, guys, it's been a blast.

But first, we've got a job to do — remember? We're gonna run a ruler over The Mount, see if Edith lives up to her own diktat, or will she be hoisted by her own petard?

At the time of publication, *Italian Villas and Their Gardens* was the first of many about Italian gardens, but Edith's book is distinguished by a perceptive understanding of the gardens and (obviously) its author's ability to communicate. Edith's writing is evocative but not romantic — really, you gotta see some of the stuff written at this time. She's briskly informative but not academic. In short, her book is boring but a great achievement.

1903 and she's back at The Mount, about to write the book. She's exhausted — it was a massive exercise in detective work, logistics, and bravura — but she's got every reason to be excited. Her new home is finished, and her career as a novelist fast becoming a reality. Plus she's planning her Italian sunken garden. But she's also got problems.

A drought has wiped out a heap of planting, the head gardener is drunk in the garden shed (he's been in there a while), and Teddy's got her worried. It's been a big trip, and he's starting to act a bit, well, *weird*.

And just one other teeny-weeny problem.

Edith's just realised the gardens at The Mount are a design fail. No kidding. Total. Epic. Fail.

I know, I know. You're outraged (especially the garden committee) — but please, bear with me a bit longer . . . .

Let's start with her own words. She's sitting upstairs at her desk over-looking the grounds of The Mount. She's just finished writing a letter, adding that her garden is a mess with stunted plants and bald patches: *I try to console myself by writing about Italian gardens instead of looking at my own.* And now it's back to business; she's got a textbook to finish. First Edith lists all the stuff to avoid: you can forget sundials and marble benches, they're just garden 'effects'. Ditto twisted columns and amputated statues. And definitely no sarcophagus! (I know, right? Only Edith could ask us not to put a sarcophagus in the garden.) She's saying it straight: an Italian garden is more than garden features from Pottery Barn.

So what *does* she suggest for a well-designed garden at home?

That a piece of ground be laid out and planted on the principles of the old garden craft. (You can tell I'm paraphrasing.) This won't be an Italian garden in the literal sense, but something far better, a garden as well adapted to its surroundings as the models that inspired it. Composition is everything: the subtle beauty of planning to utilise natural advantages of the site with little perceptible strain (still channelling Edith). We're looking for a sense of the informing spirit, an understanding of the gardener's purpose. We want a quality of inevitableness, as if to ask — how could this garden be otherwise? We want a garden that is born, not built.

Great. So now she puts down her pen. She's looking out the upstairs window — and what does she see? (Remember: The Mount is perched on a small rise.) Looking down, the land kind of slides away. It's like a municipal recreation ground designed by a guy with a diploma in turf management. But guess what? Edith's just written that grass should always be used sparingly, set jewel-like within clipped hedges or statue-crowned walls. Use lawn judiciously, and you'll appreciate it all the more. Such wise words — only, Edith's garden looks like a nine-hole golf course, and she's thinking holy fuck.

So, it's a fail on the lawn front. But what about the 'effects'? Well, let's have a wander outside. No sign of a sundial or amputated statue (phew!). But we've got ourselves some gravel walks and trellis, even some topiary — what do we think, guys? Everyone happy with topiary? Fair enough. But what about the fountain with carved dolphins? We're on dodgy territory with this one, and the bedding plants are an ode to American suburbia. As for the rockery and English meadow, they're very lovely, but this is like a Top 10 collection of garden styles.

But I think her greater mistake is failing to control the landform. Granted, the site's got its problems. Not only does it fall steeply from the house, but there's an awkward cross-slope. Edith employs a series of ambitious banks, but the effect is weirdly reminiscent of a ziggurat. Worse, the whole garden appears to be sliding sideways like a sailor's lunch. In her defence, awkward topography will challenge the best designer, and Edith knows enough to recognise success at Villa Gamberaia, noting the skilful use of levels. You gotta wonder what she thought arriving home.

And, meanwhile, she's writing that composition is everything, 'the subtle beauty of planning, to utilise natural advantages of the site with little perceptible strain'. But she wrote this while looking down on a zip-wire avenue stretching across the hill face. At one end her Victorian flower garden floats untethered in the middle distance. To fix this, Edith countersinks an Italian garden at the other end of the lime walk, but the result is something like a see-saw. To be fair, the Italian Garden is pretty good, and here's the point: she designed this *after* writing her treatise. I think we can all agree it's the best part of the garden and shows the designer she will become.

But overall?

The garden is laboured and clumsy, no sense of inevitability. A garden built, not born. Little wonder Beatrix Farrand (niece and landscape architect) restricted herself to the kitchen garden and some drainage on the driveway. When esteemed gardener Ambassador Choate stepped onto her terrace, he roasted Edith by saying: Ah, Mrs Wharton, when I look about me, I don't know if I'm in England or in Italy! What a killer. Edith was supposed to be an authority on interior design and now gardens. She had her professional reputation to maintain. But the gardens at The Mount? They lay out her shortcomings for everyone to see.

A quick back-track to Sainte-Claire — this'll only take a minute, promise.

Designed sixteen years after Edith laid out the gardens at The Mount, it shows an amazing response to place. A garden adapted to its surroundings. It's got an informing spirit and understanding of the gardener's purpose. A quality of inevitability — as if how could it be otherwise?

A garden that was born, not built. Yes, my friends, she got there in the end. Don't get me wrong, I'm not saying Mrs Wharton fled to Europe to escape her garden — believe me, it's way more complicated. But, boy, she must have relished the chance to start again.

And don't think my snarky comments about The Mount undermine its beauty or importance. Sure, it's a bit of a mess — the style and structure — but the same can be said for *Sense and Sensibility.* No kidding. Ms Austen was still finding her way around in that novel. It's called 'learning on the job'. No shame in that, people.

Here's another way to look at it. The curator of a museum doesn't necessarily select items for their beauty or perfection, so why should a historic garden be any different? The gardens at The Mount are a hugely important piece in the complexity of Mrs Wharton's life, as well as tracking her growing understanding of garden design. The garden embodies the inner Mrs Wharton at a specific time — a display garden of splendour, striving to hold its own in this wealthy district. Victorian in style and in convention, it reflects a woman raised in a strict and conventional society. A woman who hasn't had much (how shall I say?) *life experience.* Are you starting to see what page I'm on? This garden represents her *Teddy years.* And let's have a shout-out for that guy, because he poured his heart and soul into this place.

And you know what? It's a truly beautiful garden, a fresh loveliness in a stunning landscape. A garden that provides spiritual refreshment to the visitors who experience its beauty. But it's also a garden she left behind. Let's be honest, shall we? Edith only spent six years at The Mount.

Not long after she headed for Paris to live, and after the war, she developed two very different gardens. The first, on the outskirts of Paris,

Is inspired by everything good about this city. Pavillon Colombe is stylish and elegant. Let's call this her Walter garden.

Remember Walter?

He was like a kind of consort. An international diplomat, a real cool customer. Establishment. Impeccably dressed. Cultured and (no, wait, that sounds like yoghurt, let's try a thesaurus). Elevated. High-minded. Lofty and rarefied. You get the picture? Now think of a garden — yes, that's right, you've got Pavillon Colombe. Indisputably lovely, it's also guarded and well-behaved, adhering to strict conventions. A garden of form and good breeding.

But don't forget, Paris is also the city of love — and, boy, did Edith take this to heart. After having a mid-life *grande passion* with bad-boy Morton Fullerton, she's a changed woman, burning with the afterglow. Now every winter she heads down to the heat of Hyeres. No surprise this garden is openly emotional, flagrant and flaunting. Yes, folks, this is her Fullerton garden.

In summary. One of her French gardens is trapped by custom and circumstance, the other a free spirit and harbinger of the future. One reflects the esteemed and irreproachable Mrs Wharton, always immaculately presented. The other is a hot mess, all the confusion and passion of a writer. A dichotomy so familiar to those who read Wharton's work. Two gardens that represent the internal conflicting emotions of the great woman herself.

And I'm telling you this for free: they both deserve better recognition and care.

*

Their boarding call was delayed, no reason given. Austen headed off in search of coffee, warning that he might be gone a while. Their gate was at the end of a far-flung concourse, isolated by stretches of moving walkways and empty lounges. Sara could see the lights of their airline through the large glass windows, the reflection of other travellers crowded in the departure lounge. All the seats were taken, bags piled between the rows. A group of schoolgirls had formed a circle on the carpet to play a game, their laughter loud and explosive. Sara pushed the carry-on luggage under her feet. She was watched by an Indian woman sitting opposite, her gold silk sari exposing soft folds of brown flesh. Sara turned her attention to their boarding passes, aware she was still under scrutiny. They had decided to change their flights and leave Italy a week early. They were flying directly home.

Home. A picture formed in her mind of bulbs forced into ill-fitting holes. Everything would be parched in the heat of summer. The roses would be in flower, but she had no idea what colour. Her garden. She was surprised by her own anticipated pleasure. But not for much longer. The house would be on the market by autumn. Austen had agreed — no point carrying on just for the sake of it. *Best cut our losses*, he said, taking on the idea as his own. Sara didn't think it a loss. Just something that didn't work out. No shame in that. Better to fail than die wondering.

She had briefly considered a villa in Italy — maybe they could live the dream. But speaking it aloud would have exposed the ridiculous idea for what it was. One step at a time. Singapore, probably. After Austen's phone call this morning, it might even be Bangkok. There was plenty to do. The usual sorting and packing, dealing with utility companies and banks, insurance and relocation people. And this time there would be realtors and lawyers. Austen had warned that he might have to leave first. That didn't worry her. They weren't expecting any farewell parties.

Bernard had rung. The whole place was in an uproar, particularly the sponsors and volunteers. And the publishers were furious. The board had called a special meeting and were waiting for a legal opinion on defamation. But Bernard said not to worry — he'd told them she was a weirdo and hadn't meant to be malicious. As for him, he was heading back to New York; he had a friend with an art gallery. Personally, he didn't care about the uproar, he always thought they should follow up on the Wharton affair. That would've been more interesting than gardens. But whatever. He was over the whole thing and happy to leave. And Sara should avoid The Mount for a while. Take up something else — had she thought about golf? He rang off, wishing her well.

Sara sat back, recalling their first meeting in the library, Bernard's energy and excitement. For what? Had his enthusiasm for Edith been genuine? Or was the blogging idea nothing more than a vehicle for self-promotion? Maybe Bernard was just opportunistic, taking his chances when they came. And who was Sara to judge? Only Medora emerged with any honour.

Austen had said that Houston was suggested, but he turned it down. And he would stay away from management, wanted more flexibility and time for travel. There was an outside chance his retirement bonus might be reinstated. No promises. But definitely Asia — remember that great resort in Malaysia? Sara nodded and said maybe they should get a bigger apartment than usual, just in case the kids wanted to stay. Austen was careful to keep the surprise from his face, but Sara could read something that looked like hope.

In those first few hours together, when Austen arrived back to the mocking luxury of their hotel room, they had examined the ruins of their marriage. Austen asked if she wanted a divorce, the words catching in his throat. His shirt was hastily tucked, and his hair tousled. There was evidence of Medora all over him. Had the girl helped him to dress, smoothing his hair?

Sara waited, expecting to hear his remorse, a stumbling confession of sorrow and regret. But Austen continued to speak flatly, saying divorce was probably for the best, and it shouldn't be too difficult. Dragging his eyes from the floor, he stared at her with defiance, and Sara felt a body-slam of horror. He regretted nothing. No remorse for spending the night with Medora. On the contrary, Austen wore the drug-somnolent triumph that came from a night of hard fucking.

Reeling, she steadied herself against the window frame. She would fight this. She wouldn't lose him — not along with everyone else. She heard herself say, 'But I don't want a divorce. I want us to stay together.'

Silence followed. Longer than anything she had ever experienced.

She turned, forcing herself to look directly into the bloodshot, rebellious eyes. Slipping the wrap from her shoulders, she moved closer, willing Austen not to turn away. His eyes widened as she leaned forward to kiss him, savouring the taste of Medora.

It was Sara who first began to re-imagine their future together, and Austen tentatively agreed. Gradually they began adding layers to the fabrication of their new life until it gained substance, and what began as a lie became a truth. Conversely, their life in Lenox became more insubstantial, less believable, until it was almost a nonsensical conceit. An unspoken question. *What on earth had they been thinking?* Now they could face each other directly without irony. They were safe within the limits of their own self-justification, the soundness of their own reasoning.

Last night Sara even mentioned her name. They were having dinner when she said, almost naturally, 'I wonder where Medora is.' Austen studied his meal — *osso bucco*, in a restaurant just off the Piazza Navona. Gently he tilted his glass of wine, a Chianti. He watched the ruby glow cast on the white tablecloth, swirling and diaphanous. With suppressed violence, he threw back the glassful, swallowing hard. He blinked. Sara could almost feel the alcohol hitting his synapses, numbing and anaesthetic. He appeared to roll a little, regather, refill his glass. She understood, nodding as if to answer a question. Medora's name was not to be mentioned again. Lifting her own glass, she felt the hollowness of terror, the suck of an open window in a storm. Could she survive this? Did she have the strength?

A crackle came over the speaker, the boarding call made in Italian and repeated in heavily accented English. It was time to go. Sara got up, gathering their bags and looking around. The area was clearing quickly, a rush to reconfigure into the long line that snaked towards the water fountain. She could see Austen coming, carrying two cups of coffee. From here she could almost believe he was a stranger, his head lowered in concentration. She could detect the signs of ageing — the sloping shoulders and sideways shift. As if the weight of the future were already imprinted on him. She had a sudden sense of the length of the years that stretched before her. *So this is what it will be like*, she thought. She felt herself straighten as if to compensate. It would be different this time. She knew her own strength. Enough for both of them. Enough to get them through.

the end

CHAPTER X

Edith rocked slowly in her chair. She had enjoyed the themes of conformity in the novella, of characters not taking their chance at love. And she had recognised fragments of her own writing, even some notes from her love diary: *this is like being happy* — although she had the feeling this phrase might come from somewhere else; no matter. And while references to the affair were numerous, they weren't salacious. More for promotional purposes, the prompting of modern interest in a woman believed to be a sexually repressed Victorian. Edith nodded to herself. She could never have predicted what might eventuate when she left her love diary behind, but this novella would do nicely.

The fire crumbled in the grate, sending up a shower of sparks. No, she wouldn't burn the manuscript; the novella should be published. It was almost midnight. She must hurry because there were things she didn't yet understand. Smoothing her skirt over swollen knees, she said, 'Please, Trix, tell me how you heard of "Terminus".'

'Your Italian friend.'

'I assume you're referring to Elisina.'

'Mrs Tyler became very close to you in later years.'

'I'm too tired for insinuations, Beatrix. What are you saying?'

'You were very generous to her.'

'She was a dear friend.'

A stir from the shadows, and Walter observed, 'You two were magnificent in the war.'

'Indeed, we even made you sweep floors at our sewing factory — remember? Nobody was spared, not even you.'

A low chuckle, and Edith joined in.

The sewing factory was their first response to war, but as the streets filled with refugees from the Battle of the Marne and Ypres, Edith and Elisina began setting up hostels. Providing beds was, however, just the beginning; they also arranged for lunch rooms and grocery distribution, clothing depots and a free medical clinic. The list went on: coal delivery, an employment agency, a day nursery for the children.

But they needed money. Elisina became chief organiser, while Edith became a war writer. She and Walter travelled to the front line with Charles Cook, eventually making five trips. As well as delivering medical supplies to makeshift hospitals, Edith delivered the grotesque reality of war to America: a series of articles retelling experiences beyond anything she could have imagined: the long marching columns of muddy soldiers, white puffs and scarlet flares across a wooded valley, the flame of enemy fire. It was like being at the very gates of Hell. One evening, Edith came across the strangest scene: a priest taking Mass in a village church converted to a hospital. Rows of beds were filled with the sick and shattered, incense floated over pale heads on pillows, while the local villagers stood between the beds and wailed songs. Another night the checkpoints were unexpectedly shut after heavy fighting. Driving from village to village, Edith and Walter finally found a single room, leaving Cook to sleep in the car, wrapped in Red Cross dressing gowns with his head on a pile of gauze pads. They were unusual times. Edith described a soldier dozing in the silver moonlight of a bombed village, tea service on a table strewn with war maps, standing at the front line and *almost feeling their breath on our faces.*

The Belgium situation was even more shocking. In response to a government request, Edith and Elisina housed a thousand Flemish orphans, nuns, and the elderly. It was all-consuming. Edith arranged benefit concerts, rummage sales, and fundraising art exhibitions. She kept herself busy every minute of the day lest the horror be too much to endure. She wrote that *as soon as peace is declared I shall renounce good works forever!* As friends lost sons at the front, a black cloud hung over the world, and her spirit was heavy with loss.

In recognition of their war efforts, she and Elisina were made Chevaliers of the Legion of Honour in 1916. By then Elisina was doing a magnificent job of running the committees, Edith writing, *Dear Good Fairy, I really can't wait till tomorrow afternoon to tell you how I thank you & bless you & admire you for all you've done!* Edith was in charge of fundraising and endlessly entreating America to join the war. Their last charity was a cure programme for returning soldiers with tuberculosis. Then, finally, it was over.

Twenty years later, Edith called Elisina. She had suffered a stroke while travelling north from Hyères. Thankfully, she hadn't known it would be her last stay at Sainte-Claire — that would have been unbearable, saying goodbye to the heavenly beauty and quiet of her home, a moon rising over silver seas, the wheeling of the great winter constellations. The *Cielo della Quieta.*

Elisina had swept her up, once again becoming her Good Fairy and taking charge. Edith spent her last few months with her at

Pavillon Colombe. They spent their days reading and remembering the past, watching summer drift into early autumn.

'Aunt Puss left her home in Hyères to Mrs Tyler,' Trix was saying to Walter. 'And a good deal of money.'

'Sainte-Claire?' said Walter in disbelief. 'My God, woman, what were you thinking?'

Edith rounded on him. 'You — of all people! Need I explain the disproportionate importance of those at the end? How they overwrite everyone before?'

'You mean my nephew Harry.'

'I'm sorry.' Painful reminders lay everywhere, hidden like land-mines, and so difficult to avoid.

'But Sainte-Claire?' persisted Walter.

Trix was unpleasantly obliging. 'After falling ill, Aunt Puss became unduly influenced and changed her will. I never did trust that woman; she had an unsavoury past.'

Her own niece was such a prig. It was their upbringing decreeing women must possess a studied innocence. Edith, however (unlike Trix), had forced herself to recognise the dark places within. As one of her characters once posed: *Is it anything to be proud of, to know so little of the strings that pull us?*

She said coldly, 'I make no apologies for leaving Sainte-Claire to Elisina. I saw so little of my *family*.'

'She didn't want me to see you when I came to Paris . . . I mean — towards the end.'

Edith was taken aback. 'Oh, my dear, it must have been a mis-understanding. Elisina would never—'

'There was no misunderstanding.'

Could Elisina have been so difficult? She knew Edith's relationship with Trix was occasionally strained but also that she was much-loved family. Turning the question over in her mind, Edith said, 'Elisina stayed when I needed her most, and I repaid her as I saw fit.'

'With family money.'

Edith shivered. 'No, please, don't say — you didn't contest my will? Beatrix?'

'The court found in my favour.'

'Good God, how dare you? My wishes should have been observed. I deserved better, Trix. I deserved *respect*. You know how badly I was treated by my family, how painful the legal fight. And now I hear you've dragged my name through the courts again, all because you wanted money? How dare you? I *wanted* Elisina to have the money — and no, it wasn't family money, it was mine. I wanted her to have Sainte-Claire.' Edith sat back, frightened by the hammering in her ribcage. Such traitorous behaviour by her niece.

Trix, too, was trembling with mutinous anger. 'She had the place stripped. Only four years after your death.'

'I'm sorry?' Edith blinked. She must have heard incorrectly; Trix wasn't making sense.

'The property was subdivided and the furniture auctioned. The silverware and linen were pawned and the books sold.'

'No, stop it.' Edith covered her ears, but the words continued to penetrate.

'Wall coverings torn down, balustrades dumped in the garden. Perhaps that explains the condition of the house today.'

Edith shook her head, speechless.

'I'm sorry,' said Trix, 'but you said our possessions shouldn't matter now.'

Edith paused; that was true, if difficult to accept. Hearing about the condition of her home was deeply painful, but nothing compared to the knowledge of Elisina's actions. A sudden thought: 'But Trix, what about dear—'

'Alfred? He was allowed to stay in his house on the estate, and I don't believe he paid rent.'

'Thank goodness.' Edith bowed her head. So Alfred had been treated well, his last years peaceful — and what more could anyone want? Unlike poor Grossie, who died before Edith did, placed in an asylum for the insane, hair tangled around a scarlet face and clutching a kitchen knife. Grossie was like a mother, but Edith watched her dragged from the house.

'Elisina and I agreed to split the money.'

'Thank you.' Sadness seeped into her soul.

'I always loved you, Aunt Puss. Even if we—'

'I know, Trix, dear.'

'And I greatly admired your career. Perhaps I didn't always approve of you, but that was a failing on my part. And you loved Mother almost as much as I did.'

Dearest Minnie.

Trix folded her hands. 'Your loyalty to us meant going against your own family. We were always grateful, knowing how much pain it caused. Not to mention your generosity. We often depended on your financial support, but you never accepted our gratitude.'

'All in the past.'

'But no less appreciated. I only wish Mother were here.'

Edith smiled sadly. 'So do I, my dear.'

It was several minutes before Katharine said, 'Did Henry ever see "Terminus"?'

'I've no idea.' She had never considered this, not having known that Morton copied the poem. But it was an intriguing possibility,

Morton showing the poem to Henry like a prized exhibit. Henry had been the patron saint of their affair.

Trix gave a low laugh. 'I'm not sure Henry would have enjoyed your description of Rye.'

'Poor Henry.' Katharine's mouth twitched with humour. '*A harbourless wind-bitten shore, where a dull town moulders and shrinks.*'

Henry had been waiting in the foyer of the Charing Cross Hotel the following morning, whisking Morton away. He took delicious delight in his role as elder statesman, a stamp of propriety for his frolicking protégés. He adored Morton, the 'dear boy', with a paternal pride . . . along with something more unspeakable. Edith, too, had felt Henry's deep affection, hidden beneath the theatrics. She was never offended by his cowed demeanour when she arrived at Lamb House with a motor-car, his protesting terror and exhaustion in advance of yet another motor-flight with his Angel of Devastation. He would always write after her departure, his letters wistful and tender: *I cling to you, dearest Edith, through thick & thin, & believe that we shall find ourselves in some secure port together yet.*

Yes, they both adored Henry, but neither of them liked Rye.

'A little unfair,' said Katharine, light refracting from her glasses. 'With Henry such a loyal cover for the whole business.'

Edith held still. The clock on the wall continued to tick. Another bulb in the light fitting had gone out, the edges of the room shadowy. Linky was now curled by Teddy's feet, and they both appeared to be asleep.

Had Katharine always known about the affair, even in the cab — surely not? Her family would have kept the truth from her until after her marriage to Mr Gerould. Edith was aware of being examined, the woman's homely façade disguising something far more complex. Morton would never have upset his innocent young sister by revealing their affair. And Katharine's parents would have protected their religious child from Will's sexual indiscretions: the blackmailing landlady, his affair with the famous Mrs Wharton. Katharine would never have guessed the truth while sitting in the cab, staring at the note held damply by the oceanographer as rain streamed down the windows. And yet so much was unexplained. Why did Katharine write about Morton's stay at The Mount? How could she write with such startling detail? She even remembered the date. Why did Katharine ask about Edith's return to America in the early summer of 1908? It was as if she knew of Morton's silence. What did Katharine mean: *It's a mistake to think history can be viewed in its entirety. There are always unknown factors and other points of view.*

Edith's mind swam with confusion. She kept reaching for a truth, but it would always slip away like a fish, sparkling and winking. She must concentrate. There was something she must understand — how could Elisina have known about the poem? Did Morton show his own copy of 'Terminus' to Elisina? And why did she tell Trix? They were adversaries. Edith said, 'I don't understand, Trix. Everything is so confusing. You must explain how Elisina knew about "Terminus".'

Trix drew her brows together. 'I don't . . . Well, it was a difficult time. My husband was very ill.'

'I understand, but why did Elisina tell you about the poem?'

Trix turned to Katharine. 'It was your brother, Mrs Gerould. In the later years, Mr Fullerton contacted Mrs Tyler. He was black-mailing her.'

'I don't believe it,' burst Katharine. 'My brother would never blackmail anyone.'

Edith didn't believe it either; that was not Morton's style.

Katharine was flushed. 'You can't make accusations without explaining yourself.'

'That's all I know,' said Trix.

'Please, Trix,' pleaded Edith. 'This is very important. You must remember something.'

Aversion hardened Trix's features. 'Mrs Tyler was concerned about your reputation. You had left evidence about a love affair.'

Her secret diary. *L'Âme Close*.

Trix continued. 'Mr Fullerton showed Mrs Tyler the poem, saying it was worth money. That's when she contacted me.'

Morton was right, the poem *was* worth money.

'Barely amounts to blackmail,' said Katharine mildly.

'Mrs Tyler employed a lawyer to negotiate with Mr Fullerton, but he wouldn't part with anything, saying he had many more papers of interest. He didn't share her concern for your reputation, calling her efforts pious.'

Yes, that sounded like Morton.

Finally — Edith had the answer to a question that had haunted her all night, an answer that lay in wait as she thrashed stupidly in a fog of confusion. It had been waiting in the pages of the novella.

The author had known about her poem 'Terminus'. Perhaps a copy of the poem (in Morton's handwriting!) was on the desk as the author wrote of Sara not wanting to be *whirled down the ways of the world like dust-eddies swept through a street*. Edith had recited these very words this evening, but she had missed this telling detail, had not been paying close enough attention. She had been too caught up in knowing her love diary existed in the world of modern literature and was being used in the pages of a contemporary novella. Alarm bells should have rung when Morton was described as a 'bad-boy'. The author was drawing on much wider material than just Edith's love diary — or even her poem. The author was reading her letters to Morton.

The letters survive.

Morton never destroyed her letters.

The letters survive.

No, he didn't keep them for money; she knew him too well.

The letters survive.

Morton would have enjoyed their existence, knowing the power they held, even if he chose not to use that power. It wasn't blackmail, simply the satisfaction that they belonged to him. And who knows, maybe they meant something more to him than monetary gain?

Edith roused herself, saying, 'What happened to the letters?'

'Letters?' repeated Trix, looking puzzled.

Edith rephrased the question. 'You said Mr Fullerton had many more papers of interest. I would like to know what happened to all this material.'

Trix hesitated. 'I'm not sure.'

'You must have some idea.'

'A ridiculous story.'

Edith waited.

'I heard through friends in France — the name Morton Fullerton caught my attention. Elisina was gone by then. An armed hold-up occurred when Mr Fullerton was an old man.' Trix swivelled in her chair towards Katharine. 'You mentioned his wife, Camille.'

'That's right.'

'But there was another woman. A common-law wife. I believe they lived together for many years.'

Katharine nodded. 'Hélène Pouget. Handsome, but a common woman. Unlike Camille, she didn't object to Will straying.' She glanced at Edith. 'Will referred to her as his housekeeper.'

Edith rapped her fingers impatiently.

Trix resumed her story. 'Camille armed herself with a revolver and went to the house to rob Hélène of papers. An armed hold-up between two old women in their eighties. I understand there were at least two suitcases of papers, but I've no idea what.'

Edith did.

Her letters to Morton, there must be three hundred; she knew they had survived well beyond an armed hold-up.

Above her, the lights strengthened, as if in response to the clarity in Edith's mind. Carefully, she ordered her thoughts. During that springtime month in Paris, she had written in her love diary: *This must be what happy women feel.* Three years later, while sitting on a promontory high above the deep-blue inlets of Portofino, she had written to Morton that it was *like being happy.*

A phrase repeated in the novella. Sara had thought to herself: *This is like being happy.* Edith had initially mistaken this for an entry in her love diary. But no, the author had been reading her letters to Morton and had re-used them in the novella. It was irrefutable proof that her letters existed in the modern world.

Edith rested back into the chair, feeling the warmth from the fire. Such small things that brought comfort now. *The letters survive.* Letters that contradicted her retelling of the affair. Letters that revealed *L'Âme Close* to be nothing but a self-delusional joke. Letters that revealed her bleeding, shredded soul.

Soon after their night in a railway hotel, Edith and Morton spent a month travelling around England, Henry their gloriously majestic chaperone. It was the happiest month of her life. She wrote, *I have been completely happy. I have had everything in life that I ever longed for, & more than I ever imagined!* She had been through Hell, and now she was basking in the autumn of her affair. Back in France, their lovemaking was as intense as ever, but matched by periods of leaden silence. She was sent into an indescribable abyss of desire: *I can only think of one thing . . .*

To one pleading letter, Morton sneered: *I will be all you have the right to expect.*

Their affair became a sickness. He called only when he wanted her, and she couldn't refuse: *What you wish, apparently, is to take of my life the inmost & uttermost that a woman — a woman like me — can give, for an hour, now & then, when it suits you; & when the hour is over, to leave me out of your mind & out of your life as a man leaves the companion who has accorded him a transient distraction. I think I am worth more than that . . . .*

But such honesty was always followed by quick retraction: *the tiresome woman is buried, once for all, I promise, & only the novelist survives!*

Every day she re-invented herself: as a literary comrade, sexual partner, pleading mistress. Reality fused with storytelling, and she recorded everything, even the tender moments of complicity: *my heart ached to see you so tired today, and to think I was part of the tire . . . I love you even better than I knew.*

Even her fragments of happiness were shadowed with sadness. Regret for lost years and apprehension for the future. *Now I am asking to be happy all the rest of my life.* Humiliation as she tried to remove herself . . . *it is a misfortune to love too late, & as completely as I have loved you. Everything else grows so ghostly afterward.*

Unable to leave him, she begged for release. *It is impossible that our lives can run parallel much longer. I have faced the fact & I am not afraid, except when I think of the pain & pity you may feel for me.* She apologised for calling when he was busy and harassed. *I want to love you in any way that gives you peace, & not bother!*

Life at home was unbearable as insanity gripped Teddy. Sometimes she cried all night at her fate, but her greatest concern was for Morton's wellbeing: *I can be anything, do anything, to help you!* And — always — she wanted her letters back: *some day next week — before Wednesday.*

Only one thing remained constant, her determination to elevate Morton. She adjusted the fulcrum of their relationship, re-weighting their balance of power. She created a man worthy of her own grand passion, worthy of heroic heartbreak, worthy of *herself*. Idealising Morton protected her from the humiliating truth: that she was debasing herself. Her love was fraudulent. A fanciful, self-deceiving indulgence. If Morton was not the man she wilfully believed him to be, then her pain and behaviour were incomprehensible. *Dear, that I know how unequal the exchange is between us, how little I have to give that a man like you can care for—*

Thinking she had reached the bottom, she managed to find grace and dignity within herself. She became gently reproachful, telling him even her friends stayed in touch. *But I do ask something more of the man who asks to be more than my friend; & so must any woman who is proud enough to be worth loving.* And finally she began to find the strength to move away from him. *Be happy and love me a little, when you have the time, and let the heart tell you . . . .*

But he wouldn't let her go so easily. Almost a year after their night at the Charing Cross Hotel, she was more lost than ever. *I am sad and bewildered beyond words . . . I can't go on like this! . . . I don't know what you want, or what I am! You write to me like a lover, you treat me like a casual acquaintance! . . . My life was better before I knew you. And it is a bitter thing to say to the one being one has ever loved d'amour.*

By now she couldn't leave Teddy for more than a few hours at a time. Her whole world was a madness, and Morton's behaviour was equally unreliable. *I have borne all these inconsistencies because I love you so much . . . I can bear no more—*

Knowing she could no longer satisfy Morton's sexual needs, she applied herself to his failing career. She drew on her contacts and reputation to secure job opportunities with publishers and the foreign service, even arranging a meeting with Teddy Roosevelt. But the truth couldn't be avoided. She was Morton's superior in every way. It was increasingly challenging to ignore or explain his shortcomings: he was lazy and ill-committed; he lacked ambition and application; he was — in a word — a ditherer.

Morton might have impressed President Roosevelt at Edith's apartment in Paris, but he failed to show at a following meeting, later explaining that he might undermine his first impression. Edith thought him a fool. *My personal inconvenience . . . was nothing compared to my regret at having been importunate in trying to help you.*

This was the beginning of the end. Given Teddy's precarious mental state, they could no longer find a mutual opportunity to meet, Edith saying drily, *Don't see in this any ruse to regain possession of your time.* She could now dispassionately re-appraise their relationship, beginning with his visit to The Mount, standing glossy and reptilian in her foyer.

At the time she believed Morton to be an influential journalist with powerful and influential friends. Tracking back, however, she learned that Morton had failed to receive a tenured position at Harvard. Heading to Europe, he became the Paris correspondent for *The Times*, but success was beyond him. Constantly overlooked for promotion, he was moved to Madrid (a branch office!); when this closed, he arrived back in Paris (with debts and an estranged wife) to pick up again with his landlady. At forty-three, he was still writing home asking for advice and money. This was the Mr Fullerton who strolled insouciantly into the low-lit *salon* of Rosa de Fitz-James asking to be introduced to the rising American novelist Mrs Edward Wharton.

Morton wasn't sexually attracted to her, but her instincts weren't entirely wrong; his attraction to her was genuine. He was attracted to her wealth and status. There was no preconceived plan (with Morton there never was). To pursue the inimitable Mrs Wharton was a natural response, and when she left for The Mount that summer he simply forgot about her. There was nothing personal about his silence. On hearing she would soon be in Paris, he wrote that everything survived. Of course it did. He didn't have the necessary application to end the thing. No, the dynamic Morton Fullerton never existed. He simply reacted to opportunities that arose and moved on when bored. His love affairs were ill-fated by neglect. This revelation finally gave Edith strength to leave him, knowing the end must come sometime. *Dear, there was never a moment, from the very first, when I did not foresee such a thought on your part as the one we talked of today; there was never a moment, even when we were nearest, that I did not feel it was latent in your mind. And still I took what you gave me, & was glad, & was not afraid.*

They stayed in touch, and Edith recovered her inner self and humour. *I herewith graciously accord you the privilege of gazing on my countenance when it once more rises on your horizon.* Her letters became busy with travel and friends, her struggles with Teddy. She described her garden, knowing it held no interest: she even chided Morton for his silence: *I should have had a letter from you, if only a postcard.* And she didn't completely lose faith in him, but continued to offer career advice, hoping he could still find his *raison d'être*.

However, her greatest triumph was the act of transforming her pain into *The Reef*, a story of sexual jealousy, betrayal, and humiliation — even an affair in a shabby railway hotel called The Terminus! She wrote her novel while trapped with Teddy, his insanity and scandalous affairs now public. She examined her pain and humiliation with surgical precision. *There it lay before her, her sole romance, in all its paltry poverty, the cheapest of cheap adventures, the most pitiful of sentimental blunders.* She wrote about the entrapment and sexual subservience. And finally, while struggling with the last six chapters of her novel, she sent a note to Morton, inviting him to tea — she was keen to read the chapters to him! She had survived. From Portofino she wrote of her recovery: *I am staying in this unimaginably beautiful place to rest & to steep my soul in light & air.* And two years later, from Algeria, she wrote evocatively of the people and landscape, finishing, *Is this the kind of letter you like to get from me? It would do very well in a memoir, wouldn't it? Only I don't know how to sign it—*

Their affair was the emotional capital she called on for the rest of her writing life: love and sadness, bitterness and loss, longing and desire. It was like an infinite glory box, always offering up something new — another insight, a different way of seeing. Even as a young woman she had known it would be necessary to acquire wisdom through experience. In an early novella she wrote, *wisdom unfiltered through personal experience does not become a part of the moral tissues.* But she couldn't have predicted the emotional gains from an affair with Morton Fullerton. Riches that belonged to her alone. Morton may have shared the experience, but it didn't bind them. And yet only Morton had known what she felt and what she was capable of giving to a man. His laughter had been coarse with pride when he called her insatiable, and she hadn't been ashamed.

The letters survive, and everything survives.

Finally she understood. When Morton wrote these words, the past was stored in the basement of a town library or the desk of a public servant, a shelf in the crematorium office. Places sought by only the most committed researchers spending days in draughty reading rooms. But now? It seemed everything was available to anyone. Her inner self would be splashed across the internet like a human sacrifice to the lions.

Edith hesitated before addressing Katharine. 'Your brother kept so many papers, never throwing anything away.' After another pause, she continued, 'But I never understood what, exactly, the landlady had in her possession. What hold did she have over Morton that he paid her for so many years?' Edith held Katharine's scrutiny; she was ready to understand.

'He hoped she would provide for him in her will. I don't believe that happened.'

The question had been left unanswered, and Edith felt sure this was intentional. 'I understand that an affair with the Ranee of Sarawak would have been awkward, possibly expensive, but to my knowledge Morton was not the only man to have enjoyed her.'

A small smile. 'That was also my understanding.'

'You're deliberately avoiding my question.'

'I'm not sure you'll like the answer.'

'Nothing about Morton can surprise me now.'

'I'm not so sure.' Katharine pondered and then said, 'Did you know that Oscar Wilde asked Will for a loan? It was only a year before Wilde died in Paris, living in destitution after his release from prison.'

'I didn't know they knew each other.'

'Oh, yes, but Will didn't pay him anything.'

'It's unexpected that he should have encountered Wilde — they didn't move in the same circles.'

Katharine's gaze was level and considered, as if she expected Edith to pursue this line of enquiry. But why? The room felt heavy with meaning. When Edith finally spoke, her voice was overly forceful. 'If you have anything to say, please say it. I don't care for concealment.'

Katharine laughed. 'Concealment was the basis of your writing career, not to mention your private life.'

Edith could feel thoughts starting to form and coalesce.

'My brother did not want a similar prison sentence, Mrs Wharton.'

Dry-mouthed, Edith could do nothing but stare.

'Did you know Lord Ronald Gower?'

Edith nodded her head. Morton had been proud of his association with Lord Gower, a great friend of Henry's. There had been a group of them. This fleeting thought took weight.

'I believe the landlady, Madame Mirecourt, held love letters written from Lord Gower to my brother. They must have been explicit enough to establish a physical relationship. My brother was bisexual.'

Edith turned away, her head churning. It was like watching a slow wave coming closer, the tumultuous crash no less shocking. So many fragments that could be pieced together: Walter casually asking about the dear boy while studiously looking away; Henry unable to tear his eyes from Morton's physical beauty; a book Morton once lent her, the inscription from Lord Gower, *Amica amicis*; and — of course — Henry saying Morton would never pose long enough for the camera of identification. So Henry had known all along.

Trix re-adjusted her scarf, and Walter stirred uneasily. Percy and Sybil were almost indiscernible as the edges of the room crept closer.

Katharine continued, her voice low and insistent. 'I have an amethyst ring given to my brother by Lord Gower. My family understood he was Will's lover. And there were others; we believe Bliss Carman was also his lover.'

The room was filled with dark silence. Unable to speak, Edith closed her eyes and, without warning, the brilliant lights of her memory blazed on a stage in her mind: the dining-room of a grand hotel — The Belmont on Park Avenue, October 17, 1910. She was dining with friends on a Monday evening. There were just the four of them.

She had been in residence at the hotel for a month, endlessly waiting for Dr Kinnicutt to come and examine Teddy. It was an awful place: only four years old, built by August Belmont, who installed a private entrance to the new subway beneath the building. Twenty-two storeys high, it was reputed to be the tallest hotel in the world. The room was infernally hot. Edith looked out across a landscape of brick and iron towards a river of pitch. She translated these surroundings into a novel, the hotel becoming the Stentorian, owned by ruinous banker Julius Beaufort.

Teddy was intolerable. Recently he had confessed to embezzling her money and being unfaithful. Everyone thought he should be put under restraint — everyone, that is, except his family. Unable to cope, Edith arranged for Teddy to travel around the world with a paid companion. Only that afternoon, she had delivered him to the pier before he could change his mind.

Now she was stricken with nervous exhaustion, and tomorrow she sailed for France. She had passed beyond fatigue: the travel and Atlantic crossings, responsibility for The Mount, Teddy's insanity. She knew a final showdown was coming. Soon her life would be transformed, and she would become a divorced woman living in Paris. But that seemed a lifetime away; there was so much to endure first. And tonight there was dinner.

Her dining companions, when they arrived, were in similarly low spirits. No one knew this would be the last time they would all be together.

Walter, Henry, Morton, and Edith.

They were in an unusual, uneasy accord, each in a transitional passage of their life, anxious about their current circumstances and apprehensive for the future. But tonight they found themselves together — and where better for these wavering souls than the vast Belmont? The hotel was a monument to transitory life.

Edith felt an intense sense of reality. The dining-room details were etched on the silver photographic plate in her mind, later to be transcribed into a notebook and, later still, into a novel. She described the dining-room as sumptuously stuffy, where dinner fumes hung under the emblazoned ceiling. The other diners were pallid and richly dressed, eating their way through the bill of fare, the chef having ransacked the globe for gastronomic incompatibilities. And in the middle of the room a knot of equally pallid waiters were engaged in languid conversations, backs turned on the persons they were supposed to serve.

Delighted by her disdain, Henry was fulsome in his praise, declaring the hotel extremely luxurious: *prodigious & unutterable*. He saved his highest praise for the dining-room, which he likened to a Renaissance Italian palazzo. Dear Henry — massive, slow-moving, and awe-inspiring — but deeply sad. He had come from his brother's place in New Hampshire, having been with William when he died six weeks earlier. Now that his stay in America was coming to an end, Henry couldn't bear the thought of returning to England. Lamb House was taking the form of a prison in his mind. Edith was fearful; seven months ago in London she had been alarmed by one of Henry's depressive episodes. He had cried of unspeakable loneliness and the blackness of life, his craving *not to wake — not to wake —*

And Walter? His mood was reflective. Ill-health had forced his resignation as an international judge, and his career was faltering, the pinnacle had been passed. Now he was in the process of packing up his life and moving to Paris.

Even Morton was not his usual dazzling company. Having resigned from *The Times*, he was unsure of his future and deeply disturbed by the marriage of his sister Katharine. He couldn't understand it; she had known he was coming home, he told her to wait. But no, Katharine's fiancé had insisted they marry before Morton's return — and she had agreed. He was hurt and bewildered. To the others he explained: Gordon Gerould had a minor position at Princeton University; his most distinguishing quality (according to Morton) was to wear a store-made business suit to his wedding.

Edith had heard all this before: the wedding was four months ago, and Morton was still churning over events. She was tired of it.

What about her? She was only just emerging from their affair, bruised and agonisingly aware. To know his failings (and her own) brought no comfort, and it was painful being so close to him. She could think of nothing but her letters — several hundred, some written as recently as six months ago — all in Morton's possession. Now she understood: he would never release them. The letters exposed her soul with unguarded honesty. Edith was carefully composed, trying to ignore the pitiful words that scrolled through her mind: *I am sad and bewildered beyond words. I don't understand. It was not necessary to hurt me.*

So many currents ran deeply that night.

Picture them: Henry rousing himself to deliver a roiling oratorical triumph, mired in sorrow yet delighted to be in the company of old friends. Walter smiling with restraint and good manners, his worldly views peppered with vicious anecdotes. While Morton, in the unique position of knowing their secrets, is hungrily watched by the rest. He would have enjoyed that.

They fell into familiar ways. Edith pretended to ignore the Morton–Henry comedy act. She had always thought Morton malicious to tease poor Henry, leading him on, playing satyr to his impotent ardency. Earlier that year in London, Henry had said: *Down there, alone at Rye, I used to lie & think of Morton, and* ache *over him.* Of course Edith had written this to Morton, thinking it would amuse him.

But, for all her knowing ways — and her love for both men — she had misread the situation. There was an undercurrent between them, an unspoken understanding, a truth Edith had never suspected. Henry was excited by Morton, the sexual libertine. Did he know he was Lord Gower's lover? Quite possibly.

Walter was parrying with Henry as always, their witticism covering something more urgent and base. What was Walter thinking as he chewed delicately on canvas back duck? Was he recalling Henry's visceral, lusting letters: *I shall have nothing for you but a great gaping mouth.*

And what was Walter thinking as he reached for his wine glass, watching Morton with a dry-mouthed, unquenchable thirst? Years later, Morton would speak publicly of Walter's fine culture and high irony. He would mention Walter's immense and varied contacts of life, of which he was a rare connoisseur. Had this been a subtle joke, some high irony on Morton's part? Did Walter know the truth about Morton? Quite possibly.

Yet Edith never suspected.

Now everyone turned to her, concerned about her travails with Teddy; they understood how difficult things were. But did they really? Did they see her pain when Morton laid his hand on the table, so close to her own? Perhaps Henry understood, but Walter would have been too preoccupied with his own concerns. It was becoming increasingly likely that Edith would soon be a divorcée living in Paris. Was he worried about her expectations? Afraid she would demand more than he could give?

And all the while, in the eye of this sexual maelstrom, Edith busily held forth, believing herself to be in the know. How wrong she was. How blind to the impulses and desires that throbbed between the four of them. A mutual admiration society. So complicated, and she had been so weary.

She was weary now. The events of this evening were beyond anything she might have expected. There had been nothing to indicate the turns that would take place, and only in retrospect could she understand. She had once written: the turnings of life seldom show a signpost; rather, though the sign is always there, it is usually placed some distance back, like the notices that give warning of a bad hill or a level crossing.

The clock continued to tick. Another bulb popped and went out. The edges of the room were dimming, and she could only just make out Linky curled by Teddy's feet, a reprimand in the way her head lay on his foot. She tried calling, but Linky gave no response. In panic, Edith rose from her chair, stumbling towards the dog. Pain shot through her chest, numbness in one arm. Her feet stalled. In fear, she called Linky again, her voice rasping. Linky looked up, contrite, and Edith felt a flood of tears. The little dog limped across the room, as if shadowing Edith's own afflictions.

Relief drained her, and she sank to scoop the animal up, holding her close, feeling the soft patter of a heartbeat. She was holding Linky against another farewell. It had been such a terrible evening. Why hadn't they stuck to Yeats? Ambition had ruined everything — and for what? She had no right to meddle in the modern world, there was no way to control her own story. It was beyond her; her letters would be pored over and analysed. She mightn't like her image as haughty and imperious, but, by God, it was better than a broken woman debasing herself for a worthless man. With fury, she straightened, depositing Linky on her chair to collect the novella from the floor.

'No,' cried Katharine with premonition. 'You mustn't.'

'Why not?' Drawing to her full height, Edith gained strength from her intention. 'I've no wish for this to be published now.'

'Because of the letters?'

'Because of everything.' A stumbled step, and she was by the fire, papers held in outstretched arms.

'For heaven's sake, woman,' snapped Walter. 'You'll burn the place down.'

'*No,*' cried Katharine again. 'Please, don't burn the manuscript.'

Edith ignored her pleas; she would not be deceived. 'You want it destroyed. You've been my adversary all night.'

Katharine shook her head. 'I only wanted you to understand the consequences of being published. To know what it meant, what would be revealed about all of us.'

'This has nothing to do with you. All night I've suffered your insinuations and veiled warnings. I've had enough.' Leafing the top page into the fire, Edith watched it ball into flames, her forehead prickling with heat.

'No, let me explain.'

'Explain what?'

Katharine looked back with quiet confidence. Earlier this evening, Edith had been irritated by her sly and expectant hinting, but there was truth in Katharine's demeanour now, and kindness. Katharine said, 'You asked about my interest in Will staying at the The Mount, why the date was etched in my mind.'

Edith nodded, pages ready to slip into the flames.

'I remember the date very clearly because the night before—'

'Yes, I know,' said Edith wearily. 'Morton stayed at your college giving a talk on Henry.'

'We hadn't seen each other for nine years.'

Nine years?

Katharine continued softly. 'I was only nineteen when he left for Europe. You can imagine his surprise when we met again.'

A creeping sense of foreboding kept Edith quiet.

'He stayed overnight at The Mount before we met again in Brockton. We wanted to confront the storm together.'

Edith swallowed. Her heart was beating so violently that there was a rush in her ears. It was contrary to reason, yet it must be true. But still she didn't understand.

CHAPTER XI

A spark caused Edith to jump. She had been dreaming — the ice-blue crunch of snow, bending to collect a golden flower spilling scarlet seeds like blood. Ink-black writing on thick vellum: *The letters survive, and everything survives*. Shadow-mouths melted to one. The swell of an ocean liner. A stolen whisper: *you are mine, mine, mine!*

Just one bulb remained, a low, ghostly glow. Katharine was regarding her calmly. She now seemed the only one with any presence. Her face was like a book of which the last page is never turned, where there is always something new to read. Edith smiled. Despite her initial misgivings, she was pleased Katharine was here tonight.

Katharine began to speak. 'After my brother stayed at The Mount, we met again at home. We wanted to tell our parents together.' She paused a moment, folding her hands. 'To announce our engagement.'

'I don't understand.'

'I think you do.' The round tortoiseshell glasses gave Katharine a homely air, but her expression was brutal with honesty. She continued, relentless and calm. 'We were lovers.'

Edith swallowed, the room was revolving.

Katharine continued. 'Incest was something that interested you. I always wondered about your father—'

'*No!*'

'Of course not.' The same devastating calmness.

Edith tried to make sense of it, saying slowly, 'When Morton stayed at The Mount—?'

'We were engaged the night before.'

Edith felt a rush of air: Morton's treachery still had the power to overwhelm her.

'That's why Will was so preoccupied when you dropped him at the station. We told our parents that night in Brockton.'

Edith shook her head. She could feel herself sliding into a world of darkness. 'I don't understand. He was your brother.'

'I adored him all my life, but not until the age of twenty-five did I learn that I was adopted. His father was my uncle. Two brothers.'

Edith stared.

'You've no idea what a gift it was. In a single moment our love was transformed from a perverted sickness to something pure and right. A love to be celebrated by others, including the Church. Finally we could act on our long-suppressed feelings. My love for Will was lifelong.'

Edith felt the dizziness that follows a physical blow, a shock of wonder. There was always something unfathomable about Morton. She had known this, repulsed and yet fatally drawn to it. Katharine was speaking the truth: there was nothing Morton was incapable of. In that strange and intimate relationship, he told his sister everything about their own affair. With reluctance, Edith raised her head to Katharine. Triumph remained, but it was fading to something more enigmatic. Something almost resembling pity.

The room was quiet. Edith felt deadly tired yet alert to this extraordinary revelation. 'Please continue. As a writer, you'll understand the human condition is an endless fund of material, and your brother was so inexhaustible.'

Katharine smiled. 'I also had the appetite of a writer who wanted to experience everything.'

Edith recalled Morton in the foyer at The Mount, all charm and compliments. Passing his hat and cane to the butler, while Grossie fussed about his train journey — all the way from Philadelphia!

Now Edith wondered about Morton's journey: it must have taken six hours, longer if he dined at a railway station in New York awaiting his connection. What was Morton thinking? He had just proposed to his beautiful young sister and was now on his way to Brockton to face his parents. However, first he makes a brief detour, less than twenty-four hours at The Mount, to visit the best-selling American authoress.

Katharine spoke. 'As you know, Will came to college to give a talk on Henry's work. You can imagine how the girls adored him. Not only was he handsome and charming, but so clever — and a friend of Henry James! I swear all the college girls fell madly in love with him. Afterwards Will came to my rooms in the residential hall and we talked for hours.' Her eyes clouded with distance. 'I have lived a rich life, Mrs Wharton, but there's no feeling like being young and in love and knowing it's reciprocated. I think it must be like climbing to the top of a mountain on a glorious day. A giddy headiness and shortness of breath, horizons wide and beautiful, full of infinite possibility.' A small shrug. 'But then I have never climbed a mountain.'

'No,' responded Edith. 'Neither have I.'

'Of course, by its very definition, young love can't last.' Katharine turned to the fire, a low crackle of dry wood; memories flickering across her face. 'Will said he'd loved me for years, since I was eighteen. He held my hand with such exquisite sadness, saying that without marriage there was no life for either of us.' Her gaze met Edith's. 'When we told our parents in Brockton there was quite a storm.'

Brockton. Morton had written from his parents' house thanking Edith for her hospitality, a letter in which he had enclosed a sprig of witch hazel. Had he written the note while his mother was weeping in the kitchen, pleading with Katharine? Had he left the house to post the letter while his father stood rigid with outrage at the window? The same sprig of witch hazel that had fallen from the envelope onto her desk, the symbolic beginning of their affair. She had begun *The Life Apart: L'Âme Close*, opening the pages with such trusting honesty, the hesitancy of impending love. Edith sighed; it felt like a fresh wound. She said, 'I cannot imagine what your poor mother went through.'

'She loved Will with a passion that was almost unnatural. She thought he'd simply taken pity on me; likely I was to blame. Mother always defended Will against every accusation, supporting his confessions. Of course, there was more to come.' Katharine had turned away again. Edith was reminded of her as a beautiful, shy young woman awestruck by the famous Mrs Wharton. 'Perhaps it was our religious upbringing that made Will so fond of confession, but I do believe he could have spared our parents. It was not a normal love affair.'

'It certainly wasn't.'

'But you can imagine — as a writer — how it heightened every sensation, feeding our desire for a grand passion. It was an illicit love, almost immoral, fuelled by the religiosity of our childhood. In my love letters, I called him my brother.' A pause, and she spoke more slowly. 'I enjoyed the perversity. I wrote of our wonderful, wretched fate, that ours was a love needing God more than most.' The sunshine of a smile broke across her face. 'The fanaticism of youth, exacerbated by a religious upbringing.'

Yes, Edith could understand this strange attraction, stepping from the stage of life into the shadows. How could Edith, as one of Morton's women, judge another? Curious, she asked, 'While you were at college — with Morton living in Paris — you continued to write to each other?'

'Of course — we were engaged.'

That was the blissful first month of her own affair: taking a train to Montmorency; climbing the small wooden stairs in a country hotel; and, afterwards, looking into the layered loveliness of a flowering chestnut. When Morton lay in bed watching her — was he thinking of his fiancée? Was he remembering his beautiful young sister?

Katharine looked down at her hands, tracing a deep crease across her palm. Edith had heard enough — she felt a soul-saddened weariness — but Katharine seemed keen to continue. 'His first letters idealised my virtue as something he wished to protect, but he soon became very explicit about his desire for me. Sometimes I was frightened by his intensity.' She paused. 'I later realised Will was seeing you in Paris at the time.'

Edith nodded: May 1908. How could she forget: driving through the countryside past old grey towns piled above rivers, through the melting spring landscape all tender green and snowy-fruit blossom; strolling up to a cathedral together, the quiet moment outside, sitting on the steps in the sunshine as he asked, *Dear, are you happy?*

Edith shook away the memories to say, 'Earlier you mentioned my return to America in late May. You guessed correctly that Morton never wrote. I couldn't believe he'd forgotten about me, but now I remember — you were in Europe on sabbatical leave.'

Katharine nodded. 'Will and I spent every day together; it was blissful. Until the terrible night when Will told me about you.

I could hardly believe it. I was heartbroken that he could be so duplicitous and cruel. And with you, of all people. How could I possibly compete with the great Mrs Wharton?'

'You were doing rather well until then,' said Edith drily. 'Meanwhile I was in despair at The Mount, waiting every day to hear from Morton, months spent listening for the mail cart. I couldn't sleep, and, for once in my life, I couldn't even write.'

Katharine's features were strained. 'When he told me about you, I fled to a convent to work on my novel, but it was impossible to concentrate. I couldn't write either.'

'But you came back to Paris.' The following year — 1909, Edith's affair having resumed — desperate and debased.

'Yes. Will came to see me with the usual lies and romantic sadness. He wanted a copy of a poem I'd written. I came to Paris for the day, and he dropped your note in the cab. From your expression, I could tell it was a love note.'

Edith laughed bitterly. 'I was terrified you would pick it up and be devastated with shock. The little sister, so young and devout.' But no. Katharine was engaged to her brother and knew all about the affair. Edith shook her head. The power of William Morton Fullerton to corrupt all those who loved him. Including his own sister.

'You were very kind to me,' said Katharine, 'even praising my poem.'

'But you married Mr Gerould a year later.'

'Oh, you know Will. He maintained just enough contact to secure my love, but nothing more. He said his life was too confused for marriage. Which was true. The old landlady was blackmailing him; possibly they were still lovers. And he was trying to dissolve his marriage, plus there was a slovenly young woman called Doll. And you, of course.'

Edith tried not blanch, to be associated with such women. To think that she played such a small part in Morton's busy days.

'And then, like you, I was treated to silence. I wrote and wrote, imploring him to respond. I still can't understand how he allowed me to degrade and humiliate myself — his own sister, a woman he claimed to love. I wrote, *I do not believe you have ever treated another woman so ill*.' Katharine grimaced. 'But I may have been mistaken.'

'Perhaps.'

'And then I married a good man. We had a long and fulfilling life together.'

'You became a published writer and reviewer. You were very generous when reviewing *The Glimpses of the Moon*, calling it a magnificent gift of storytelling, pure and simple.'

'Along with your ability to produce a best-seller whenever you felt like it.'

'Henry always sniped about that, but I had a large staff to feed.' Edith stopped, saddened at the thought of Henry in his later years, writing himself into knots, distraught as the world turned away. Rousing herself, she said, 'Please carry on; I imagine the wedding was awkward.'

'Poor Gordon. He couldn't understand the business with Will, and I didn't expect him to. My children were later perplexed by the whole thing. Will wasn't much of a topic of conversation in our household, particularly as the male lovers came to light.' Tiredness drew lines down Katharine's cheeks.

'Katharine?'

There was no response: she appeared to be dozing.

Darkness smudged the corners of the room, and Teddy was no more than a vague shape. This existence seemed to be closing in. Edith was aware of a chill, Linky no longer a warm presence on her lap but something cold and unresponsive. With panic, Edith tickled Linky's ears, harder than she intended. The dog shifted and weighed more heavily, thank goodness. Now she noticed Percy and Sybil had lost substance, pushed away like discarded stage props. She was relieved to see Walter's legs remained stretched before him. He was leaning back in his chair, hidden in the shadows.

Edith was mortified beyond reason at what they had endured this evening. She regretted everything — and for what? Did she really want the novella published and her work rediscovered? She was disconcerted to find herself again scrutinised by Katharine. What could be read in that calm implacability? Something almost . . . yes, collegial. The look of a woman who had been with the same man, known the complexities and limitations of the same lover. Intuitively, they understood each other. Edith had written of lying with him afterwards, looking into his eyes, *to read where we have been*. It was singular to know Katharine had done the same, lying satiated next to Morton, looking into his eyes to read where they had been.

The fire was nearly out: a low ripple of flames, the occasional flare of resinous blue. The pages of the novella were piled untidily on the rug, so close to the flames.

'Do you want the novella published?' Katharine asked.

'I'm not sure.' Did she want it published? At first she had been beguiled by possibility, but there had been too much pain and damage tonight. She hadn't meant that to happen, particularly not to Walter. The revelations had been terrible. After a lifetime of concealment and evasion, she now understood she couldn't control how posterity viewed her. Her legacy was apart from her, another beast entirely. To Katharine, she said, 'You were right to say it's not my story to tell.'

'I said it's more than your story. There's a difference.'

The fire crackled, letting off a brief flare. Edith shook her head.

'Your family — extraordinary they all knew about Morton. Your parents and husband, even your children.'

Katharine's face was serene.

'To have lived life so openly, with such honesty . . . .' Edith looked down at the manuscript on the rug. Could she do the same? Several pages were torn, a reminder of Walter's anger and Percy's unexpected help. Such a peculiar evening. She had learnt more than she might have wished. Morton had never been a perceptive person or a great writer, but he had been at his best when writing, *The letters survive, and everything survives.*

She raised her head, wanting to repeat this to Katharine — knowing she would enjoy the mischief of her brother's words — but the room had darkened and Katharine was no longer discernible. Edith understood that she was alone again, without even the comfort of Linky. The air flowed around her like water, ripples lifting her. Closing her eyes, she thought, *life is the saddest thing there is, next to death.*

THE END

Author's Note

Edith Wharton always denied that her characters were based on real-life people. Writing in her memoir, she said nothing was more trying than to have 'a clumsy finger pointed at one of the beings born in that mysterious other-world of invention, with the playful accusation: *Of course we all recognise your Aunt Eliza!*' However, she went on to say that 'it would be insincere to deny that there are bits of Aunt Eliza in this one, of Mrs. X in that . . .'.

Later on, she explained: 'Experience, observation, the looks and ways and words of "real people", all melted and fused in the white heat of the creative fires — such is the mingled stuff which the novelist pours into the firm mould of his narrative.'

Just as Wharton drew on the raw materials of her life to create her fiction, *The Night of All Souls* draws on her fiction to re-create passages of her life. It is like a reversible reaction: transforming the melted and fused material back to an approximation of their original state. It's an amorphous process that provides — at best — a general sense of authenticity, some specifics of scene, and the occasional hint of Wharton's inner workings.

Of all her work, the poem 'Terminus' is surely the most revealing. Using Wharton's metaphor of alchemy, consider it this way: in transforming life into art, this poem barely reworks the substance, producing a matter that is little modified. With startling directness and honesty, 'Terminus' relates a night spent at a railway hotel: *Wonderful was the long secret night you gave me, my Lover.*

This affair — with Morton Fullerton — would inspire her later novel *The Reef*. When praised by her editor, Wharton replied that his words went to her innermost heart *because I put most of myself into that opus.* In this novel, she performs a delicate self-splicing operation to present readers with her two opposing selves: the sexually curious Sophy; and the older, guarded Anna. In an act of self-laceration, Wharton examines her feelings: *There it lay before her, her sole romance . . . the cheapest of cheap adventures . . . .* She also documents the details of a railway hotel room: *the framed card of printed rules under the electric light switch.* Morton Fullerton is re-imagined as the sexually expedient Darrow, chronically unreliable and a liar; while Anna's deceased husband — a cool aesthete — brings to mind Walter. There is even a mother-in-law called Lucretia, about whom Wharton makes no attempt to disguise the fact she was 'gumming the snapshot of a real person into the vibrating human throng of a novel'. The pious Lucretia has very expensive tastes when it comes to fashion.

It is interesting to compare *The Reef* to her poem 'Terminus', particularly her portrayal of the hotel room. In her 'morning-after' poem, Wharton illuminates the 'commonplace' room with her wonder at having joined the union of other women: *And thus some woman like me waking alone before dawn, While her lover slept, . . . Some woman has heard as I heard the farewell shriek of the trains . . . .* Contrast this with the hotel room portrayed in her novel, published three years later and weighted with her disabused knowledge of Fullerton. Now the hotel room (transplanted to Paris) is sordid and dispiriting, with *grimy carpet and wallpaper.*

Along with her fiction, Wharton wrote letters, diaries, and memoirs; as did many of her friends. This permits us the luxury of expanding our viewing lens, using all this material to corroborate and 'flesh out' the fragments of real people and experiences in Wharton's writing.

Take the aforementioned night in a railway hotel: Henry James recorded this event in his pocket diary for June 4, 1909, reminding himself to *Dine with Morton Fullerton and E.W. Charing Cross Hotel.* Meanwhile Fullerton, while making a handwritten copy of 'Terminus', noted in the margin: *. . . we went up to London, and were met at dinner by Henry James. I took apartment No. 92 (two chambers & salon) in which I left her alone the next day at 10 with only time to have sent to her room a bunch of roses.*

Many years later Fullerton wrote to Elisina Tyler: 'She was fearless, reckless even, in her frank response to her companion. I shall send you soon a striking proof of this in a long poem addressed to me on the morning of the long night we spent together in Charing Cross Hotel. I had left her in the early morning and as I lingered she took up her pen to write.'

In this way, *The Night of All Souls* draws on many sources of information. The selected material is treated equally, despite varying degrees of opaqueness and veracity, everything of value sifted and layered into the narrative.

This should not be confused with psychoanalytic literary criticism. Such an approach seeks to interpret codes embedded in literary text, believing the novelist has expressed secret unconscious desires and anxieties in their work. Wharton's work is often subjected to such a technique — perhaps unsurprising given the discrepancy between her public persona and the often sexual nature of her writing. But the approach taken in writing *The Night of All Souls* is not interpretative; rather, it reworks her writing.

This novel is built on the bedrock of a biography written by Hermione Lee, a monumental work to which I am greatly indebted. But there have been a number of biographies written on Wharton, each with differing perspectives and emphases — and sometimes different 'facts'. I have deliberately selected versions of events that helped shape the story I wanted to tell. For example, the R.W.B. Lewis biography states that Fullerton travelled to Brockton immediately after his stay at The Mount in 1907, meeting with Katharine to break the news of their engagement to the elder Fullertons. Other accounts, however, suggest his parents weren't told of the engagement for several months. For similar reasons, I chose the R.W.B. Lewis version that assumes Fullerton is the father of his wife's child. This may not be the case.

I have also simplified some events. Wharton wrote *two* poems after her night with Fullerton, but the allegorical 'Colophon to the Mortal Lease' is less useful to the story — except for the beautiful line, *to read where we have been*. After her death, Wharton *did* leave behind some letters from Fullerton. Discovered by Elisina Tyler, they were (presumably) destroyed after being shown to her son Bill Tyler. However, as they were romantically stored in a small velvet-lined casket, it's unlikely they contradicted the idyllic version of events portrayed in her Love Diary.

Several other small liberties have been taken for the benefit of the novel. While Elisina may have contacted Trix over her dealings with Fullerton and the poem 'Terminus', it seems unlikely. Similarly, Trix may have heard about the armed hold-up over a suitcase of Fullerton's letters, but probably not. And how much Edith came to learn about Fullerton's true character, we will never know.

As for the mechanics of integrating all this material into the text, generally speaking, material sourced from writing intended for publication (fiction, non-fiction, memoir, and biography) appears in roman type. Writing not intended for publication (diaries and letters), along with Wharton's poetry, appears in italics. Ultimately, all decisions have been made based on what best serves the novel.

With respect to quotes from Wharton's fiction, they are seamlessly integrated into the text so as not to distract, but they appear as italic when readers are alerted to a phrase having been written by Wharton for publication. Non-fiction sources are also used to retell passages of Wharton's life, usually paraphrased and integrated into the novel using roman type, with italics used only to indicate dialogue or thoughts or to highlight a phrase that comes from a letter or diary.

In a more general sense, countless Wharton expressions are integrated into this novel to give a sense of authenticity. This is extended to the novella, which also contains some allusions to Wharton's writing. When Sara 'takes her clothes from their hangers, watching herself fold them to perfection', this echoes Wharton when packing after her spring romance with Morton in Paris. And the walk-on role of Edith Wharton as Mrs Newbold is a trope that Wharton occasionally used, most memorably in her short story 'Roman Fever', where 'A stout lady in a dust coat suddenly appeared, asking in broken Italian if anyone had seen the elastic band which held together her tattered Baedeker. She poked with a stick under the table at which she lunched, the waiters assisting.'

Finally, I would like to thank the Watkins/Loomis Agency for checking the rights to the quotes I have used. I would also like to thank Harriet Allan and Jane Parkin; Ian, Edward and Kate.

Notes

The quotes are listed in the order they appear in the novel.

Pages 5, 111, 246, 247, 305, 306, 307, 312, 322, 330: *The letters survive, and everything survives.*
From: Mainwaring, p.165.

Page 7: 'When I get a glimpse, in books and reviews, of the things people are going to assert about me after I am dead, I feel I must have the courage and perseverance, some day, to forestall them.'
From: Wharton's personal diary kept spasmodically 1920–1937, Lewis, p. xii.

Page 13: 'It's all been *good*, hasn't it, my dear?'
From: Letter from Walter Berry to Edith Wharton, 25 February 1923 (adapted):
'— for it would all have been good.' Held in the Beinecke Library; quoted in Benstock and Lee p. 64.

Page 17: '— that she could imagine a ghost more wistfully haunting a mean house in a dull street than the battlement castle.'
From: Preface to *Ghosts* (adapted): 'I can imagine them more wistfully'.

Page 18: *'he fed my mind and soul.'*
From: *A Backward Glance*, 6.1. p.119 (adapted): 'He found me when my mind and soul were hungry and thirsty . . .'

Page 44: 'Walter wouldn't remember his last days in hospital when he wanted her so close; holding her so fast that all the old flame and glory came back in the cold shadow of death and parting.'
From: Letter to John Hugh Smith (adapted), Lewis and Lewis, p.504: 'The sense of desolation (though of thankfulness too, of course) is unspeakably increased by those last days together, when he wanted me so close, & held me so fast, that all the old flame & glory came back, in the cold shadow of death & parting.'

Page 48: 'their sense of humour and irony pitched in exactly the same key.'
From: *A Backward Glance*, chapter 8, Henry James 8.1, p.173 (adapted line she wrote about herself and Henry James): 'The real marriage of true minds is for any two people to possess a sense of humour or irony pitched in exactly the same key.'

Page 55: '. . . they had grown more and more distinct, giving out a light of their own.'
From: 'The Eyes', chapter II short story: '. . . but as I looked the eyes grew more and more distinct; they gave out a light of their own.'

Page 73: 'Edith had always believed the air of ideas the only air worth breathing — but Sybil's ideas were as dull as cold mutton.'
From: *The Age of Innocence*: 'The air of ideas is the only air worth breathing.'

Page 74: Anecdote about calling the waiter Twilight.
From: Lubbock, p.117.

Page 74: *'I have been practicing liking it for 24 hours and am obliged to own that the results are not promising.'*
From: Letter to Mary Berenson about Lady Sybil Cutting's marriage to Geoffrey Scott, Lewis p.409: 'I have been *practicing liking* it for 24 hours now, & am obliged to own that the results are not promising.'

Page 74: 'Apparently, so the story went, Percy had inadvertently dropped his cigarette down the back of Sybil's dress — and on fishing it out, Sybil had fainted romantically into his arms.'
From: Lewis and Lewis, p.487.

Page 77: 'Later she would write: *Every sensation of touch and sight was thrice-alive in her.'*
From: *The Reef*, chapter XI.

Page 78: 'Edith listened to herself speak, aware of a glowing consciousness drawn around them.'
From: *The Reef*, chapter XI (adapted): 'She seemed to listen to herself speaking from a far-off airy height, and yet to be wholly gathered into the circle of consciousness which drew its glowing ring about herself and Darrow.'

Page 82: '. . . the soft weight sinking trustfully against her breast, the rosy blur of the little face, the folding and unfolding fingers.'
From: *The House of Mirth*, chapter 13 (adapted): '. . . and Lily felt the soft weight sink trustfully against her breast . . . wondering at the rosy blur of the little face, the empty clearness of the eyes, the vague tendrilly motions of the folding and unfolding fingers.'

Page 91: 'Catching her reflection in the mirror, she recalls a line written this morning (a short story that's coming along nicely): *it was a face which had grown middle aged while it waited for the joys of youth.'*
From: 'The Pretext', short story.

Page 103: '— a dazzling motor-flight over blue mountains and through avenues of amber-gold.'
From: Letter to Sally Norton, Lee, p.309 (adapted): 'a dazzling run across blue mountains, through arches and long vistas of gold & amber.'

Page 104: 'She sits back, so intensely aware of Morton's nearness that there's no surprise in the touch he lays on her hand. They look at each other in silence.'
From: *The Reef* (adapted): 'Anna sat silent, so intensely aware of Darrow's nearness that there was no surprise in the touch he laid on her hand.'

Page 120: 'Percy says you were dry and supercilious . . . But that you were an insatiable reader and a hard worker, a good linguist and traveller. That your practical experience often helped Edith . . . But none of your friends thought you better for the surrender of your spirit to the control of such a man.'
From: Lubbock, chapter 3, pp.43–44 (adapted): 'None of her friends, to put it plainly,

thought she was the better for the surrender of her fine spirit to the control of a man, I am ready to believe, of strong intelligence and ability — but also, I certainly know, of a dry and narrow and supercilious temper. He was an insatiable reader, a true glutton of books; he was a hard worker, . . . he was a good linguist, and a traveller who searched and mastered art and culture of many lands.'

Page 121: 'Percy writes that I have the harshness of a dogmatist, the bleakness of an egotist, and the pretentiousness of a snob . . . And a deep vault of egotism sealed against the currents of sympathy and humanity. . . creating a chill that lowered the temperature of life all round it, deadening its charm and cheapening its value.'
From: Lubbock (adapted): chapter 3, p.44: '. . . the harshness of a dogmatist, the bleakness of an egotist, and the pretentiousness (I can't help it) of a snob' and from chapter 14, p.230: '. . . a deep vault of egotism within, spacious and cool, sealed against the variable currents of sympathy and humanity . . . the chill from within pervades the outer climate, lowering the temperature of life all round it, deadening its charm, cheapening its value.'

Page 122: 'He was drumming on the arm rest with a long, bloodless hand; a red seal ring on his small finger.'
From: *Hudson River Bracketed*, chapter XXXIX (adapted): 'His hands were bloodless . . . he wore a dark red seal ring on his left fourth finger.'

Page 122: He was usually the embodiment of Old New York, a tribe of people who dreaded scandal more than disease, and placed decency above courage; and who considered nothing more ill-bred than 'scenes' — except the behaviour of those who gave rise to them.
From: *The Age of Innocence*, chapter XXXIII (adapted): 'the way of people who dreaded scandal more than disease, who placed decency above courage, and who considered that nothing was more ill-bred than "scenes," except the behavior of those who gave rise to them.'

Page 122: 'she was too fashionable for Boston, and too intelligent for New York'.
From: *A Backward Glance*, chapter 6.1, p.119 (adapted): 'I was a failure in Boston . . . because they thought I was too fashionable to be intelligent, and a failure in New York because they were afraid I was too intelligent to be fashionable.'

Page 122: 'That she despaired at American hotels — such crass food, crass manners, crass landscape! *What a horror it is for a whole nation to be developing without the sense of beauty, & eating bananas for breakfast.*'
From: Lewis and Lewis, p.93: 'Such dreariness, such whining sallow women, such utter absence of the amenities, such crass food, crass manners, crass landscape!! And, mind you, it is a new & fashionable hotel. What a horror it is for a whole nation to be developing without the sense of beauty, & eating bananas for breakfast.'

Page 123: 'No doubt Percy mentioned the *bons mots* that had been so spontaneous and witty at the time; but they would be worn and unpleasant when recounted with such a deadened hand. She knew the stories: her enjoyment at the expense of her wealthy uncultured neighbours in Lenox. *The XYZ's, they tell me, have decided to have books in their library.* Or being shown around an opulent home, the owner saying, *And I call this my Louis Quinze room*, to which Edith replied, *Why, my dear?* The Frenchman who

approved of The Mount but disliked the bas-relief in the entrance hall, to whom Edith said, *I assure you that you will never see it here again.*
From: Lubbock, the XYZ's anecdote told on p.17, the bas-relief anecdote told on p.24; and the Louis Quinze anecdote from Lee, p.152.

Page 124: 'In her diary she wrote, *Looking now & then at the way the hair grows on your forehead, at the line of your profile turned to the stage.*'
From: *The Life Apart* in Lee, p.313.

Page 124: '*That's something you don't know anything about.*'
From: *The Life Apart* in Lee, p.322.

Page 124: '*I have found in Emerson just the phrase for you — & me. 'The moment my eyes fell on him I was content.'*'
From: Lewis and Lewis, p.129 (adapted): '*I have found in Emerson (from Euripides, I suppose) just the phrase for you — & me. 'The moment my eyes fell on him I was content.'*'

Page 125: 'Always the writer, she relived the events in her diary, adding: *This must be what happy women feel.*'
From: 'The Love Diary' in Lee, p.313.

Page 139: 'Old New York: a place where the unusual was regarded as either immoral or ill-bred, where people with emotions were not visited; where authorship was still regarded as something between a Black Art and a form of manual labour. Yes, Trix was a fitting representative; she was so resolute in her determination to carry to its utmost limit that ritual of ignoring the "unpleasant" in which they had been brought up.'
From: *The Reef,* chapter IX (adapted): 'the unusual was regarded as either immoral or ill-bred, and people with emotions were not visited.'; and *A Backward Glance,* chapter 3.3, p.69); '. . . authorship was still regarded as something between a black art and a form of manual labour.'; and *The Age of Innocence*, chapter III: 'Nothing about his betrothed pleased him more than her resolute determination to carry to its utmost limit that ritual of ignoring the "unpleasant" in which they had both been brought up.'

Page 141: '*What being married was like.* At her mother's look of icy disapproval, Edith persisted, *I'm afraid, Mama — I want to know what will happen to me!* The coldness of her mother's expression deepened to deep disgust — surely Edith had seen enough pictures and statues to know men were made differently? To Edith's confusion, she ordered: *Then for heaven's sake don't ask me any more silly questions. You can't be as stupid as you pretend.*'
From: *Life and I*, chapter II.

Page 144: '*It is easy to see the superficial resemblances between things. It takes a first rate mind to perceive the differences underneath.*'
From: *A Backward Glance*, chapter 6.1, p.117.

Page 144: '*Can this be me? Can this really be happening to me?*'
From: *The Reef* (adapted): 'Is it true? Is it really true? Is it really going to happen to ME?'

Page 146: 'She would later write of the large double bed as a fiery pit scorching the brow of innocence. She would describe the new bride's dull misery as she endured her husband's rough advances. It was a cruel experience.'
From: 'The Old Maid', in *Old New York* (adapted): 'there was the large double bed; . . . through the dressing-room door which had once seemed open into a fiery pit scorching the brow of innocence.'; and *Beatrice Palmato*: 'That experience is a cruel one.'

Page 147: 'Several years before his death, he wrote to Edith recalling that day at Bar Harbor: canoeing in the bay and dining at Roddicks. Walter wondered why he *hadn't* proposed, for it would have all been good — and then the slices of years slid by. He wrote that he never "wondered" about anyone else, *and there wouldn't be much of me if you were cut out of it. Forty years of it is yours, dear.'*
From: Letter from Walter Berry to Edith Wharton, 25 February 1923, held in the Beinecke Library; quoted in Benstock and Lee, p.64.

Page 154: 'He gallivanted about the place with his women, signing them into hotels as his wife. Edith once came across her name in the register of an unfamiliar hotel and noting the previous entry of a "Mr and Mrs Edward R. Wharton", said wryly to a friend: "'Evidently, I *have* been here before.'"
From: Lee, p.395, a story told by Daisy Chanler to Louis Auchincloss and retold in *Edith Wharton: A Woman in Her Time.*

Page 176: *'forty years of it is yours, dear.'*
From: Letter from Walter Berry to Edith Wharton, 25 February 1923, held in the Beinecke Library; quoted in Benstock and Lee, p.64.

Page 183: *'You are victor, winner, master, Oh Irresistible One — you've done it, you've brought it off and got me down forever . . . I must feel your weight and bear your might.'*
From: February 8–14, 1912, *Letters from Henry James to Walter Berry.*

Page 183: *'I shall have nothing for you but a great gaping mouth . . . think of me therefore as just a waiting, panting abyss.'*
From: Previously unpublished letter from James to Berry, quoted in Novick.

Page 184: 'Damn you, Percy Lubbock, no better than a parasite, living off the crumbs of others.'
From: *The House of Mirth*, chapter 14 (adapted) '. . . Gerty has always been a parasite in the moral order, living on the crumbs of other tables . . .'

Page 185: *'If I could find a fairy who would suit you I should secure her at once.'*
From: Lee, p. 654, and p. 536 *'I shall try to import fairies from Cannes.'*

Page 186: 'She had once written (shortly before her death) of the difficulties for a ghost: their need for silence and continuity, their preference for the small hours; the impossibility of finding standing room in a roaring and discontinuous universe.'
From: Preface to *Ghosts.*

Page 206: 'Even Henry, always a defender of Teddy, was horrified by one such scene, writing later, *you must insist on saving your life by a separate existence.'*
From: Lee, p.386.

Page 207: 'She had been the star in her own drama, playing lead role of adulteress. The streets and *salons* of Paris became a theatrical setting, the secrecy of longing staged in a Parisian season. *I don't suppose you know . . . the quiet ecstasy I feel in sitting next to you in a public place . . . while every drop of my blood in my body whispered "Mine-mine-mine!"* She had been radiant with love, glowing with sensuality. For the first time she felt truly beautiful. Morton ripped through her ordered life, turning it upside down. She experienced everything, mad with desire. Morton said: *We are behind the scenes together.*'
From: *The Life Apart* in Lee, p.313.

Page 209: 'with advertisements screaming: *Was She Justified In Seeking A Divorce?*'
From: Lee, p.588.

Page 213: 'She felt like a passenger on an ocean steamer who is told there is no immediate danger, but that she had better put on her life-belt.'
From: 'Xingu', short story.

Page 230: 'The most wonderful piano player, even as a child. She'd just finished playing for the Whartons when Edith said loudly, *Well, Teddy, it may be just as well that we never had any children. Just think, one of them might have been musical!*'
From: Lee, p.701.

Page 230: 'Always the outsider. All her life *the soul sits alone and waits for a footstep that never comes.*'
From: 'The Fullness of Life', short story (adapted): 'a woman's nature is like a great house full of rooms . . . and in the innermost room, the holy of holies, the soul sits alone and waits for a footstep that never comes.'

Page 234: '*That's something you don't know anything about.*'
From: *The Life Apart* in Lee, p.322.

Page 242–3: '*Hold me long & close in your thoughts. I shall take up so little room, & it's only there that I'm happy.* Playfully she recalled their first luncheon together, observing other guests, *the moist hippopotamus American with his cucumber-faced female — do you remember?* Often her letters were distraught: *You chained at one end of the world, & I at the other.*'
From: Lewis and Lewis, June 5, 1908, p.149: '. . . hold me long & close in your thoughts'; Monday, June 8, 1908, p.150: 'the moist hippopotamus'; Friday June 5, 1908, p.149: 'You chained . . .'

Page 243: '*Dear, won't you tell me the meaning of this silence? . . . What has brought about such a change? Oh, no matter what it is — only tell me! . . . didn't you see how my heart broke with the thought that, if I had been younger & prettier, everything might have been different . . . But this incomprehensible silence, the sense of your utter indifference to everything that concerns me, has stunned me. It has come so suddenly . . . This is the last time I shall write you, dear, unless the strange spell is broken. And my last word is one of tenderness for the friend I love — for the lover I worshipped.*'
From: Lewis and Lewis, p.160–2.

Page 244: '*Nay, lift me to thy lips, Life, and once more/ Pour the wild music through me.... and into my frail flanks, Into my bursting veins, the whole sea poured/ Its spaces and its thunder; and I feared.*'
From: 'Life', in *Artemis to Actaeon*.

Page 245: 'There were moments when she almost argued herself into thinking Morton's silence more natural than his continuing to write. She couldn't allow herself to believe he'd forgotten her, that the whole episode had faded from his mind like a breath from a mirror.'
From: 'The Letters', short story, chapter iv.

Page 245: '*Only sit tight yourself & go through the movements of life. That keeps up our connection with life — I mean of the immediate & apparent life, behind which, all the while, the deeper & darker & the unapparent, in which things really happen to us learns, under that hygiene, to stay in its place ... Live it all through, every inch of it — out of it something valuable will come — but live it ever so quietly; & — je maintiens mon dire — waitingly!*'
From: Powers, written Oct 13, 1908, also in Lee, p.329.

Page 246: '*You have — if they still survive — a few notes & letters of no value in your archives, but which happen to fill a deplorable lacuna in those of their writer.*'
From: Lewis and Lewis, p.170.

Page 248: '*How dangerous to care too much even for a garden!*'
From: Lee, p.558.

Page 254: 'it's a quote about how much she loved this place, especially the garden, that it's a paradise like no other, the *Cielo della Quieta* to which the soul aspires when the end of the journey draws near.'
From: Letter to Bernard Berenson, December 12, 1920, in Lewis and Lewis, p.434 (adapted): 'Meanwhile the heavenly beauty & the heavenly quiet enfold me, & I feel that this really is the Cielo della Quieta to which the soul aspires after its stormy voyage.'

Page 256: But Edith hated spending winter here so... *when winter comes, and rain and mud possess the Seine Valley for six months, I fly south to another garden, as stony and soilless as my northern territory is moist and deep with loam.*'
From: *A Backward Glance*, chapter 14.2, p.363.

Page 265: 'It was quieter outside now, the shops closed and Vespas gone; a dry wind was blowing across the doorway, small dust-eddies in the air.'
From: 'Terminus' (adapted): 'Whirled down the ways of the world like dust-eddies swept through a street.'

Page 271: 'as if the scene of the offence added to the guilt of the couple.'
From: *New Year's Day*.

Page 271: 'She had always been protected by her age and her past — and the image her mirror gave back to her.'
From: 'The Pretext' (adapted): 'She was protected by her age, no doubt — her age and her past, and the image her mirror gave back to her ...'

Page 272: '*I have drunk of the wine of life at last, I have known the thing best worth knowing, I have been warmed through and through, never to grow quite cold again until the end.*'
From: *The Life Apart.*

Page 274: 'retreating into a rage of conformity'.
From: 'The Long Run', short story.

Page 274–5: 'She could feel the rumble of a train deep within the bowels of the building, the shriek of a departure from below her window. *The shaking and shrieking of trains, the night-long shudder of traffic* ... Only now did she become aware that it was still raining. It had rained all night. *The black rain of midnight pelted the roof of the station.* Rising from the bed, she pulled tight the belt of her night robe and crossed to where rain streamed against the high-perched windows, reducing their vast prospect of roofs and chimneys to a black oily huddle, and filling the room with the drab twilight of an underground aquarium. She could see the face of a clock in a tall building beyond the railway. Seating herself at the writing desk, she began to make order of the strewn sheets of paper. She heard Morton go through to his own room, collecting up his suitcase and belongings. She switched on the red lamp, flushing the common-place room with magical shadows. Now Morton was back in front of the mirror and pulling on his jacket. He flicked an imaginary speck and tugged at his sleeves. *Here, in this self-same glass, while you helped me to loosen my dress, And the shadow-mouths melted to one* ... His case was placed on the armchair by the fireplace. Edith studied the blotched marble top of the chest of drawers, the electrolier overhead. She committed to memory everything about this dull and featureless room, allowing it to take possession in her mind, every detail pressing itself on her notice with the familiarity of an accidental confidant. Whichever way she turned, she felt the nudge of a transient intimacy. *Yes, all this through the room, the passive and featureless room, Must have flowed with the rise and fall of the human unceasing current, And lying there hushed in your arms, as the waves of rapture receded, And far down the margin of being we heard the low beat of the soul* ...'
From: *The Reef* (adapted) and 'Terminus' (italics).

Page 276–7: The poem 'Terminus'.

Page 283: 'Sara smiled and thought, *This is like being happy.* She allowed her fingers to lightly feather the beautiful cheek.'
From: Letter to Morton Fullerton, 1911, Lee, p.357, (ref p.789).

Page 283: 'Medora's face fading like breath on a mirror.'
From: 'The Letters', short story, chapter iv: 'like a breath from a mirror.'

Page 288: '*I try to console myself by writing about Italian gardens instead of looking at my own.*'
From: Letter to Sara (Sally) Norton, June 5 1903, Lewis and Lewis, p.85.

Page 288–90:
From: *Italian Villas and their Gardens* (paraphrased).

Page 290: 'When esteemed gardener Ambassador Choate stepped on to her terrace, he roasted Edith by saying: Ah, Mrs Wharton, when I look about me, I don't know if I'm in England or in Italy!'
From: Lubbock, p.20.

Page 296: 'She had a sudden sense of the length of the years that stretched before her. *So this is what it will be like*, she thought.'
From: 'The Pretext', short story (adapted): 'She had a sudden aching sense . . .'

Page 299: 'Edith described a soldier dozing in the silver moonlight of a bombed village, a tea service on a table strewn with war maps, standing at the front line and *almost feeling their breath on our faces.*'
From: Lee, p.486.

Page 299: '*as soon as peace is declared I shall renounce good works forever!*'
From: Sept 13, 1914, Lewis and Lewis, p.341.

Page 299: '*Dear Good Fairy, I really can't wait till tomorrow afternoon to tell you how I thank you & bless you & admire you for all you've done!*'
From: April 1915, Lewis and Lewis, p.354.

Page 299: 'a black cloud hung over the world and her spirit was heavy with loss.'
From: *A Backward Glance;* chapters 14.3 and 14.4, p.368: 'But still the black cloud hung over the world . . . My spirit was heavy with these losses'.

Page 299: '. . . saying goodbye to the heavenly beauty and quiet of her home, a moon rising over silver seas, the wheeling of the great winter constellations. The *Cielo della Quieta.*'
From: Lee, p.542 (adapted): '. . . sun & moon risings & settings, & the wheeling of the great winter constellations.'

Page 300: 'As one of her characters once posed: *Is it anything to be proud of, to know so little of the strings that pull us?*'
From: *The Reef*.

Page 303: '*I cling to you, dearest Edith, through thick & thin, & believe that we shall find ourselves in some secure port together yet.*'
From: Powers, p.164.

Page 305: 'Perhaps a copy of the poem (in Morton's handwriting!) was on the desk as the author wrote of Sara not wanting to be *whirled down the ways of the world like dust-eddies swept through a street.*'
From: 'Terminus'.

Page 307: '*This must be what happy women feel.*'
From: *The Life Apart*, in Lee, p.313.

Page 307: 'Three years later, while sitting on a promontory high above the deep-blue inlets of Portofino, she had written to Morton that it was *like being happy.*'
From: Letter to Morton Fullerton, 1911, Lee, p.357 (also p.789).

Page 307: 'She wrote, *I have been completely happy. I have had everything in life that I ever longed for, & more than I ever imagined!*'
From: August 12, 1909, Lewis and Lewis, p.189.

Page 308: 'To one pleading letter, he sneered: *I will be all you have the right to expect.*'
From: Letter to Morton Fullerton, Winter 1910, Lewis and Lewis, p.197.

Page 308: *'What you wish, apparently, is to take of my life the inmost & uttermost that a woman — a woman like me — can give, for an hour, now & then, when it suits you; & when the hour is over, to leave me out of your mind & out of your life as a man leaves the companion who has accorded him a transient distraction. I think I am worth more than that . . .'*
From: Winter 1910, Lewis and Lewis, p.197.

Page 308: 'But such honesty was always followed by quick retraction: *the tiresome woman is buried, once for all, I promise, & only the novelist survives!*'
From: May 10, 1909, Lewis and Lewis, p.179.

Page 308: *'my heart ached to see you so tired today, and to think I was part of the tire . . . I love you even better than I knew.'*
From: May 10, 1909, Lewis and Lewis, p.179.

Page 308: *'Now I am asking to be happy all the rest of my life. . . . it is a misfortune to love too late, & as completely as I have loved you. Everything else grows so ghostly afterward.'*
From: Late summer 1909, Lewis and Lewis, p.189.

Page 308: 'It is impossible, in the nature of things, that our lives should run parallel much longer. I have faced the fact, & accept it, & I am not afraid, except when I think of the pain & pity you may feel for *me.*'
From: Late Summer 1909, Lewis and Lewis, p.189.

Page 308: 'She apologised for calling when he was busy and harassed. *I want to love you in any way that gives you peace, & not bother!*'
From: Early Jan 1910, Lewis and Lewis, p.195.

Page 309: *'I can be anything, do anything, to help you!'*
From: Tuesday, Winter 1910, Lewis and Lewis, p.196 (adapted).

Page 309: 'And — always — she wanted her letters back: *some day next week — before Wednesday.'*
From: Nov 27, 1909, Lewis and Lewis, p.193.

Page 309: *'Dear, that I know how unequal the exchange is between us, how little I have to give that a man like you can care for —'.*
From: Late Summer 1909, Lewis and Lewis, p.189.

Page 309: *'But I do ask something more of the man who asks to be more than my friend; & so must any woman who is proud enough to be worth loving.'*
From: Winter 1910, Lewis and Lewis, p.198.

Page 309: *'Be happy and love me a little, when you have the time, and let the heart tell you . . .'*
From: March 18, 1910, Lewis and Lewis, p.201 (translated from French).

Page 309: *'I am sad and bewildered beyond words . . . I can't go on like this! . . . I don't know what you want, or what I am! You write to me like a lover, you treat me like a casual acquaintance! . . . My life was better before I knew you. And it is a bitter thing to say to the one being one has ever loved d'amour. . . . I have borne all these inconsistencies because I love you so much . . . I can bear no more —'.*
From: Letter to Morton Fullerton, mid-April 1910, Lewis and Lewis, pp.206–8 (adapted).

Page 310: *'My personal inconvenience . . . was nothing compared to my regret at having been importunate in trying to help you.'*
From: April 27 1910, Lewis and Lewis, p.212.

Page 310: *'Don't see in this any ruse to regain possession of your time.'*
From: April 1910, Lewis and Lewis, p.214.

Page 311: *'Dear, there was never a moment, from the very first, when I did not foresee such a thought on your part as the one we talked of today; there was never a moment, even when we were nearest, that I did not feel it was latent in your mind. And still I took what you gave me, & was glad, & was not afraid.'*
From: June 25 1910, Lewis and Lewis, p.218.

Page 311: *'I herewith graciously accord you the privilege of gazing on my countenance when it once more rises on your horizon.'*
From: July 19, 1910, Lewis and Lewis, p.221.

Page 311: *'I should have had a letter from you, if only a postcard.'*
From: Oct 16, 1911, Lewis and Lewis, p.260.

Page 311–2: *'There it lay before her, her sole romance, in all its paltry poverty, the cheapest of cheap adventures, the most pitiful of sentimental blunders.'*
From: *The Reef*, chapter XXXV.

Page 312: *'I am staying in this unimaginably beautiful place to rest & to steep my soul in light & air.'*
From: Letter to Morton Fullerton 1911, Lee, p.789.

Page 312: *'Is this the kind of letter you like to get from me? It would do very well in a memoir, wouldn't it? Only I don't know how to sign it —'.*
From: Letter to Morton Fullerton, April 9, 1914, Lewis and Lewis, p.316.

Page 312: 'In an early novella she wrote: *wisdom unfiltered through personal experience does not become a part of the moral tissues.'*
From: *Sanctuary*, chapter IV.

Page 315: 'Edith looked out across a landscape of brick and iron towards a river of pitch.'
From: Letter to Bernard Berenson, Belmont Hotel, Oct 3, 1910, Lewis and Lewis, p.222 (adapted).

Page 316: 'She described the dining-room as sumptuously stuffy, where dinner-fumes hung under the emblazoned ceiling. The other diners were pallid and richly dressed, eating their way through the bill-of-fare, the chef having ransacked the globe for gastronomic incompatibilities. And in the middle of the room a knot of equally pallid waiters were engaged in languid conversations, backs turned on the persons they were supposed to serve.'
From: *The Custom of the Country,* chapter IV (adapted).

Page 316: 'Henry was fulsome in his praise, declaring the hotel extremely luxurious: *prodigious & unutterable*.'
From: Lee, p.383.

Page 316: 'Dear Henry — massive, slow-moving, awe-inspiring, at dinner with two gentlemen and a lady.'
From: Lee, p.384 (adapted).

Page 316: 'He had cried of unspeakable loneliness and the blackness of life, his craving *not to wake — not to wake —*'.
From: March 19, 1910, Lewis and Lewis, p.202.

Page 317: '*I am sad and bewildered beyond words. I don't understand. It was not necessary to hurt me.*'
From: Mid-April 1910, Lewis and Lewis, p.207 (adapted).

Page 318: '*Down there, alone at Rye, I used to lie & think of Morton, and* ache *over him.*'
From: Letter from Edith to Morton Fullerton, reporting what Henry said, sent from the Berkley Hotel, London, March 18, 1910, Lewis and Lewis, p.200.

Page 318: 'Years later, Morton would speak publicly of Walter's fine culture and high irony. He would mention Walter's immense and varied contacts of life, of which he was a rare connoisseur.'
From: Mainwaring, p.238.

Page 319: 'She had once written: the turnings of life seldom show a sign-post; or rather, though the sign is always there, it is usually placed some distance back, like the notices that give warning of a bad hill or a level crossing.'
From: *The Custom of the Country*, chapter XVI.

Page 321: 'Her heart was beating so violently that there was a rush in her ears.'
From: 'The Pretext', short story.

Page 322: 'Her face was like a book of which the last page is never turned, where there is always something new to read.'
From: 'The Moving Finger', short story (adapted).

Page 323: 'the dizziness that follows a physical blow.'
From: *The House of Mirth*.

Page 323: 'A shock of wonder.'
From: *Ethan Frome*.

Page 324: 'a low crackle of dry wood; memories flickering across her face.'
From: *A Backward Glance*, chapter 14.7, p.379: '. . . and I still warm my hands thankfully at the old fire, though every year it is fed with the dry wood of more old memories.'

Page 326: 'driving through the countryside past old grey towns piled above rivers, through the melting spring landscape all tender green and snowy-fruit blossom; strolling up to a cathedral together, the quiet moment outside, sitting on the steps in the sunshine, as he asked, *Dear, are you happy?*'
From: *The Life Apart*, Lee, p.317 (adapted): '. . . through the grey old towns piled up above their rivers, through the melting spring landscape, all tender green and snowy blossom . . . the quiet moment outside sitting on the steps in the sunshine (*"Dear, are you happy?"* he asked, to her intense delight)'.

Page 328: 'I wrote, *I do not believe you have ever treated another woman so ill.*'
From: Letter from Katharine Gerould to Morton Fullerton, 5 Jan, 1910, Mainwaring, p.56 (adapted): 'I do not think any human being has the right to hurt another like this . . . you have treated me unpardonably ill.'

Page 329: 'Edith had written of lying with him afterwards, looking into his eyes, *to read where we have been.*'
From: 'Colophon to the Mortal Lease', poem, in Lee p.346.

Page 330: *'life is the saddest thing there is next to death.'*
From: *A Backward Glance*, chapter 14.7, p.379.

Bibliography

Letters

Letters from Henry James to Walter Berry, Black Swan Press, 1928.
Letters from Walter Berry to Edith Wharton, held by Beinecke Library, first published in Shari Benstock, *No Gifts from Chance*, 1994.
Henry James and Edith Wharton, Letters 1900–1915, ed. Lyall H. Powers, Weidenfeld & Nicholson, 1990.
The Letters of Edith Wharton, Lewis and Lewis, MacMillan, 1988.

Non fiction

Mainwaring, Marion, *Mysteries of Paris: The Quest for Morton Fullerton,* University Press of New England, 2000.
Wharton, Edith, *Italian Villas and Their Gardens*, The Century Company, 1904.
Wolff, Cynthia Griffin, *A Feast of Words: The Triumph of Edith Wharton,* Oxford University Press, 1977.
Wolff, Geoffrey, *Black Sun: The Brief Transit and Violent Eclipse of Harry Crosby,* Random House, 1976.

Biographies and memoirs

Auchincloss, Louis, *Edith Wharton: A Woman in Her Time*, Michael Jospeh, 1972.
Benstock, Shari, *No Gifts from Chance: A Biography of Edith Wharton*, Charles Scribner's Sons, 1994.
Lee, Hermione, *Edith Wharton*, Chatto & Windus, 2007.
Lewis, R.W.B., *Edith Wharton: A Biography,* Harper & Row, 1975.
Lubbock, Percy, *Portrait of Edith Wharton,* Jonathan Cape, 1947.
Novick, Sheldon M., *The Mature Master*, Random House, 2007
Wharton, Edith, *A Backward Glance*, D. Appleton-Century, 1934.

Wharton diaries

'Life and I', in Wolff, Cynthia (ed), *Wharton: Novellas and Other Writings*, Library of America,1990.
'Line-a-day' diaries, 1920–1937, held at the Beinecke Library, Yale University, quoted in R. W. B. Lewis, *Edith Wharton*, 1975.
The Life Apart (or Love Diary) Engagement Diary Feb–May 1909; American Literature, Vol 66 No 4 (Dec 1994).

Wharton novels

Sanctuary, Charles Scribner's Sons, 1903.
The House of Mirth, Charles Scribner's Sons, 1905.
The Reef, D. Appleton & Company, 1912.
The Custom of the Country, Charles Scribner's Sons, 1913.
The Age of Innocence, D. Appleton & Company, 1920.
Hudson River Bracketed, D. Appleton & Company, 1929.

Wharton novellas

Ethan Frome, Charles Scribner's Sons, 1911.
Old New York (collection: *False Dawn, The Old Maid, The Spark, New Year's Day*),
    D. Appleton & Company, 1924.
Beatrice Palmato, undated, first published in R. W. B. Lewis, *Edith Wharton*, 1975.

Wharton short stories:

'The Moving Finger', *Crucial Instances,* Charles Scribner's Sons, 1901.
'The Pretext', *The Hermit and the Wild Woman and Other Stories,* Charles Scribner's
    Sons, 1908.
'The Eyes', *Tales of Men and Ghosts,* Charles Scribner's Sons, 1910.
'The Letters', *Tales of Men and Ghosts,* Charles Scribner's Sons, 1910.
'The Fullness of Life', *Edith Wharton: Collected Stories,* 1891–1910, Library of
    America, 2001.
'The Long Run', *Xingu and Other Stories,* Charles Scribner's Sons, 1916.
'Xingu', *Xingu and Other Stories*, Charles Scribner's Sons, 1916.
Ghosts, Charles Scribner's Sons, 1937.

Poetry

Wharton, Edith, *Artemis to Actaeon,* 1909.
'Terminus', first published in R. W. B. Lewis, *Edith Wharton*, 1975.
'Colophon to the Mortal Lease', first published in Hermione Lee, *Edith Wharton*,
    2007.